Also by Gay G. Gunn

One Day. Someday. Soon: Book I, Culhane Family Saga
Might Could Be: Book II, Culhane Family Saga
May We All: Book III, Culhane Family Saga
Nowhere to Run
Pride and Joi
Everlastin' Love
Dotted Swiss and Gingham

By GiGi Gunn

Never Been to Me
Cajun Moon
Rainbow's End
Living Inside Your Love

EVERLASTIN' LOVE
II

By Gay G. Gunn

To the dynamic
Denise Brooks,
a little "tissue" to dab
your tears. :) The last of The
cultures ...... Enjoy!
Gay G. Gunn

Everlastin' Love II is a work of fiction. Names, characters, business organizations, places, events and incidents are the product of the author's imagination or are used fictitiously. Any resemblance to actual persons, living or dead, events, or locales is entirely coincidental.

2019 Different Drummer Trade Paperback Edition

Published in the United States
by Different Drummer, LLC

ISBN-978-0578513614
eBook ISBN-978-057813621

To all who have found their Everlastin' Love... Rejoice.
To those still seeking it... Persevere.

We are All loved more than we realize.

One lives only as long as one is remembered

Book IV

Culhane Family Saga

Chapter 1

1968

Music. There was none where it had always been. Singing into the mic at Champion Studio. Singing to each other as they strolled the beach stealing kisses and hidden touches, harmonizing as they furnished their apartment from Antique Row, before and after they made love. Music, as much a part of them as breathing, was yanked from their lives, and the silence screamed between them.

It was a familiar sight. A red Karmann Ghia speeding up the coastal highway from Watts to San Francisco. A guy, a girl, and a dog. The guy and girl had been inseparable since high school, since she was sixteen; now he was graduating from Stanford, law-school bound, and she was finishing up her junior year at Berkeley. You seldom saw one without the other. He, in a red baseball cap with a white S covering curly brunette hair, and a brown leather bomber jacket clinging to the torso of one of the

West Coast's most sought after athletic bodies. She, wearing her father's 1940s fudge fedora, her mane of copper hair matching the billowing of the fringe on her buckskin jacket.

Until now, the sojourns to Watts had been pleasure trips: to see family and old friends, to participate in the annual Watts Boys Club Christmas Show, to attend the New Year's party at Club Oasis, to record at Champion. But now there was loud quiet. To turn on the radio was to risk reminders of happier times when his Raw Cilk songs rivaled Motown's best. When Raw Cilk's "Everlastin' Love" and Percy Sledge's "When a Man Loves a Woman" were hailed as *the* love ballads of 1966. When the stars were in their heavens and all was right with the world. What a difference a year makes.

Now his hypnotic hazel eyes set in deep bronze skin fastened to the nothingness of the road. The car seemed guided by the stars as the moon shimmered silver on the ocean and played hide-and-seek with the terrain. She touched his hand, sadness flickering in her honey colored eyes. He managed a glance and quick smile before returning his gaze to the highway. The silence deafening, and all that could be heard was the whiz of rubber on asphalt.

He parked his car beside her 1957 pink T-Bird, a sweet-sixteen gift from her parents. They climbed the front steps of the Victorian house on Alta Vista, and she stopped to get the mail as he opened the vestibule door. After tackling the three flights in silence, he unlocked their apartment door and hung her hat and jacket on the hall tree while she went over to the wall of windows. The San Francisco skyline twinkled before her, calming her much like the ocean always did. As he went to get the dog's leash, she folded her arms and stared at the city's lights dancing below.

2

"You want some light?" Qwayz asked when he returned to the room.

"No, thanks," Jaz answered.

"I'm gonna take Akira for a walk." He kissed her cheek and opened the door for the beautiful Irish setter named for its master's old karate teacher. Her brother's handsome image superimposed itself on the San Francisco vista, and Jaz washed the windows with her cascading tears. What had TC, this young music mogul, this black genius, been doing in Vietnam, and why did he have to die? Whether he had been killed at Khe Sanh or in the Tet offensive, it was January 1968, and her big brother, Tavio Culhane, was dead. Until Qwayz's brother-in-law, Yudi Hodges, went over, Vietnam was known only as the thief who stole young black men from urban ghettos to fight yellow men in a distant land for the white man. The lure? Steady money and benefits. The catch? Few made it back, and those who did, like Yudi, were in no condition to enjoy it. When TC went, it put Vietnam right smack-dab in the middle of the Culhane-Chandler world.

Now, just back from TC's funeral, Jaz, in her mind's eye, replayed the day her idyllic life shattered. She and Qwayz had just driven back from a ski trip in Tahoe, their Christmas gift to AJ, whom they had put on a plane back to L.A. She and Qwayz called dibs on a hot shower as they raced up the steps to the vestibule, grabbing the mail before jockeying up the first flight of steps. Jaz tripped Qwayz and laughingly climbed over him until they reached the second floor. They tiptoed past two apartments before they bolted up the final flight to their love nest in the sky. When Qwayz unlocked the door, they both tried entering at the same time. Qwayz's long legs took four giant steps to the bedroom door. "Foul, foul!" Jaz protested. "Your legs are longer than mine."

"But yours are prettier," he countered. Jaz sidled up to Qwayz, gyrating her body into his. When Jake, Jaz's nickname for Qwayz's manhood, responded, she bypassed him and ran for the bathroom.

"Foul, foul!"

"You use your advantages and I use mine!" She closed the bathroom door.

"How 'bout we share?" he said through the door.

"No way, I've had enough of you guys and the cold. I'm never going skiing again."

"You didn't go this time," he joked. "I'm going to the store to get Akira dog food, anything else?"

"What I want from you, you can't buy in a store, babes. Hurry back!"

When Qwayz returned, he snatched up the ringing phone and set the groceries on the counter.

"Hey, Mr. C." He eyed the bedroom. No sight of Jaz meant she was still in the tub.

"Well, I'm clean, pruney, and hot." She stood in the doorway wrapped in her fluffy robe, her wet hair hidden beneath a thirsty towel. "How about some loud love-making on the magic carpet of our big brass bed?" Qwayz didn't respond as he finished putting things away. He's tired, she thought. "You take a shower while I rustle us up something delicious to eat." Her husband was transfixed by something out the kitchen's stained-glass window. "What is it?" Jaz looked out and saw nothing but a strangeness in her husband's eyes. "Qwayz, what's the matter?"

"Your dad called." His mouth opened but nothing else came out. Jaz thought her father had blown her anniversary gift, but the painting was to be shipped directly to the landlady. "Jaz..." Qwayz gripped her shoulders for support and it scared her.

4

"What?" she implored. His face looked as if it were going to explode under the pressure. "Qwayz, what?" She almost screamed as her heart pounded, and a queasiness churned in her stomach. And, she knew. There was only one thing her father could say that would hit Qwayz like this. "What, Qwayz?"

"It's TC."

She began to cry uncontrollably, matching the silent tears streaming down his cheeks. "No! No, no, no," she wailed like a wounded animal. Forehead to forehead, nose to nose, honey on hazel, tears to tears. They collapsed, huddled and locked in each other's arms, as Akira circled them before resting by Qwayz's side.

"It was instant, painless," he began as Jaz jerked at the idea of death being painless. "He's receiving a Bronze Star for valor. After most of his company was killed, he lay in ambush until the VC came around and took out four before they… got him." The last word mixed with a new wave of tears, and they cried together until all moisture drained from their bodies.

A horrible few weeks followed, and now with her brother buried in the Culhane family cemetery in Colt, Texas, Jaz just wanted her life with Qwayz back to normal. She just wanted him to finish up his prelaw studies and she her premed. She just wanted the fun-loving, optimistic, crazy Qwayz back. The guy whose handsome face would split into a wide smile, whose laughter would fill his eyes and then the room. Her Qwayz. Girls wanted Quinton Regis Chandler IV, and guys wanted to be him. His gait as easy as the licks he'd put on Amber, his dad's old guitar. She wanted popcorn and old movies on TV in their brass bed on Saturday nights and bubble baths in their claw-foot tub illuminated by a thousand candles. Chilled apple cider and satin sheets. She wanted to make love again anytime, anywhere. Didn't matter how much lovin' they enjoyed through the week,

Saturday night was always a marathon and twice on Wednesdays, their hump day, when afternoon delight between classes was capped with an after dinner flesh-fest. She wanted lazy rides north to Napa or south to Carmel, where love pulled them off the road, demanding release. She wanted strolls along the beach, special celebrations at Giuseppe's, cuddling by their fireplace munching pecan bark from Ghirardelli Square, and purchases from Fisherman's Wharf to be cooked and devoured in the privacy of their own home. She wanted her perfect life back when it was all sunshine, laughter, music and love.

And Qwayz's lovin' was… supernatural. He knew the how, where, and what of pleasuring her, talented, adventurous, and insatiable, crediting his West Indian heritage for his "gift." After all this time, being with him remained magical. Making love in their big brass bed was like climbing onto a magic carpet, Qwayz her passport to ecstasy. Soaring high above the earth, they flew among the stars, tumbled through heaven, and somersaulted into paradise as Qwayz brought her to an indescribable, unendurable pleasure. He was her FLO—First, Last, and Only love. It had taken him a full year and a half to consummate their relationship because he wanted it to be special for her. "You're only going to have one first time, Jas-of-mine. It's gonna be magical like we are. No back seat, sand dunes, or green grass motels for us." Jaz's best friend, Gladys Ann, told her that Qwayz could pull it off since he'd "already had enough poontang to last him till he's thirty!" Jaz and Qwayz'd discovered inventive ways to relieve sexual tension while maintaining her virginity. Finally, during her graduation trip to visit her aunt and uncle in Paris, France, Jaz was deflowered in the Fluellen limo parked outside the Chateau Jazz during the Fourth of July celebration while TC's "Night Moves" tape played, followed by various times in the chateau's gatehouse.

They had intended to make love all across Italy, too, but the Watts riots called them home.

Jaz blew her nose and walked into their bedroom, running her fingers across the "friggin' heirloom," as TC had called their gleaming brass bed with its ornate curved head- and footboard. It had been the first bed she and Qwayz'd ever made love in. Over the last few weeks, they'd existed in an isolated togetherness, still sleeping intertwined as usual, but brought together by comfort, not desire, and Jaz missed his touch, spontaneity and craziness. She missed coming home to a passel of balloons after a tough exam or a candlelit dinner set for two with a centerpiece of pink roses. Or a cord of wood obstructing the doorway and lining the walls because he thought two cords would keep "his lady" really warm in the winters. Or coming home and finding him stretched across the hearth wearing nothing but a smile, strumming Amber. He'd put the guitar beside the driftwood from Paradise Rock, open his arms, and say, "Show me you know me, girlie." And she would.

Yeah, she wanted her Qwayz back so they could "not mourn," like TC said in his tape. TC, the big brother Jaz followed everywhere for years. Before he went to Vietnam, TC was her only blood relative here on the West Coast, but TC and Qwayz had been womb-close since they were ten and eight. Despite a two-year difference in age, Qwayz was TC's equal athletically and musically. Closer than most brothers, once Qwayz revealed his newfound feelings for Jaz, both guys often reminded her that they shared a relationship "over and beyond" her, which she had to recognize and respect.

With her parents in Italy, where her father was ambassador, her sister Mel in New York, and her jazz diva aunt Selena and Selena's husband, the legendary saxophonist Zack Fluellen, back in Paris, Qwayz was all she had in this world. He'd always been there for her and promised that he always would be; she never had reason to doubt him. He needed time to grieve TC's loss and to heal.

"I'm back," Qwayz said as he hung his red cap and jacket on the hall tree and headed for the bathroom. Jaz only wished it were so as Akira stretched out in her usual posture. "Ready for bed?" he asked coming from the bathroom, climbing in and opening the covers for her.

Jaz crawled into him, and he enveloped her body with his. They lay in the darkness, the reflection of San Francisco bouncing back at them from the dresser's mirror. A distant foghorn bellowed as she paced her breathing with his. They both feigned sleep, begged for it to come and go, come and go, signifying the passage of time when all would be right with their world again.

The next day Jaz pulled into a space and noticed Qwayz's car already there. For their first anniversary, she'd stored their wedding portrait in the seldom used bedroom closet. As Qwayz kissed her goodbye early this morning, had he wished her happy anniversary or Happy Valentine's Day or good luck on her BioChem exam? After such a weird few weeks, with both of them preoccupied with TC's death while trying to catch up on their studies, Jaz hoped today was the day they would find their way back to each other.

Opening the door and announcing her arrival, she stopped, then convulsed with laughter. In her grandmother's rocker, a few steps from the door, sat a gigantic teddy bear holding a red and purple balloon bouquet in one paw and a dozen pink roses in the other.

"I couldn't find gardenias to save my life," Qwayz said, leaning against the bedroom doorjamb.

"You're a trip." She fell into Qwayz's waiting arms. "I love you."

"Me too you. Happy Valentine's Day, Jas-of-mine."

"That sounds so good." Jaz let her head drop against his neck, soaking up his Jade East scent.

"And this feels good, too, but we've got reservations at Giuseppe's at six."

"Oh, boo coo de bucks."

"Nothing's too good for my lady." He flashed his familiar smile, even-toothed over a sensuous bottom lip.

They dined royally at their favorite neighborhood bistro, where Mama Abruzzo always hired a roving violinist and gave each woman a rose for Valentine's Day. When Qwayz told her it was their anniversary, she announced it to the entire room and gave the couple a bottle of champagne.

They staggered lazily up the hill to their apartment. Inside, they patted Teddy on the head, and rounded the fireplace to the bedroom, where Qwayz had more champagne on ice… water.

"No more champagne," Jaz protested weakly, "or I'll get a headache, and I don't want a headache tonight." She began peeling off her clothes as Qwayz threw the champagne out of sight. "Oh, I look a mess." Jaz stood in front of a freestanding antique cheval mirror, absently moving a big red bow from her field of vision. "I always loved that mirror." She flopped on the bed.

"Happy first anniversary." Qwayz stroked her bare brown thigh.

"Ah!" Jaz said, jumping up as she realized the antique mirror she'd admired for so long was hers. "You devil!" She fingered the beveled glass as Qwayz sidled up behind her, his image captured behind hers.

"It's hard to shop for the girl who has everything." He brushed his lips across her cheek and kissed her.

"As long as I have you, I do have everything." She squeezed her hands over his.

"Well, I'm gonna give you something memorable every anniversary."

"That reminds me." She wrestled herself loose of his grasp and rolled the television out of the way.

"Hey, watch it." He ran to help. "What's in there?"

"My gift to you. Put it over here. On the bed. Now, you unveil it."

"Oh, sweet!" He fell speechless.

"Oh, Qwayz, it's beautiful. We're beautiful." They both stared at their wedding day image captured in oil, their eyes shining brightly. Jaz remembered his proposing during one of their study breaks.

"Valentine's Day has always been super special for us, and I think we oughta do something extraordinary to commemorate it," he'd said, his sensuous bottom lip tucked under even white teeth, devilishness dancing in his eyes.

Jaz straddled him and murmured, "Yeah? What?"

"Marry me." He rode her to the other side of the couch, her questioning eyes never leaving his. "Why not? I love you, you love me, I can't see any part of my future without you in it. Somewhere on this planet, I want it written that you and I cared enough about each other to make it legal. I've thought about it a lot since your father discovered our living situation, and it's what I want. You and me for eternity, Jaz. I want you to be my wife." He kissed her.

"Qwayz, you're a trip. In a time when folks are running from marriage and commitment—"

"I've never gone along with the okey-doke, Jas-of-mine. Isn't that why you're so crazy 'bout me?"

"You're pregnant!" Jaz teased. "In love and trouble, tsk-tsk."

"I'd be in trouble if you said no, Jaz. That'd mean I was wrong about us all along. Am I?"

"No, Qwayz. I'd be honored to be your wife for the rest of my life." From behind the bathroom door, Qwayz then sprang on her the ecru Victorian tea dress with the leg-of-mutton sleeves that Jaz had loved in Memories Boutique. "How can I refuse?" She smiled through tears of happiness.

Qwayz was willing, but Jaz nixed the idea of inviting her parents, knowing her father would be vehemently opposed to his daughter marrying so young. So, they swore their friends to secrecy, and the Chandler wedding party took off for Tahoe one weekend. TC orchestrated the ceremony with Nat King Cole's "Too Young" as their wedding march. TC hosted the wedding dinner before dangling the bridal suite keys in front of the newlyweds. Qwayz carried his bride away from their friends and into the suite, where the first thing they noticed after he staggered across the room and dumped her on the bed was the beamed ceiling... a reminder of the first few times they made love in that chateau gatehouse. They'd convulsed with laughter and fell asleep in their wedding clothes... she in that gorgeous lace dress with the gardenia wreath on her head and he in his tux.

And now, a year later, their wedding-day images stared back at them. Two blissfully happy newlyweds with a glimpse of the gardenia bouquet. The artist had captured Qwayz's full lips, the little indentation between his top lip and his narrow nose, his high cheekbones, hazel eyes, skin tone, and curly hair.

"I didn't expect this masterpiece." Jaz moved closer to inspect their larger-than-life selves. "You are one fine brother!"

"It's perfect of you." Qwayz mesmerized by his wife's intelligent, honey eyes, hooded by dense, long eyelashes and topped by her thick, naturally arched eyebrows. Her curly mane, which fell below her shoulders, was crowned by the halo of gardenias. "Unreal. Who did this? Michelangelo?"

"Close. Luchesi Tretoni. He did the painting of us as children that hangs in Dad's office. It's as awful as this is magnificent."

"He captured us, Jaz... the love, the hope, the promise. This is a for-sure bonafide heirloom. You hadn't seen it before?"

"No." Jaz slid her arms around Qwayz's waist. "I wanted us to see it together for the first time on our first anniversary."

"Our kids are gonna laugh." He chuckled. "What is it about you, me, and Italy? We're gonna get there one of these days."

"Our second honeymoon. I'll get pregnant there." They laughed into each other's arms.

"Oh Jaz, thank you. I needed this... to remind me of how sweet our life together is."

They made slow, deliberate love, with not an inkling of urgency from the weeks of deprivation. "Welcome back," she said, as they lay spent and satisfied.

"It's good to be home." Qwayz kissed her as he interlocked his legs with hers. "If I'd played my cards right, we'd be making love at Paradise Rock for our first anniv—"

"Everything I want I have, whenever you hold me tight," Jaz quoted the Drifters' "This Magic Moment."

"We are magic, Jaz, and we'll last until the end of time." They giggled and kissed. He thought of the place they'd found after one of their trips to Carmel, where they had regularly stopped to make love until somebody built a house on it. "But it was perfect, Jaz. That secluded granite peninsula jutting out over the Pacific. The sound of the ocean pounding five hundred feet below."

12

"We have a lifetime to discover another special place. Maybe even the Myrtle Beach your dad was so crazy about."

"Yeah, but he hadn't seen Paradise Rock. If I'm ever missing, that's where I'll be. Our one-bedroom hideaway from little Q-5 and Amber and Shane."

"Oh, Negro, please. We'll name our daughter after your dad's guitar, but I'm not naming our second son after a movie. I'm thinking of resurrecting Seth Culhane Chandler."

"Shane Chandler? Sounds… athletic."

"Sounds doofus."

"As cool as we are, we'd never have doofus kids." He stretched out his long brown legs and Jake protruded. "I'm kinda cool, how 'bout warming me up?" Qwayz said, and Jaz climbed on top of him, covering his body with hers. She rose above him and held on to the brass headboard with San Francisco's diamond sky approving beyond. She let her engorged breasts fill Qwayz's passion-soaked eyes. "Have mercy, girlie," he managed before treating each of her chocolate drops to the rough-smooth texture of his tongue. "I love you, Jas-of-mine; don't ever forget that."

"Don't ever stop. Promise?"

"Promise."

Chapter 2

The NCAA basketball final drew an SRO crowd to the immense stadium and Jaz pried Denise Chandler Hodges, Denny, away from the house to see the last game of her brother's college career. As they settled into their seats, Jaz recalled sadly that last year TC had been there, and Yudi, Denny's husband, was expected home from Nam. This year TC was gone, and Yudi had disappeared somewhere into America, a broken shadow.

Qwayz's second cousin, AJ, who preferred being called his nephew, sat with Jaz and Denny. Qwayz's mother and sister, Ma Vy and Hanie, and AJ's parents, Melie and Big Aubrey, sat in front of them. Qwayz's boys from Champion Record Studios, the neighborhood, and Roosevelt High kept up noise and spirit to the far left. The excitement high. All those who had scored the coveted tickets reveled in their good fortune and felt privileged to witness the final game of "Magic" Chandler's college career.

The TV commentators transmitted plays secondhand to folks unable to beg, borrow, or steal a ticket and bantered on about how Magic Chandler's leaving would hurt the team. How before him, Stanford had not played in the NCAA since '42, but Magic had taken them there twice. How he epitomizes grace under pressure, even with seven-foot Alcindor on his back, "Magic just adjusts and scores." Now he was giving up the game to go to law school.

Even though Stanford lost to UCLA, Qwayz was high scorer with 38 points, 12 short of his personal goal to tie with Wilt Chamberlain's 1962 record. As the two teams shook hands, Stanford ran off while UCLA remained on the floor.

It began on the far right, a hum like a swarm of unearthed bees and became rhythmic and distinct. "Qway-z! Qway-z! Qway-z!" Like a Zulu chant, it spread through the crowd until everyone in the bleachers stood, chanting his name. "Qway-z! Qway-z!" Spectators stopped in their tracks, in the aisles and at the entrances, and on the floor, the UCLA team joined in to give a great one his due. "Qway-z! Qway-z!"

The crowd wasn't going anywhere until it got another glimpse of Number 24, the best college player of the century. Qwayz appeared and the crowd thundered with applause, cheering and whistling. He raised both hands over his head like a prizefighter who'd just been declared champ, his clenched fists alternating with waves. When the crowd refused to cease, he threw kisses to his mother and his wife, bowed graciously from the waist to his adoring fans, and jogged off. Tears of pride, joy, and pain graced Jaz's cheeks as her husband bid farewell to a segment of his life he'd lived and breathed ever since she'd known him. He'd surely miss it and basketball would miss him . . . and TC had missed it all.

Even though UCLA won the NCAA championship that year and Alcindor was named Player of the Year, it was the picture of Qwayz "Kissing Basketball Goodbye," that made the cover of Sports Illustrated.

~*~

"I think we oughta move," Qwayz said casually as they prepared fondue for guests one night.

"Where did that come from?" Jaz swirled the melted cheese as Qwayz arranged seafood around the vegetables.

"After graduation." She eyed him curiously as he continued, "It'll be better for you once I start law school. I don't wanna worry about you coming and going from campus to here."

"I do it now."

"Yeah, but I'm here now. I thought we'd move to Berkeley. A nice apartment with a balcony for Akira, maybe a fireplace in the bedroom." He yo-yoed his eyebrows suggestively, but Jaz wasn't amused. "I'll get it." He answered the door for their dinner guests.

Jaz loved this Alta Vista apartment, their first home, with its hand-picked heirloom furniture, beamed ceilings and fireplace.

She assumed they'd stay here until they bought a house. She wasn't sure what to make of this move idea, but maybe he would read her reaction and drop it. Things were much better between them since their anniversary celebration, but he still kept more to himself than usual. She thought that after the basketball season and his last game he'd be more the old Qwayz, but he remained slightly preoccupied. For all she knew, she was as well. They were still adjusting to the lack of TC in their lives. Things would happen, and after sharing it with one another their natural reaction was to "call TC." Maybe this apartment reminded Qwayz of TC, maybe San Francisco did. Maybe it was Qwayz's attempt to move on.

If Qwayz brought it up again, she wouldn't balk. He'd always been there for her. He was there when her parents threatened to move her to Connecticut so the family would be closer to her dad in Washington. When her aunt and uncle came from Paris to take care of her for her senior year, he'd called her every night at eleven throughout that year and came down from Palo Alto whenever he didn't have a game. He was there at her prom and graduation, taking pictures, and beside her every step of the way as she discovered Paris. He was there when she had her first brush with prejudice in her Phi Sci class. It was Qwayz who comforted and told her, "Jasmine Bianca Culhane has the GPA, SAT scores, and the right to be in any class on Berkeley's campus... and the only relationship you have to worry 'bout is between you and the teacher. Period." He'd held her and said, "Some of us are born to ride against the wind. I guess we're just a pair of the lucky equestrians." He was there for her when TC died. He'd be there with her forever. It was her turn to be there for him. While she loved this apartment, she loved Qwayz much more.

Qwayz's graduation was full of pomp and circumstance. His mother and his sister Hanie stayed in her parents' suite at the Fairmont, Melie and Aubrey in a room at the Mark Hopkins, and AJ on Jaz's and Qwayz's sofa. Jaz's father, Hep, hosted a reception for his "son" in the Riverton Room, where members of the old L.A. crew came up and mingled with the academicians, former team mates, and college friends.

Jaz still had a few more weeks of school, so Qwayz took it upon himself to apartment hunt. He often waited for her at school after an unsuccessful day of inspecting possibilities. She didn't know which was worse, his apartment hunting or his going off to L.A., which he'd done twice without her. They never did anything apart except during basketball season, and that was over.

"I found the perfect place!" he told her one day, beaming with excitement, and took her by.

"It's new!" was her first objection to the apartment. "It's a year old and really close to campus."

When the door swung open, she hated it instantly. Straight ahead was the balcony. To the left was a closet door; the next opening an exposed kitchen with the countertop, just like her childhood home on Alvaro Street. To the right was a closet door, then another door to the bedroom. The living room was the space in front of the balcony, and the dining room was the space in front of the kitchen counter. It was small, with no character and thin white walls. "It has a dishwasher, a disposal, and a washer and dryer," he pointed out. "The bedroom has a fireplace."

Jaz took the two giant steps from the front door into the decent-sized bedroom with a long window on one wall and the two closets and bathroom doors on the other. "Where are we going to put all our furniture?"

"Well, the bed on this wall opposite the fireplace and the armoire and wardrobe… over here. We'll work with it, Jaz."

She stepped back into the living room, shaking her head at the thought of all their gorgeous pieces being crammed into this tiny apartment.

"Over here we can get that new dinette set you wanted. The all-glass one on the brass pedestal and the matching chairs." ·

"Where do we put our parlor set?"

"On the balcony."

"The balcony?" Jaz smelled a rat. Was Qwayz so anxious for this move that he was bribing her with the "too expensive" glass and brass dinette set? If only she could determine why he wanted to move so badly, then she could counter it, ease his worries, and they could stay on Alta Vista. But this was as animated as he'd been since graduation. His sister, Denny had said that the death of TC probably conjured up some long-buried feelings from their dad's death. Stir in his giving up basketball and ending his musical collaboration, graduating and beginning law school; this all must weigh heavily on his mind. As his wife, Jaz would have to adjust and make the transition more palatable for them both.

"Is this the best you've seen?"

"Trust me." His hazel eyes locked with her honey.

Jaz swore she saw him flinch.

What they didn't cram into the new apartment, they put in storage. The bedroom accommodated all their furniture including the lingerie armoire and the cheval mirror, but the living room had to forfeit furniture. Still, once they hung their wedding portrait over the couch, it seemed like home.

"I could stare at it for hours," Qwayz mused, sitting on the coffee table facing the painting.

"Why do that when you got the real thing?" She kissed him on the nose, pivoting into the kitchen to unpack condiments. "Think Scoey and Tracy will be as happy as us?" She spoke of their best friends who were about to marry. Scoey had unselfishly expanded his friendship with TC to include Qwayz from their days at the Watts Boys Club right on up through Raw Cilk, to Scoey's receiving a football scholarship to USC and beyond.

"No one could be as happy as we are. I gotta go down to L.A. to make the last plans for Scoey's bachelor party."

"Can't you do that by phone?" Jaz had noticed the frequency of his trips to L.A., including the one last week.

"I've got final fittings for the tux and a bunch of us are helping Scoey move into his new place. 'Sides, you'll be busy. You are taking that special program at the hospital? That's quite an honor to be recommended as an incoming senior."

"That's only because I'm so brilliant and talented," Jaz teased, returning to sit next to him on the coffee table. "I thought I'd

19

pass it up and we'd spend the summer together: Carmel, Napa, Tahoe—"

"The program is only six weeks. Think how far ahead of everyone you'll be with this project. A shoo-in for med school."

"I just thought it was important for us to spend some serious time together." Always so in tune, it bothered Jaz that she couldn't read his expression.

They both returned to L.A. where the wedding was gorgeous with Tracy, radiant in the most elegant gown and train ever to grace St. Theresa's. Jaz as matron of honor, a maid of honor, six bridesmaids, and a flower girl were all decked out in a symphony of muted pink and green. Scoey, his best man, Qwayz, and the other groomsmen regally handsome in their black tuxedos.

Jaz took the bouquet from her old friend, Tracy Renee Summerville, the petite, pretty girl with the graham cracker complexion framed by black hair, whom she'd met in dance class before Mrs. Terrell put Jaz out. A parochial school girl, Tracy refused to attend an all-girl high school and ended up at Roosevelt with Jaz and her best friend Gladys Ann... the notorious pair. At first sight, Tracy'd set her designs on the older star football player, Ellis Carlton Scofield, and slow-walked him until she got him. "Shoulda given that girl more credit," Gladys Ann once said of the quiet, naive but tenacious Tracy.

From the packed church, guests followed the limo to the reception, where the champagne flowed from fountains like water and the food as plentiful as the cache' of gifts, which required their own room.

"Did I tell you I've just bought and revived a pepper farm with a pimiento plant?" Hep asked Qwayz. Next to his children there was nothing Hep Culhane enjoyed discussing more than his investments, and Qwayz was the only interested family member. "Besides my Orsini holdings, my foreign assets now include the cocoa plantation in South America, tin in Sumatra, bauxite in the Caribbean and in Sri Lanka—" Hep chatted on as Qwayz drank pink champagne and watched his wife posing with the bride. "Don't-give-a-damn gorgeous" had been used to describe her physical beauty: the copper skin, the voluminous nutmeg hair shot with blond from the California sun. The Cherokee rise in her profile responsible for her pronounced cheekbones, which plunged into hollows, only to be rescued by full lips that rendered her mouth in a perpetual pout. Jaz had always been mature-looking, even at ten, when. tired of the constant comments, she had plopped her father's too-big fedora on her head in an effort to hide her looks, but instead drew more attention.

Jaz took no responsibility and therefore no credit for her looks, and had no time for folks who responded to her based solely on her appearance. Jaz hated the comparisons others made between her and TC to Mel. At seven, to the delight of Hep and the chagrin of Lorette, Jaz punched out older classmates for calling her big sister, Mel, "bug-eyed," "gorilla nose," or "adopted." But Miss Thang found her beauty niche when she went off to Juilliard. In the gene-pool roulette black families inherit, Mel would never have mountains of long hair like her sister or her height or her "apple-jelly eyes," as AJ called them, but Mel learned to play up her features. Those "bug eyes" rimmed with professional makeup became her trademark, she grew into her nose and adorned it with an eighteen-carat-gold ring, and the hair her mother had croquignoled every Saturday now formed a short, airy, natural halo around her mocha skin. The Culhane sisters favored each other, but the most beautiful was his wife, Qwayz thought.

21

"Young man, you haven't heard a word I've said," Hep chastised Qwayz, who smiled unconsciously at his wife. "But I approve of my competition. You love her very much."

"More than life itself."

"I hope you don't have to prove that one day."

"I hope I prove it every day, Mr. C."

"What are you two jawjacking about?" Jaz insinuated herself between her favorite men.

"We're buying a house in San Fran, Punkin. Three bedrooms on Nob Hill. The head of Culhane Enterprises needs a house in the city," Hep informed his daughter.

"Are you keeping the Connecticut house museum?"

"No, my New York business will be moving to the coast, too."

"What about that poor old fossil you brought out of retirement to run it for you while you were in Italy... Kyle? Was that his name?" Jaz watched her father's eyebrows knit together in a question, then relax with recognition.

"Tipton Kylerton has been a trusted friend and associate—"·

"Can he still walk, Dad?"

"So like the young to have no mercy for the old."

The photographer called for the best man, and Qwayz left to pose for pictures with Scoey. Jaz couldn't help but remember that it used to be three extraordinary black men: TC, Scoey, and Qwayz— the trio.

And then there were two, Jaz thought.

"Glad this circus is over," Qwayz said, watching the bride and groom get into the limo to catch a plane bound for Hawaii.

"You'll do the same for our daughters," Jaz said.

"No question, and they'll be as beautiful as their mama."

"This is just what the doctor ordered." Jaz slid her arms around her husband, thinking of the changes and horrors of 1968, beginning with the death of her brother in January.

In March, Howard University crowned a homecoming queen with a natural, like the one Mel had been wearing since her days at Juilliard. In the My Lai massacre, the United States had slaughtered a whole village of unarmed South Vietnamese, and fifteen days later LBJ announced he would not seek reelection. Four days later, on April fourth, Dr. Martin Luther King Jr. was assassinated on the balcony of the Lorraine Motel in Memphis and died an hour later; inner cities erupted. Two days later, seventeen-year-old Black Panther Bobby Hutton was shot and killed by police in West Oakland. On May thirteenth, delegates from the United States and North Vietnam held their first formal peace meeting in Paris. Then Robert Kennedy was killed at the Ambassador Hotel. One step forward, then two steps back.

But personally, all was not lost. Mel had the lead and hit song with a nightly standing ovation in the Broadway hit *Hair*. Qwayz had graduated with honors from Stanford, and Mr. and Mrs. Ellis Carlton Scofield, Scoey and Tracy, had entered the ranks of the blissfully married. "Well, after six long months this year is finally looking up," Jaz said, to which her husband made no comment.

~*~

The alarm blasted and Jaz opened her eyes. Ugh! This hateful apartment, she thought. She missed the wall of windows at the headboard, and making love with their silhouettes reflecting in the bureau's mirror, lit by the starry San Francisco skyline as their backdrop. She missed the wide open spaces. Here poor Akira had a balcony, but she had to sleep on the threshold between the bedroom and the living room. It was awful, but

Qwayz made it bearable. The move was good for him; he seemed to be coming around.

Jaz stood on the balcony watching him wash their cars down below. Akira sprinted back and forth in the park across the small one-way drive. Jaz observed Qwayz's biceps ripple as he applied pressure to her car's roof, the way the sun caught and ricocheted off his brunette curls. "Hey, foxy mama," Qwayz greeted, swinging his arm up over the roof in pure adoration of his wife's beauty. She wore her sleep T-shirt with scanty panties underneath, her hair still tousled from last night's lovin'. "Have mercy! Girlie, you do look fine in peach."

"Everything you buy me is peach." She teased by rocking her legs and body suggestively.

"You wear it well next to that deep brown skin."

"Thanks for the wake-up alarm." She leaned over taunting him.

"Your interview is at three."

"I don't need three hours to get ready. What else did you have in mind?" She licked her lips.

"I'll be up in a few." He winked as Mr. Sanchez, the super, greeted them both. An embarrassed Jaz quickly disappeared.

Showered, dressed in jeans and a sweatshirt, Jaz answered the ringing phone, and talked to Denny as she seeded a cantaloupe.

"I report directly to the chief psychiatrist," Denny said. "I've only got my thesis to complete. Gotta keep busy." The name of Yudi hung unspoken between them. "As for you, I hear it's quite a coup to even be approached for Dr. Brock Williams's summer research program."

"True, but I was hoping Qwayz and I could spend the summer together, maybe even in Myrtle Beach."

"Where is that baby brother of mine, anyway?"

24

"He should be hanging his cap and jacket on the old hall tree any minute now. How does he seem to you?"

"How do you mean?" Denny hedged, and Jaz heard it.

"He moved us over here, for one. At least he stopped his solo trips to L.A., which means the other woman lost to the wife."

"Nothing like that."

"You know somethin' I don't and should?"

"No, he's been taking care of things... with the recording rights for TC's—"

"Denny, what's going on?"

"Hey, girlie." Qwayz and Akira came through the door, hanging his cap and jacket on the brass knobs.

"Saved by the bell," Jaz said to Denny. "Catch you later."·

"Who was?"

"Denny."

"So how's she doin'?" he asked evenly as Jaz surmised that blood was thicker than semen.

"Okay, but I still can't get her here to visit. So we gonna get AJ before or after his summer in camp? He's a teenager. How long do they think this camp crap will last?"

"His parents don't think. That's why he has us... at least—" He stopped. "I thought we'd spend some time together, just the two of us."

"I like the sound of that." Jaz slid her arms around his neck as he sat on the coffee table facing their portrait. "I'll make you blaff tonight. I'll pick up the ingredients on the way home from the interview." She kissed the side of his salty cheek.

"I better go shower."

"Good idea." Jaz released him. "Qwayz," she called after him, "you don't have anything to tell me?" Her honey eyes fixed on his hazel; the longer the gaze, the more worried Jaz became.

"Well." Qwayz could hear his sister's voice prompting him: You better tell Jaz. "It can wait."

"Why don't you tell me now." She walked slowly to him, not blinking once. Bad vibes began in her toes and he looked uncomfortable. Quinton Regis Chandler IV never looked uncomfortable.

"Okay." He relented, motioning for her to take a seat on the couch. He sat facing his wife and their oil images upon the wall.

This was going to be far worse than Jaz had thought. Was Qwayz deathly ill and dying or impotent? Nope. The area of lovemaking remained supernatural. If anything, their problems began once their feet hit the floor. Were they broke? Impossible. He wasn't going to law school? That was his choice, and not as grave a situation as he was making her feel. "Qwayz, you're scaring me."

"How do I begin," he said as he played with her folded hands.

"At the beginning."

"I've spoken it in my mind a thousand times."

"No more dress rehearsals. This is it, spit it out."

"Better or worse," he chuckled, twirling her circle-of-diamonds wedding band. "I've already lost two people I cared about most in this world. Don't be number three." His eyes speared hers.

"I'm not going anywhere, Qwayz."

"It has to do with TC's death. I've remained more tied to it because I've handled most of his affairs. A complicated and talented man." He sensed Jaz's disguised impatience. "I know you've noticed my preoccupation at times and that's partially the reason for it that I couldn't put it to rest as quickly as you thought I should have."

"So what you have to tell me is about TC?"

26

"Yes and no. I mean, I couldn't believe that he had so much to give here in the States, but he wanted to give in Vietnam, where his country needed him."

Jaz didn't hide her confusion. His eloquence had served him well as a songwriter and would do so as a lawyer, but right now it was driving her up the wall.

"I've felt the need to do more." He raked his hands through his curls, rose, and strutted across the room, looking out of the balcony window down at their cars parked predictably side by side; the red Karmann Ghia and pink T-Bird. "Before TC went over, we knew about Vietnam from Yudi going over and the guys we knew who came back and didn't. We saw it on television, able to turn it off if we wanted. We saw the demonstrators, passed right by them with their handouts and protest songs. What did it mean to us, the future doctor and lawyer? But TC's death brought the war right into our house, sat it down, and said, 'What are you gonna do about it?' And I gotta do something, Jaz." He looked back at her from the sliding glass door. "I just haven't felt comfortable with this whole thing; that TC died fighting to protect our freedom over there while we enjoyed it free of charge here. I just had to do something."

"I think that's admirable." Jaz joined him at the door, stroking his arm and taking his hand. "Everyone has their own way of contributing to the same cause—different roads to the same end. We're all fighting for freedom. Your role in life isn't in Vietnam; it's here, fighting in the courtrooms for justice. It's to protect Ma Vy, me and our children."

"But how do I look our children in the eye when they ask about Uncle TC and ask what I did?" He broke from her grip and paced the room. "How did you get out alive, Daddy?"

For the first time in their relationship, Jaz felt as if she and Qwayz were seriously out of sync—a bizarre twilight zone of lapsed communication. Something that seemed so important and all-consuming to him didn't mean diddly to her.

"Qwayz, it'll be all right. We're talking years from now; the war will be long over. There are peace talks in Paris now, LBJ isn't running again, we'll elect a president who'll stop the war—"

"I need to do something *now*. Something definite, concrete; something I can feel good about as a man, so I can contribute and move on with my life." He led her back to their original position, with him on the coffee table and her on the couch. "I feel confident about my decision. It's your reaction to it that has me worried."

"What? You volunteered to work with... vets?"

"I want you to look at the long-term benefit of this for me as a man, a husband, a father. It's important to me, and I really have no choice. It's something I have to do if I am to look at myself in the mirror with any pride for the rest of my life. It'll throw our plans off for about a year, no more than two, tops, but we'll be healthier as a couple, a family, because of it."

So he'll work a year or so before going to law school, Jaz thought, could be worse.

"I've joined the Air Force." Hazel eyes unflinchingly pierced honey-brown ones.

"What?" Jaz managed without blinking, her face frozen, and Qwayz repeated his statement with such calm relief it was frightening. Qwayz seemed almost boyish after the release of the news, and Jaz felt ancient.

He continued eloquently as if presenting a case before the Supreme Court. Jaz felt as if she were trapped in a nightmare that grew more macabre as she caught snatches of his soliloquy, such as "As an officer... equivalent to law clerking... trying cases of military indiscretions... court-martials... a special task force... Saigon is a fortress... well-protected..."

28

"What did you say?" Her horror found voice. Qwayz had mistaken her quietness for reluctant acceptance. She slid her hands from his as if his were contaminated with acid. "You're crazy." She rose from the sofa, pacing the room's perimeter like a caged feline.

"I've made up my mind, Jaz."

"You're certifiable." Her heart pounded and her head split wide open. "Didn't you see TC? His body riddled with bullets, smell the jungle funk that filled that room. Did you hear the sobbing? The words? Did you see the pain? And you're signing up for more of the same?"

"Jaz, I told you this place is a secure—"

"That's what Yudi told Denny; all he'd be doing is what he did at the funeral home, and she hasn't seen him since he left their house! No one gets back alive from Vietnam. Haven't you learned anything from the neighborhood? Zombies come back. Their minds gone, the body parts missing, and the flesh that survives is hooked on morphine and heroin. If you wanna kill yourself, just get a gun and blow your brains out. Save us the prolonged agony and trouble." Tears streamed down her face, and she yanked a napkin from the Lake Tahoe holder.

"Jaz, I can't imagine living without you. You are my world, but something heinous has crawled into it and I have to deal with it the best way I can... or it will destroy us both."

"Save it, Qwayz." She resumed pacing. "You're going off to avenge my brother's death. It would be funny if it weren't so sad. This isn't back-in-the-day when some rival cross-town team sold wolf-tickets to the Dragons so y'all gonna go over there and whip ass for the big payback!"

"I'm doing this for both of us, Jaz." Qwayz stood.

"Don't hand me that shit! And please spare me the Gary Cooper 'a man's gotta do what a man's gotta do' bullshit. Well, I

29

gotta another quote for you, Qwayz." She posted her face inches from his. "I think it's from Dr. Zhivago. 'Only an unhappy man volunteers to go to war!' If life is so bad for you here with me, you don't have to go to Vietnam to get away. No! I release you." She began throwing things into an overnight case, and Qwayz followed her without realizing what she was doing. "You selfish bastard!"

"I could say the same about you."

"You're doing this because it's right for you. To hell with everybody else! They don't count, they don't get a vote. Jaz is strong. Jaz is resilient, she'll bounce back. Jaz heats up and cools down. She'll adjust, she'll get over it. Hell, I'll be back home by that time. Well, little Jaz isn't going along with the same-o, same-o shit this time." She yanked her shoulder bag, fedora, and jacket off the hall tree. "Let Qwayz go off to war so he can feel better about himself. To hell with me, Ma Vy, AJ… those you leave behind."

"Jaz, where are you going?"

"Like you even care." She shifted her shoulder bag. "Tell me, shall I bury you next to TC so I can visit both graves at once? That'd be real considerate of you."

"Jaz, I'm comin' back."

"Yeah? Think so? In what condition?" she challenged, and when he started to speak again she yelled, "Stop it! Just shut-up, okay? You are leaving me for no good reason but to chase some macho male bonding shit thing you had with my brother. Well, I can't compete with my dead brother's memory. I have sense enough to know that."

"Jaz, let me go with you."

"I have to learn to live without you… might as well start now." She dodged his attempt to hold her. "You still don't get it," she said with precise clarity. "I don't want to be around

30

anyone who cares so little about me and my feelings... as a wife, a person, a human being."

"I'll make it all up to you."

"That is so typically male of you." She laughed wryly and stopped. "You have demonstrated to me just how much you care for me—the living." She opened the door. "It's too late already. You can never make this up to me. Never in a million years." She slammed the door shut.

From the balcony door, Qwayz watched her sling her things into her car and drive off without a backward glance.

Jaz tore around the streets of San Francisco before she ended up at Ghirardelli Square for a chocolate fix. Absently munching on pecan bark, she strolled too close to Antique Row, where she and Qwayz had spent most of their Saturdays shopping for furniture, dreaming of their apartment. She hopped into her car. What the hell am I doing? She gassed up and headed down the coast, turning off the radio, which played too much Raw Cilk; TC's music and Qwayz's lyrics against his soaring tenor voice. Jaz needed to talk, but Tracy was still on her honeymoon and she wouldn't understand anyway, not like Denny, whom Jaz resisted seeing. She longed to talk to her oldest best friend, Gladys Ann, but she was in Washington, D.C. at Howard University. They'd joke about the "stiff-dick club"—the way guys stuck together no matter what.

Unconsciously, she drove to Gary's Seaside Restaurant in Carmel, where she cried in her soup, played with her lobster, passed on dessert, and was propositioned by the waiter as she left. She meandered through Carmel's quiet streets before ending up on Ruidoso Canyon Road. She pulled carefully off the main highway, taking the treacherous turn with aplomb, cruising to a stop about a mile from Paradise Rock and the house that occupied it now. The couple who lived there came out and

31

peered in the direction of her '57 T-Bird perched on the lookout before they climbed into their car and pulled off.

Jaz gazed out at the ocean, searching for answers, not knowing how long she'd been there. The sun had set long ago, and the moon rays skated on its dark glass. *What is it they say about full moons and crazy people?* she thought as she drifted off to sleep. Awakened by the chill in the air, she got out to retrieve the quilt from her trunk and thought she saw the outline of a car farther down the road, but decided it was a rock formation. She locked her doors and let the ocean's roar soothe her back to sleep.

"Dag," she said aloud, waking the next morning and unfolding herself. She rubbed her stiff neck, vowing no more nights spent in the car. Maybe she'd head south, stop at the coastal sights she'd always whizzed by in the last few years. The couple hadn't come back last night, and the tap on the car window startled her. "What do you want?" she asked, rolling the window down only a crack.

"I want you to come home," Qwayz said simply. "So we can talk this thing out."

"As I see it, the time for talk is over. You're going. Goodbye." Jaz started up her car and drove off, a cloud of dust swirling around him.

He wouldn't follow her. To what point? When he called to postpone her interview, he found that Jaz had already canceled it. He just had to wait for her to come around, to see his side. He hoped it would happen before he left for Saigon.

"Hi," Jaz said simply as the door whined open.

"I've been expecting you." Denny smiled.

"I took the scenic route, Big Sur, San Simeon. You ever been to Hearst Castle?"

"Nothing on the Culhane estate in Connecticut," Denny said, with an awkward chuckle.

"I've always liked this house." Jaz looked around the cozy decor as Denny poured soda over ice.

"It's been four days. Folks are kinda worried."

"You mean Qwayz."

"And your father. Qwayz thought you'd caught a plane to Italy."

"Left my passport at the apartment. Besides, Pops was the first one to leave me. Then TC, now Qwayz. Seems I can't hold on to a man."

"Yeah, I know the feeling."

"Oh. I'm sorry, maybe I shouldn't have come."

"Nonsense. I want you here. Who else would understand better than me?"

"Is this Denny the friend, the sister-in-law, or the psychologist?"

"A little of all, but more of the first."

For a couple of days, the two women just lounged around, goofed off, and went to the movies—

Barefoot in the Park and *The Graduate*, enjoying each other's company and steering clear of the old gang, who'd ask after Qwayz. Jaz called her father and convinced him not to leave the embassy in Italy. Denny convinced Qwayz of the same.

"I don't know when I lost control of my life," Jaz confessed quietly one afternoon. "When it all shattered into a million pieces." She grabbed a throw pillow, cradled it in her hands as Denny sat across from her. "The very foundation of our marriage; the love, the honesty, the trust was all a sham, violated and replaced with deceit and manipulation. That whole Berkeley move was part of it. He knew back then, but didn't tell me. I was happy on Alta Vista." She bit back tears. "You know, I shoulda

33

laughed that night on Papa Colt's porch when he told me he loved me. Thrown this gold star in his face." She fingered the necklace he'd given her. "I woulda been spared all this. I wonder where I'd be now. Umph. TC used to say, 'Same thing makes you laugh can make you cry.'"

"I think you've had many an enviable time or two, as I recall."

"Yeah, we did have a charmed life—a crystal stair," she borrowed from Langston Hughes.

"You all were the couple everyone wanted to be," Denny said before leaving Jaz to remember the good times while she fixed them a snack. A faint, sad smile graced Jaz's lips when she returned.

"During his weeks of soul-searching, Qwayz turned to me, his sister," Denny explained. "With TC gone, I guess I was second pick. He wasn't moving past the death of his best friend, his brother. He didn't say it, but I knew he felt six years old and powerless again. And there's nothing worse for a man to feel. So without judging or offering guidance, I listened to him try to make sense of it, sort it out, and then self-prescribe his course of action." Denny stopped staring out the window. "It was hard to hear. As his sister, I couldn't endorse it, but as a psychologist, I understand that it is important for him to do *something,* and this is what he elected to do. What he needs now from us is the unconditional love and support that our grandmothers gave our grandfathers. The way our mothers did our fathers—when they came up with cockamamie ideas. Guess that's why we're here now, because of forgiveness and compromise." Denny looked at her friend, who didn't respond as she twirled the glass of soda on the coaster. "It's easy to love somebody when everything is smooth and cool runnin'. The test of real love is when you can hold on through the rough, insane times. Better or worse… until death do us part." Denny looked at the door. "It's hard to sustain love with no contact, but I still love Yudi. I always will, couldn't stop if I wanted. If he were just to walk through—" Denny's voice broke.

"How do you get past the hurt and anger?" Jaz asked.

"Maybe you don't. Maybe you just put it on hold until later, the way a parent, crazy with worry when their teenager has broken curfew, does. You imagine all sorts of grisly things, but then you see them, that they're all right and you're instantly relieved and mad at the same time. Maybe you can put this aside until Qwayz comes home safe and sound, then give him hell for the rest of your lives." Denny chuckled. Never have two people been so much alike as my brother and his wife, she thought. "Worst scenario," Denny continued, "he leaves with you all like this. Him guilty, you mad... and he doesn't come back at all." Jaz jerked her head toward Denny. Bingo, Denny thought. "Then all the guilt and anger will be yours alone, my friend." She touched her sister-in-law's shoulder. "The nicest thing you all did for TC was to put aside personal feelings and give him a good send-off, with great memories... a reason to come back."

"Lotta good it did," Jaz mumbled.

"You'll never know. I just hate to think of you and Qwayz wasting this time apart when you two should be building memories, not tearing them down. Don't regret forever not spending these last few weeks—"

"Few weeks?"

"You didn't know? He's leaving on the third of July."

"July! But I thought August... like TC. Oh shit!" She scrambled for her things. "He'll miss his birthday."

As Jaz tore up the highway the anger melted, evaporating with her need to see Qwayz, to be with him. "Oh, please be there," she prayed when she stopped for gas and called home.

No answer. "I'm coming home, Qwayz, just as fast as I can."
The faster she sped, the more it seemed as if the car were stuck
on a treadmill to nowhere.

Chapter 3

"Qwayz! Qwayz!" Jaz slammed open the front door, jarring Akira to her feet. "Where is he?"

"Right behind you." He let the towel fall around his neck and over his bare chest.

"Oh, Qwayz!" Jaz flew into his arms. "I'm so sorry I acted that way. I was so mad and scared."

"Jaz, Jaz." He rocked her in his embrace, as happy for her safe return as for her changed state of mind. "I was scared, too; not about going, but that I'd lost you in the process of finding my answer to this crazy mess. I never meant to hurt you or make you feel—"

"I know, I know." They stood wrapped in each other's arms, joy filling their hearts and the week-long separation creeping into their groins.

They began kissing while Qwayz removed Jaz's shoulder bag, then her outer jacket. As they dropped to the floor, the knowledgeable Akira took her seat next to the balcony window. Undressing each other, they remained connected by tongue and tongue, tongue and neck, tongue and nipple, until he lifted her in his arms and carried her the few steps to the couch. While they made love bathed in the moonlight, their wedding portrait over their heads, Akira yawned at the familiar scene.

Luxuriating in each other's embrace, they sat on the floor with the couch as their backrest.

"What will I do without you?" Jaz asked, nuzzling his chest.

"I'll be back before you can figure it out." He brushed his lips across her forehead.

"I'll never understand, Qwayz, but I don't have to. Just come back so we can get on with our lives."

"I will, Jaz. We've got degrees to get, children to have, and a lot more memories to make."

"Promise?" Jaz implored with her honey eyes.

"Promise. Never broken one yet, have I?"

"No! And now's not the time to start."

"No argument here."

Satisfied, secure, warm and protected, Jaz fell asleep with the familiar rhythm of Qwayz's heartbeat as her lullaby. With nothing between them now, only the cloud of Vietnam hung over their heads as they crammed a year of life into two weeks. They went up to Napa, over to Tahoe, down to Carmel and past Paradise Rock. They ate out most nights, sometimes capping the evening with a movie. Paul Newman's *Cool Hand Luke* for her, and Sidney Poitier's *In the Heat of the Night* for him. It was the theme song of "To Sir with Love" that moved Jaz to tears as Lulu sang about someone taking you "from crayons to perfume." That's what Qwayz'd done for her, helped her grow up and allowed her to be.

Sometimes they stayed home partying on their own, playing old records and dancing all the moves of their youth until the wee hours. Mostly they went to bed early and slept late until the time drew nearer and nearer.

"We'll go down to L.A. tomorrow." Qwayz adjusted the covers over Jaz's bare behind.

"No, you go. I think you should go say goodbye to your mom and sisters alone. I've had my private moments with you and so should they."

Reluctantly, Qwayz went alone to L.A. and spent a couple of days before returning to Jaz. He had nixed a farewell party, proposing instead a big all-out Welcome Home bash upon his return.

"With a devil's food cake with white icing, balloons, flowers, champagne, and tickets to Myrtle Beach," he murmured into her ear.

"You got it," Jaz giggled with delight. "What did AJ say?"

"He wanted to know who was going to take care of Aunt Jaz and Akira. Not necessarily in that order." He chuckled.

Seemingly only moments later, Jaz clung to him at Alameda Air Force Base, the airplane engines threatening their last moments.

"This is so weird. Send me your hair." She felt his sides that would soon be shaved.

"What about the rest of me?"

"It's not too late to go AWOL."

"You decide where you wanna go for our R&R: Tokyo or Hawaii."

"Hawaii, no question. I want that place Elvis had in *Blue Hawaii*, with the single cottages so we can make lots of noise."

"Have mercy, girlie." When the commanding officer gave him a final stare, he kissed her.

"Stay safe." Jaz held his hand, then his fingertips until the very last touch possible.

"I will. I got promises to keep." He walked backwards, hazel eyes on honey, a sensuous bottom lip tucked under even white teeth. Up the steps and at the opening, he wriggled his index finger, threw a kiss and yelled something Jaz couldn't make out but guessed. The more tears she wiped away, the more came, and they blurred her vision as the watery image of the plane shivered down the runway.

"And babies to make." She held her stomach, hoping that she was pregnant. It would make it all so much more bearable.

~*~

In short order, like a seasoned opera goer, Jaz came into the immense amphitheater and took a seat in the middle on the aisle, knowing that to be her best vantage point, not in the first few rows where the eager-to-impress sat. Qwayz'd taught her that. Though two weeks late due to some family crisis, Dr. Williams awaited the arrival of Jasmine Chandler, partly because of her academic reputation and partly because she was black, the only one in this highly selected class of sixteen.

Jasmine Chandler sat poised, with glasses perched upon her nose and a tell-me-all-you-know attitude. She took few notes, her intelligent eyes absorbing the words before he spoke them, and she jotted down a word here and there. When something was complicated, she'd lean a little forward, asking pointed and focused questions, sitting back only after she had a complete understanding. She acted visibly impatient when another student masqueraded inquiry as an opportunity to show off his knowledge; she resented his wasting her time. The doctor would lose her to daydreams out the window when he repeated something a pupil should have already known. It was always hard to draw her back in after one of her interludes.

In the lab, the white coat accented her copper skin, and Dr. Williams stared at the long braid that divided her back as she worked tirelessly with accuracy and precision, staying as long as it took to render textbook results. She needed little assistance, and of her own volition, she made up the two weeks of lab work she had missed. Jasmine Chandler was unlike the other black students he'd taught in this advanced placement course: the too few, too hard women and the men who felt the brother-man should cut them some slack. The rigor of this program took its toll on minorities, and they became obsessed with achievement, an admirable quality in the classroom when balanced with some normalcy. Miss Chandler didn't seem obsessed, only quietly enthusiastic and supremely confident without arrogance. It was a delight to have her in his class, with her quick grasp of new material, her dedication, and commitment to problem-solving. Dr. Williams was smitten with Jasmine Chandler, and no one would believe it was only her mind that excited him.

Time crawled on and Jaz breathed easier after Qwayz's first letter. From a local florist, he'd sent her flowers on his August birthday, pink roses and a card in his handwriting saying, "Happy birthday to me! I love you!" She'd hoped to surprise him for his birthday with an announcement of her own, but apparently it had been only stress and nerves that delayed her period, not a little Chandler.

Jaz talked to him twice by phone and was cautiously reassured by claims that his assignment was far less dangerous than combat. He was in "the American Embassy in Saigon, for chrissakes!" He talked, laughed, told weak jokes, and made kissing sounds goodbye like he had when she was in Malibu and he up the road at Sanford. She hung up and stared at their wedding portrait. He was safe and challenged by the work; maybe he would be all right. Jaz just wanted him to make it past November: TC survived only four months over there, so if Qwayz made it past that, she promised herself to relax about it.

"Excellent as usual, Miss Chandler." Dr. Williams marked her lab work as she was leaving one evening. She always wore the same jewelry: the gold star around her neck, gold earrings, and her watch and gold bracelet of interlocking hearts on her left wrist. But he never seemed to notice the thick, initialed gold cigar band ring mounted by a circle of diamonds.

"Mrs. Chandler," Jaz corrected for the umpteenth time.

"Are you considering research as a career?"

"No. Pediatrics or OB-GYN."

"Good choices, wide open for a woman. I hope your husband doesn't mind your long hours here at the lab."

"No. He's in Vietnam. Good night, Dr. Williams."

A stunned Dr. Williams sat frozen and puzzled by her information. He wondered how a young, beautiful, brilliant girl ended up with a husband in Vietnam. Had he misjudged her? Was she so academic that she'd fallen for the rap and game of a street dude? Maybe he was in ROTC and was over there as an officer. It did not correlate.

When the summer was over, and Dr. Williams's recommendations on candidates were made, he offered Jaz a work-study in his lab. But, she declined. "I've enjoyed your mind, Mrs. Chandler. I hope you'll return to the program next summer."

"I'm going to apply for the surgical program, but thank you, Dr. Williams. I've enjoyed your class." She extended her hand and they shook. Dr. Williams watched her saunter down the hall. "Have a nice life, Jasmine."

The temperature changed as fall approached and Jaz began her senior year along with CC and Sloane. The three had been friends since freshmen year. CC, Chiam Cooper, the rambunctious product of an East Indian mother and a black military father who had retired after a stint at the Presidio, challenged Jaz's sensibilities. Being the fourth daughter born next to the coveted first son, CC had learned early to work her personality and the art of making and forgetting friends fast. She presented as a study in soot-black from her waist-length wiry hair to her lips; the only white was around her ebony eyes and in her smile. The depth of her skin color seemed to offer her freedom from it. CC dated any boy she took a fancy to, black or white. A constant bone of contention for Jaz, but "no biggie" for CC.

"Keep dating gray boys and no decent black man will have you," Jaz seethed.

"Honey, there are forty-nine other states and several continents where I can be a born-again virgin. I am not pressed," CC had replied.

CC was the first truly free spirit Jaz had ever encountered, and she did so with awe and envy. The pretty "high yella" Sloane Yeager with the sandy-colored hair, hailed from Atlanta, where her father had unsuccessfully run for mayor in 1967 and was regrouping for a win in 1969. Sloane and her matriculating brother at Morehouse would be the third generation of Yeager college graduates. Sloane, a dedicated officer of the Black Student Caucus, recruited her two reluctant friends. During Qwayz's road games the two girls would visit Jaz on Alta Vista. They'd eat junk food, talk about folks, do hair and nails, and party, which often started with forty-fives and ended with CC asking Jaz to sing something like "Tell Mama" or "Bye Bye Baby." On Sunday mornings, CC would leave to attend church with her family and then jet back to be with her friends until Jaz put them out.

"Y'all got to go, my man is coming home," Jaz would say, changing the sheets from blue percale to pink satin.

"I guess we've served our purpose," CC'd tease as Jaz opened the apartment door while singing "Dr. Feelgood" to them, much to CC's delight.

But now, Alta Vista was gone, Qwayz was gone, and Jaz purposely took an overload of courses to keep her mind occupied. She sprinkled her premed studies with architectural courses, hoping to repeat her success when her model of South Hall won a first place blue ribbon, heralded as one of the most exquisite replicas of a building from any student, architectural major or not.

Once home, she received phone calls from Denny, Tracy, and AJ, who would call to ask a homework question in biology and then talk on as if he were just around the corner. Her father called to discuss process and progress on the Culhane building and his Frisco house. He'd already planned to be in San Francisco and host their traditional Christmas and New Year's Eve parties from this new house. Mel was coming and Jaz agreed to as well, since she "had nothing else to do."

Jaz didn't betray Mel's confidence, that she'd finally left Hud, the actor who'd lured her from Juilliard to audition for a Broadway play. Her three-octave range outshone his, and while they had a son, nothing could stop Mel's meteoric rise or Hud's descent into despair. So, Mel moved into a three-story brownstone in the Village with Hud, Jr. Gladys Ann and Jaz kept up their coast-to-coast correspondence while CC and Sloane remained her closest friends, but sometimes any human contact proved too much to bear, whether by phone, at home, or on campus. None of them was the right human being.

"Mrs. Chandler," Jaz halted at the super's insistence. "There is something for you in your apartment. From the florist. I let them in. I hope you don't mind."

"Anytime, thank you." Jaz ran up the steps, knowing exactly who sent her flowers on this Monday, the fourth of November.

"Hi, Akira," she said, and then stopped in her tracks to admire the two dozen pink roses arranged in a vase poised on the coffee table under their wedding portrait. Jaz cried as she reached for the card, which unfolded into a letter of familiar handwriting.

"The jinx is off, Jas-of-mine. We broke the curse! I'm still here, though you are there, but I couldn't love you any more. I miss you goo-gobs. Much love always, your husband, Qwayz.

P.S. Tape to follow."

"He's a fool," Jaz said to Akira. "A crazy, wonderful fool." She inhaled the fragrance of the roses, imagining what it took for him to arrange all this with the florist before he left. "I wonder how many more surprises Marchetti Florist has for us."

The tape full of news and sentiment arrived two days later. Slowly she was beginning to believe in his safety as well. He sounded like he was just visiting Ma Vy or away at law school. "The work is meticulous, tedious but invigorating," his voice revealed. "There are horrors and atrocities, but I'm not given those cases. I'm on the Tan Sun Hut basketball team and we're crushing all opposition. I help the guys write letters home to their girls. I write and record songs for them using the base piano, a far cry from the studio equipment. I know you don't understand," he continued, "but I feel I am making a contribution here. I'm not fighting, not in the bush or running up against Charlie, but I am giving something, Jaz. Contributing, and that makes me feel good. Once off the U.S. compound you don't know who to trust. Kinda like being in Watts, ain't it?" He chuckled. "Make no mistake, I'd rather be with you, but just think, I'm four months closer to being with you forever. I love you so much. I wish I could show you." At the sound of his kiss, she wiped her tears, traced his image on the Malibu picture of the two of them. She popped into bed and wrapped herself around Qwayz's pillow, pretending she heard his heartbeat, felt his body envelop hers, the faint aroma of Jade East and Lifebuoy soap… and fell asleep.

Jaz awoke in the Berkeley apartment even though she always hoped it'd magically turn into Alta Vista. A quiet, cloudy day, Jaz couldn't help recall this bed and her man and a wall of windows. In her half-awake ear she could hear Sarah Vaughn singing, "Just A Little Loving Early in the Morning," although Qwayz preferred "Early Morning Love" by Lou Rawls. She stretched and lay there recalling how much love they'd made in this bed. Anytime, day or night. Discovering they favored early morning love under a dusky gray, gunmetal sky before dawn broke. Jaz would reach for the already awake Jake and stroke him, eliciting a welcoming moan from her husband. They'd soar, soothe and satisfy each other to the inevitable climax and fall back to sleep for a few hours before Qwayz rose to take a run with Akira. He'd come back, shower and kiss her goodbye with a "Have a good day. I love you." Her human alarm signaling the time for her to wake up and start her day. She missed it… she missed him… the loving and familiarity of it all. A routine she knew they'd never tire of.

Northern California sent forth a crispness to the air in time for Thanksgiving, hoping to lure Jaz into a holiday spirit. But Jaz and Akira drove to Carmel for Thanksgiving, declining festive invites from Mel, her dad, CC, and even AJ, who'd invited her on his usual ski trip. On the way back home, she stopped by Ruidoso Canyon Road, taking the murderous curve with ease and parking on the same lookout where she had blasted Qwayz for his betrayal. Jaz got out and let Akira relieve herself on a nearby rock. She wished there was some way to access the beach below during high tide, but that's what they'd liked about the property, the natural prohibitive boundaries. The owner's car wasn't in front of the house on Paradise Rock; a lifeless aura hung around the property. Jaz summoned Akira to the car and drove slowly up the private driveway to the house perched on the tongue of granite. As Jaz passed the front entrance she noticed the setting sun shining straight through. White folks never use drapes, she thought. No cars in or out of the garage, and when Jaz peered inside, the house looked uninhabited.

"I'll have Daddy check this out," she said to Akira as she returned to the car and started the motor. "Wouldn't that be fine? What a surprise if I could get Paradise Rock for us. He'd come home and I'd take him to our new address. He'd love it!"

The following week, greetings, presents, and salutations from her parents, Selena and Zack, from Paris, Mel and her son, and AJ, marked Jaz's twenty-first birthday. Qwayz'd sent her the most exquisite authentic peach kimono that shimmered into a pale lavender, with intricately embroidered birds and flowers and a note: *"You're legal now, girlie. I have something for you to wear under this during our second Hawaiian honeymoon. Love you beyond all words. Your husband, Qwayz. XXOO ."*

Red and purple balloons came from Marchetti's. Her girlfriends threw her a surprise birthday party at the Black Student Caucus, complete with a devil's food cake with white icing and chocolate ice cream.

As Jaz devoted her time to finals, her parents made the final arrangements to occupy their San Francisco house and return from Italy for their two-week Christmas vacation. Fifty-year-old Joe Virgil Tennyson, the valued Culhane butler from Connecticut, consented to move to San Francisco with his wife Mildred as the maid. The seasoned Tennysons comprised the Culhanes' sole staff for the house's day-to-day operation, additional staff hired on an as-needed basis for special occasions.

Jaz managed to stay clear of the house until Mel and her son, Hud Jr. arrived. Jaz entered the small semicircular driveway hidden behind a stone wall in front of a substantial, elegant, old brick house with gracious draperied windows and a small flagstone stoop. Immediately inside the front door entrance a stone wall, where indirect lighting highlighted its granite texture and showcased brilliant red poinsettias in a flower box. To the left, an immense living room with sophisticated yet comfortable furniture and a beautiful split-rock fireplace wall as its focal point. A series of sliding glass doors led out onto a long, narrow side yard, well secured by the eight-foot brick wall that surrounded the entire property. Across the room, opposite the fireplace, was the door to Hep's office.

To the right of the entrance, black and white Harlequin tile provided the base for a two-story foyer. A curved staircase cradled a mammoth Christmas tree. Through the archway, Jaz saw an ample-sized chic, stylish dining room with sliding glass doors that revealed a flagstone patio and a small, manicured yard beyond. The kitchen reminded Jaz of a ship's galley until the neat built-ins gave way to a vast but quaint breakfast room of sturdy white wrought-iron and glass tables reminiscent of bistro furniture during her trip to Paris.

Jaz climbed the stairs, using the ornate, thickly braided rope on the non-banister side of the staircase, noting the master bedroom to the left, two good-sized bedrooms with baths, and the back stairs down to the kitchen or up to the Tennysons' apartment.

"Merry Christmas, baby. So, what you think?" Mel hugged her sister hello.

"They done good." Jaz eyed her father as he beamed. "Where's my nephew?" Jaz started to the bed.

"Don't wake him!" Mel and Hep whisper-yelled in unison.

The Culhane New Year's party was going full swing, the sound of the band wafting up to where Jaz and Hud played peekaboo for the zillionth time. The pair had used the backstairs to raid the goodies and steal back upstairs unnoticed. Jaz liked Millie Tennyson: salty, hard and tough on the outside, but a soft touch for babies, dogs, and sensible folk.

"Jaz, won't you come downstairs?" Lorette sighed. "You didn't used to be so antisocial."

"I don't know or care about those folks down there." Sloane had gone home for the holidays. CC was going to come and spend the night, but had fallen victim to the same malady that cut AJ's annual Christmas ski trip to Sun Valley short—the Hong Kong flu.

"As a doctor, you're gonna have to work on your bedside manner." Lorette smoothed her hands over her dress, pirouetting at her reflection in the mirror without looking at her daughter.

"I don't think any of your friends will be having babies when I'm a doctor," Jaz said. She'd tried to be nice, but her mother was already tap dancing on her last nerve.

"You can bring Hud down," Lorette said as she left.

"C'mon, sis, it's not right for me to be partying while you babysit." Mel came in and lifted Hud.

"Lorette send you up here?" Jaz asked as Mel wiped her son's mouth with a wet washcloth. "I've been damn tolerant, staying here when I have a perfectly good apartment of my own."

"Akira loves the yard."

"I've endured the Christmas carols, the celebrating 'all together as a family,' the whole bit. Well, I'm twenty-one, and it's a new year in about an hour. So tell yo' mama to back off!"

"Look, I accept this thing you and Mama have. You don't see me tryin' to change a thing. Now, when are you coming to New

York to see me and your nephew's new house? You have your own room this time."

"Jaz!" her father boomed over the crowd, the phone in one hand, summoning her down to him. Jaz sauntered down and took the receiver from his hand. "Hello?" Jaz couldn't hear, so Hep pushed her into the powder room under the main stairs and closed the door behind her. "Hello?" she repeated.

"Hello yourself. Happy New Year, girlie."

"Qwayz?" Her voice lifted and tears fell.

"Jas-of-mine, you partyin' while I'm here all alone on the telephone?"

"You're crazy."

"'Bout you, yeah. How you doin'?"

"I'm doin'. Boy, I miss you."

"Boy?"

"Come show me different."

"Oh, how I wish I could."

"Yeah?"

"Don't taunt me. I can't take it. It's been too long."

They talked as easily as they could with the pressure of time hanging over their every word. They discussed family and friends; she tempted to tell him about the possibility of buying Paradise Rock. About how Hep found out the property was a discovered love nest now tied up in litigation as part of a divorce settlement. She could easily swing it solo from their savings, which included Raw Cilk royalties and the money inherited from TC. Coupled with the money Qwayz sent monthly, she'd have enough to furnish it with flair without giving up that godawful Berkeley apartment.

"I got a surprise for you." He shocked her, and she loved how much, even thousands of miles apart, in sync they were once again. "But I'll tell you when I see you."

"Okay. They do much holiday celebratin' over there?"

"They celebrate anything over here—the riots at the Democratic Convention in Chicago. They weren't too crazy about Nixon being elected, but nothing got 'the bloods' fired up more than the stand John Carlos and Tommie Smith took at the Olympics in Mexico City."

"That was in October."

"So? It beat the hell outta a Christmas or New Year's celebration."

"Qwayz," Jaz heard the hoots and hollers from the other room as the band ordered the chaos with "Auld Lang Syne." "It's 1969 here. Happy New Year."

"Happy New Year, Jas-of-mine. This will be our year, you'll see. And we'll be together in just two short months."

"Nothing short about sixty days."

"Closer than it has been. I'm planning something very special."

"Just being together will be special enough."

"You just wait…" His voice faded out, then back in again. "How's Akira?"

"Horny as hell, like her mistress."

"Well, her mistress better stay horny until Friday, March seventh."

"You better."

"You kidding? These women over here got stuff that thrives on penicillin and asks for more. No way, Jose, not this man. Do without before I do and die."

"Well, if the disease don't kill you, Jaz will."

"My mama didn't raise no fool. I've had to revert to taking matters into my own hands, but at least I know where they've been. That's a habit I don't need no methadone to break—"

"Qwayz, you're fading out on me!"

"Guess that's our cue from the government, huh? I love you!"

"Happy New Year, Qwayz. I love you, too." She held the dead phone and wasn't sure how much he'd heard. She sat on the commode holding the receiver. They can send men to circle the moon on Christmas Eve, but can't put an end to a war right here on earth.

Shoulda sent Apollo 8 to circle Vietnam, she thought as she hoisted herself up and looked at her reflection. "Hang on, girlie. March seventh is D-day for you. De day you get it regular for ten days." She laughed at her own joke before opening the door on the party revelry. "These saps don't even know there's a war on."

~*~

Jaz glided across the crowded campus after finding her name on the roster for the Summer Surgical Program. The bounce in her step had little to do with her acceptance into the program and more with her early morning call from Qwayz wishing her a Happy Anniversary and Valentine's Day and sharing the final plans for their Hawaiian celebration next month. She laughed aloud, recalling his saying he had a Hawaiian disease only she had the cure for, "lack-a-nookie."

Returning to the apartment, she found the remnants of Mr. Sanchez's wayward key. Jaz kneeled before the huge box addressed to her and stamped with Oriental writing. She opened and flung packaging material everywhere while Akira sniffed its contents. Inside the box was another box, then a box within a box, until finally she found a music box.

"Is this one of Qwayz's jokes? Are snakes gonna jump out? Oh, my!" Jaz held up the most exquisitely carved Oriental music box and, lifting the lid, tried to decipher the delicate tune. "Ahh," she sighed, recognizing Nat King Cole's "Too Young," their wedding song. "What a special man." Attached to its bottom, a tape and a letter.

"Jas-of-mine, this will be the first and last anniversary we spend apart. I hope you love and treasure this gift as I love and treasure you. It wasn't easy getting mama-san to get the tune just right, but finally perfection prevailed. I'm looking forward to Hawaii. Till then, here are some songs from my heart to yours. I love you, Jaz. Shortly, you'll see how much. No one will disturb or come between us then. See you soon! XXOO."

Jaz put on the tape and listened to her husband's pure voice as he accompanied himself on the piano. She heard only "Too Young," "Everlastin' Love," "My Funny Valentine," "I'm Glad There Is You," "Unforgettable," and "I'll Be Seeing You" before drifting off into the most restful sleep she'd had since he'd left.

~*~

Jaz brushed her teeth in the tiny bathroom and returned in time to fasten her seat belt as the plane banked and made its final approach. The weather was balmy but dry; the breezes whirled her hair as she walked into the cool, open-aired airport, searching for that first glimpse of Qwayz. She threaded between couples, men in uniforms and women in their Sunday best. A minor panic overcame her as she realized for the first time that she didn't know the specific arrangements, and if Qwayz weren't here due to some glitch, she'd be doomed to spend precious time in the airport until his arrival.

Then over by the wall she saw a man clad in tan slacks and a loud Hawaiian-print shirt with a bouquet of peach roses hiding his face. As she inched closer, there was no question: it was

53

Qwayz! She ran to him, pushing the roses out of her way and planting a kiss born of a thousand lonely nights upon his sensuous lips.

The roses dangled across her back as he drank her in, the faint smell of Jungle Gardenia, of freshly washed hair cut with a lemon rinse tickling the back of his arms, of soft brown flesh surrendering to him, of familiar and long-desired curves conforming to his as if there had never been any separation.

"Oh, Qwayz." They finally came up for air and she soaked up his essence. His hazel eyes not dimmed by the war he'd left behind, but were happy with the sight before him. A mustache shadowed his upper lip, while the hair on the sides had disappeared.

"You're bald!" She laughed.

"It'll grow back in the next ten days 'cause I don't intend to waste time shavin'."

"Don't I have anything to say about that?"

"Yes... more, Qwayz... oh, don't stop... oh yes, Qwayz... yes!" he teased, squeezing her even harder in an embrace.

"You feel so good to me." Jaz closed her eyes to all around her, wishing that upon opening them, by magic, they'd be in a hotel bedroom.

"These are for you." He presented the two dozen roses.

"I expected you to be in dress blues." She took them and slipped her arm through his as they promenaded off.

"Never wear a uniform unless you absolutely, positively have to."

"They'd beat that bama shirt," she joked as he hoisted her luggage into the jeep.

"You crackin' on my attire?"

"Soon you won't be needin' any."

54

"Great minds… great minds." He kissed her as they sped off to a secluded part of the island. Jaz couldn't take her eyes from him, for there was no rival in tropical fauna that could compete with her handsome husband.

They approached the Honeymoon Cove desk and Jaz observed how open everything was, a roof but no walls.

"How long have you been here?"

"Just a few hours."

"Where is the hotel?"

"It's not a hotel, its cottages, nosy. Maybe you should be the lawyer."

"Mr. and Mrs. Chandler? This way, please." A robust native escorted them down winding paths toward a canal. "Please?" The man directed Jaz to a raft in the middle of the water. Jaz looked at him like he was crazy.

"Surprise! Remember Blue Hawaii? Elvis and Joan Blackman?" Qwayz placed a ring of gardenias upon her head and a matching lei around her neck. After he kissed her, Jaz noticed the bed of flowers on the raft and the strolling musicians waiting on either side.

"Oh, Qwayz."

"The stuff that memories are made of, Jas-of-mine. The memory of a day like this can get you through the rest of your life." He pecked her on the lips. "Nothing is too good for my lady."

The only other occupant of the raft steered, as two young Polynesian girls tossed more flowers into the water they coursed. Then Qwayz sang, "Can't Help Falling in Love," putting Elvis to shame.

Qwayz carried Jaz over the threshold of the immense A-frame thatched roof hut with a bed as its centerpiece.

"My kind of place," Jaz said as Qwayz dumped her on the bed, where they remained in various stages of undress for four straight hours of unbridled lovemaking. Qwayz scurried across the cool tiled floor opening, then poured champagne for them both before returning to the bed. They consumed it thirstily along with the complimentary hors d'oeuvres. Jaz pulled the white sheet about her brown body, denying Qwayz any cover.

"Just looking at what's mine." She eyed Jake. "I mean, I felt him, but I haven't seen him for a long time."

"There he is… still risin'."

"I can handle it. Can you?"

"You are so bad." He whipped the sheet over himself and stuffed a melon ball into her pouting mouth.

"This place is paradise on earth." Jaz snuggled against his hairy chest.

"Sorry, no fireplace. There are a few beams."

"I like that ceiling fan. To cool our body heat, in our little grass hut in Hawaii," Jaz sang, and they fell asleep. Qwayz stirred at sunset admiring a sleeping Jaz, kissing her into wakefulness. They walked through the glass doors out on the lanai into their private lagoon, where they swam under the setting sun which reduced them to silhouettes against the fuchsia sky.

"Hungry?" Their nude bodies intertwined, Jaz's legs wrapped around his waist, perched atop him.

"Ravenous." She drew in his bottom lip, alternating licking and sucking as if devouring the most luscious of delicacies. Qwayz moaned as the fluid, warm water made their movements tantalizing.

"What do you wanna eat?" Qwayz managed without breaking the rhythm of their foreplay.

"You."

A lesser establishment might have been concerned at not seeing the Chandlers for the next three days, but the staff of Honeymoon Cove honored the Do Not Disturb sign for as long as it reigned over Hut 3. Though the staff could never clean the rooms or change the sheets, an abundant supply of fresh towels always appeared some time during the day. Only room service caught a glimpse of the male Chandler as he cracked the door open far enough to receive and sign for a food tray, later left outside with discarded linen and three never-read newspapers.

On the fourth day there were sightings of the Chandlers by the beach, but they still relied on room service for sustenance. They'd stopped the world, constructing one of their own, and refused to be invaded by any modicum of reality.

By the fifth day the Chandlers made dinner reservations for the Tiki Room, which they didn't actually honor until the sixth day, causing some of the staff to lose bets that they wouldn't show at all. Reports from maid service indicated that no bags had been unpacked and everything remained spotless and basically unused except for the bed and the shower.

The couple, sitting across from one another in wicker chairs made famous by Panther Huey Newton, sipped on Singapore slings, nibbled on poi, and vanished before the main course arrived.

On the seventh day they made it all the way through the salads before they were interrupted.

"Hey, Qwayz!" A black marine greeted, slapping him on the back and Jaz's heart sank.

"Buzz! Hey, man!" Qwayz stood and Jaz knew the real world had just crept in.

"This is my wife, Roberta."

"This is my wife, Jaz... Buzz McLeish."

"Hi." Jaz tried hard to be gracious, but they could rap back in Nam. Jaz had only forty-eight more hours.

"You comin' or goin'?" Qwayz asked.

"We're 'bout to have dinner."

"Join us," Qwayz suggested.

If looks could kill, Jaz would have been a murderer and a widow.

"Buzz, maybe they want to be alone," Roberta said, and Jaz smiled at her new friend for life.

"Qwayz, Mr. Popularity? Roberta, this is the guy who whipped my buns at B-Ball and wrote that love song for me."

"Really?"

There goes my friend for life, Jaz thought.

"You're very talented." Roberta shrugged her shoulders at Jaz in defeat.

Jaz enjoyed the stories about Qwayz's wartime environment, but barely endured the rest.

"So how long you been here?"

"Not long enough." Qwayz took Jaz's hand.

"We've only got two days left," Jaz said her comment lost on Buzz.

"She's as pretty as your pictures, Qwayz."

"Don't I know it?" Qwayz kissed her fingers.

"Newlyweds, huh? Robert and I've been married six years, have two kids and another on the way."

"Congratulations!" Qwayz said.

"That's what these jaunts are for," Buzz winked at his friend. "Us lifers live for these R&Rs, man."

The next day, the Chandlers ventured into town for a few souvenirs for her to take back home; a few boxes of chocolate-covered macadamia nuts served for most, but she wanted something special for Ma Vy. Jaz twirled around the jewelry display but met resistance. When she tried to move it again, a cute little boy giggled at his playful ploy and darted away. Jaz only glimpsed his leaving. "Cute little devil," she remarked.

"Who?" Qwayz asked, sporting a new pair of aviator sunglasses. "Cool?"

"Too handsome for words," Jaz picked up a cowrie shell dish and Qwayz gestured that he was walking over toward the outer kiosk to get something for AJ.

Jaz nodded and looked up and over at an attractive woman... A Black woman? Jaz visually dismissed her, but her mind thought, LeLani Troop. Quickly, not seeing Qwayz, Jaz followed the woman out the door into the mall corridor. "LeLani?" Jaz walked to catch up. "LeLani Troop," Jaz called after the woman who stopped and turned around. "It is you. How are you? Imagine seeing you here."

"Yes. How are you, Jaz?"

"Just fine. You live here?"

"Yes, I have for a few years now. My mother is here, and I have a great job. Sorry to hear about TC."

"Yeah. I'm here with Qwayz on R&R. Can you believe he volunteered?"

"No. I cannot."

With the mention of Qwayz's name, LeLani became visibly nervous. "Listen. It was great seeing you, but I've got to run. Tell the gang back home hello for me." She hurriedly began rushing off toward an older man with a little boy. The little boy from the store. How odd, Jaz thought as the three scurried off. Tell the gang back home...LeLani didn't have a clue about what was happening in the states. There was no "gang back home" left. Weird, Jaz thought as she began looking for Qwayz. She turned back around in time to see the little boy climb into a black SUV.

The little boy smiled over at Jaz and waved.

Her heart caught. OMG! OMG!! She knew that face. "LeLani!" Jaz stepped into the street, the car screeched and wheeled around her.

"Jaz!" Qwayz called from the second level and ran down to where she was. "What's going on?"

"That was TC's little boy."

"What?"

"With LeLani. It was him. He looked just like my brother."

"TC has a son? No way."

Jaz woke from her nap. "Feel better?" Qwayz rubbed her neck. "Do you still think it possible?"

"I know you don't but suppose TC didn't even know. Suppose that's why she left... she was pregnant."

"Doesn't make any sense why she would keep it a secret from TC or your family. While you were napping, I already checked with information and looked in the phone book. There is no LeLani Troop. Suppose the dude with them was her husband and the son was theirs."

"But why run away from me. From us." She crawled up into his arms. "You didn't see him."

"No. I didn't. But maybe just seeing her, one of TC's old girlfriends, got your mind playing tricks."

"I dunno. I am exhausted just thinking about it."

"Then let's think about more immediate, for-sure things." He yo-yoed his eyebrows.

Jaz chuckled... then relented. After another passionate lovemaking tryst, Jaz lay brusquely over him. "Still thinking about it?"

"Not so much. I have the rest of my life to do that and only a short time to do what we do."

60

"You going to tell your dad?"

"Tell him what? That I saw LeLani with a man and a little boy that resembled TC. Same coloring, curly hair? The boy at the concierge desk looks like him too...but he was as old as TC."

"I don't think we'll ever stop seeing TC around us."

"We have to keep him alive in our thoughts and prayers. No one should be forgotten."

"He'd be happy that we are here together now."

"Yes he would."

"Handle your business," they quoted him together and laughed.

Their last forty-eight hours passed like wind through a latticed porch, and all too soon, Jaz clung to Qwayz like a wisteria vine to a southern trellis.

"Jaz, I thought my second surprise would make you super-happy."

"It did at the time you told me, and it will when you come home for good in August, but it don't do doo-doo for me right now, Qwayz." He looked handsome in his blue Air Force uniform, though she preferred him in the buff. She held him as the military planes readied behind him.

"Time to go, Qwayz, my man. Nice meeting you, Jaz," Buzz said in passing, without breaking stride.

"Jaz, I'll be home for good on an early-out in just five short months, and I got big plans for us."

"Yeah?"

"Maybe we should explore LeLani's kid. Just to make sure. To see. Your dad and his resources could find her in a New York minute, faster than you and me... he'd talk to her dad in Watts. Or quiz her brother. He used to sing with Tavares," Qwayz pondered momentarily.

"Your mind goes a mile a minute," Jaz noted.

"I wasn't going to use any of our precious time chasing a pipe dream that TC could have a kid."

He embraced her again, kissing her cheek. "We'll never be separated again. I promise with all my heart and soul and every fiber of my being." The engine gunned, signaling the final call, and Qwayz began backing away.

"Qwayz..." Their fingertips touched until the very end and he reached down and picked up a smooth gray stone polished by some ancient volcano.

"Here, this will be our life, Jaz, from now on... smooth and solid as this rock. A symbol of our love. Just five funky little months, tops." He palmed the flawless stone in his hand as if energizing it before placing it lovingly in her hand. "Take care of that. I'll ask for it when I see you. Set it on our nightstand next to our Malibu picture so it'll be there when we make love my first night home—providing Mother Nature cooperates." He smiled and winked. "I love you, Mrs. Chandler."

He jogged up the steps, wriggled his index finger, threw kisses and flashed his patented smile until the door closed between them. She hung on the chain-link fence, watching his plane take off, returning to Southeast Asia. She stood there a long while, tears drenching the stylish Yves Saint Laurent pantsuit Selena had sent. Opening her hand, she looked at the curiously smooth gray-black rock, the "symbol of their love." She held it to her breast as she made her way to the gate for her plane, bound in the opposite direction. Back to her world, a world without her best friend, lover, husband, protector, confidant. A world without Qwayz.

~*~

"So what'd you bring me?"

"Thesis Denise-es," Jaz said before continuing, "nunca, nada, zip."

"Figures. Sure you didn't bring back a seed that will blossom in, say, nine months?"

"I wish, but your brother wants at least one full year of just me and him before we become parents."

"Selfish devil, ain't he?" Denny said. "And you can drop that 'thesis Denise-es.' I submitted my dissertation yesterday! Fifty-six pages of psychological brilliance."

"Well, all right! Guess I have to call you Dr. Denny now."

"Not until that June date. Thereafter, I'll answer to nothing but."

"I'll be there with bells on."

"How so? You graduate the day after."

"I don't need to walk to get my degree. I'm already in med school."

"You're fooling yourself if you don't think Ma and Pa Culhane as well as auntie and uncle from Paris and a sister straight off the Broadway stage won't be there to see the first Culhane college graduate get her degree."

Jaz had never thought of it that way. Her family was so accomplished without a college education. Her grandfather Papa Colt, the ex-slave cowboy, had founded an all-black Texas town. Her dad had risen from beat cop to President Eagan's chief of protocol before he'd been appointed ambassador to Italy. Her aunt, the toast on two continents. Her brother a musical genius and her sister an accomplished Broadway star. They'd had vision and determination, but not a degree among them.

"But they were just here for two weeks at Christmas, and Dad gave up the Kentucky Derby in early May and the Indy 500 on Memorial Day to spend two weeks at the Cannes Film

Festival in mid-May. Then he'll go to the World Cup soccer games in Italy soon—"

"And they'll be here for their daughter's graduation. Get ready, girlie." Denny used Qwayz's sobriquet playfully. "Who's in that Frisco house while they're in Italy?"

"The Tennysons, Joe Virgil and Millie. I had a hell of a time getting Akira away from Millie when I came back. I thought AJ was bad."

"That is one loved doggie."

Jaz didn't have time to consider any of that now. Spring blossomed around her, a time for rejuvenation, growth, and new beginnings. She'd been energized since she'd seen Qwayz in March followed by her official acceptance to med school. Three factors ensured a perpetually blissful state: Qwayz's early out in August received its authorized, official stamp, she had settled on Paradise Rock, and accepted the honor of being godparents to Tracy and Scoey's child expected early next year.

Jaz delighted in transforming Paradise Rock from an illicit love nest into a home. She redid the sunken couch upholstery with ecru raw silk, matching the drapes and complimenting the new carpet that lay before the fireplace. Huge pillows in muted earth tones scattered around the glass and brass coffee table finished the formal sunken living room. The parquet floors buffed and gleaming. Jaz had a wall of shelves built around the archway to the bedroom's hallway for Qwayz's component set and record collection and for their books. In the bathroom, she papered the walls in foil seashells and found linens to match the raised aquamarine tub. The wicker bed situated so they could lay back and look out at the ebb and flow of the tides, watch sunrises and make love in the diminishing rays of the sunsets. She knew once Qwayz got a glimpse of Paradise Rock, the Berkeley Heights apartment would be history.

64

Her graduation, a formal intrusion on her planning for her husband's homecoming, a mere ceremony to be endured. Although the pictures, the dinners and the gifts were more fun than she had anticipated. CC would still be around, but Sloane was returning to Atlanta for grad school. Hep took a picture of them all, and Jaz began more painful farewells to many college friends. But for everything you lose you get something else...Quinton Regis Chandler IV was coming home.

Chapter 4

"Good girl," Jaz complimented Akira as the dog ran the sandy beach, retrieving a stick and returning it to her. Jaz already benefited from being at Paradise Rock, where she spent her weekends far away from her summer surgery program. She liked the five-foot-five and brilliant Dr. Nussbaum but avoided the chief of staff, Dr. Brewer, his racist attitude legendary.

All was well with her family and friends, she reflected, dodging the cold surf. Tracy wore maternity clothes needlessly but proudly. Jaz threw the stick for Akira again, smiling as she thought of Gladys Ann's pink and green letter announcing that she'd been accepted to med school. She'd joked on their exchange of graduation pictures, saying, "At least we both know we can look better than this!" Jaz chuckled as they began winding back up to the house, using the path Qwayz had forged past rocks and windswept cypress. Every now and again she thought about LeLani and her family in Hawaii, deciding to leave well enough alone.

As her tea brewed, she rechecked the way she stocked their kitchen, ready for immediate habitation with rows of popcorn, cocoa, seasonings for blaff and callaloo, bread pudding makings, and chocolate. She planned to kidnap Qwayz from the air base and bring him directly here. He would call his mom while she hit the stereo, already primed with Nat King Cole and Johnny Mathis, on the way to warming up the pasta with seafood sauce and popping the cork of the 1945 Lafitte-Rothschild, compliments of her dad. They'd rush through the meal and get on to the main activity. They wouldn't eat anything hot again for a couple of days, so she had a list of cold cuts and s'more makings to buy the day before he arrived. The perfect reunion for the perfect couple, she thought, fishing the smooth stone out of her sweater pocket. Unable to decide whether to leave it at the Berkeley apartment or at Paradise Rock, most of the time she left it in her shoulder bag. Each night she fell asleep to the anniversary tape he'd sent of him singing Raw Cilk hits on one side and all their other favorites on the other. She drifted off to sleep looking at their picture from that Malibu summer in 1964, when Selena and Zack rented the beach house and the photographer captured their images: Qwayz in a peach banlon setting off his deep bronze arms as they enveloped Jaz. Their smiles as bright as their futures. The Malibu picture, the music box that played "Too Young," and the smooth stone stood sentry on her nightstand—a trinity of love. "The stars are in their heavens and all's right with the world."

~*~

"Hi, Daddy. Happy Fourth of July!" Jaz kissed her father, and waved at Millie and her mother, who were officiating on the patio outside the dining room. "Mel and Hud here?"

"Will I do?"

"Selena!" Jaz ran halfway up the staircase to embrace her aunt. "Oh, it's so good to see you! Where's Zack?"

"Napping."

"What about the Fourth of July at Chateau Jazz?"

"Child, didn't you learn nothing from me?" Selena guided her niece back downstairs. "Give the wolf a taste and leave him hungry."

"You'll be back for Qwayz's welcome home party in August?"

"My baby comin' home from the war? Wild horses and an airline strike couldn't keep me away."

The house brimmed with smiley-faced people as Hep manned the Texas barbecue, complete with apron and tongs, while Lorette played the gracious hostess. CC chatted with Selena while Hud Jr. ran through the flowers, dodging the sculptured garden medallions and creating havoc. When everyone was full and satisfied, the guests sought the comfort of cushioned wrought-iron and hushed conversations.

"I really admire you, Mel, caring for a child and being a single parent," Jaz told her sister.

"You do what you gotta do. He's the joy of my life when he's asleep like this. I'm one of the lucky ones able to be home with him during the day. Even my matinees coincide with his naptime, and I'm usually home before he wakes up. I'm there to put him to bed at night before I leave for the theater. I couldn't imagine being pregnant again now, like Mom was with me and TC, or me and you."

"Well, she did have a husband to help her."

"I'll talk to you when you have a child. Then and only then can you understand what I'm saying."

"What's this new play?" Jaz changed the subject.

"*The Reverend*, a black musical about a southern church with a show-stopping tune for me. I'd star, of course."

"Of course, 'Miss Thang.'" Jaz used Qwayz's pet name for her.

"Be doing some show stoppin' yourself in a few weeks. The Big Q comin' home. You two always had it all. While the rest of us had to run tests on a buncha triflin' dudes, you found yours from the git-go."

"I went through a few frogs before I found my prince."

"Oh, sure. Jesse Ramsey who's now the Chicago Bears' star running back."

"That turd. Saw what he did two years ago when the black athletics asked him to join them in support of Muhammed Ali and protest of the Vietnam War."

"I'm not black. I'm Jesse Ramsey," Mel quoted the infamous statement.

"He always believed his own hype."

"Is he still married to Cherish Harley-Ramsey?"

"Far as I know. He probably cheats on her. No prize there. Dodged that bullet." Jaz stroked Hud's sleeping cheek. "Look at Dad. Mr. Girambelli and sons must be here with the fireworks."

Jaz watched the display with mixed emotions. It wasn't like those she and Qwayz enjoyed in Paris at Chateau Jazz in '65 or from the boat in the Caribbean with TC before he shipped out. Last year there were no fireworks at all for her. The Fourth was just another dismal day. But this Fourth of July filled her with hope, possibilities and new beginnings. Jaz clapped and shouted just as much as Hud did from her lap.

"Might as well stay the night, Punkin." Hep tempered his insistence.

"No thanks, I've said my goodbyes and I wanna get back to the beach."

"Will I ever get an invitation out there? I flushed the address as ordered."

"Maybe, if you're good, but I want Qwayz to be the first man there."

"Coming back for dinner tomorrow? We'll only be here for two more days."

"Okay, Daddy." She kissed him goodnight, leaving him in the doorway as she settled Akira safely in the front seat. She drove directly to Paradise Rock. "Qwayz , we're home!" Jaz called out as she slid the door closed and turned on a light. Akira stopped in her tracks, looking at Jaz, then looking down the hall. "Sorry, girl, just practicing. But when would I be going anyplace without him, huh?"

Jaz reset the security system, a caveat from her dad that came with the thousand-dollar bottle of "welcome home" wine. It was the only way he'd leave her alone in this secluded beach house. She surveyed the comfortable and inviting room as she turned off the light. The house that love built.

~*~

Her nocturnal ritual complete, teeth brushed, hair braided, attired in one of Qwayz's old shirts, she set the tape, grabbed the stone, and climbed beneath the sheets. The moonlight poured onto her face like daylight and she stared at it as Qwayz's voice filled the room. Her eyes located their star and she looked at it, marveling that this same star had shone on Qwayz the night before and the night to follow. Soon they'd be lying in this bed together, looking at it. In many ways, Qwayz was already here. It felt like he was just in the kitchen fixing cocoa; any minute he'd spring around the comer and cannonball into bed beside her. With his spirit here, now Jaz waited for his body.

"The stars are in their heavens and all's right with the world," Jaz repeated with Qwayz at the end of his tape, and drifted off into a peaceful sleep.

On his birthday, August second, Jaz shopped for his presents. He wasn't going to be here, but she wanted to be involved on the anniversary of the day that brought Quinton Regis Chandler IV into the world. She purchased a Rolex watch inscribed "Till the End of Time" and a pair of first-class round-trip tickets to Myrtle Beach, South Carolina.

"I couldn't get a line out," Qwayz apologized over a static-riddled phone line.

"Doesn't matter," Jaz yelled into the receiver and Akira looked up. "I think I celebrated in a fashion you'd approve of." Now the voices faded in and out, some words louder than others.

"Yeah? Meet me in Hawaii and we can return to our little grass hut for a week of debriefin'."

"I got something much better planned for you right here. Guaranteed." She'd waited this long. What was another week?

"Yeah? You have our rock?"

"Yep, I keep it with me most of the time along with the music box." The line crackled static, threatening to separate them. "Qwayz?!"

"I love you, Jaz! See you soon—when the stars will be in their heavens and all's right with the world!"

"I love you, too. Bye!"

Qwayz replaced the receiver and mopped his face with the drenched handkerchief. Jaz was his number one priority, but a cool climate with hot showers, cold wine, and ice cubes that didn't melt on their way to the glass also appealed to him. As he sauntered across the base, dust whirled around him from a passing jeep.

"Hey, Short-time! This'll all be history for you in five quick ones, huh?"

"You got it, man." Qwayz jogged over to Major Tapp in his AC-47. The tall, dark man jumped from his plane, waving off his co-pilot and crew. They'd become fast friends once Qwayz learned he was from Virginia and had summered in Myrtle Beach as a teenager.

"Paperwork?" Major Tapp noted the paraphernalia in Qwayz's hands.

"Nope, mailed a Christmas package to my wife. It's due out the thirteenth. I thought it would be a kick to mail stupid stuff and be there to open it together."

"I think the man loves his wife."

"No question. You gonna make a run?"

"Just got back, running visual recon along the Laotian border. Just so Charlie knows we're interested."

"Sounds like soft time to me."

"You had the cushy job in JAG," he said, referring to the judge advocate general's legal department of the armed services. "You gotta let me buy you a drink before you set off, Q."

"I'll be a drunk by the time I get back to 'the world.'"

"Popularity costs, man. Never did take you up in my jet."

"Hey, I've been up in Hueys, a F-4 Phantom, a F-105 Thunderchief, a Cessna A-37, and a Cobra—can't be any different."

"Aw, rankin' now that you're checking out? Listen, I got to go up again tomorrow. Why not meet me, let me take you for a ride, then dinner?"

"Deal." They slapped five. "Later."

Qwayz ate with the guys, listening to Buzz still talking about how "fine" Qwayz's wife was. He turned in late, but was there bright and early, to greet a waiting Major Tapp.

"Didn't think you were gonna show, Chandler," Tapp teased. "You forcing me to rethink my assessment of you."

"Beautiful day for a flight." Qwayz sniffed the already hot, stale air, squinting his eyes against the blazing sun. "Won't be long before these recons are a thing of the past, huh?" He accepted the helmet and snapped it on.

"You talking about Nixon's announcing the first troop withdrawals? All remains to be seen, my man. Hop in," Tapp invited.

"Just us?" Qwayz's surprised eyes peered over his new aviator sunglasses.

"Not to worry. You can't get more routine than this," spoke the seasoned pilot, who'd flown over 146 missions in his five-month stint. "'Sides, Charlie isn't even up yet." The jet soared and sliced the clear blue sky. "Really beautiful country from up here," Major Tapp mused.

"Reckon it would be if I could see it right side up," Qwayz cracked on the major's aerial displays. "Glad I didn't eat first."

"Man, you haven't seen nothing yet." And Major Tapp took his pride and joy through five minutes of celestial acrobatics. "I thought you said you and your father-in-law were gonna take up flying so you can pilot your own jets."

"If I survive this," Qwayz chuckled. "What's that?" he asked of a distant sputtering.

"Ummm, Charlie is up. Myrtle Beach to control. Myrtle Beach to control, we're receiving some fire from the northwest quadrant. Over."

"Fire? You mean like artillery?" Qwayz questioned as Tapp signed off.

"Not to worry, just letting base know where they are. We're way outta range for that lightweight action."

Before the words left his mouth, a thunderous jolt hit the plane, engulfing it in fire. The jet exploded upon impact, careened downward, belching puffs of black smoke miles back into the tranquil air that had just released it from its safe, protective grasp.

~*~

A bloodcurdling scream awakened Jaz and she bolted straight up. Akira was up on all fours, growling. Jaz wondered if she had been the screamer. Was it a nightmare or a clap of thunder or the crash of glass signaling an intruder? Jaz's heart raced; she couldn't catch her breath and her drenched nightclothes felt clammy. What the hell? She stared into the darkness of the quiet apartment. Her stomach cramped and churned. She slid across the bed, hurrying to the bathroom in time to vomit chartreuse bile into the toilet. She hugged the porcelain bowl, recalling that she hadn't thrown up since she and Gladys Ann drank Bali Hai at the party in the Boondocks, only to be rescued by Qwayz, who lectured them both all the way home. She and her fifteen-year-old friend had argued over which was worse, the cheap wine or Qwayz's sermon.

Jaz brushed her teeth clean of the burning film, chasing it with a long drink of cold water straight from the faucet. She stepped over Akira to go into the kitchen, trying to remember what she had eaten that would tum on her. She eyed the front door and the balcony. All secure and undisturbed, except for the gnawing sick feeling in her stomach and an uncontrollable shivering, as if she were cold.

"Weird." She crossed back over the canine to the bathroom, where she shed her clothes, showered, and returned to bed. Lying there wide awake with a knot in the pit of her stomach, she hoped she wasn't coming down with anything. Qwayz'll be home in three days, Mother Nature's cooperating, so what was this? she thought. She went from the chills to the sweats and back again. She finally fell into a fitful sleep and dragged herself to the last day on the surgical unit.

"Hallelujah! It's over. Come on, Qwayz, I'm ready for you!" She almost skipped across campus, singing the Marvelettes' "My Baby Must Be a Magician."

Hours later, Jaz hoisted the bags of munchies from the car while Akira jumped out, relieved herself near a tree, and reached the concrete steps at the same time as her mistress.

"Mrs. Chandler, there was a soldier here to see you," Mr. Sanchez informed her as he returned to his hedge clipping.

"Thanks! He's surprised us!" Jaz and Akira raced up the steps.

"Captain Bradford, United States Air Force," Jaz read the card stuck in the door. "Right branch, wrong soldier. They wouldn't even let Qwayz get home and spend time with his wife before they started looking him up, which is exactly why we have Paradise Rock."

Jaz entered the apartment and surveyed the already packed bags containing Qwayz's civvies, his birthday Rolex, the two tickets to Myrtle Beach, and the Paradise Rock deed. She wouldn't have time to pack anything later. Her dad was in from Italy to inspect the Culhane Building, and she'd promised to tour the masterpiece with him, dine with her parents, and spend the night.

As she stood wondering if she had time to drop everything off at the beach house first, there was a knock at the door.

"Mrs. Jasmine Chandler? I'm Captain Bradford," the middle-aged white man informed her. "May I come in?"

"Sure." Jaz scratched the looking-up-an-old-buddy scenario and figured the Air Force must have forgotten to give Qwayz something.

"You know my husband won't be here until Thursday?"

"Yes, well that's the reason I'm here. Ordinarily you'd be notified in writing and you still will be, but because of his . . . scheduled arrival so soon—" he breathed deeply and exhaled with, "I regret to inform you that your husband, Quinton Regis

Chandler IV, was reported MIA- Missing In Action as of August—"

"There must be some mistake." Jaz stood, and the captain rose with her.

"The details are still sketchy," he continued as if she hadn't spoken. "But your husband boarded an AC-47 with Major Tapp on a routine harassment run along the Laotian border. There was enemy fire. There's been no word since the last radio contact."

Jaz let this cold, distant man, the complete antithesis of her Qwayz, finish his spiel. As he droned on, she thought someone other than this tactless man should be conveying such sensitive information.

"The mission covered quite a large area and the exact area where the plane went down has not been determined. It is believed from official sources that a VC rocket, which means they were flying low, hit the jet. The area was swept for aerial observation, but with that mountainous jungle terrain it's almost impossible to sight anything... even the remnants of a burned plane can be swallowed up whole and completely covered by that jungle brush in a matter of hours. The Air Force will try to locate any clue as to your husband's whereabouts," he concluded in textbook manner. "His personal effects will be sent to you shortly. We regret your loss." He almost saluted at the end.

"Captain Bradford," Jaz began. "I'm sorry you've come all this way, and equally sorry for the person for whom this information is intended. My husband was not a pilot or a co-pilot and was in no way connected with any missions, routine or otherwise. He was in intelligence, detailed to the judge advocate general stationed in Saigon. So you see, there has been some military foul-up."

"Mrs. Chandler, I assure you that this Quinton—"

"Captain Bradford," Jaz cut him off by escorting him to the door. "There must be another Quinton Chandler whose family is awaiting this horrible news. My husband will be home Thursday as planned. He would have no reason to jeopardize himself or our future by taking a flight. I know how overworked the Air Force is, but a less understanding person could be quite devastated. Perhaps you should reconfirm the identity of your personnel more closely before reporting falsely on them. Now, if you'll excuse me. Good day, Captain Bradford." She closed the door behind him.

Jaz pushed all the bags by the hall tree near the door so that when she returned from visiting her parents she could just grab them, along with Qwayz's red baseball cap and bomber jacket, and split for the airport. Showering again made her late for the meeting with her father, and on her way out she yanked up the phone, thinking it was him.

"Jasmine?" the unmistakable lilt, muffled with tears, in the voice of Qwayz's mother asked.

"Ma Vy. Hi, how are you?"

"A Major Thurman just came by—"

"Ma Vy, don't worry, it's all a mistake—"

"But Jaz—"

"Ma Vy, don't pay them any mind. They're wrong! You'll see on Thursday. They'll all see on Thursday. I don't mean to be rude, but I gotta go. I'm meeting my father and I'm late. Catch you later."

Ignoring the ringing phone, Jaz locked the door and proceeded down the hall. Waving to Mr. Sanchez, she let Akira hop in the car and headed for San Francisco.

"Oh, God, Dad'll have a shit-fit." Jaz eyed her watch as she quickly changed the radio station from "an upcoming Raw Cilk classic" and instead, sang along with Stevie Wonder's "My Cherie Amour."

In Jaz's absolute, deep, and utter denial, one centimeter in the quiet of her heart remained noncommittal and silent against all the outer refutations; it calmly awaited more documented reality—for time to tell.

Hep's car waited in the semicircular driveway as Jaz parked her T-Bird on the outside plaza.

"There's my Akira," Millie opened the side gate, letting her in.

"Thanks," Jaz said to Millie. "Sorry, Dad," Jaz apologized before her always punctual father could razz her. "Nice car."

"Needed a little something to get around in when I'm in town."

"Stylin' and profilin', Pops." Jaz teased him about the stares they received as they pulled the Rolls Royce into the driveway on Kearny Street in front of the prestigious Culhane Building.

"Ooo-wee!" Jaz looked up the height of the edifice, only able to see thirty stories, as the top five were recessed by design. "A marble sidewalk?"

"Polished granite from Seattle," he said as Jaz eyed the gilded C in a starburst on the two plate-glass doors. "On the other side of that guard kiosk will be twenty street level executive parking spaces." He handed Jaz a hard hat as a worker opened the door to his knock.

"Good googa-mooga!" Jaz's chin stretched toward the ceiling as she looked up. "It's a cathedral of rose quartz marble." She walked slowly down the colonnade past the mammoth columns, her sneakers squeaking on the marble floor. "Holy moley!"

"You like? It has a fifty-foot foyer like the old banks in New York. I want to convey strength, dependability, endurance, and power. Now, over there is going to be the executive elevator, mahogany paneling, an express right to the top, first stop thirtieth floor unless otherwise programmed. These six will be your regular elevators." They stepped into the construction elevator. "All these will be Culhane Enterprises offices. The employee cafeteria and lounge on the twenty-eighth floor. Gym on the twenty- ninth, and thirty through thirty-four will be my indispensable staff—finance offices, legal department, construction force, my prize corps of engineers, architects, and interior designers, and my summer intern program for talented Black college students."

"That's a real groove, Dad."

"If not me, then who? Gotta give back and help our own. Ah! The thirty-fifth floor! Here is the secretarial pool. Notice it's in a horseshoe shape, for luck. Surrounding it will be executive offices, joined by a concealed corridor. I know it's hard to imagine—"

"I can dig it, Dad. Good use of function and design."

"Why, thank you. This way." He pointed to the left.

"My office. My small conference room through here, and my washroom complete with shower, sauna, and clothes closets and here—" Hep stepped outside his office and walked into another marked opening—"my right-hand man's office, with his own shower and closet, but not as big as mine."

"Of course not. You're the boss," not that white man Kyle, she thought.

They finished the tour by the executive elevator shaft and Jaz thought of how she preferred the smaller corner office with the two windows over them all.

Hep said, "I know you're hungry. So we'll stop by the wharf and pick up a half-dozen lobsters."

After Millie prepared and served a delectable meal, Jaz curled up on the couch in front of the television and asked, "Dad, how long are you staying?"

"Just long enough to look into the hazel eyeballs of my son-in-law and give him a welcome back bear hug," he said as Lorette chuckled, joining her husband on the couch. "Why? Were you going to invite me to the before party?"

"No way."

"But we'll be back for his big welcome home party," Lorette chimed in. "Mel's flying in, too." She smiled at her daughter.

"Great." Jaz turned her gaze back to Richard Pryor, who told bittersweet jokes about growing up black and poor in a Peoria ghetto.

"Mr. Culhane?" Millie interrupted, handing him the receiver.

"Yes... hello, Vilna! Yes, she's here, excited as all git-out about Qwayz's—" Hep listened intently to Qwayz's mother, turning his back on Jaz and her mother. He swung around, answering the woman with "Yes, she's fine." He looked at her laughing at the comedian, her feet tucked beneath her, a Royal Crown cola in her hands. "Oh my God!" Hep whispered into the phone. Hep hung up and disappeared into his office.

Jaz saw his extension light up red.

Hep contacted an Air Force friend of his in Washington, General Forsythe, for information. In a matter of minutes, he returned Hep's call with the grim confirmation. Qwayz was MIA.

"Meaning what, Bill?"

"It means there's no body, no remains to ship back. In layman's terms, it means that your son-in-law is either dead or a POW. Being dead is more humane. Off the record, Hep, the plane was hit by a VC rocket. He was burned to death. What wasn't incinerated on impact, the animals will finish off. Sorry, but I know you like your medicine straight."

"Is it at all possible that he escaped unharmed?"

"A fairy tale. Pray that he is dead, Hep. It's his only salvation."

Hep sank into his chair. What a hideous way for a brilliant young black man, so full of promise, to end his life on earth. It was the second time he'd lost a son to that Vietnam war. It was over for them both, TC and Qwayz, but it had just begun for Jaz, for his mother, sisters, and all who were touched by him. Hep called Ma Vy back.

~*~

"Where's Jaz?" Hep asked Lorette, shutting his office door behind him.

"You took so long, she went on to bed. Why? Something wrong?"

"It's Qwayz. He's reported missing in action."

"What!" Lorette's hand flew involuntarily to her mouth as she sank on the couch. "Oh no, no," she wailed quietly. "Not Qwayz, too. Not again. Jaz! Poor Jaz."

"She knows. She's known all day."

Hep scaled the steps, leaving his distraught wife at the newel post below. Knocking gently, he walked past Akira, who stood at attention, wagging her tail.

"Jaz? You awake?" he inquired, sitting on the bed.

''I'm really tired, Daddy,'' she said, without turning toward him. Silence swirled around them, her back a barrier to any discussion.

"I know about Qwayz."

"Oh, Daddy." Jaz rose on her elbows. "You don't believe that, do you?"

"Punkin, I checked with General—"

"I don't care if you spoke to the president himself. Qwayz is alive. I know it. I can feel it. You'll see on Thursday."

"Jaz—"

"I need you to believe it, Daddy. I can't have any negative vibes. You're either for us or against us."

"Jaz, the facts say—"

"Don't you ever believe in feelings, things beyond facts and reports?"

"What if he isn't here on Thursday?"

"He'll be here on Thursday. If not this Thursday, then the next or the next, but he is coming home. He promised. He's never broken a promise to me." Jaz fell back on the pillows, turning her back to her father once again.

"We'll talk tomorrow."

"There's nothing left to say."

Jaz intentionally slept late, rising after her father had gone off to the Culhane Building. Turning away from her mother, she told her she'd be out all today and driving to Travis Air Force Base tomorrow.

"Qwayz and I'll pick up Akira in a few days. You know he'll have to see his dog." Jaz chuckled as she walked to the door.

"Jaz—" Lorette looked into her daughter's clear determined eyes. "Drive carefully."

"Thanks, Ma." Honey eyes locked with ebony pools of maternal sincerity.

Jaz spent her last day alone at Paradise Rock. She walked along the beach, climbed the granite formations, and rechecked the house for every conceivable creature comfort. She soaked in the tub of hot pink bubbles, gazing at the setting sun over the ocean. Qwayz is gonna love this, she thought. On her last night solo she slept restlessly, bathed in the rays of a full moon as the waves crashed below. Tomorrow we'll be lying here together, looking at our star.

Gorgeous day for a flight, Jaz thought as she drove to the airport base, hoping he wouldn't be upset because Akira wasn't in tow. She palmed the Hawaiian rock and waited the ten torturous minutes that the plane was late. Finally, it landed and taxied to a halt. The door opened and uniformed men poured into the waiting arms of teary-eyed families and friends. Jaz craned her neck to focus on the last few stragglers. It was like Qwayz to be last, or to leave in a laundry sack so he could surprise her from behind. Her heart raced and her breath shortened as she looked in earnest for his distinctive, easy, streetwise swagger. C'mon, Qwayz, don't dance with me now, she pleaded, absently singing the Drifters' "Some Kind of Wonderful."

"Jaz?" Her head jerked at the sound of her name.

"Buzz McLeish from Hawaii."

"Sure… Roberta?" Jaz offered his wife's name.

"Late as usual."

"Where's Qwayz?" Jaz watched the smile drain from his brown face.

"You're not here to— Oh, no. Damn Air Force was supposed to contact you before today."

"Is Qwayz on this plane?"

"Jaz, he isn't on this plane."

"Have you seen him? Do you know where he is or which one he will be on? I wasn't home yesterday, so if he called, I missed it." Jaz could feel her nose burn the way it did when she was going to cry. Buzz's image got wavy in the water that sprang uninvited to her eyes. Shoving the wetness from her cheeks, she defiantly awaited his answer.

"I haven't seen Qwayz since he and Milton left for a flight early last week. Jaz, they didn't come back. A bunch of us volunteered to scout the area. They were both liked a lot . . . but I was hopin' to see you. Qwayz gave me this to have the clasp fixed. Said you'd kill him if he showed up without it." Buzz dangled the gold ID bracelet she'd given Qwayz for his high school graduation. "First time he was without it. They'll be shipping his stuff home, but I didn't wanna leave this to chance. Things like this walk."

Jaz took the shiny bracelet, rubbing her finger across the deep engraving: Quinton Regis Chandler IV. She'd won her battle with the tears and now, dry-eyed, she looked at her husband's name in the palm of her hand.

"This picture, too," Buzz said. "It was the one he kept by his bed."

"We were just kids then... Malibu summer," Jaz whispered.

"I'm really sorry. He was one real special guy." The words offered to comfort caused Jaz to bolt after a quick thank you. "If you ever need anything just look me up!" Jaz heard him call to her back as she ran to her car.

Jaz drove furiously down the highway, trying to outrun reality. Her hair streamed in the wind, and her eyes shone red from tears of fear and frustration. The radio betrayed her, and she flipped from "a Raw Cilk classic, Everlastin' Love," smack-dab into the middle of their wedding song, "Too Young." Finally, she cut the radio off.

She took the turn from the main highway onto Ruidoso Canyon Road a little too fast and sped up the driveway to a halting stop. She jumped out, turned off the alarm, and slammed open the sliding door, stripping off her clothes as she went. Pulling on sweats and braiding her hair, she wound down the path to the beach, seeking the calm of the ocean. High tide prevented her from venturing too far, but the sound of the water began to quiet her, becoming a life-support system.

She remained perched on those boulders until the dawn of a new day; remaining at Paradise Rock for two more days before calling her father to assure him that she was fine and insisting that he go back to Italy. Jaz returned to the apartment a day before her med school classes began, searching in earnest for any mail from the Air Force or from Qwayz himself. Instead, the news Captain Bradford had verbally extended was now in official black and white on United States Air Force stationary.

What do *they* know? Jaz thought, as she lovingly placed his red cap and bomber jacket back on the hall tree. She slid his still-packed suitcase with his civvies, the Rolex, and the tickets to Myrtle Beach into his closet. We'll be packed and ready to go when you come home, she vowed.

"I'm fine," Jaz resigned herself to saying whenever anyone caught up with her to ask. She had read them all the riot act...her parents, Aunt Selena, Grandma Keely, Aunt Star, her sister, Denny, Tracy, Scoey, CC... even Gladys Ann and AJ whenever she heard pity creep into their voices. If you couldn't believe he was still alive, at least have the common decency to keep it to yourself, her stance.

School proved a welcome distraction. Her academic reputation preceded her, and no one knew or cared about her private life as long as she kept volunteering for extra emergency room duty so the less gifted could cram for exams or spend holidays with their families.

"You know, you have family too," Hep chastised Jaz for taking another student's shift on Thanksgiving. "I know it's an honor to qualify for that ER course as a first-year student, but—"

"Maybe I'll come by afterwards, Dad." They both knew better.

Hep hung up from his daughter and immediately called Denny. "How's everybody down there?" Hep asked.

"Ma Vy's formidable on the outside, ripped to shreds on the inside. My sister Hanie's still pretty shaken, but AJ's destroyed. He doesn't understand why Jaz won't talk to him. I'm not a good substitute. He's beginning to close off like she has."

"I'm concerned about her. I know you said it would take time, but—"

"She's not ready to accept Qwayz's loss. She's in complete and absolute denial, and we can't force her to think otherwise."

"That won't happen. She won't allow it. If you're not a believer, she cuts you off completely. You've been through this, Denny, and you counsel vets and families. Don't you think Jaz could use some?"

"Yes, but she isn't ready. Some people zip through the grieving stages, while others take months, years even. You have to remember, Mr. Culhane, that Jaz and Qwayz were best friends and confidants before they became lovers or husband and wife. A lot of who Jaz is, is tied up with my brother. They were very much a part of each other for many years, and he was Jaz's first love—the kind fairy tales are made of. She hasn't begun to mourn Qwayz or their relationship… what was… what will never be again."

"But this isolation—"

"Her way of coping with trauma. It's classic Jaz Culhane. She did this when we were kids. She withdraws and insulates herself, during which time she nourishes and fortifies herself. Then she reemerges when she's ready to face the music."

"What if it takes years? She'll waste her life."

"Healing, Mr. C. She has to reintegrate herself into a world without Qwayz."

"It just hurts to see my daughter in so much pain."

"She's not in pain yet. She's in denial. The only time she feels pain is when someone jabs her with reality. Right now, all her emotions and feelings are on hold. She's numb, a little angry, even sad, but hope is her strongest ally, her life preserver. Hope is what keeps her going. When she stops denying and accepts that Qwayz won't be back, then our work is cut out for us."

"An uphill climb to the bottom," Hep lamented.

Chapter 5

Jaz opened the door and her heart stopped for just a moment when she spotted the large package with the Oriental writing. But, she wasn't falling for it this time as she had before. In early October, Qwayz's metal locker stood in the middle of the floor, and she'd run through the apartment screaming his name, sure he was there, hiding in the shower stall or out in the hallway. She'd gone out onto the balcony looking for him when Mr. Sanchez yelled up to her, asking if she had seen the package the deliveryman had left. The cruelest words Jaz had heard in a long time. It took her an entire day and a half to open it, things Qwayz'd packed himself enshrined in the putrid smell of heat, sweat, and jungle. A military jacket with CHANDLER stenciled in black lay on top as if to protect treasures underneath: her tapes and letters tied with red ribbon. You're such a neat freak, Jaz thought. His composition book full of thoughts, song titles, and song beginnings. Presents wrapped with his mother's, sisters', AJ's, and her name on them. Letters from all his boys from Watts, even her father, and a tape recorder with a tape still in it. Jaz pressed play, and the sound of his voice tore her apart.

"…And lots of perfect beautiful brown babies. Rethink the four and let's go double or nothing. It'll be fun to try." His laughter filled the empty room and she cut it off before he could continue. She slammed the lid shut and shoved it into his closet, putting it under the packed suitcase with his civvies.

Now this package stood in the same place. His own handwriting could be seen amid the flurry of ornate stamps and strange characters. She cut the twine and unraveled the brown paper wrapping.

"I'm writing to myself 'cause I know I'm here to receive it," was scribbled in his familiar penmanship. "Lots of goodies in here for us, Jas-of-mine. Another set of kimonos 'cause I know we've worn the others out!" After reading the next sentence, Jaz shut her eyes tight as if screening out a harsh, painful light: "Are we pregnant yet?"

Jaz couldn't bear to look any further, and she hurriedly pushed another entry into Qwayz's bulging closet. Only then did she realize it was Christmas 1969 and she had no tree. She dressed for ER duty, refusing to think of her first season totally alone.

At her shift's end, Jaz walked back into emergency to discover a white boy lying on the cold linoleum floor, turning blue while a resident and an intern argued procedure and liability over the non-breathing victim. In a reflexive swoop, Jaz grabbed a scalpel from the tray, pushed a screaming girl out of the way, slashed open his throat, and barked for the tubing she saw dangling in the resident's hand. Jaz inserted the tube amid spurts of blood as Dr. Islip rounded the corner, taking charge of the just-trached young man.

"Dr. Mahler had been summoned, Chandler," the resident spat at Jaz.

"But he's not here, is he, Snyder?" Jaz sniped back.

"You'll hear about this!" the resident threatened as he followed Dr. Islip.

I'm sure I will, Jaz thought, washing the blood from her hands before signing out. Truth was she didn't give a fat rat's ass about Snyder or medicine. A scary revelation grabbed ahold of her; that something she had wanted for so many years all of a sudden didn't mean diddly. Medicine no longer interested or challenged her. It was a diversion… a way to fill her time.

"Miss Chandler!"

Good news travels fast, Jaz thought, turning into the cold stare of Dr. Brewer, the chief of staff, who apparently couldn't resist an opportunity to belittle her in front of the crowd.

"The idea that a first-year med student would have the audacity to think herself capable of performing an emergency tracheotomy is absurd. Your cowboy antics have surely opened us up to a multimillion-dollar lawsuit and ended your short-lived medical career," he concluded, happy that another darkie had been put in her place.

"It's not that I even care," Jaz later said to Mel as they drove down the coast. "It doesn't have as much to do with Brewer as it does with me and what I want."

"What do you want?"

"That's a Qwayz question: 'If not medicine, then what?'" Jaz laughed, imagining his smiling face and warning finger as she drove up the driveway.

"Whose pad is this?" Mel asked as her sister cut the engine in front of Paradise Rock.

"Ours. Mine and Qwayz's."

"Aw, shucks now, gimme the tour." Mel flung open the car door and took the tour with her mouth agape. "This is some humdinger of a house."

90

"I'm glad you came." Jaz served her sister tea in the sunken living room after she settled down.

"Well, Christmas and family are important. I want Hud to be close to his grandparents the way we were. Even if it's just for two days. Lemme call Dad and tell him where I am." Mel rose to use the phone and returned. "Is this some coup? Dad couldn't believe I made it to 'Paradise Rock.'"

"You're our first guest." Jaz didn't notice her pronoun usage. "Got something else to show you." Jaz rose, key in hand, with Mel following as she opened the garage door.

"Wow!" Mel entered the studio, one of its walls removed and replaced with a shatter-proof glass panel and view of the rolling ocean. "This equipment is first-rate."

"We bought the basics and figured Qwayz could add what he wanted later."

"TC's piano," Mel identified as she touched the carved wood reverently.

"Everybody thought Qwayz should have it."

"Yeah," Mel agreed, fingering the upright instrument that had been given to TC one Christmas by Selena and Zack.

"Here, sing your showstopper song for me." Jaz flipped on the mic and Mel obliged, singing her heart out. "Forever the ham." Jaz stood, giving her sister the usual standing ovation. "Miss Thang." Qwayz's word for her suspended between them.

"Now you," Mel prodded. "C'mon, you know you got a voice. I was always thankful you left singing to me, but you're just as good. TC and Qwayz agreed. You know one song I used to love to hear you sing, "Bye Bye Baby." For serious. You could really raunch it up."

Jaz sang it for Mel, who took another request from Jaz, and then they sang together. They emerged from the studio hours later. Mel spent the night and they talked until dawn and slept past noon.

Mel and Hud made Christmas dinner with her parents more palatable, but Jaz spent New Year's at the Berkeley apartment alone. She crumpled up the letter that notified her of a "change in status of Quinton Regis Chandler IV from MIA to KIA, Killed in Action." She threw it across the room, and it bounced and landed inside his guitar, Amber. "Two points! I don't believe a word of it. They wrote off my husband, but I know he is alive. I know it," she said aloud. That little stubborn piece of her heart wiggled, and Jaz took another swig of champagne to squelch it as the revelers outside the window yelled, "Happy New Year!"

"Know what I decided, Akira? We're gonna move back to San Francisco. We'll tell Mr. Sanchez so he can tell Qwayz where to find us. Then I can get our furniture out of storage and get Qwayz's Murphy chair and hassock out." Jaz took another swig of bubbly. "The love we made in that big ole chair and the things we did with that hassock. Ha!" Her laugh out loud turned to a scream, "Qwayz, where are you?" She dissolved into tears on her bed, a bottle her only company.

After assessing her finances, the checks from Champion that Qwayz received as well as his Air Force pay, their bank account could support a modest move. The next day Jaz called her father, asking if he knew a good black realtor who could help her move back to San Francisco.·

"Sure, what do you want?"

"I want a small, well-built Victorian house. Three floors so I can rent out the bottom two apartments for income."

Hep smiled. Not only was she moving on, but her business acumen was showing.

"I want the top floor. Unobstructed views. Large rooms, a fireplace, beamed ceilings, sunny, bright, and no trolley car tracks."

"Like Alta Vista."

"Yep, and a porch for Akira."

"Fine. If there's one in San Francisco, my people will find it."

"Thanks, Daddy. Remember he's got to be a brother."

"Yes, Jaz, I'm well aware of your politics." Hep hung up the phone with a wide grin. His daughter was coming around.

~*~

"Dr. Brewer must be proud of you!" Another student and friend, Farrell, ran up to Jaz with a copy of the campus newspaper.

"Hardly. I'm on my way to see the old bastard now." Jaz didn't break stride.

"For congrats, I'm sure. It's in the paper. The guy you performed the emergency tracheotomy on was Scott Carlisle, son of the Carlisle chain store family, who was visiting a friend for the holidays. Old Papa Carlisle is so grateful, he's giving a million-dollar wing to the Berkeley Medical Hospital Center that saved his boy. Listen, and I quote, 'It renews my faith in the medical profession and humankind that there are some dedicated doctors who place human life over bureaucracy, hierarchy, and red tape. Courage is the word I use to describe Dr. Chandler.' Oooh, gimme your autograph, girl!"

Jaz smiled.

Dr. Brewer kept Jaz waiting for more than twenty minutes, then joined her without apology.

"In retrospect," he began, "I suppose I should commend you for your quick action in the performance of the emergency procedure last week. There may be some hope for you yet." He offered a quick, insincere smile. "With a lot of hard work and my help, you may become a doctor. You were lucky this time, but don't try any of that foolishness again. Dismissed." He fanned at her.

"My becoming a doctor has very little to do with any help from you," Jaz countered without moving. "I bet the more input you have into my career, the less likely I am to succeed." Jaz rose towering above him, her honey eyes piercing cold blues. "Had it not been for my 'foolishness,' you, your department, an intern, and a resident would have egg on their faces, a corpse in the morgue, and the multimillion-dollar suit you were so eager to give me credit for. What I did had nothing to do with luck. It was skill." She turned on her heel and left his office door open as wide as his mouth.

"Damn uppity black bitch," he said.

"Racist honky bastard," she said.

~*~

"Hello!" Jaz yanked up the receiver to answer the jangling phone.

"Hit me with your congrats! I'm a daddy!" Scoey yelled.

"It's too early."

"She didn't think so. It's a girl, Jaz, the most perfect little black baby you ever saw."

"Oh, Scoey, congratulations. How's Tracy?"

"Sore. Won't be gettin' no nookie anytime soon."

"Typical! I'll be down there tomorrow."

"Hoping you'd say that."

"Give Tracy my love. Need anything?"

"Just your presence."

"Is that presents?"

"Them too! Gotta call her mom now. Make sure you come 'fo har," he did in his best Ma Vy imitation. "See ya tomorrow, Squirt."

94

Jaz relished the drive to L.A. As she tiptoed into Tracy's hospital room, Scoey bounced over to greet her, and Jaz gave him the flowers.

"Mama and daughter are a little busy." Scoey teased as the baby suckled at his wife's breast, "Wish it was me."

"Aww, look at how tiny she is." Jaz bent over without touching either Tracy or the baby. "Tracy, she's beautiful."

"Weighed six pounds six ounces!" Scoey forgot to whisper.

"That's your loudmouth daddy. Get used to it," Jaz whispered.

"Only family allowed," the nurse announced without ceremony.

"This is my sister," Tracy said. "Say hello to your aunt Jaz, Amber."

"Amber?" Jaz stood erect.

"Yes," Tracy said quietly, looking to her husband.

"We hope you don't mind. We thought it would be like her Uncle Qwayz named her. When he comes back and you two get started—well, we'll just have two Ambers."

"I think that's just… great." Jaz smiled through tears. "Thank you for that." She hugged them in turn, for naming their firstborn after a name their friend loved so. Thanking them for joining her in the hope that one day he would come back.

Aunt Jaz stayed with Amber and her parents for a full week, watchdogging their rest, making sure visitors didn't stay too long or get too close. Tracy's mother, Mrs. Summerville, brought over meals each night, and Scoey hired a nurse.

"You done good, Attorney Scofield," Jaz toasted him late one night as mother and daughter slept.

"Thanks." He looked around his barren house. "Maybe next year we can afford furniture. The pool's got water." He sipped wine. "Thanks to your dad throwing some major business my way, things are good. Money begets money, and as long as white folks keep making elevator music out of Raw Cilk classic hits, some of that kicks back to me, thanks to your brother."

"Yeah," Jaz said quietly. "Couldn't happen to nicer folks."

"Everything'll be okay, kiddo. Hang tough."

"I'm hangin '."

"Talked to Ma Vy recently?"

"We had a parting of the ways." Jaz rose, crossed her arms and stood by the fireplace.

"About Qwayz's memorial service?"

Jaz walked to the terrace door, gazing at the shimmering light reflected from the pool. "How can you have a funeral without a body?"

"Maybe she needs this to put it all behind her."

"I'm not putting Qwayz behind me, and I'm takin' names of those who do. I'm not letting anybody bury any part of him or my life with him. She'll look damn foolish when we drop by to see her."

"I think she'll be glad to be a 'damn fool' in that instance. That was pretty cool of you signing over Qwayz's air force pay to her."

"Dag, do you know everything?"

"For a change, good news traveled fast."

"Well, she's got Hanie's college tuition soon. And I got plentay mon-ay." Jaz sipped the wine, looking up at the star she and Qwayz shared.

"Denny and AJ know you're here in L.A."

"Big mouth. Maybe I'll drop by and see AJ. He graduates this year."

"I know. Denny's been given a professorship at USC."

"Time sure does fly. Just yesterday, AJ would sit in the back of Reds on our way to POP or Disneyland. Now he'll be off to college."

"He couldn't be any worse than you at that age."

"Say wha?" Jaz challenged playfully.

"You needed more than a little rescuing. I was always pulling you and Gladys Ann outta some mess your mouth started. Your mouth? Always writing checks your body couldn't cash."

"Ooh, you lie! It was you, Colt 45, and all them gals you were lovin' on in the back seat of that Impala. Condom city—we found enough rubber to make a pair of tires."

"Shush! Tracy thinks she married a virgin."

"And so do you." Jaz had to laugh.

"What you mean by that?" He shot her his patented mock-angry look.

"It scared me then, only humors me now."

"As I recall, nothing scared you then. That was your problem. What is so fascinating out that window?" He got up to join her.

"That twinkling star. It belongs to Qwayz and me. We declared it ours that Malibu summer. It's the same star that shines in Vietnam." Jaz looked up at her old friend. "You 're the last one, Scoey—the last of the trio."

"I can't take the weight, Jaz. Those guys were something fierce."

"So are you," Amber cried out and Jaz responded, "Lemme go, I'll be leaving in the morning."

Jaz picked up the sweet-smelling baby, all swaddled in pink lace and cotton, and walked with her until the bottle warmer heated the milk to perfection.

"You're a nighthawk, like your aunt Jaz and uncle Qwayz." She sat in the nursery's rocking chair. "Actually, your uncle

Qwayz never needs much sleep. That'll be good when we have our own children. Maybe you can babysit, huh? He's gonna be crazy about you."

Tracy and Scoey watched the pair from the doorway with a bittersweet irony. Jaz and Qwayz had been the first to date, to fall in love, to marry, destined to name their first girl child, Amber. Yet Jaz was here with a child named Amber, not her own.

~*~

Jaz found the perfect old gingerbread house perched high atop a San Francisco hill with two rentable apartments beneath hers. It took her only a couple of months to convert the ex-hippie house into a Victorian of distinction, and with great relish, Jaz left the Berkeley Heights apartment.

"Home." She cut the engine and walked the three flights to her door, lovingly hanging Qwayz's red baseball cap and leather bomber jacket on his brass hook of the hall tree. "It won't be removed until he does so himself," she vowed as Akira headed straight for the open sliding glass door to the covered porch.

The apartment was big enough to resurrect all their bulky antique furniture from Alta Vista, yet small enough so that Qwayz would only be a reach away. From that back porch a spectacular view of the bay crowned the living room, flanked by the kitchen on the left and the bedroom on the right. Jaz's carpenter built bookcases on either side of the one bedroom window creating a padded seat where she could bask in the sun. Jaz imagined her and Qwayz sipping cappuccino from their prized machine in the kitchen's bay window or rubbing derrieres in passing as they cooked.

Their wedding portrait hung over the brass bed. On the nightstand, an anniversary music box that played "Too Young" sat in front of a picture of two young people in love one Malibu summer and a smooth volcanic rock—the last thing Qwayz had handed to her. The movers placed all of Qwayz's clothes plus his trunk, locker, Christmas package, and the suitcase Jaz'd packed with his civvies in his closet. Jaz never touched them as she closed the door. All was in place. Jaz now comfortable and pleased with her new home, but all the challenge and purpose of buying and remodeling was gone. Once again, loneliness set in and she felt lost. She longed for more.

Well, what now, Jaz? she asked herself, joining Akira on the covered porch. A Qwayz question that needed answering, especially since she'd officially dropped out of med school. Doctors Lochner, Williams, and Islip had called her in for a conference, trying to convince her to stay and wanting assurance that Dr. Brewer wasn't the reason she was leaving.

"One monkey don't stop no show" came out of her mouth before she realized it. "His attitude is actually motivation for me to stay and teach him a few things about unearned entitlement and minority superiority, but that would be my only reason for staying. I would never let anyone else steal my dream, but it's no longer medicine," she had told them.

"Okay, Jaz, you don't want medicine, what do you want?" Jaz asked herself aloud, and Akira looked up at her. It was June, and she didn't have a clue. "Let's go for a ride."

Jaz and Akira cruised around town, ending up across from the Culhane Building. She pulled out of the traffic to absorb all thirty-five floors of its grandeur.

"I have a B.S. degree and could get a job there when it's completed, but what'll I do now?" she asked Akira, when another Qwayz question insinuated itself into her psyche: What would you like to do whether you got paid for it or not?

There in the midst of noise, traffic, the clang of a trolley car, and fumes, the answer shone clear as it bounced off the gold steeple atop the Culhane Building.

"Of course." She started her motor along with the beginning of a new challenge and life.

~*~

In just a few months, all the Johnny Mathis and Nat King Cole records were returned to their jackets and placed on the stereo stand. All the doors and windows secured. When he found out, AJ would have to battle Millie for custody of Akira. Jaz took one last glance at their wedding portrait and the nightstand shrine formed by the trinity—music box, Hawaiian rock, and Malibu picture—deciding again that this was the way she wanted Qwayz to first see this room, intact.

Europe. Paris. She had decided on the Sorbonne over the Ecole des Beaux Arts. Her friends didn't understand why she had to go to Europe to study architecture, and Jaz couldn't articulate the razor-sharp pain she felt trying to cope with life without Qwayz, no matter how temporary. She couldn't explain the anger provoked by the news, whether it reported on the war in Vietnam or the war on poverty. The shootings of her people, the urban blight, the racism, the prejudice she felt walking the streets, in department stores or the hallowed halls of the American educational system.

The height of government anarchy and arrogance occurred when Governor Reagan tear-gassed Berkeley students protesting at Sproul Plaza. In May, she knew the entire United States was an obnoxiously unwell, repugnant society feeding upon itself when national guardsmen fired on students protesting the U.S. invasion of Cambodia, killing four at Kent State. Everything here was reduced to race, ignorance, power, or the lack thereof.

Jaz, like her aunt Selena before her, was sick of America. She longed to be treated as a human being, and garner a break from racism at every level. Not just the sanctioned armed assassination of Fred Hampton by "law enforcement" or this crazy mess brewing with George Jackson and Angela Davis right over the bridge, but black men deemed expendable cannon fodder in Southeast Asia while the white man pulled strings for his own son. Jaz remained bone-weary of the status quo where all white folks, although none alive were responsible for slavery, benefited from it. Just as all black folks were continually scarred by it. Jaz needed a vacation from the hypocrisy of America.

The iron bird soared slicing through the puffs of clouds, and Jaz dared to put the headset to her ears. America gave her a farewell concert; the social commentary of the Temptations in "Ball of Confusion," the assault from Edwin Starr's "War," what is it good for? and a plea from Freda Payne to "Bring the Boys Home," but it was the prayer from Stevie Wonder's "Heaven Help Us All" that pierced Jaz's heart, rattled her sad soul, and sent tears streaming down her cheeks. "Help the boy who won't reach 21. Help the man who gave that boy a gun…"

Chapter 6

Jaz's leather flats clicked across the highly polished parquet floors, echoing in the faded elegance of this sixteenth-century Rome apartment building with the colorful past. The resident manager explained that it had gone from housing heads of state to a famed brothel and back again to an address of repute.

"*E troppo grande,*" Jaz sighed, leading the manager to the elevator.

She'd lived with her parents in the embassy's private quarters for five days now and had less than a week before her classes at the American Architecture Academy, AAA, began. She'd fought coming to Italy because her parents were here, but it was the only place for a serious architecture student who had the means and money to study in Europe. Paris had turned on her for not bringing Qwayz back, and conjured him up in every nook and cranny of its being. Jaz saw them buying candy from the comer confectioner's, climbing the steps of Notre Dame, her posing for him in front of the gargoyles. Visions popped up of Qwayz coaxing her into the Eiffel Tower elevator then sharing Berthmillion ice cream as they sauntered across Ile St. Louis. Images of him plucking the perfect bouquet of sunflowers while charming the vendor or presenting Jaz with a passel of helium-filled balloons before they walked through the park, giving them to children. The loving picnickers by the Seine seemed hokey and obnoxious since she and Qwayz were not among them. Qwayz's essence blossomed everywhere in the parks, the streets, the markets, the shops and the museums. Her heart, mind, and soul ached for him in Paris, more than it ever did at home. So, she had to come to Rome.

Even with no imprints of Qwayz here in Italy, the world remained coupled: her parents only bothered her occasionally; Gladys Ann had married Dr. Ulery Menair, a native of St. Bart's; Sloane was engaged; and CC had run off to Maine with someone she met at Woodstock. What intelligent black woman goes to Woodstock? Jaz didn't have to ask what color he wasn't. Seems she and Denny remained the stalwarts. The last true-blues, who waited for their men to reappear. Qwayz should have called or come home by now. Qwayz was late. Quinton Regis Chandler IV was never late. So, while she held a silent vigil for his return, she'd immerse herself in the study of architecture, take a loft apartment, and furnish it with the bare necessities, because when Qwayz called… she was gone.

Ensconced in her classroom, immediately inspired by the pace, the challenge and the work of the core curriculum, she jumped into her studies full-force. She'd finally decided on the top floor of that faded hotel formerly used for a greenhouse and storage and turned into an ersatz one bedroom flat perfect for her. Centrally located up a steep hill that she could neither ride her bike down or up. Clearly a vesper, the native Italian choice of transportation, was in the cards for her. The building lay at an angle up the hill so that its top floor actually formed the first floor apartment of the alpine village where the now defunct ancient aqueduct had provided the water. Her flat, the only one

103

of the structure protruding above ground. The door opened onto an immediate 15 steps which led up to the L shaped room.

A bright picture window dominated the front, looking onto shops although a floor up, providing privacy so no one could look in without a ladder. Directly opposite that front picture window was another plate glass window-wall with a full display of the magnificent Victor Emmanuel, referred to as the Wedding Cake, which looked like a photograph when lit up at night. Walking through to the bathroom, she passed an opened, alcove-bedroom, consisting of a double bed and a dresser. If looking out of the window, you'd miss it altogether. The bathroom, small, efficient with a tub, shower, basin, commode and small window like Alta Vista. Jaz bought a toaster oven for the minuscule, almost non-existent kitchen with a small under the counter refrigerator and a two-burner stove. Compact-cozy, she needed function not fanciful, a place she could vacate at any given moment. From necessity, she purchased a drafting table, which she set in front of the picture window facing the village shops. She splurged on a beautifully crafted, ancient apothecary cabinet with its plentiful and deep drawers to house all her drafting materials, slide rules and other essential equipment. There was no place for junk. She swapped out a new mattress for the platform bed and added a small couch and coffee table on the Victor Emanuel side, which served as living and dining room. It suited her perfectly.

Once she reiterated to her parents that her prime reason for being in Rome was to study and not to attend every state or official dinner/reception/tea they hosted, they left her to her academics. Jaz accepted an invite perhaps once a month when she craved a sumptuous meal and could manage being sociable. She spoke with some regularity with Aunt Selena, Grandma Keely, and Denny, who promised to come for a visit, and saw

Keely J, still based in Paris, a couple of times. She kept up letter correspondence with Sloane, AJ and Gladys Ann like they did when they were in college. Jaz was living a life without Qwayz but wondered how long this alternative and temporary plan would last for her. Despite being happily consumed by her studies and limited social obligations, it didn't take long for Fabrizio to locate her and begin his campaign about her modeling. He extended perfunctory condolences regarding Qwayz, ending with what a wonderful "specimen of a man he was…" which pissed Jaz off. She avoided his cards, letters and flowers until finally he relented a little. One thing he said stuck with her… the gargantuan amount of money she could make with little time or effort. "A couple of print ads could pay for all her bills back in California." Jaz thought of that when the management company informed her that boiler in the basement of her new San Francisco Victorian house needed replacing and reminded her that next year she'd have to paint the wooden façade which would be ravished by the salt and sea air of the bay. She would love to send additional money for Hanie and AJ's college. While AJ's parents paid his tuition, Jaz knew a college student could always use more money…he'd gone to Stanford like his Uncle Qwayz. Amber and Hud Jr. would be approaching before she knew it and she envisioned herself being a good aunt and godmother.

Fabrizio continually promised that any modeling would not intrude on her academic life. After swearing Fabrizio to absolute secrecy, Jaz peppered him with her terms and conditions; noninterference with her life, no direct contact with any client, no pedigree disclosure as she didn't want it known that she was the daughter of an ambassador or where she was from; no U.S. ads as she planned to keep Qwayz or anyone else in the dark about this little side venture she was getting ready to embark

105

upon. Her parents would gladly give her the money, but Jaz relished being on her own for the first time and wanted to be a grown, independent, self-sufficient adult who could handle her life and expenses.   Seen as a temporary solution, she finally relented. "Don't make me regret this Fabrizio. I need a Vesper. Biking to my sites is getting old and tired."

"Ah! You will be able to buy your entire family scooters."

"Just one will do."

With her permission, the pushy Italian bon-vivant was off and running. Or so it seemed. It was weeks before he returned with a couple of weekend shoots which did not interfere with her plans. In the company of other models, photographers shot around the Trevi Fountain. Up the Spanish Steps, at the Forum and Colosseum. Jaz showed up, they did her makeup, hair, gave her wardrobe, placed her...and it was over. She appreciated that Fabrizio always accompanied her and, while she spoke Italian, it wasn't as fast and furious as Fabrizio who she knew made demands on her behalf that the client didn't always agree with. "Got to teach people how to treat you," he told her.

Her first check shared post office space with a letter from Gladys Ann, which she read first before opening it...as per Jaz's directive, in keeping with her anonymity, it came through Fabrizio. "What the hell?" She called him immediately. "What is this?"

"You like? Too much?" He gleaned.

"This is outrageous! Is this all for me?   Just standing in place?"

"Less my twenty percent of course, but yes. Now you can buy a car instead of a scooter."

When available, Jaz became far more cooperative. Visions of her paying off her new Victorian house danced in her head and how delighted Qwayz would be with her business acumen; he and her father subscribed to the edict… "don't sell nothing." After a picture of four models appeared on the cover of European Vogue…a thin, pale white girl, Jaz, a Japanese girl and a Negro girl, Jaz's stock vaulted into a highly desirable category. The camera loved her and shone on her as if she was the only model gracing that cover. Deep copper-skin, light eyes, wild hair shot with gold, pouty lips, full eyebrows and savage cheekbones. Exotic. A love-fest ensued. She was everything most models weren't, and the photographers loved her. The clothes loved her. Even at an American size 8-10, she refused to lose weight. "I'm not giving up pasta or gelato." All bookings went through Fabrizio and he savored the exclusivity of it. "Your name is Tawny now."

"Say what?"

"I had to call you something. Can't use your real name or make any connection between you and your parents or even America. You know they've never heard you speak. So there is much speculation and mystery as to who you really are. It's outshining the clothes."

"Is that good or bad?"

"Are you kidding? You can't create this kind of buzz, my dear. Oh! The latest of 'who is she?' A Brazilian heiress who is doing this for fun."

"As good as any bio, I suppose."

On the way to a sketch site Jaz glimpsed a picture of the magazine with her image on it. She diverted her Vesper to inspect her solo image on the cover. That's me, she thought. Not that you could immediately tell with all the makeup, the hair piled high in a topknot upon her head and the bored facial expression they coveted. Funny what folks saw. Back home preparing for bed, she'd washed her face and French-braided her hair like she'd always done. She looked in her tiny bathroom

107

mirror... all she saw was a black girl from Watts California who had two black parents and four black grandparents. People saw what they wanted to see, she supposed. She cut the light and climbed into bed.

~*~

The night, young and staid, as Jaz sat with her parents and other dignitaries at their table, one of five with ten guests each, in the well-appointed embassy ballroom. Luckily, not an elaborate ornate affair but the food as sumptuous as any she'd tasted while in Italy. She chatted amiably while wishing she could eat and vaporize back to her flat and settle in and ready for bed. Instead she accepted the pro-offered hand of Prince Omar. She hadn't known he was there until that very moment. More handsome than she had remembered, they danced once, twice before walking out onto the terrace. Distant orchestral stings could still be heard as he asked the mundane questions; when did you come? How long will you be here? Sorry to hear of your husband's disappearance in action. She accepted his expressions of caring about Qwayz and did not correct him that the classification was Missing in Action. What did an Arab care of the Vietnam war?

"Perhaps you will let me show you around Italy while you are here."

"As I said, I've been here for a while and will be here until I complete my studies. I don't have any time to socialize. And to what end?"

Startled by her directness, he smiled charmingly. "I suppose at some time you have to eat."

"I do. Often with jeans on and a pencil in my hair."

"Allow me to take you to the opera—"

"I don't care for the opera," she stated flatly, bored with the conversation and ready to go home.

108

"Jaz," her father called.

"Excuse me. It was great seeing you again. Take care," she dismissed the crown prince.

The after-dinner banter was brutal and as Jaz escaped and stuck her key into her door, she mused that she may never need a meal that badly again. Chinese would suffice. The next day she didn't notice a strange car following her on her vesper as she darted in and out of traffic. She met Fabrizio and rode with him to her next shoot. Like the metamorphosis of a butterfly, she was transformed from a grad student into Tawny. She assumed her place, took direction and vanished after the shoot, not fraternizing with the other models…feigning that her Italian was "not so good."

For the next two shoots, a black limo appeared and disappeared as did she. Finally, Fabrizio asked, "So how long has Prince Omar been stalking you?"

"What?" The oblivious Jaz asked him.

"You haven't noticed? I've seen him the last three times. I suspect there have been others."

Jaz looked across the street at the long limo. "Well why?"

"C'mon, Tawny. The man is smitten."

"Don't be absurd."

"I'm not the absurd one. Tawny and the Prince. That has a nice ring to it. Imagine what folks would do with that?" Fabrizio gleaned. "The publicity alone would up your captivating appeal."

As Jaz sat in the grass sketching the Pantheon, she noticed the limo again. She took a long swig from her water bottle, flipped her sketch book closed and marched straight for the back passenger side door. She tapped on the window. As the glass slid into the well, revealing inch-by-inch of his handsome face in the process, Jaz said, "So it is you. Why are you following me around town?"

"I can see you are indeed very busy. But perhaps we can at least dine together once or twice. You must be hungry. Sandwiches, Chinese food, pizza... not very healthy." He smiled and dazzled her. "What would be the harm? Surely you don't fear me."

"I fear no man," Jaz quipped.

"Well, then..."

"I suppose you won't leave me alone until you find out how utterly boring I am and move on."

"Yes. That is it."

She side-eyed him and they chuckled.

"OK. One meal—"

"Fair enough. What time do I pick you up?"

That's how it began... One dinner turned into two, then three, then a lunch, then a limo ride to her next sketch site, sometimes he waited. Other times, he would leave her, then pick her up for yet another eating date. He'd even taken her to a few shoots where Fabrizio beamed at seeing Tawny emerge from the limo of a crowned Saudi Prince. What a publicity coup I could create with this but Jaz would never permit it, he mused, preferring their friendly alliance over a breach in their contract.

Once Prince Omar jetted her away to an elegant yet whimsical place where they dined on a terrace overlooking the Nile. "This is beautiful. And the food exquisite. I haven't had a burger like that since I left California."

"I had them make it especially for you."

"Did you now?"

"I saw your Aunt Selena last week in Paris—"

"You didn't tell her we were friends?"

"Of course not. I want to stay 'friends.'"

"Good answer."

"I've never known your kind of pretty before. Both inside and out. There is not a calculating bone in your body, which is why I am so taken with you."

No black brother talks like this, Jaz thought.

"I was thinking perhaps we can change our status. Escalate it to the next level."

"You don't want to be my friend anymore?" Jaz teased, thinking, here it comes.

"We're both married. With a wife and children, I'm not going anywhere. You are married and when your husband returns, you are going back to him. Let us just enjoy the time we will have together."

Jaz smiled. Not really at Prince Omar or the distraction he could offer her, but that he understood. He too believed Qwayz was coming back.

"You would be the only other man I have ever been with in my life," Jaz confessed.

"Ah! A virgin," Prince Omar teased, pristine white teeth blazing in a rich, Arab complexion.

Jaz laughed at his harmless proposition. "You know I love me, and I'd only consider it if you use a prophylactic." She smiled thinking that telling him a condom was required would be a deal breaker. Did a prince even know what a condom was? He paused as if thinking it over. Gauging whether she was worth the trouble or not.

"You know when a prince takes a concubine or second wife, she is subjected to a rigorous health examination and a background check before we...can proceed. I cannot be blackmailed or made sick by diseases."

"That may be all well and good. But I am not your concubine and not applying to be your second wife. So if we... you and

I… are going any further, that is my term. No glove. No love."
Jaz waited for him to huff off with the sheer absurdity of her
mandate. He stared long and hard, silently considering her
again.

"You understand that this will be an exclusive relationship.
Just you and me. No other man."

"Of course. And only your wife."

"You will help me with the apparatus?"

Jaz smiled. "Yes, I will." He's bluffing, she thought.

"Then 'let's do it' as you Americans say."

To cover her shock, Jaz asked, "So how would this work
otherwise. When you enter into these kinds of 'beyond
marriage' liaisons?"

He smiled. "If I found someone I wanted to spend more time
with. We'd flirt a bit. Then I'd send my emissary to work out the
details: the physical examination, the non-disclosure
confidentiality agreement, obtain a suitable address for her
during our association and decide on a monthly allowance for
services rendered."

"How romantic." She volleyed his smile back and
indicated," Of course I'll need none of that. I am my own
person."

"Which makes you so tantalizingly intriguing."

"That's me."

They dined on his yacht crowned with the helicopter on its
rooftop pad and the Bentley in the hull ready for anything on
land they wanted to do that struck their fancy. On deck, after
their dessert dishes had been removed, beneath the night sky's
studded stars, he stood, extended his hand and escorted her to
the master stateroom. His skin smelled of frankincense and
myrrh, he tasted of spices curry, cumin, saffron, figs and dates,
his flesh beneath her fingertips subtle, firm and warm but… so

112

hairy; his legs, his chest, his arms, his back. Her people, the African and Indian, not so apportioned. Pacing himself, he stopped kissing her and retrieved the glasses of champagne beside the ice bucket. Years of privilege showed in his carriage, his bearing, his regal attitude passed down from generations; the governesses, the servants, the education teaching him the seven languages he spoke fluently. The lack of concern about finances of any type. But one male constant showed itself. Protruding from its hairy home, an anxious and engorged love muscle throbbed. They toasted and sipped before he removed the flute from her hand and renewed exploring her with his lips. Oddly enough he was patient and tender, and when the time came, trying to don the condom provided a playful source of mirth and relief.

Thus the relationship escalated... a studied affair of terms. Neither looking for permanency, a future or the three words...unless they were Do Not Disturb. A freeing and satisfying friendship for them both. Nothing beyond the present. Their liaison met where curiosity and diversion converged. Shortly after her graduation, and not ready to return to the United States, she immediately began studies on her second master's degree so that the men in her life: Fabrizio and Prince Omar, would continue to respect her boundaries and not threaten to engulf her. Fabrizio brokered a deal of total exclusivity with Alonge' Cosmetics whereby Tawny only worked 20 days per year and for no one else the rest of the time, giving her considerable freedom to pursue another degree and spend time with Prince Omar. She had merely to express curiosity about a place and he'd whisk her away...by private jet or yacht. From Timbuktu to Thailand to Tahiti, Jaz had visited them all. The only limits, her imagination. Jaz's favorite destination, the villa on Lake Como due to its proximity to school, work and her parents. She and Prince Omar settled into the lake villa and used it as their base. Despite the enormity of the 15th century villa which appealed to Jaz's penchant for architecture, they used only a few rooms. Bedroom and its terrace, the dining room on occasion, the cooks made use of the kitchen where anything she wanted would magically appear. She told him of her fondness for Georgia peaches and the next morning he presented her with a crate shipped overnight from America. Frequently, she would lift a breakfast cloche, expecting a frittata, brioche with butter and apricot preserves, grapefruit juice; but finding an expensive bauble from a jeweler to match her eyes or further adorn her. "You must stop this. I have nowhere to wear such opulence."

"The jewelry is here to serve your skin. It is the lucky one." The safe of the villa brimmed with his generosity. "This is how an Arab man shows he cares. That you are special."

"I know," she teased. "But really. Stop."

For her birthday he presented her with the deed to the villa. "I cannot accept this. What will I do with it when I go back to America?"

"What you wish. It is yours." He kissed her toes. "It is now called Villa Nubia. After you."

Jaz looked at him and blinked.

"It is our *nido d'amore.* Love nest. We could not call it Villa Jazz... there is already Chateau Jazz outside Paris where we first met." He nibbled her behind the calf of her legs. "Years from now when they refer to it as Villa Nubia... I will think of you. And smile."

At Ambassador and Mrs. Culhanes' farewell dinner, Lorette broke from her guests to greet her daughter. "Ah, I'm delighted you came... Tawny," she whispered as Jaz eyed her mother nervously.

114

"Every mother knows her own. Of course your hair is pulled back and the clothes not as expensive." She smiled. "I will not tell your father. But now I can stop worrying about how you are managing. You are rich."

"Not quite." Jaz quipped.

Jaz and forty-nine other guests dined at the American Embassy while the orchestra played softly. After dinner, Prince Omar approached and bowed, inviting her to dance. As they glided across the polished marble floor with the other revelers Jaz said, "I don't think this is a good idea."

"No one knows but you and me. It is fine. Two old friends sharing a waltz. Unlike when we dance nude at our villa."

That night marked the first time Prince Omar stayed in Jaz's tiny apartment. Victor Emmanuel lit up between their legs. "Do people really live like this?" he asked, venturing to the bathroom.

"I live like this. You are a snob."

"Not really. This is just not my reality."

One week later, Prince Omar answered the summons from his father. Entering the office, he greeted his father customarily and his father wasted no time. "You have been remiss in your duties."

"I have not," Prince answered. "I have been at every meeting required."

"Ah. You are the crowned prince. You must do more than just what is required. Your legacy must be protected." He motioned for his son to sit and join him. "It has come to my attention that you do not always wear the regalia. That sometimes you are in the jeans and knit shirt of western wear."

"Not when on duty."

"A crown prince is always on duty." He watched the butler leave their refreshments and when he backed out of the room,

115

the king continued, "I understand you are keeping company with a model and architecture student. Please tell me they are one in the same."

"They are."

"She was vetted through the normal channels?"

Prince Omar swallowed before answering, "She is fine, my father."

"Umm. I wasn't concerned initially. We all have our dalliances. Appetites to be satiated. It is expected. But discretion does not seem to be your ally."

"I still pray to Allah five times a day. I am careful."

"Not as I witnessed the night of the Culhane farewell dinner at the American embassy. Both your mother and your wife suggested that I speak to you. Perhaps you are getting too familiar. I thought so when I saw the expense of the Lake Como villa."

"A mere birthday gift. I give her no other remuneration."

"I could believe this if I did not know of the fixation you have for this girl since she was sixteen. Is she returning to America with her parents?"

"I hope not. She is a grown woman with her own mind."

"I suppose that is what attracts you. She is different from the others."

"Father. We both know what this is. I am married as is she. It is nothing more. I assure you."

"Your wife says you have not been home."

"I go home one week in the month."

"You think this is sufficient?"

"For now. It suits me. There will come a time when it does not. I know this."

"Careful, my son. Sometimes the hunter gets captured by the game."

With her parents and friends a continent away, Jaz completely succumbed to the charms of Crown Prince Omar Al Khalifa Sidar. He was funny; not like Dickie Peckingpah, Richard Pryor or Watts-funny, but he had a sense of humor and an endless desire to pamper her; just what Jaz needed. The prince continued to romance her. An intense lover, predictably his maleness dominated the tryst often so heavy upon her, Jaz could barely move. Once Jaz took control, flipped herself, mounted him and brought them both to a never-ending climax. "Well, you are just full of surprises," he grinned.

"It is a participatory event," she joked as he arranged the covers to expose her nude body. A true voyeur, he loved watching her walk, or inch by inch, devouring her brown form with his smoldering, passion-soaked eyes. He seldom made demands and did not interfere when Jaz invited her friends to Italy for a visit. She often gifted them with a first-class airline ticket and a stay with her; One side of a double bed for the ladies and the couch for AJ. Tracy and Scoey never made it over, but she showered them and Amber with the latest fashions. Jaz loved showering her family and friends with special treasures; she inundated Grandma Keely with imported yarns and materials for the quilts she now made and Aunt Star with the thin brown cigarettes and hard ginger candies Jaz had once sent to Star's beau, but her aunt confiscated. Although closer in distance than they'd ever been, Jaz and Aunt Selena seldom saw one another but kept up with their weekly phone calls. Jaz saw Keely J more, who opened her own restaurant, Keely's Soul Food in Paris. Jaz'd connected with Hanie, who forwent college in California for Parson School of Design in New York City's Greenwich Village. Years of watching Ma Vy support the family as a seamstress, the skill ran through Hanie's veins and upon graduation, she received a design award for inventing clothing for children and young adults with cerebral palsy and other ailments that limited mobility. This innovation caught the eye of Maximo who flew her to London where Hanie has been ever since, marking her territory in the design world. "Qwayz would be so proud," Jaz told her.

Two weeks with AJ was magical, and they did Europe and Egypt and glacier-skied in Cortina and St. Moritz. During his stay with Jaz, AJ met Avia Checole, Hep's embassy assistant, prior to his permanent return to San Francisco and Culhane Enterprises. The pretty, slim-faced girl, whose coal-black hair sprang back into curls moments after it was brushed, was the color of a wet ginger-snap, compliments of her French mother and Cameroonian father. Jaz watched the blossoming of an authentic relationship.

Jaz enjoyed all of the visits from her friends and relatives except the one from Denny. It gave her pause. She'd shared with Jaz that psychiatrist Dr. Lloyd Winslow had proposed, and she accepted. It took Jaz three conversations to express happiness and invite her to Rome to get her wedding dress. Jaz'd hoped that this gesture would keep Denny from asking Jaz to fly to L.A. to attend her wedding.

When Denny flew to Rome, they spent a fabulous two weeks searching for the perfect dress for her friend's upcoming nuptials and decided on a beautiful, elegant, midi-length dress. "It's my second marriage," Denny quipped. Knowing Jaz wasn't ready for a return to the U.S., but not able to get married without her friend present, Denny asked anyway. "I want you to be my maid of honor."

"Matron," Jaz corrected quietly. She'd forgotten how wonderful it was to spend time with her best friend. Calls and letters couldn't replace the eyeballin'. Late one night as they lay in bed and looked at a lit up Victor Emmanuel, Jaz finally asked, "Why, Denny? I thought you and I would never give up waiting for our men."

"I know. But I'm tired of being lonely, Jaz. Not alone but lonely. Yudi decided for me. I don't think there was any pain as hard as declaring your husband dead when you know he lives under a bridge."Jaz eyed her, unable to imagine her friend's inner agony.

"But that isn't my Yudi Hodges. That person is not my husband." Denny wiped away a tear and continued, "I've come to realize that life works out best for those who make the best of the way life works out." She looked into Jaz's eyes. "Lloyd is good to me and for me. I love him—not like I did Yudi, but I do love him, and it will grow stronger in time, I am sure of it. Especially once the children come."

"When did you know?"

"When I realized that life without him would not be worth living." She smiled weakly, but Jaz could not return the gesture. "You'll come?"

"I will."

This one and only time Jaz returned to America, she did not let anyone know. Luckily, her parents were on travel, Scoey and Tracy vacationing, AJ away with Melie and Aubrey for a Caribbean family reunion, as if her friend Denny had arranged for them all to be gone. She wanted Jaz there and to make it as easy on her as possible. But there was only one person with whom Jaz had to deal. Ma Vy. Jaz hadn't seen or talked with her since their row about Qwayz's memorial service. Jaz avoided her for most of the small affair, held in Denny and Lloyd's new Baldwin Hills home, but she caught her by the punch bowl. "I want to thank you for signing my boy's pay to me, Jaz."

"You're welcome. Qwayz would have wanted that. We'd discussed it before... he... left."

"Well. I appreciate the follow-through."

"Sure." She didn't reference Hanie who was not here for her sister's ceremony.

Jaz stayed overnight at a local hotel and couldn't wait to return to Italy and the adoring arms of Prince Omar. She was not ready for the United States.

~*~

Jaz nibbled on a kumquat, relishing the sweet peel and the sour citrus inside, as she looked out over the lake. Peaceful, calm. The breeze on her skin... delightful. The sun shimmered on the still water ruffled by the passing of an occasional yacht. Prince Omar will return tonight, she thought. He never liked being around her while Mother Nature visited. Must be an Arab observance, she pondered.

The quiet was pierced by a commotion and Jaz looked down at the driveway partially obstructed by trees. A man shouted at a woman as four children cowered in the fold of her garment. Jaz wondered why they chose her driveway to have such a domestic discussion. Circumventing the upper terrace, she scrutinized the man and realized it was Prince Omar in his full regalia. He was early and not in jeans and a shirt. In one shocked instant, Jaz realized that the woman and the children were his. Two cars. Apparently, his wife had followed him here with their children in tow. So furious at her breech, Prince Omar railed against his wife's indiscretion, his voice rising in a way Jaz'd never heard as his murmurings evaporated in the air. Seeing the wife cower under his ire unsettled Jaz. She didn't recognize this man. Jaz leaned against the cool of the marble

120

terrace. This was not a woman "accepting" of her husband's traditional wayward ways. Jaz was an interloper. Cast as the "other woman." In her mind's eye they were but an illicit couple sneaking around. Raised better than this, Jaz deserved better than this. Her inner reverie interrupted by Prince Omar calling to her as he came into the house. She couldn't answer. Finding her on the terrace he said, "Ah, there you are." Having shed his flowing garments, probably left on the steps for the servants to retrieve, he presented her with an armful of the sunflowers she loved. . She stared at him and he dropped the happy yellow flowers with the brown centers by his side and asked, "How much did you hear?"

"Enough. I cannot do this anymore." She brushed passed him and reached for her valise.

"It is just a misunderstanding. She over-stepped. It will not happen again," he mandated.

"She is your wife!"

He looked at Jaz curiously. "Yes. We both know that."

Jaz then realized her complicity in this debacle. She had fallen for the rap of an Arab man and jumped in feet first, thinking there would be no ramifications or repercussions... and there weren't for her or Prince Omar. But the wife and family... Jaz felt such shame, embarrassment and so stupid. He and their relationship now, instead of sheer pleasure and hedonism, made her feel badly. Her ancestors, surely as disappointed in her choices as was she.

He pled with her to be reasonable as she packed. She walked down the stairs and into a waiting car. She never responded. There was no argument. She was gone.

Despite his extravagant displays to win her back, Jaz'd made her decision. Exotic flowers piled up outside of her tiny apartment, chocolates and once he drove by and saw the locals pillaging the gifts, he ceased supplying them. His calls went unanswered until Jaz changed her number, giving it only to her parents, friends and Fabrizio. She wished she smoked. On a spring day, while deciding her next move an image appeared on the television screen. Turning up the volume, she heard the anchorman report... "Saigon has fallen. The war is over." The verbal commentary accompanied images of Vietnamese rushing a helicopter on the roof of the American Embassy to get out. Jaz watched the imagery and it was crystal clear. It was time for her to go home. Return to America. Surely, if Qwayz was ever coming home, it would be now.

Chapter 7

In the spring of 1975, Jaz slipped back to California as quietly as she had left. All of her friends and family anticipated her return after a five-year absence, but no one knew exactly when. Though anxious to see Paradise Rock, Jaz gave the cabdriver her apartment's address. When they passed the street to her parents' house, she thought of how put out her father would be for not being privy to her plans. She had given him an inkling during their last conversation, telling him she didn't have definite projects beyond helping Tracy with her new baby. Hep warned her not to consider working anywhere except Culhane Enterprises. He even promised her the corner office with the two windows.

Mel and Hud Jr. had relocated to L.A. so that Mel could star in her own variety show, and she'd made wedding rumblings about the show's producer; Denny, Tracy, and AJ were ecstatic about Jaz's homecoming.

Italy was less accepting of her departure. Jaz had shipped her drafting table, apothecary cabinet, three pasta machines, record collection, and "Tawny" wardrobe home before flying back. The cab paused for a light in front of a travel agency, and Jaz caught a glimpse of an Amalfi coast advertisement. She smiled and thought of Italy and how much she missed it. Life there was as good as it got without Qwayz, who remained part of her every thought and breath. She would have given it all up in a heartbeat just to feel his arms around her again and hear him say, "The stars are in their heavens and all's right with the world."

As the cab pulled behind a trolley car, she thought of the lifestyle she'd acquired in the past five years. None of her friends would believe it. Earning two master's degrees, Tawny's invention and modeling career with Fabrizio, and the exclusive contract for 1.2 million with Alonge's, which had two years left—all unbelievable. Jaz had no regrets beyond leaving Villa Nubia which she gifted to the Lake Como district and made Fabrizio sole curator. Perhaps she had one regret, that she trusted a man who didn't deserve it. A handsome, spoiled more than selfish man used to getting what he wanted and had never been told "no" in his life. Their unholy alliance started with an expiration date and stamped when his wife showed up with their children. Despite all his princely wealth, pedigree and status, he proved to be just a lyin', cheatin' man. Jaz cut him loose on the spot. Easy enough to do when he only had loan of her body. The prince hadn't touched her mind, heart, or soul—they would always belong to Qwayz.

As the cab inched a few blocks before being caught in another rush-hour snarl, Jaz muttered, "Welcome to San Francisco." The plane ride home had been different from the initial one to Italy in 1970 and from the anxiety-produced trip home for Denny's wedding. This trip held some maturity, some healing, and was full of rekindled hope, of beginnings and continuing. Jaz was ready to embrace a new career and a renewed spirit of waiting.

It was not the America she'd left, but she, too, had changed. The United States had come to its senses about some things. In

124

1973, on the heels of Watergate and the Agnew resignation, sanity in dealing with the armed services and human rights emerged. The draft ended and a volunteer army began, and Roe v. Wade gave a woman the right to determine command of her own body. The new black cinema probably started in 1970 with "Mandingo," redeemed itself in 1971 with "Shaft," and forged on with "Lady Sings the Blues," as Earth, Wind & Fire kept their "Head to the Sky." In '74, Cicely Tyson portrayed Miss Jane Pittman, and Duke Ellington left this world for the next. Jaz missed the U.S. oil crisis, Nixon's resignation, and Patty Hearst becoming a bank robber. Ali beat Foreman in Zaire, and Hank Aaron hit his 715th home run. A lot had changed in the United States, but one thing remained constant...it'd still be an existence without Qwayz. The passage of time didn't make her miss him any less.

Jaz stood at the threshold of her apartment. She tipped the driver carrying the last of her luggage and sighed, "Home." The apartment wasn't stuffy, but she flung open her porch door, welcoming in the refreshing San Franciscan air. Inhaling deeply, she spun around, noticing the Johnny Mathis and Nat King Cole albums sitting on top of the component set. Without dwelling on whether she'd left them out years ago, she put them away, along with the opera albums shipped from Italy. Qwayz's Amber was still perched against the fireplace, with Papa Colt's pearl-handled guns and TC's Grammy on the mantel. Going into the kitchen, she pushed the empty apothecary chest into place at the end of the counter. She caught sight of the distant shipyard and watery horizon through her bay window. "Home."

She crossed the kitchen threshold, walking straight past the porch to her bedroom. Then Jaz noticed its absence. Her head jerked up before she flattened her body to the floor to see if it had fallen. She searched the closets and corners for it. She called her father.

"Jaz? Where are you?" Hep asked.

"I'm here in San Francisco!"

"Lorette! Jaz is here," he yelled out. "I can't believe you didn't call us."

"It's okay, Dad, I just got here, really."

"Well, you almost missed me. I'm just here to pick up a few things before I fly to Houston—"

"Hello, Jaz," Lorette's voice interrupted on another line. "Welcome home! Are you coming for dinner?"

"I won't be here," Hep told his wife through the phone.

"You don't have to be here for Jaz to come to dinner, Hep. My goodness, if she waited for that to happen, it could be months."

"Folks, I'm home and I'll be here for a while," Jaz interjected.

"Thanks to Kyle, your father's doing only the domestic travel."

"He's aces, Jaz, you'll have to meet him, though I don't know when, he's always out of the country. He traveled with me through the Orient and they love him. He picked up some of the language and dialects, and negotiated contracts for us to build two luxury hotels in Hong Kong and Singapore." Hep stopped as Tennyson informed him the limo was ready to take him to his jet.

"He must be one giant liver spot by now," Jaz sarcastically poked at her father's continual adulation of the Great White Bwana. "How does he do it?"

"Huh? Youth, I guess," Hep said, "Now, Jaz—"

"Hep, let the girl relax, she just wants to be home," Lorette said.

"Dad, I called you because my wedding portrait is missing."

126

"What?"

"My Tretoni oil of Qwayz and me is not hanging over the headboard. I'm here and it's not."

"Oh. Where's my head? It's in the shop."

"What happened to it?"·

"It fell and the frame was damaged. I forgot all about it. Don't worry, it's with a reputable dealer who did our Monet and—"

"When will it be ready?"

"Listen, Punkin, I don't have time to call right now, but I promise I'll pick it up myself when I get back."

"Thanks, and congrats on making the Fortune 500 list. Unprecedented."

"You ain't seen nothin' yet. Gotta go, Punkin."

"Have a good trip, Dad. Bye, Lorette." Jaz fingered the picture of Qwayz and her in Malibu on the night table. "Guess you'll have to do till then." She opened the lid of the music box, which delicately began "Too Young," and palmed their Hawaiian rock to her heart. "Home."

~*~

In less than one week's time Jaz accepted Sloane Yeager Copeland's invitation to join her in Atlanta. Her old college roommate's timing impeccable as Jaz was inundated with requests and expectations since being back in the United States. When she visited her parents, Akira had run to her with excitement, jumping on her, barking before the dog went to the door through which Jaz had just come and whine-barked with anticipation that Qwayz too would follow. "No. He's not with me, girl," Jaz stooped and told her sadly, but the dog's eyes remained fixated on the door. "I know. I've been waiting too. Would love for him to come through."

Despite the whiplash of daily activities and phone calls with old friends, Jaz's nights filled with a sharp loneliness she never experienced in Italy... a place Qwayz'd never been. They'd never been. She jumped at the chance to see her old friend and explore another topography, new and non-Qwayz filled. In the airport, the two college roomies squealed like school girls upon sight before being surrounded by her husband Dane and three children. Her father had become the first black mayor of Atlanta and her husband its city manager. Jaz accepted the invite to an epic yearly Atlanta fundraiser to keep the coffers full and legitimate. Uncharacteristically, Jaz acquiesced to stay with the Copelands in their spacious home and welcomed the distractions of their rambunctious children; riding shotgun with Sloane as she maneuvered her days with finalizing arrangements for the event from catering, creating ambience to school pickup and feeding, homework, bath then story-time. "I am in awe of you, girl."

"All in a day's work. Somebody's got to do it." Sloane smiled pure delight. "Life is good, girl."

"Have you kept in touch with Farrell, Hilson or that crazy CC?"

"The very single Hilson, like her daddy, is on the road to a judgeship, and Farrell married a fourth generation raisin farmer in Fresno. Big bucks." Sloane changed lanes. "Our girl CC is married with five children living in a lighthouse on Cape Cod."

"Say wha?"

"We were on vacation and went over. She's really happy. Lady Madonna with all those children and her husband on a little secluded island in the middle of the Atlantic Ocean."

"Need I ask you what race her husband is?"

"You know no black man is going to live in a lighthouse with his wife and children for long."

128

The following night, resplendent in a ball gown befitting the occasion, Jaz sat at the Copeland table with the Yeagers, Sloane's parents, her brother and his wife and a few cousins. The elegant room decorated and festooned with a combination of old and new money, this affair was the place to see and be seen, as livered waiters circulated with hors d'oeuvres before everyone settled at their tables and listened to speechifying of the highest degree. Dinner served, then awards, when finally all were released to tap their toes to the musical stylings of a local band. As Jaz stood chatting with a couple, she heard from behind, like an old familiar chant… "Jasmine Culhane…"

The sound of her name falling from those lips catapulted her back years … like the time-warp of a sci fi movie. When she'd picked up her order at Berkeley's Purple Hippo. She smiled at the timbre of his voice and braced herself for the sight of him… she turned into his warm, welcoming smile: still tall, fine and as deep Hershey-chocolate as he ever was.

"Solomon Noble," Jaz identified. They both stood and soaked in one another's essence.

"As I live and breathe. You look good."

"You too."

As the band played "Shining Star," they stood and gawked.

"Sloane told me you'd be here."

"Well, she told me nothing," Jaz admitted and thought, wait until I talk to her.

"I'm sorry to hear about your husband."

The smile on Jaz's face froze as she tried to cover and regroup at the reference to Qwayz. She honestly didn't know how to respond. A long explanation about how much he meant to her or just a pleasant acceptance for the acknowledgement, temporarily baffled her. She didn't have to think long as a beautiful, caramel-colored lady slid up next to him, claiming him with a hand-loop through his elbow. "Ah, Jaz. This is my date Logan. Logan Mitchell this is Jasmine Culhane Chandler. An old classmate from Berkeley."

"Pleasure," Jaz said.

"How nice," Logan managed before announcing, "Vernon Jordan wants to see you."

"Ah great. Listen, are you going to be in town for a while?" he asked Jaz. "I'd love to catch up."

"Sure."

"Great. I'll be in touch. Really good seeing you, Jaz."

"Likewise."

"That Negro is still fine," Jaz enthused once Dane left to take the babysitter home.

"I thought you'd like connecting with him again." Sloane spooned ice cream into waiting cups. "Not married. Not really dating. I mean Logan thinks they got something going, but he doesn't. He's always super-busy, but I'd bet he'd slow down to squire you around."

"She looks like a Pekinese."

Sloane laughed out loud. "I forgot how funny you are."

"I mean her features are all scrunched together in the middle of her face," Jaz clarified while Sloane continued to chuckle. "No problem, Solomon's features will rectify that, and they'll have decent looking children."

"He ain't studin' 'bout no Logan," Sloane reassured Jaz in her best Ebonics.

Jaz spent a restless night and was dead asleep when he called the next day. "Oh, not a lark?"

"Not at all. I am the undefeated champ of sleeping in," she said as a grinning Sloane left the room.

"Good to know," he intoned. "So what are you doing today? I've cleared my calendar in hopes that you'd join me for a late lunch."

"Sounds good. Where should we meet?" Jaz grabbed the pencil and pad from the nightstand.

"No, no, no. A gentleman picks up a lady for a date."

Jaz dropped her pencil and blushed.

"Say in an hour?"

"That'd be good."

"Great. See you then."

For three days straight Jasmine Chandler accepted the constant companionship of Solomon Noble... exploring the old times like they never could and enjoying the present with no plans for the future beyond her two more days in Atlanta before she returned to D.C. The couple seemed giddy with the newness of their association. The second night after dining in the home of friends of his, Solomon walked her to the door and asked, "May I kiss you good night?"

Kinda fast, she thought, but said, "That'd be nice."

He took her face in his hands and bent down as she met him halfway. Their lips brushed one another's playfully, toying before parting into a sensuous kiss that sent Jaz's toes to tingling. It surprised her. "Well, that was nice," said he.

"Yes it was," she agreed. Like her, he was staying with friends, so there were no invites in for a nightcap, and going to a hotel seemed too forward and a little reckless, so they parted ways with plans for a picnic at noon tomorrow.

He spread a blanket on the grass as she opened the basket to see what deliciousness he'd brought. Assuredly, none as tasty as last night's kiss.

As he discussed himself: where he'd been since Berkeley, what he'd been doing since graduating Georgetown Law School, where he planned to go and be, Jaz only caught words here and there...living on Capitol Hill, making inroads in the community...while she noticed the smoothness of his sable-black skin and speculated if he shaved. His thick, perfectly coiffed natural hair picked then patted into place above matching eyebrows and long lashes, his eyes sparkling with excitement about his future and he broke into that fabulous big smile, full of big Mandingo-sized white teeth that drew her in. She couldn't help wonder what else was Mandingo-sized. She'd forgotten how tall and sturdy he stood. "What about you?" he'd come to an end, asking her a question.

Watching boats bob on the water, she shared the highlights of living in Italy, her pair of advanced degrees in architecture, the food, the sights and sounds ...everything minus Prince Omar and Tawny. After lunch they strolled the park and surrounding area before dinner time rolled around and they ducked into a quaint café. "Do you mind French?"

"Not at all."

"I'd like to travel like that," he admitted.

"You really should. There's nothing like it."

After they ordered she asked, "So you never married?"

"Nope. Haven't found the perfect mate yet."

"Perfection doesn't exist. You know that right?"

"I think you can come pretty close." He reached over and brushed crusty breadcrumbs from the side of her mouth. Sensing she didn't want to discuss her husband or his situation, he turned his attention to the jazz combo.

After dinner when the group took a break, "I've got to stretch my legs," he said, unfolding his tall frame. "Let's walk."

Jaz took his hand and he never let go. They meandered hand-in-hand, Jaz not really knowing or caring where they were.

132

It'd been so long since it was this easy being with a like-minded man.

"You're heading back tomorrow?"

"Yep. Going to spend some time with my girlfriend Gladys Ann. She's a doctor who married one, so their time is really limited."

"Where is she… northern or southern California?"

"She's in D.C."

"Is that where you're going?"

Jaz shook her head.

"So am I!"

Jaz side-eyed him.

"No really. I live there."

"Why sir, are you stalking me?" Jaz teased with a southern drawl and fluttering eyelashes.

"Couldn't think of better prey. I live at The Envoy Towers on 16th Street."

"Um, across from Malcom X Park?"

"Yeah. You know D.C.?"

"I've spent some time there in my youth. Went to the March on Washington, stayed in the city with Gladys Ann's people. So you're only a few blocks from the Kalorama Skating rink."

He reared back. "Don't tell me you skate?"

"Had my own."

"So how long are you going to be in D.C.?"

"Just a few weeks. Got to get back to San Francisco."

"Why?"

Jaz looked at him and blinked. "I didn't come home from Italy to hang around D.C. I need a job… to live, plus my friends are having a baby and I want to reconnect with my goddaughter, Amber. I've only talked to Denny… I have to go to L.A. and see her—"

"Stay in D.C. long enough to attend the Black Caucus in September."

"September? No. That's months away."

"Only one. I think we could find some way to spend the month of August."

Jaz smiled at him and said, "There is a lot to do and see in D.C. "The Nation's Capital."

~*~

The tropical breeze tangled with the palm trees and made them rustle and sway. LeLani heard the thud of a car door and looked up. There outside the little gate, a man erect and dressed casually in slacks and a Hawaiian shirt stood on the other side. LeLani exhaled. The jig was up. The man reached down to open the gate. LeLani, tired of running, hiding, pretending and denying, wouldn't scoop her son and take him to his kupuna wahine's for a few days until Hep Culhane went home. Besides, he had the time and money to wait her out; had money and connections to find them in the first place. In a way, LeLani was relieved.

With no bell, Hep knocked on the wood of the screen door. LeLani stared at him. Her lover's father, her son's grandfather. Maybe if she didn't move, he wouldn't see her and just go away. LeLani knew better. She went to the door and opened it. "I've been expecting you," she said quietly.

"I'm here," Hep replied.

She saw him wander in and glancing around as if saying my grandson can't live here, like this. LeLani followed his gaze and every place he looked she did also with her inner voice countering his argument with...here he has love. No, it's not as palatial as where you live, but he is surrounded by loving, caring people who give him guidance and friendship.

"You have a nice home here," he said.

134

Surprised, she said, "Thank you."

Just then, Cully ran in excitedly, "Mama, can I go fishing with kupuna kane?'

The boy stopped at the curious scene and looked from his mother to the man standing there. His mother did not introduce them, so he pushed on, "Can I?"

"May I? And yes. Have him bring you home before dark."

"OK. Thanks."

He was gone, leaving tears standing in Hep's eyes. "I guess a DNA test is unnecessary."

"Yes. It is," LeLani answered. "How'd you find out? "

"Watts is a small community."

"I saw you at my father's funeral. You didn't say a word."

"You didn't bring him."

"No. I didn't. I thought it was all over for me... for us... that we'd pulled it off."

"Why would you want to do that?"

LeLani really didn't know why except she wanted to keep him...keep TC to herself. "I thought you'd take him away from me," she confided.

"Why would I do that? You don't know me."

"No. I guess I don't."

"I would like for him to get to know his father's people. Whenever you are ready. Or you think he'd be ready."

"And if the answer is never."

"Why do that to him? To us?" Hep stood tall and ventured, "You may be mad at TC for leaving... for dying... but I assure you we didn't know that Cully existed. Or I would have been here sooner."

"I know that's right."

"As his mother, I'm sure you want what's best for your child. If he ever wants college, a study abroad program or to go on a field trip to New York—"

"From Hawaii? I assure you the only field trips around here are to the taro and pineapple fields."

"I'm not here to cause you trouble or problems. We both love that little boy... you longer than we have. I am just offering any resources I have to make his life better. That's all. If TC had known, he would have set up a trust for him. I'm sure of it. We are not adversaries, Ms. Troop. I assure you."

LeLani folded her arms protectively.

"Promise you won't disappear with him," Hep gauged.

LeLani leveled her eyes at him. "I have... *We* have a good life here. Surrounded by the love of his grandparents, aunts, uncles and cousins. I would never take him away from that—"

"His other grandparents, aunts, uncles and cousins would also like to meet him. Would you deny him that?"

Hep took a business card from his pocket and handed it to her. "Do you need anything now?"

LeLani glared at him.

"If you do, just call," Hep said and left.

~*~

D.C. remained as hot as Jaz'd remembered; a heat and humidity sandwich with her in the middle. She and Gladys Ann caught up only three times since Jaz'd come to town, but she quite understood the time restraints on her doctor-friend. "You're living my life, huh?" Jaz teased.

"I guess I am. Who woulda thought I'd be the doctor?" she asked.

"Not me," Jaz countered. "But you look so happy."

"I am. A far cry from my Tony Culbreath days."

They slapped five.

"No kids yet?"

"No time, gurl. Not just here at the beginning, but what will I do with them after they're here?" she laughed. "I hear Denny and her man and son are doing just fine."

"Yep. I've only seen pictures, but I'll rectify that once I get back home." They walked toward Garfinckel's department store. "I love this store."

"I know you do," Gladys Ann agreed as they entered the elevator and got off at the lingerie department.

"It's nice to see all my friends and my sister are doing well."

"Yeah, she's slated to marry the executive producer of her variety show."

"The only black male executive at NBC. Lee Harker. He seems well-suited for her."

"It's your turn, Jazzy," Gladys Ann used Aunt Selena's sobriquet.

"I'm working on it. Slowly but surely." She held up an animal print teddy.

"Really?" Gladys Ann prompted without prying. "That's good. It's later than we think."

Jaz piled her heavy hair up off her neck in a high ponytail and fanned with the program at the Carter Baron Amphitheatre. Solomon brought her a cool drink which she grabbed with both hands offering a fervent thank you. "It is hell-hot out here." She wafted the hem of her T-shirt to create a breeze between her breasts. But when Earth, Wind & Fire took center stage, Jaz jumped up with everyone else in the audience... heat forgotten.

By the time the concert ended, Rock Creek Park had been bathed in summer-cool reprieve for only a few hours until dawn's early light. Solomon slung his arm affectionately around her shoulder. "Wanna go get a drink?" Twelve-thirty a.m. found them at Mr. Henry's on Capitol Hill listening to Roberta Flack's second set. He drove her to the Trask house in LeDroit Park. Jaz's Grandpapa Colt had rescued Seth Trask, an orphan from River Bend, and raised him as his own son. Sending him to Howard University undergrad then medical school where he'd met and married and become one of the most prestigious players in the sickle cell anemia fight. His son, Dr. Strudwick Trask, followed in his father's footsteps and kept the family home, happily hosting Selena and her first husband and now Jaz. Even after Papa Colt's death, Seth Trask remained in touch with Keely. Now, like college students, Solomon sat Jaz on the retaining wall as he went in for a few more kisses. "I had a great time."

"Really." He kissed her again like back-in-the-day teenagers they were never allowed to be with one another. "You'll have a better time tomorrow.

"Really."

"Um humm. I'm going to cook for you. My place."

She looked into his liquid obsidian eyes. "You can cook?"

"I can burn."

"That's what I'm afraid of. Should I bring a back-up meal?"

"I can cook in more ways than one." He kissed her again. Slowly, deeply and she savored his essence. "Bring an overnight bag. It's a slumber party—"

Unintentionally, Jaz inhaled a gulp of air.

"Too soon? Well, you decide. No pressure."

Oh *hell* yes there was pressure, but not *from* him... *for* him. Jaz wanted him badly. She'd learned she was a sexual being. Qwayz'd made her one. She couldn't imagine what would have become of her had she not married such a skilled and fabulous lover. Her life would have been ruined by inept, wifely-duty sex, which would mean nothing under less skillful hands. She recalled asking Qwayz if she were a nymphomaniac. "I want you all the time. Nothing feels better than your hands all over me." He'd smiled and said, "That's the way it is when you love and trust so completely. If you're a nympho then so am I, which means we are perfectly suited for one another. Compatible." Jaz smiled remembering.

As she selected earrings, she rationalized that Solomon could satisfy her body and mind, but her heart and soul remained untouchable. Jaz, school-girl giggly all morning, anticipated the night ahead and all it promised. She'd hardly given any thought to Uncle Charles' offer that she take a position at Howard University's School of Architecture for the next semester to pinch-hit for a professor facing a family emergency. It had been a soft sell to the school to temporarily replace him with an accomplished black woman straight from earning master's degrees in Italy to center stage for a basic second-year design course. "It'd be a great fit, Jaz," Uncle Charles said over the phone. "Win-win. Look good on your resume." When she hedged with logistics, he'd sweetened the pot by offering her a third floor apartment on 16th street and a Volkswagen beetle. As Jaz shimmied into her Garfinckel's animal print teddy and snapped the crotch, she asked him, "Do I have to tell you now?"

She hung up, bid goodbye to Dr. Trask, and with a "don't wait up," hailed a cab and headed for the Envoy Towers. She stopped on U Street for a bouquet of flowers before walking the two blocks up, and catching the elevator to the fourth floor. She checked her lipstick, situated the flowers and did a visual on the condoms in her purse although she couldn't imagine Solomon not having his own. He answered the door with that lustrous Mandingo smile and an apron that read, Kiss the Cook. He poked out his luscious lips and she obeyed the apron's directive. With his naked mahogany biceps on display, he turned to get a vase for the flowers and she noted he was in his boxer briefs. "Oh my… did you forget something?"

"It's the way I cook. I'll put on pants when we eat."

"Certainly not on my account."

"Maybe you'll join me."

"Maybe I will," she sassed and surveyed his apartment. "Nice digs." She looked out the window, and smiled that his place faced the trees on Belmont Street, and not the hustle bustle of 16th street. Great for sleeping in, she thought.

"Taste… Preview," he poised a sample of the sauce for her.

"Oh. That is good," she admitted. She wondered if Qwayz would have become a cook. "Stop it," she self-admonished.

"I have a cabernet breathing over there. Make yourself at home."

Jaz sauntered over feeling like a heroine of a saucy light romantic comedy as she poured the red liquid into its goblet.

He noticed she hadn't brought an overnight case, but her purse was big enough to accommodate things. I guess I'll have to see how this plays out, he thought. Regardless, I'm in.

She lit the candles as he escorted the piping hot frutti de mare serving dish of seafood pasta. She went to the refrigerator and retrieved the salad.

"How'd you know?" he asked surprised.

"Look at you. Man does not survive on pasta alone. I knew you had greenery somewhere," she quipped and sat in the chair he'd pulled out for her.

"Smart and beautiful. We are in sync."

"We'll see." He shook out his pants slung over the couch's back. Slipped them on and turned away from her to zip them up.

"Tease."

"Hardly. Enticing, maybe."

"I like your boldness. Serving pasta to a girl who has spent the last five years in Italy."

"I know *al dente*," he whispered, brushing the side of her ear with his lips, doused with the aroma of red wine.

They devoured the cuisine as they laughed, swapping stories about Berkeley, the state of the black man, women and children… families in America, talking rings around all subjects except Vietnam and Qwayz, which suited Jaz just fine. After dessert of chocolate tiramisu, he announced, "Got to stretch the legs." He stood and inclined his hand, which she took as they walked to the couch facing the unlit fireplace.

"I bet that comes in handy about Christmas in D.C."

"Hope you'll come back and find out."

"Funny you should mention that," Jaz began telling him of her offer of a temporary professorship.

"You're going to take it," sprang from his lips, more of an order than a question.

"I'm thinking about it. It's intriguing."

"Ripe with all sorts of possibilities."

Frank Sinatra's "Didn't We?" serenaded them quietly from the sound system as he slid closer to her. "Did I tell you how fabulous you look tonight?"

"Too little too late, Noble," she teased, calling him by his last name.

He chuckled. "I like you."

"I know. Many do."

They began dancing to the slow jams wafting through the room, their bodies meshed as their lips met with Luther Van Dross urging them on with "So Amazing." They maneuvered into his bedroom. Without stopping, he deftly unzipped her dress, falling in a puddle around her ankles, revealing the leopard teddy. She reciprocated by unbelting the leather around

141

his trousers. He smiled and they gazed into one another's eyes. He stopped.

"Jaz. If this is too soon…"

Look boy, her body shouted; *now*, you want to do this? But managed, "No. Not too soon." She resumed lick-kissing his luscious Mandingo lips as his hands explored her and they fell onto the bed. Rolling, kissing, urging, sucking and moaning nosily until both were nude. As the moon shone over her body, he tenderly kissed her eyelids, her cheekbones, her neck down to her breasts, inhaling one taut ripe nipple after the next as his trek continued. Jaz felt his succulent sable lips trace the outline of her body and his skin felt supple yet soft under her fingertips. The sensations all tactilely overwhelming.

Every place his ample dark chocolate hands touched, electrified her in uncommon ways. Deep in the recesses of her veins, tribal drums beat, making her heart vibrate and jump and her need of him throb. The ancestors spiriting, shouting, rejoicing, exhaling through them both. From the tingle in her toes rushing up to the tippy-top of her head, each pore of her entire being shook. DNA of the ancient, pulsing through to present day forced her to shake, rattle, roll and explode the only way a black man can make you feel. She'd forgotten how exquisitely a black man could love a black woman. They lay suspended in air, space and time as Jaz floated in gelatinous ecstasy. Jaz hadn't felt anything this completely since Qwayz. Didn't know if she ever could again. She not only enjoyed Solomon Noble, but he was teaching her things about herself.

"Look at us," he directed her eyes to the color of their intertwined legs. "We're like a Reese's peanut butter cup," he declared, and she laughed.

She awakened to his singing coming from the bathroom. A song she couldn't recognize but made her chuckle. He couldn't carry a tune in a bucket, but she was happy. For the first time in a long time, Jaz felt true contentment. At least Prince Omar hadn't filled their silences with inane professing of what they could be if they were free; he just acknowledged that both were married and committed, although he plied her with expensive baubles she never wore, whisked her off to exotic beyond-reach places and gifted her with the deed to Villa Nubia on Lake Como, her name the only one that appeared on the gift-wrapped deed. All was exciting, but Prince Omar never got it. Never got her. Would never truly have her. Never understood it wasn't about him or the things he gave her. Jaz wasn't the least bit confused. It was *all* about her—she knew the moment Qwayz returned, she'd be gone without a backward glance. But with Solomon Noble it was different, familiar and comfortable, with a smile, a touch, an innocent intimate gesture like reaching to guide her safely across the street. He "got her" like Prince Omar never did. Never could. Never would.

She stretched and turned onto her stomach as the water in the shower and the singing stopped. She eyed the tops of the beautiful trees outside the window and knew she loved Qwayz *still* and when he came home, she'd go, but maybe she'd look back at Solomon Noble and say, "Goodbye."

~*~

After the Labor Day picnic, as they folded the blankets at Haines Point, the playful summer came to an end and, with September, came responsibilities, his old ones and Jaz's new. She found the classes stimulating and the students challenging although disappointed that there were very few females in the entire school and none in her class of 22. Once she quelled their curiosity about living and lifestyle in Italy, she redirected their interests to architecture, convincing a few students that the fact that their mothers were a few years senior to their dads had

143

nothing to do with the course in or outside the classroom, after which, they focused on restoring a house in Martha's Vineyard bequeathed to the school by an alumna.

Jaz and Solomon continued their relationship, deepening it, although both were busy during the week, the weekend belonged to the couple. Jaz spent hours catching up with Denny and Tracy long distance by phone as well as her parents who wanted her to return to Colt, Texas for Christmas as Keely and Star wanted to "eyeball" her. Jaz still spoke with her Aunt Selena weekly and to her grandma Keely every few weeks, but felt no pressure from her beyond the fact that she was always glad to hear from her granddaughter; the press to visit for the holiday, seemed clearly orchestrated by Hep Culhane. A lot hadn't changed with her family, but now she did share her weekends with a handsome, "up and coming" man about D.C. She admitted she liked being part of a couple again even though they didn't seem to enjoy as much private time as she liked. He was always taking her to this reception, that party, this opening, that concert. She began growing weary of the "see and be seen" milieu of a Washington "mover and shaker." Going to catch Roberta Flack at Mr. Henry's or Phyllis Hyman at Blues Alley, seldom its own reward as there was always someone joining them. Or to the Foxtrappe, Jaz impressed with external architecture more than the internal cast of characters. Going to pool parties where few people swam. At one such affair in North Portal Estates, Jaz dove into the water without splashing and swam four laps before she grasped that she'd unwittingly become the entertainment. She got out of the pool dripping wet, dried off and wrapped a sarong about her waist which fell to her bare feet before realizing it. She found it odd that Solomon smiled proudly at her. After their evening lovemaking session she'd asked, "Was there something wrong with swimming in the pool?"

"You know black women and their hair. They're not going to get it wet. But you—"

"I'm from California. You see a pool and it's hot, you jump in."

~*~

Solomon picked her up and escorted her to the Black Caucus dinner at the Washington Hilton Hotel. The black couple cut a stunning image; him tall, dark and handsome in a classic Armani tuxedo and she, copper-colored and smart in a Givenchy. The ultimate, young power-couple in D.C., topping everyone's A list. After dancing the night away, they made early morning love. Jaz found constantly being with people tedious and they'd managed only once to get away just the two of them to Annapolis, Maryland. Splendid. By the next weekend, they were part of a sextet at a Highland Beach house party. One morning after at her place, Solomon jumped up from bed, "Where are you going now?"

"Reese, remember I got that softball game with the firm. Wanna go?"

No I don't 'wanna go.' I want you to stay, she thought but asked, "Do you ever just lay and linger? It's Sunday for goodness sakes."

"I'll be right back afterwards."

She knew that meant 4 o'clock after they played the game, and win or lose, they'd go to Georgetown for beers and pizza.

For his birthday, their first birthday together, Jaz cooked a candlelit meal for him at her apartment as a surprise. She'd bought new lingerie and a giant bow to adorn his gift… her. He said he'd be there at 6 and hadn't called or shown by 7. At 7:30, he called saying, "I'm down at McGinty's. The birthday happy hour turned into a little party for me."

Jaz was tight. "I've planned a celebration for you here. A private one. Our first."

"Oh. How great. I didn't know. Listen, why don't you come join us. You know almost everyone here... We can have our private celebration tomorrow."

Silence.

"Jaz?"

"I'm here. But I won't be there. You just carry on with your birthday party. Catch you later. Not Noble, Solomon."

Click.

He had apologized profusely, arguing that had he known she'd gone to all that trouble, he would have come home. He intended to make up for it by taking her to a little B&B on St. Michael's the following weekend, but he had to change plans because of work. Jaz went anyway, which miffed Solomon. "It was bought and paid for and I needed to get away," Jaz said simply. "The Eastern shore is beautiful even in the fall. I had a great time. Thank you, Noble."

"How could you do that? Go without me? That makes no sense."

"I like me. I can amuse myself and I did." One monkey don't stop no show, she heard her Papa Colt say.

"Alright," he said in that crisp articulate voice of his where his words are so precise, he whistles at the end of them. "At least we'll be together for New Year's Eve at The Mayflower Hotel —"

"Noble, I told you I wouldn't be here for New Year's. I have to return to Italy for ten days. Why don't you go with me for a change?"

146

"Reese, I can't just take off for ten days and travel around Europe."

"If you wanted to, you could." Jaz was already arguing with her father and family regarding the same issue. Now that she was stateside, everyone expected their celebrations along with Keely, Star and even Aunt Selena would resume. This would be the last of her Alonge' contractual obligations to fulfill, but she didn't see the need to explain any of this to them. Besides, if she didn't show, Fabrizio would kill her.

"Do we have to discuss this now? I'm late for class," Jaz said and opened the door.

"Are we still going to S.O.M.E. to serve the homeless for Thanksgiving?"

"Of course. I am looking forward to it."

That night neither of them called the other. Not the next night either. Jaz called Denny for a chat and midway through her friend asked, "What's wrong, Jaz?"

"Nothing," she'd answered. "Listen. I'll call you later this week."

Jaz awakened in her bed, in her apartment and realized she was running late. She showered, grabbed an English muffin, a Carnation Instant breakfast, the briefcase Gladys Ann had given her and walked around the corner to Corcoran Street into the bright, brittle sunshine. Momentarily blinded, she fished for her sunglasses, put them on, but kept walking down the skinny side street. She could see someone leaning against her car. Casually, hands folded, waiting for her...was he waiting for her? As she approached she slowed a little. The figure gave her pause. Eerily familiar...he waited the way Qwayz used to wait for her after classes at Berkeley. She kept walking towards him and removed her sunglasses. Her heart caught. Oh My God! She dropped her purse, her attaché scattered its papers and glasses

147

flung off as she called out "Qwayz! Qwayz! Qwayz!!" She ran to him as tears drenched her face. Oh! My God!! MY God!! He caught her in his arms. She melted into his being...the smell of Jade East cologne and Crystomint lifesavers cascaded over her. His skin, his touch. Home... she was home. He was home...Home!! "A Beetle, Jas-of- mine? When you have a perfectly good tarp-wrapped Karmann Ghia at Paradise Rock?" He joked and held her tightly. She laughed into his ear and they looked at one another... their gaze... honey on hazel. He wiped tears from her cheekbones. She hugged him again... the embrace loosened... his touch... loosened... fading—he was disintegrating, evaporating from her grasp. "Qwayz!" She held on tighter, but it didn't matter. "Qwayz, no. Don't go." She squeezed her eyes tighter... not wanting to wake up. Not wanting to stop the dream. She put the pillow over her head. "No.no.no.no.no... don't go... "

If she could have followed him from this dimension to where he was...she would have.

Chapter 8

He'd seen the tall black man around a few times. His mother usually upset but this time, she introduced him. He eyed her for a cue, but she seemed calm now. His kupuna wahine, grandma, nowhere in sight. It was odd. Cully didn't know what to make of it, so he kept quiet, silent and observant.

"I've been talking to your mother," the man began. "And she …we … think you should meet your father's side of the family. If you'd like," the man quickly added.

"I have a father? Will he be there?" Cully asked simply, as his mother's lips turned in upon themselves and wet gathered in her eyes without falling.

"If he could be here. He would. But he is in Heaven," the man explained. "I am your grandfather. Your father's father."

Cully scrutinized the man. He had a grandfather, uncles and cousins. He'd wanted a father. He'd never bought a Father's Day card. Luckily, it was not a holiday widely celebrated in Hawaii, but still he wanted a Dad. He never knew he'd even had one until now.

"We were thinking you'd like to come to Colt, Texas and meet more of your father's people. They would surely like to meet you."

Cully remained silent, not knowing what the point would be. Not knowing you could have a grandfather without having a father. He was not versed in the relationships of fathers and sons. He'd seen other boys with their fathers and only knew he did not have one. But now this kupuna kane, "grandfather," said he did.

"Your mother is invited too. When your school lets out, you could stay the entire summer…or just a few weeks. Whatever you'd like. You have a cousin who is your age, Hud. You all could ride horses and swim and do all the things your father did with his friends."

"What was my father's name?"

Hep and LeLani looked at one another. "Tavio Culhane. We called him TC."

Cully thought before replying. "My name is Cully Troop."

"Yes. It is," Hep agreed.

"My initials are CT."

Hep squelched back tears at the intelligence of the eight year old man-child. LeLani had done a good job with him.

"On your birth certificate your name appears as Culhane Troop. Did you know that?" LeLani asked her son quietly. The boy shook his head, no. "As a baby, your great-grandfather, kupuna kane kuakahi, began calling you, Cully."

He blinked a few times before speaking. "I like CT."

"Will you come to Colt, Texas for a visit?"

"I've never been on a airplane before."

Relief washed Hep's face. It had been a long arduous road to get here. After he got wind that TC may have had a son with LeLani Troop who'd moved to Hawaii, he began searching for

TC's son hoping it would not take as long as it had to find his sister, Star. LeLani denied the notion at first, but once he arranged to meet her and finally saw Cully… no paternity test was necessary although Lorette'd insisted. LeLani wanted no part of subjecting her son to this test and no part or intrusion from the Culhanes in their lives. It took months and a restraining order to keep Hep and his emissaries at bay. Her own mother, Cully's kapuna wahine, had asked LeLani, "Why keep the boy from his other family?" LeLani had no answer. When only four, Cully had gone to the airport to pick up his cousin from work, and, watching the tourists descend from the planes to come to the island for vacation, innocently asked his mother, "What is it like on the mainland? Do you think we can go there one day?" LeLani had intentionally kept Cully away from music, but he was smart and intuitively mature in other ways… just like his father. "You shouldn't punish the boy because you loved his father and he didn't love you back," her mother told her. A year after Hep Culhane had contacted her, LeLani withdrew the restraining order and called him. He came immediately.

~*~

Thanksgiving came late that year, and Solomon and Jaz agreed to meet at S.O.M.E. (So Others Might Eat) volunteering to serve the homeless the holiday meal. They'd only seen one another once for dinner since their disagreement and both begged off with having an early day tomorrow. Jaz'd already submitted her official notice to Howard University, and despite a tempting offer to stay, decided that she'd returned to the United States to be home. A Californian girl needed warmth and perpetual sunshine that the east coast was stingy with during the winter months.

While serving the patrons their turkey dressing and giblet gravy, the couple fell into their familiar routine and by the end of the evening seemed simpatico again. They'd begun as friends and friends they'd stay.

"Give you a ride home?" he asked with his Mandingo smile.

"I drove."

"Right," he smiled at her again. "So you think we—"

Jaz shot him an incredulous smile.

"This isn't going to work is it?" he broached.

"Not a chance." They both laughed and relaxed.

"Right after Italy. First of the year, I'm going home where I belong. And you'll stay here and continue to set the world on fire."

"You think?"

"False modesty does not become you, Noble."

He laughed out loud. "You do know me."

"Little bit." Jaz stuck up her fingers, measuring an inch apart.

He grabbed her two fingers playfully in one hand, held them before he began swinging them to and fro. "We almost made it this time, didn't we?" he began singing. "We almost made the pieces fit—"

"Almost... but no cigar," Jaz quipped. "You can't sing."

"I can sing. Just not well," he corrected, Jaz acquiesced, and they chuckled.

Other volunteers left the building bidding the couple Happy Thanksgiving.

"We gave it the old college try."

"Victims of our own ill timing."

"Maybe we'll have better luck next lifetime."

Honey saw her reflection in his obsidian pools of darkness.

He held her gaze while tenderly caressing the side of her face with the back of his hand, etching her into his memory. "I must say this is the most... pleasant breakup I've ever had."

"We're at different places."

"True. Women have that biological clock ticking...although you don't seem concerned at all."

"I'm young," Jaz offered.

"Men have their own clock. A financial clock and these early thirties are crucial to us. We have an idea of where we're supposed to be by forty. Then we'll settle down and take a wife. Children."

"You'll get there."

"Just not with you, huh?" He let his fingers tangle in her hair. "You'll be the one who got away, Reese."

"You're a good guy, Solomon Noble. You'll succeed at anything you do. That's your nature. That's what you do."

"Everything but us?"

Her eyes brimmed with suspended tears. She dared not blink.

"I never said it before... but I love you, Jasmine Culhane Chandler."

"I know. Same here."

"I wanted you to know because I never wanted you to look back and wonder."

Jaz shook her head. "Thanks."

"Maybe we could—"

"No. Our time is up. We don't fit. Let's not force it." She took his hand in hers. "Delaying the inevitable... We deserve more."

"Just one of the many things I love about you. Straight—no chaser."

"For future reference when you're in a relationship and it's your birthday...plan to spend it with her."

"Got it."

"When the time comes for me to cast my ballot for the first black president of the United States? You got my vote."

He bent and kissed her forehead. "The senate first. Maybe governor next."

She smiled up at him and said, "I wish you well, Solomon Noble." She kissed him on his cheek and began to back away. "Bye."

He folded his arms across his chest and watched her walk away, get into her car and drive away from him.

"See you next lifetime," he said sotto voce.

~*~

Hep's commanding all to join them at Cherokee Ranch for a Christmas surprise was preempted by Zack's sudden death. He hadn't been sick or ailing and one morning he didn't wake up. A shocked Selena beside herself with grief, denied Jaz's offer to join her in France. "After all the 'faldara' here—I'm bringing my man home. He always loved Colt, Texas." And everyone in Colt, Texas loved him. They couldn't mourn his full and exemplary life, he'd lived a long one, but his spirit was mourned sufficiently. Days before the new year rang in, the legendary Zack Fluellen, was buried on the hill with Papa Colt and his boys and TC. Selena could feel her husband's happiness with his eternal company.

Having completed her contractual agreement with Alonge', Jaz stayed on a few weeks with Aunt Selena at Cherokee Ranch before her aunt told her to get on with her life. "It's shorter than you think, Jazzy." But being with the matriarchs of the family: Grandma Keely, Star, Selena and Orelia, proved to be a restorative and reaffirming experience for Jaz as she caught up with those she loved and had left five years ago. All of whom had experienced "loves of their lives." Selena twice. Jaz would

154

have preferred not having a membership in that group. Wishing that, like Aunt O, she still had her man waiting at home for her. In an alternate universe, maybe Qwayz couldn't get away because of a big case and Grandma Vy, savored the chance to go up and take care of her accomplished son and her grands; Q, Shane and Gabrielle. If only, Jaz thought and sighed. She was ready to go back to San Francisco and resume her life.

Landing in LAX, Jaz rented a car and drove to San Francisco. She'd forgotten how scenic ride between the two destinations could be and thought how many times she and Qwayz had taken the trek together and, before that, he'd gone to and from to visit Jaz while he was in college and she still in high school. Opening the windows wide, letting the rush of air through the window calmed her; she rode on. With the ocean on her left and a chocolate milkshake between her legs, she momentarily wondered about Solomon, but not enough to call or start something up all over again. She dismissed Prince Omar as pure fantasy. Qwayz was committed and very competitive, but Solomon Noble was… driven. Now, with some distance to their relationship, she admitted that eventually she could have fallen for Noble, but she couldn't be more social, and he couldn't be any less. No one should have to sacrifice the core of themselves to make a relationship work. The price is too high. She believed in mutual compromise, but not a total makeover. If they'd married and had children, the situation would only grow worse. She wanted her husband and father to be present and had no desire to be a married, single mother.

Like TC, Jaz'd decided to take a body and heart break. She needed time and space to regroup and concentrate on herself. Her career and not consider a man for a while. With the history of the men in her life…father, brother, husband… Jaz wasn't going to settle for anything less now. Either it worked or it didn't. She didn't have the time, inclination or desire to concede or reconcile her hopes, dreams or vision for her future. She may end up by herself, no future husband or children. Maybe she'd peaked early and all the happiness she had with Qwayz was all the good Lord was going to give her. She was all right with that. Some people lived lifetimes and never had what they had. As San Francisco appeared before her, this man-weary woman smiled and decided to count her blessings and take her father up on his offer to join CE. The distraction of work had always been the perfect panacea for what ailed her.

~*~

The ringing phone demanded attention in the empty apartment. The door flew open, and dropping the groceries on the couch, Jaz yanked up the receiver. "Who knows I'm back? Hello!"

"It's a girl."

"Scoey?"

"And another girl."

"Wha? Twins? You and Tracy had twins?"

"Where you been, Squirt? I called Italy, the phone is disconnected. It rang and rang in D.C. Couldn't find your parents' number, and CE wouldn't give me squat—"

"I'm just back from Colt."

"Oh right. Where is my head?"

"You've been a little busy."

"I was sorry to hear about Zack."

"May we all live so long and so well. I stayed on a while with Aunt Selena and the tribe. So babies. Congratulations! They're early. Were you expecting twins?"

"Hell no. I turned around with the first baby and the nurse says, 'There's something else up here,' and it was another baby! Three weddings, Jaz—I'm giving a bonus to the ones who elope.

156

When you comin'? We got Ma Summerville the first week and everybody else who thinks it's so wonderful. We could really use you the second week after the cuteness wears off and everyone leaves us alone."

"I'm not waiting until then. You'll see me when you see me."

"Be like that."

"You're just the father. You've done your do, now step aside, my man."

"Don't break bad with me."

"Tracy's busy, I take it?"

"Both breasts."

"Bye, Attorney Scofield, my love to your po' wife." Twins, Jaz mused as she put her food away and began packing for L.A.

Mrs. Summerville, fresh diapers in tow, let Jaz in, excusing herself all at the same time. The babies howled without shame as the uniformed nurse ran up the stairs behind the grandmother. Jaz, in no rush to join the chaos, set her overnight and shoulder bag down, and then, beyond the glass, alone by the pool, she saw Amber. The little girl's feet hung in the pool, her body wet from a recent swim, and waterlogged braids dangling next to her ears, rounded out Jaz's first glimpse of her goddaughter since infancy.

"Hi!" Jaz approached and the little brown body straightened at the sound of a human voice.

"Hi." Her eyes darted at Jaz, then away again. "They're up there."

"Who?"

"The twins, Bethany and Brittany. All they do is cry, cry, cry."

"Mind if I join you?" When Jaz rolled up her jeans, the little girl looked at her for the first time. Big, pretty, round black eyes wondered why this lady wanted to sit with her instead of seeing the twins. "I'll see them later." Jaz took off her gold sandals and sat next to her. "I'd rather talk to you. Oooh, this feels good." Jaz kicked her feet lightly in the cool water. "You like to swim?"·

"That's all I've been doing is swim, swim, swim, especially since they came. First my mother went to have them, then came home with them and I don't even get to play with them. They just cry and eat and poop."

"What do you like to do?" As Amber recited her likes and dislikes, Jaz absorbed the prettiness of this little chocolate girl who felt replaced and forgotten. "Maybe we can do some things while I'm here. Do you know who I am?"

"No. I've seen you before, but I don't remember."

"Hey, Jaz!" Scoey bounded through the glass doors.

"Daddy!" Amber sprang to life, jumping into her father's arms.

"Hey, Ace!" He kissed his little girl. "How ya doing?

"Hey, girl." Scoey gave Jaz a peck on the cheek.

"The twins' names start with B's because my name starts with A because I was first. Right, Daddy?"

"Right, you're my first big girl." He kissed her brown cheek. "You seen the babies in question yet?"

"No, I've been hangin' out with Amber. She's gonna show them to me later." Jaz winked at Scoey.

"Oh, good idea. Well, lemme go upstairs and say hi to Mommy, okay?"

"K."

"You finished for the day?" Jaz asked.

"Naw, jury's out, gotta go back in an hour, but I thought I'd come home and see my girl, right, Ace?" He chucked her chin playfully. "You go on and hang out with Aunt Jaz."

"My Aunt Jaz from Italy? I talk to you all the time. You sent me Bobo. He's on the shelf in my room. Momma says I can have him when I get older."

"Well, we'll have to get you one you can use right now." Jaz never intended the mink teddy bear to be a museum piece. "Let's go see those babies now."

For the duration, it was Amber and Jaz. As far as the five-year-old was concerned, her aunt Jaz had been sent solely for her company. Inseparable from breakfast in the morning until a bedtime story and prayers at night. There was no place Jaz went without Amber. To buy an aquamarine Jaguar sedan with tan upholstery; she hadn't retrieved her beloved '57 T bird stored in her father's garage when she went to Italy. Like Scoey'd done with TC's coveted black Porsche, she'd re-gifted her classic car to her father's auto menagerie. She and Amber put miles on the new car as they went to see Denny and Little Lloyd, Melie and AJ, and a taping of Mel's new variety show, where Amber and Hud got to be students in a school scene. They went shopping, had lunch, and went to the movies.

"I'm heading back to Frisco tomorrow," Jaz announced to Tracy and Scoey. "And I'd like to take Amber back for a visit with me."

"Bless you," Scoey piped up, sinking to one knee. "And which other one would you like to take? Two-for-one sale." Jaz jabbed his side playfully, but Tracy's face washed with concern.

"She's supposed to start the new after-school program after spring break," she said.

"Oh, baby, she shoulda started that two weeks ago. 'Sides, being with her aunt Jaz is better than a after-school program."

"But she'd be home every night," Tracy said as one of the twins started up.

"C'mon, baby, what's Amber gonna do once she gets home? Swim herself to death? You're asleep or busy with the babies, and I'm at work. Your mama hatted up, the nurse is just here for the twins and Mrs. Dix for the housework. House full of folks, but none to tend to my Ace, I see it in her eyes. She's lucky to have Jaz pick up the slack. At least till we get this thing right. What do ya say, Bay-bay?"

"She has been kinda lost in the shuffle." Tracy tried to think over the wailing of first one, then both of the babies. "All right. Thank you, Jaz."

"Don't call us; we'll call you about returnin' her," Scoey joked, but Tracy didn't find it funny as she exited the room.

The next day with the sun and the ocean on the left again, almost matching the aquamarine Jag, two brown beauties sped toward San Francisco singing "Respect Yourself" along with the Staple Singers.

Amber had done well in the front seat for about an hour until she fidgeted beneath the safety belt and Jaz let her roam free in the back seat. She ended up where Jaz always had on those long childhood trips to Texas, right behind and in the ear of the driver. When Amber knew the words, she sang along; otherwise, she delighted in her aunt's voice. "You act silly just like my daddy. Is he your brother?"

"Almost."

The pair turned into Gary's Seaside restaurant and lunched over lobster thermidor. Amber was fascinated by the stories Jaz told of her brother, TC, who used to take her out somewhere different every May, and they often came here to Gary's, sitting right at this very table.

"I wanted a brother, but I got two sisters."

"Well, he was my big brother, just like you are a big sister. Mel is my big sister, and I'm a little sister like Brit and Beth." Jaz had fallen into using Amber's nicknames for them.

"Mel is nice." She had enjoyed her visit to the studio and Mel's house. "Where is your brother now?"

Jaz explained enough about the Vietnam War to satisfy a five year old's curiosity and not get all caught up into herself.'

"Do you miss him?"

"Very much. I think about him all the time."

Amber napped after lunch, allowing Jaz quiet for the last few miles before they climbed the three stories to Jaz's apartment.

"Ah, this is nice, Aunt Jaz." Amber surveyed the apartment as Jaz shuffled through her mail. "Where's my bedroom?"·

"I only have one bedroom and we can share, if you're not a squirmer, or you can sleep on the couch."

"Oh, wow, look a guitar." She ran toward Qwayz's treasure, hoisting it awkwardly.

"Lemme help you. Here, sit on the couch." Jaz arranged the instrument and they strummed out "Tom Dooley."

"Is this yours?"

"No, it's Qwayz's, and guess what its name is? Same as yours; in fact, your Uncle Qwayz named you." Jaz relayed the story of Qwayz, her dad, and TC and how she was named.

"Is he still in Italy?"

"I wish… " Jaz shared the less gruesome details. "So I'm still waiting for him to come back."

"Can I wait with you?"

"Sure."

"I hope he comes soon, 'cause we aren't getting any younger, you know."

"Out of the mouths of babes." Jaz fished the crumpled piece of paper out of the hole of the guitar and, read the "change in status" paper declaring Quinton Regis Chandler IV dead.

"Oh, who is that, Aunt Jaz?" Amber stood in the bedroom, pointing to the wedding portrait.

"That's me and Qwayz on our wedding day."

"Oh boy, he's some good-looking dude, just like Prince Charming."

"Well, he's my Prince Charming... always will be."

Over the next few days the pair did girly things. They washed their hair, did their nails, played dress-up, made each other up, and had tea parties with the new black doll Jaz bought, which Amber named Lucretia. They baked brownies, went shopping and sightseeing, and stayed up late watching old movies, a bowl of popcorn between them. They did whatever struck their fancy, which for Amber was riding the ferry and eating fresh strawberries at every possible hour.

"Amber?" Jaz searched for her pigtailed niece across the stalls of the Farmers Market. Walking down where two aisles intersected, she caught a glimpse of the back of Amber's blouse as the little girl stooped to pick up dropped strawberries. "Ah!" Jaz gasped as a tall black man stretched to his full six feet and offered Amber her last berry.

"Sorry. Didn't mean to startle you." His handsome face split into a wide, warm grin.

"I think that's all of them. Now I have to weigh them, right?" Amber looked between the two adults, neither of whom looked at her.

"Allow me." The man whisked her up toward the scale before Jaz could object. "One pound and three quarters."

"Is that okay?" Amber looked back at Jaz for approval.

"Fine."

162

"You gonna eat all those by yourself?" he asked, placing the little girl back on the floor.

"I sure can. All by myself, unless you want to come over and help."

"Maybe some other time," he said after an awkward pause.

"Oh, good, corn on the cob." Amber saw the ears peeking from Jaz's basket. "That's my favorite," Amber told the gentleman.

"Looks like you might have a little problem with that." He stooped momentarily to her eye level, to look at her mouth.

"I've been hearing a lot about that lately." She smiled to show her snaggle-teeth, and the two of them laughed.

"Well, I hate to break this up, but we better get our goods home, Amber," Jaz suggested, nudging her niece in the opposite direction.

"Bye." Amber looked around her aunt to the man. "Thank you." She returned his wave. "We have to get some whipped cream, too." She peeped around her aunt again. The man was standing in the cashier's line, but he saw her and waved again.

"You're a flirt," Jaz said.

"Isn't he dreamy?"

"Sounds like a Sandra Dee word."

"A what? Ooh, we need some cake cups."

"We'll get them at the bakery with the bread on the way home."

"He's gone!"

"Who?"

"My Prince Charming." She checked the aisles and other lines. "Do you think we'll see him again?"

"If fate wills you to, Cinderella." Mothers need to stop plying their daughters with this Prince Charming crap. But she is Tracy's child and it did work royally for her; she saw, wanted and married her high school sweetheart.

"Well, I'm not cleaning behind nobody, ever especially Brit and Beth."

They drove home, and as Jaz opened her front door, balancing a brown bag of groceries on her knee, she heard Amber say, "Hi."

"Hello!" a male voice replied. Jaz looked over the banister to the downstairs apartment. "Welcome back, neighbor," the blond-haired, blue-eyed man said from the floor below.

"Hello," Jaz said, ushering Amber through the door. I must tell all my friends who claim they can't meet men to rent a kid and go for it.

"Amber, didn't your parents tell you not to talk to strangers?" Jaz set the bags on the kitchen table.

"Who?" Amber climbed on the stool to get the colander so she could pick through and wash the strawberries.

"The man in the market and the guy downstairs."

"The man in the store was my Prince Charming, and the one downstairs is your neighbor, like our neighbors the Ebersoles. They don't have anyone for me to play with. Their children are grown. But they give good treats for Halloween."

"How many Prince Charmings can you have? You have the one from the market, that's enough. So you shouldn't talk to any more:"

"I don't know, I really like AJ. I haven't decided if I want him as a big brother or Prince Charming. Is he coming back over today?" Amber asked, remembering that the last time he came over they had made pasta, played records, danced, then taken Akira for a long walk.

"I don't think so, but you'll see him on the Fourth of July."

"Oh, goodie! Maybe I'll decide by then."

"It's no press, Amber, but you shouldn't go around speaking to every man you see. What about the guy downstairs? Could he be a Prince Charming?"

"No, he's not tall, dark, and handsome. My dad said only guys who are tall, dark, and handsome are good enough for me."

"He's a real smart man, your dad," Jaz grinned knowingly.

"Yeah, I like him a lot."

Chapter 9

Hep's yacht jockeyed in the bay for the choicest position for Bicentennial firework viewing. Knowing it'd be overly crowded this year, he'd sent his captain out early with most of the guests and joined them later by motorboat.

"Where's Kyle?" Lorette asked as her husband came aboard.

"He and a lady friend are entertaining on his boat—thought he'd bypass the boss and his friends this year."

"Haven't seen much of him at all," Lorette complained.

"I got him traveling so much now; I give him his space when he's here. Can't have a disgruntled employee who's not having his needs met. Hello, Punkin." He kissed Jaz before slapping five with Hud, the cool eight year old and asking where Mel was.

"In the air conditioning, of course," Jaz said as she watched her father circulate among his other guests, thankful at being spared from meeting that old coot Kyle. Loyalty. Dad must be giving Kyle a cushy position now, because he brought the man out of retirement in 1963 to help manage Culhane properties in New York while Hep was in Washington as chief of protocol, and later, while ambassador to Italy. But imagine that old guy having a date—can't be doing much but remembering, Jaz thought.

"Jaz, look what AJ brought me—squirrel nuts!" Amber gleamed.

"Yeah, I used to love them when I was your age, and a certain guy and gal kept me supplied." AJ winked at Jaz, as Amber scurried off to show someone else.

"You could bring her a handful of dirt, AJ, and she'd be elated." Jaz sipped her iced tea.

"Yeah, well, I been there, too." His mouth cut a wide smile, recalling the crush he'd had on Jaz.

"And you outgrew it."

"Had no choice. So will she." He looked out over the bay. "Fourth of July so how ya doing?"

"Actually, not bad as long as I got that little pigtailed spitfire to keep me busy. Not a lot of time for thinking." Jaz figured this would be her life if she and Qwayz had had a child.

"Did I tell you I was going to Europe for six weeks?"

"No, Melie did. But I've been waiting for the details."

"I was asked to be part of a consortium to study European surgery wards."

"I'm proud of you. One of those stops Italy?" Jaz already knew the answer. Avia had written her that AJ was coming for a visit.

"Matter of fact it is. I've talked to Avia. I hope she's free when I come through," he said casually.

"That'll be nice seeing her again." Jaz couldn't contain a smile.

"What? See, you always reading into stuff!" He fidgeted like a schoolboy.

"What? I didn't say a word."

Jaz and Amber spent the night sharing a stateroom, and the next afternoon returned to the apartment. The next day, despite Jaz's attempts to win her niece over to her favorite, Ghirardelli Square, Amber preferred Pier 39, near the water and the ferry, with its cotton candy, balloons, and the Doll Shoppe.

"Look." Amber pointed to a crowd and began elbowing and twisting her way to the front, pulling Jaz along. "What is it?" Amber asked, not seeing a clown or a movie star.

"I dunno, a car. Let's go."

"Not just a car lady, a Bugatti Royale 1931," an impressed man said as the female pair skipped toward the wooden pier.

Armed with popcorn in one hand and cotton candy in the other, Amber roamed away from Jaz, who was on a quest for a bon voyage gift for AJ.

"Hi!" Amber jerked at the gentleman's jacket, her cotton candy settling against his companion's skirt. "Remember me?"

"Well, hi there, Amber." He stooped down. "This is my friend, Amber." He introduced the little girl to the woman beside him.

"Want some?" She offered him the pink fluff, which he took while his date scoffed at the errant candy against her skirt.

"Thanks. Where's your mommy?" He eyed the crowd.

"My mommy?" Amber giggled at his mistake.

"Uh-oh, here she comes." He stood, confused by her amusement.

"Amber." Jaz spotted her and stood firm until the laughing girl joined her. "You are not supposed to wander away from me."

"Someone's in trouble," the gentleman said to his uninterested date. "Aren't kids adorable?"

"As long as they belong to someone else," his date said, taking hold of his arm and leading him away.

168

"Aunt Jaz, PC thinks you're my mommy." She was still giggling.

"Who's PC?"

"Prince Charming. He said, 'Where's your mommy?'" She laughed without stopping until they entered the Doll Shoppe.

As usual, they lingered at Pier 39, then visited Akira and had dinner with Jaz's parents before returning home. "It's late. Call your mom, Amber," Jaz directed, going into the kitchen for Amber's vitamins. "Get your new homework assignments."

"Aunt Jaz, look it's her." Amber pointed to the television.

"Who?"

"The prince's wife!"

"As the first black woman anchor for San Francisco I know you understand." The male commentator was remarking about a colleague's marriage and move.

"We wish you hearty congratulations and the best of luck at the New York network, Phil." She offered a cold smile before continuing, "Back to you, Jim."

"That's PC's wife! She's a movie star."

"You've got a good memory, Amber."

"She's pretty, but not as pretty as you, Aunt Jaz... or him," she giggled.

"Call your mama, girl!" Jaz laughed with her.

~*~

Jaz's hair billowed in the wind as she aimed her car toward Ruidoso Canyon Road. She missed her little shadow talking in her ear, but the time had come for Amber to go home. Jaz smiled, remembering Amber's amazement at how the twins had grown. She was allowed to hold them and decided they weren't so bad.

The Jag maneuvered the hairpin turn like it was a straightaway, frothing up dirt flinging it lightly in the air. Jaz paused on the bluff, the expanse of the ocean welcoming her back to Paradise Rock, a beckoning charm on the coastline. She turned right up the gravel driveway, the crunch of her tires rivaling the beating of the ocean against the granite. Jaz switched off the engine, and soaked up the sights, salty ocean smells, and sounds of the familiar. It was as if she'd never left. Of all the places she'd been or seen in this world, this was where Qwayz's spirit lived. Not in Watts, not in Vietnam, not with Ma Vy's memorabilia of medals and flags over her fireplace. This was where Qwayz was, and she couldn't wait to be with him.

She flung open the sliding door, rendered the alarm inactive, and simply stood there watching the light and shadow play on the fireplace facade. "Qwayz, I'm home!" Her heart, body, and mind ached to be free to acknowledge him, to talk with him in a way no other human would understand. She closed and locked the screen and walked around the rooms, opening the terrace door in the bedroom, breathing in the fresh air. And there Jaz remained, just enjoying the freedom that only Paradise Rock afforded her, the cleansing, the sanity and fortification needed to face the world without him.

She stayed on the terrace awaiting the moon and the stars, and when they came out, she studied them for hours more. Finally, when positioned just so, Jaz climbed into bed, her face basking in the moonlight as breezes flowed over her body. "Qwayz, are you here?" There was no voice as he drew her to his chest, his lips touched hers, and they matched the rhythms of their souls as she felt his unconditional and everlasting love.

Jaz remained in the cocoon of Paradise Rock for days, much to the chagrin of her father, who feared a psychological relapse in his daughter. Only Denny's coming to Frisco for a conference drew Jaz away from the "land of the dead," as Hep referred to it.

Denny presented her paper early on Saturday, freeing the pair to tool around Frisco, eating and acting up, and going to see *Cooley High*. Both women related so easily to the context: set in Chicago, it could have been Watts. The mood, the method, and the characters were all folks they'd grown up with. At the movie's end, they cried, remembering Qwayz and Yudi and how hard it was to say goodbye to yesterday.

"When you coming back down to L.A., girlfriend?" Denny asked at the airport.

"I best get my hind parts to working before I forget everything I ever learned. When I come, you'll know."

"You have to stay with us sometime. Tracy and Scoey aren't the only ones with guest rooms, you know. Thank your Dad again. I've never been on a private jet before. Love you." She kissed her friend.

Cooley High captivated Jaz three more times and she spent two more weeks at Paradise Rock before she called her father. "Okay, Dad, I'm ready to work," she announced. Her words, music to Hep's ears.

The corner office her father had saved for her had never been used. A smaller version of Hep's grand mahogany desk sat in front of one window facing the door. Jaz placed a drafting table at the other window; a couch, chairs, and coffee table held up the solid wall next to the door. An original Tretoni of the Amalfi coast, hung over the sofa, always caught her eye when she looked up.

Jaz carefully orchestrated her work attire to project the right corporate image. Her coppery tresses slicked back into a severe chignon, with only the ripple of waves mid-day suggested latent wildness. She wore coatdresses and suits. Her jewelry, always gold, as simple and straightforward as her professional approach. She wore gold earrings, her wedding band crowned by her circle of diamonds, a watch forever tangled with her interlocking hearts bracelet, and on her other wrist, the gold cuff bracelet her father had given her for her eighteenth birthday.

Her blouses spun from the finest silk, never a ruffle, bow, or any hint of cleavage. Her wardrobe reflected the professional person she was— no frivolity, nothing to divert the attention from what she was presenting; no room for misinterpretation or an opening for anything more than a business relationship.

As Jaz pored over Culhane Enterprises prospectuses, corporate profiles, financial analyses, current projects, and California building codes, she hadn't time to notice the subtle change in hairstyles among the female support staff. Every length of hair had been neatly brushed into a chic chignon knotted at the neck; those who could, did; those who could not improvised with a wig shop purchase. As the top professional woman in the executive suite, she set the style. When Jaz breezed in in the mornings, she had no idea that her entrance and what she wore was the talk of that floor and those below. The other women took great pride in attempting to duplicate, trying to outdo one another at least, but when Jaz came in one day with an attaché, shoes, and a handbag that had little bumps on it, all bets were off. Thanks to her boss, Addie had learned the subtle difference between crocodile and alligator, but this pimply "leather" was odd. Addie finally asked Jaz what the material was and returned to the pool with the answer. "Ostrich. The girl can rag."

"Jaz, got a minute?" Hep walked into her office.

"Sure, Dad," her lips said, but her hands and eyes kept working.

"It's about the elevator man."

"What?" Jaz looked at him unbelievingly.

"There's a bit of a mutiny among the staff. I guess it's been brewing for a while, but they've finally approached me about it."

"Dad—"

"Bear with me. Many think he makes folks coming to the building uncomfortable. No one wants to ride with him, and they wait for one of the other elevators. So what's say we put the old World War II vet on the executive elevator? He could keep his job and some dignity."

"Fine," Jaz dismissed.

"Great."

"Dad," Jaz said as Hep was leaving, "you done good." Jaz thought of the camaraderie that old World War II vets have that Vietnam vets don't.

"There but for the grace of God go I." Hep sauntered from the room and Jaz returned to her work.

"Jaz?" Addie stuck her head in. It was the first time she'd called her by her first name. "Got a minute?"

"Sure." Jaz really didn't. It was like a social club around here; if you wanted to work, you had to go home.

"I just wanted to thank you for Zeke," Addie began as Jaz searched her brain on personnel. Marc and Derek were the young, crack architects, graduates of Hep's intern program. Dory was the landscape architect. Tre' was in Finance. Zeke... who the hell was—

"The elevator guy," Addie reminded Jaz. "You were the most important vote. Kyle said yes from the Orient and you were the last one polled. Face it, if you or Kyle had said no, Zeke would be out of a job."

Jaz was no angel. She recalled herself tensing at the sight of the grotesque figure of a man holding the door open. She'd been one of those who often opted to wait for the executive elevator, but she had seen Addie talking with him at her desk, seen her wait for his elevator.

"There are too many around here who don't understand or care how hard it must be for an old man alone like that."

"Why do you care, Addie?"

"I had a mentally challenged brother and saw how everybody treated him. Zeke isn't retarded, but he suffered those wounds defending us in a war. My brother had a good soul, but all people saw was his outside and I used to worry about how he'd be treated when he grew up. Well, he died in a car accident. I'd give just about anything to have him back, to take care of him myself. I can't do for him, but I can for others." She began to tear up and stopped. "So thanks." She left.

The Culhane Enterprise clock timed Jaz at work by ten and never leaving before seven, often after eight. She usually ate lunch in and avoided dinner meetings of any kind. On Fridays, she left CE for Paradise Rock, returning from there on Monday mornings. Her weekend inaccessibility was legendary. Darkness surrounded her when Jaz walked to the elevator, saying good night to the cleaning staff.

"Ahh," she gasped at the sight of the attendant. "Zeke! I didn't know you'd still be here." She tried to hide her repulsion as she slowly inched into the small chamber.

"No reason for me to rush home."

Jaz stood behind him. His voice didn't come from his lips but from his neck region. She tried not to think about him, but there was nowhere else to look but the back of his head. She'd never noticed how small this elevator was, how dank and close, or how long the ride down was.

The smell of decaying innards and of liniment like Papa Colt kept in his barn for the horses dominated the tiny space. She watched his arm labor to work the controls and noticed the cane over his stool. He was in complete uniform, purple with gold epaulets that didn't sit right. One shoulder up, one down, gloves covering his hands. You couldn't tell whether he was black or white except for his voice.

"Workin' kind of late."

"Yes, it's quieter." She clutched her bag as if he were a robber.

"Umm-humm." He touched his hat, as crooked as his uniform. One side sat over a patch of pinkish-brown hairless skull intended to hide a malformed ear, probably the result of grafting. "Here you go." He stiff-leggedly shifted to the right, his breathing uneven and labored.

"Thank you." Jaz eased past him, as if by touching him she'd be similarly afflicted. "Good night," she threw over her shoulder. He didn't respond.

The next morning she arrived preoccupied with the newspaper. She'd forgotten all about him until the elevator door slid open, forcing her to look directly at his face before she realized it.

"Thank you," he said, presenting her with a single pink rose.

"Oh, you didn't have to—"

"I know I didn't have to, but I wanted to. Thank you for saving my job," he stated simply before closing the door.

She stared at the rose in an attempt to obliterate the vision of his face...more horrid than anything one could imagine happening to a human being. The right side a smooth pinkish-brown, looked as if it had melted and was sliding from its position had it not been caught by the chin. Every feature on that side was deformed: his eye, a hole; his nose, nonexistent. His lips fused together with just a small opening on the left through which he spoke. The left side of his face was of the same color, though not as severely deformed; the left eye shrouded with

175

extra skin and rheumy. His hairless face had no eyebrows or lashes and only patches of hair sprouted from beneath his cap on the left. He began coughing, first just rumbles in his chest, then convulsively. At a loss for what to do, Jaz grew anxious, until he managed to take a tablet and drink some medicine. He seemed composed by the thirty-fifth floor.

"You have a good one," he stated hoarsely, intending to tip his hat, but his arm didn't reach that high.

"Thank you. Thanks again for the rose."

Jaz stood there staring at the closed elevator door, thinking that this was far more than she had bargained for.

"Hey, Punkin, change your mind?' Hep asked about the mutilated vet.

"No. Anyone who wants to work as badly as he does should. Gave me this rose. Kinda ironic, a man so hideously disfigured still sees the beauty in a flower."

~*~

"Dad," Jaz barged into Hep's office, waving a folder. "When are you going to let me have a project of my own, from the ground up?"

"When you're ready."

"I'm ready. I've done additions to a library, a school, and a wing on a hospital and collaborated on two homes. I'm ready to step out on my own."

"Kyle and I—"

"Kyle?" she interrupted, letting his name drip like venom from her lips.

"Yes, he's my architectural authority and I concur with his decision."

"It's Kyle's project to begin with, he did the original house. Why can't he do the addition?"

176

"Would you have me call him back from Singapore to build onto his award-winning beach house? It won't be long, Punkin," he said placatingly, recalling how he and Kyle noticed the kind of work Jaz elicited from the builders and contractors she supervised; they loved her. When warranted, she was as free with her compliments as she was with her criticisms. "We're both very impressed so far," he soothed as his daughter rolled her eyes, which landed on the Tretoni oil painting of them as children.

"Daddy, when are you going to replace that?"

"Are you kidding? My favorite picture. Gives me great inspiration."

"I'm ten years old in this one." Jaz perused the framed pictures on his desk. "A current one of me, please, Dad."

"When you give me one like your sister did, I'll proudly display it." He rounded his desk. "Now, have you decided what you'll wear and who you'll take to the awards banquet?"

"I don't understand why I have to go."

"You're a part of this firm."

"Can't I accompany you and Mom?"

"It would be nicer if you had a date."

"Goodbye, Mr. Culhane." Jaz snatched the plans for the Santucci addition off the desk.

As Jaz left her father's office, she passed Kyle's on the way to her own and decided to look in out of curiosity. Pushing the door open, she ventured inside. The highly masculine décor of polished leathers smelled of rubbed oil. African masks watched her from the paneled walls as animal skins complemented the beige carpeting.

"The Great Bwana," Jaz scoffed, leaving the office of the old white guy fixated with the dark continent. "Figures."

"Hey, Dory," she spoke, reentering her office.

"Oh, I was just leaving you a note."

"What is the big deal with this banquet?"

"CE purchases a table for ten each year, twice a year, at a thousand bucks a pop. The American Institute of Architects in the fall and the American Society of Architects in the spring." He stopped, pondering. "Or is it AIA in the spring and ASA in the fall? Anyway, we garner most of the awards for innovation."

"Why the big press for me to attend? It's not my bag."

"Besides a proud father wanting to show off his gorgeous daughter? He always freaks out when Kyle's away—leaves two vacant seats, not good."

"So now I'm Kyle's damn replacement. Are they joined at the hip or something?"

"Practically. Hep relies heavily on his expertise. Kyle's well-respected in his field."

"Spare me." Jaz wasn't interested in more accolades for her father's idol. "Expects me to have an escort."

"He likes neat perfection and balance. His people aren't only brilliant, they're normal, too, and have time for relationships. I enjoyed the banquets when Carol and I would go. We'd make a big event out of it... limo, flowers. The works." His voice drifted off.

Over the past few weeks of their collaboration, they'd shared the stories of their mutual losses and how difficult and unaccepting the world was around them. Dory had lost his wife only two years ago, and the emptiness and pain remained acute. Hep had left him alone about the banquet the past two years, but expected him to attend this year.

"I suppose I could ask Tre', Marc, or Derek." She thought of the handsome, gifted young trio who hung together, made big bucks, and enjoyed themselves to the max. "But I'm iggin' them. Left me on the dance floor at Tramps."

"As I heard it, you were Le Freaking with Chic so fierce for so long, they couldn't get your attention to let you know they were leaving," Dory chuckled. "Heard you can really get down."

"That disco stuff isn't my thing. They gave me this, gift wrapped." Jaz held up a mood ring. "So they'd know when I wasn't pissed-off at 'em anymore." Jaz laughed at their sense of humor. "They have it made, don't they?" she pondered, top graduates of their colleges, landing plum jobs. "The world on a string."

"Listen, why not go together?" Dory said. "He wants us there, we'll be there. Have a great time and go home."

"Sounds ideal to me. Then we won't end up with a date we'd spend weeks getting rid of."

~*~

"Aw, sweat!" Jaz glanced at her watch, gathered her papers, and stuffed them in her attaché, and headed for the elevator. She was always surprised at the late hours Zeke worked.

"Working late?"

"You too," he said, sliding a little to the side. "Going to the disco? It's Friday night."

"Nope. I can't abide those discos and the music. I prefer my music of the sixties to the stuff out there now."

"I know what you mean," he finally said, after his chuckle turned into a rumble then back again.

She had gotten used to Zeke, seeing beyond his grotesqueness to his soul. His inner spirit allowed him to live past his disfigurement. Medical problems forced him to remain home on damp days and caused him to keep the elevator very warm, but it was a short ride compared with the one he'd taken from World War II to here.

"You all had some good music, too," Jaz said.

179

"Yeah, 'If You Gonna Walk All Over My Love, Baby, At Least Take Off Your Shoes.'"

"I was thinking more of 'I'll Be Seeing You' and 'Unforgettable.'"

"What a youngun like you know about those old songs?"

"My husband and I loved those old songs, old movies too. We used to have our own concerts out on the beach just singing them to each other." Jaz's eyes glazed over, remembering.

"Husband? I didn't know you had no husband."

"We're... separated." Jaz stiffened.

"Man's a dang fool wherever he is. Here you go, young lady." The elevator door eased open. "You have a nice weekend, Miss Jaz."

"Thanks, you too," Jaz threw over her shoulder as she walked toward the door and her Jag, thinking that his voice sounded like a weary old jazzman.

Jaz didn't like going to Paradise Rock if she couldn't stay the entire weekend, and since she had the opera tomorrow night, she stayed in town. She rarely accepted a client's invitation, but she hadn't seen Donizetti's *Lucia di Lammermoor* since she left Italy.

That Saturday night, Jaz wore Tawny's grand opera cape, under which a Tawny gown of bronze sequins hugged the curves of her body. Her hosts' seats were close to her parents' box, but Jaz couldn't tell who sat in the Culhane's box. During the intermission, Jaz strolled into the outer lobby with her flute of champagne and spotted Amber's Prince Charming holding court, with fans of Mrs. Charming, the news celebrity. Jaz watched until the lights flickered, and she returned to her seat. Jaz bowed out at the Conovers' after-opera soiree, and as she waited for her car, she noticed PC joining the crowd as it marveled over that old Bugatti Royale. He sat behind the wheel of the car held by the valet, tipped him via a handshake and drove away. A bemused Jaz would have to tell Amber that she saw her PC in that fancy car.

~*~

Jaz flipped through the Vanderpool specs that she hadn't had a chance to review yet, since she salvaged a Sunday at Paradise Rock.

"The Vanderpools said ten-thirty tomorrow is fine," Addie informed her as she laid a portfolio on her desk.

"Thanks. How's Zeke?" Jaz not only missed her daily pink rose, but also knew that Addie called him when he was out.

"He says 'fair to middlin',' which translates into 'not so good.' He'll probably be out another day or so."

"He sure loves to work." Jaz thought about the elevator without him. His metal stool, folded up against the panel; the crate in which he held all his paraphernalia, turned toward the wall, the bud vase he used to keep Jaz's rose fresh until she arrived, empty.

"Old guys like him measure themselves by their ability to hold a job. If they don't work, they feel useless. My daddy was that way," Addie said.

"Mine sure is." Jaz chuckled. "We could use some of those old work ethics for today's guys. Does Zeke have family?'"

"Not here. In St. Louie, where he's from."

"Seems he could go back there and live a lot easier."

"Zeke don't fly and Zeke don't want easy. He's an independent old coot and I'm sure he couldn't find another job like this with all the perks and leave your dad gives."

"True. Is your beau Bob ever jealous of you and Zeke?" Jaz teased.

"Naa. If Zeke's out a week or is hospitalized, guess who takes me to see him?"

"Sure, he's protecting his woman."

"I got no complaints."

~*~

On Dory's arm, Jaz strolled into the awards banquet, a vision of copper in Tawny's long off-the-shoulder gown, resembling poured gold. Her hair twisted in a topknot, with tendrils spilling around her face crowned her presentation. Jaz took her seat, along with the interest of every male and female in the large ballroom. Her presence added flair to an otherwise staid dinner, awards presentation, and acceptance speeches. After the banquet, Jaz and Dory went to the local White Castle for hamburgers and milkshakes before calling it a night.

Later at home, Jaz removed her makeup, washed her face, brushed her teeth, and sat cross-legged on the bed as she braided her hair and flicked on the news.

"First Phil, now you," the anchorman said.

"And now marriage is breaking up that old gang of mine," Mrs. Charming said.

"You ought to try it sometime, Bev," the weatherman added.

"Maybe I will." She swiveled her chair toward the camera. "Well, this is Beverly Nash . . . Good night." Her smile froze on the screen.

"Well, won't Amber be pleased. PC isn't married after all." She switched channels to Susan Hayward in *I Want to Live.*

Beverly Nash, her name reverberated in Jaz's consciousness as she cut the lights to go to bed. She kissed Qwayz's picture and rolled onto her side. Did she go to Roosevelt with her? Jaz thought. It certainly wasn't Berkeley. Jaz sat straight up in bed. TC. That was TC's old girlfriend, she realized. In all these years Beverly Nash hadn't married. Married to her career more than likely, just like TC. Jaz settled back into bed. There was no one to tell. That's something Qwayz would have known right away,

Jaz thought. "Hey Jaz…come here," he would have summoned. "Guess who that is? Beverly Nash."

"Who is…?"

"TC's old anchorwoman girl. She made it."

"Killed my brother to do it. Probably doesn't even think about him. Or know he's dead."

"Jaz," Qwayz would have admonished. "An old women's libber like you should be proud."

"Humph!"

"Try not to judge a person for their choices when you don't know the options from which she chose."

Her Qwayz could sound a lot like her Papa Colt.

"I got some options for you," Jaz would have teased suggestively while doing an ersatz strip tease.

"I bet you do. Have mercy, girlie."

~*~

Jaz pulled off the road onto a concrete slab designed for parking and cut the ignition. The award-winning beach house stood several feet away, like an island in the sand hoisted upon stilts, underneath its belly, the outline of a sports car. She closed the car door and stood studying the exterior façade. Other than the outer door, three staggered rectangular windows ascended the first flight of steps, to a circular window, probably at the landing, then a set of two other slim rectangular windows. There were no other windows. "A damn fortress."

Jaz cursed as her lizard-skinned heels sank in the sand. Removing them, she walked to the door, then replaced them before she rang the bell. The door swung open, and Jaz's heart leapt into her throat, stealing her breath. Nowhere in the old specs or the new, in the portfolio, or in any info on Nick Santucci did it mention that he was indescribably gorgeous.

"Mr. Santucci?" Jaz didn't know where she gathered the wits to ask, obviously operating on professional reflexes. What she wanted to say was, "Good God almighty. Hello, handsome . . . goodbye, heart."

"Miss Chandler?"

"Mrs.," she corrected.

"Please come in." He stepped back, allowing her what little space there was to maneuver the turn that led upstairs.

Jaz walked up the dozen steep steps, fighting for her composure. In her adult wisdom, she wasn't a naive believer in love at first sight; there was no such thing. But lust at first sight? She'd gotten it. She couldn't remember ever being so turned on by the sheer physical presence of a man...except maybe Solomon Noble in college. And now this guy, right after she declared she was going to take a body and heart break to concentrate on her career.

She reached the first floor, and to her amazement, it was a spectacular design, which stole her attention from Mr. Santucci. While the outer façade appeared a fortress, the back was entirely glass, revealing an incomparable view of the ocean and the beginning of a beautiful sunset. The flight of steps continued on up to the top floor, but the open pathway where she now stood divided the sunken living room, its grand fireplace reaching to the cathedral ceiling, and a platformed dining room to the left. There were no walls, and the room was as open as Mr. Santucci's waiting smile.

"May I?" Jaz resisted his easy charm as she crossed a glass bridge into the kitchen. He was an uncommonly good-looking specimen; a tan more natural than worked upon, with deep blue eyes the color of the Mediterranean, an aquiline nose, dark chestnut brown hair cut just enough to calm the curl and inspire the wave, sensuous, inviting lips, and a cleft in his chin you could get lost in. A composite of every fine Italian man she passed up while in Italy. The word "complication" stamped all over their beguiling smiles, athletically slim bodies and eager mannerisms. Thank goodness for Prince Omar.

"Kyle does good work." He flashed a smile, just the right amount of charm and sincerity.

"As I understand it, you want a study?" She almost expected him to have an accent, he looked so authentically Roman.

"And a powder room and laundry room. We bachelors need to wash clothes, too." He leaned casually against the doorjamb, his arms folded and that same inviting smile dancing on those tantalizing lips.

"May I see the upstairs?" She hated to ask.

"My pleasure." His arms extended in an "after you" gesture.

They walked back to the circle window and climbed the last flight of steps. The design surprising Jaz again with one big loft-like bedroom, the bed immediately in front of her. So, she meandered to the right, where a built-in dresser was crowned by giant louvered shutters. Mr. Santucci flung them open, flooding the room with light and a perfect view of the dining room directly below.

"Kyle's big on ventilation and light," he explained.

"Mr. Jagger regrets he cannot follow up on your addition himself, but he is in the Orient. I'm here to discuss your requirements." Jaz had the nerve to look directly into his eyes for the first time. Lawd have mercy, she prayed. "So, Mr. Santucci—"

"Nick," he corrected.

"Do you want your office up here or downstairs?"

"Downstairs, definitely."

With no need to look into the master bathroom or venture out on the adjoining, upstairs terrace, Jaz followed him down the

185

steps, and caught his backfield in motion. Not bad for a non-brother, she critiqued as he excused himself. Jaz tried to determine his accent as she jotted down notes. There was a staccato abruptness and regional enunciation to it like vintage New York, first- or second-generation Italian. "He's too cool to be all white bread." Jaz chuckled at the way she and Gladys Ann used to talk about Paul Newman. Nick didn't walk, talk, dress, or look like a California white boy.

"Oh!" Jaz was startled by the appearance of a friendly, fluffy shaggy dog. "Hey!" Jaz petted the soft, hairy animal.

"That's my roomie, Beau." He pushed up the sleeves of his sweater. "You have pets, Mrs. Chandler?"

"No." Jaz rose and returned to her professionalism.

"He doesn't usually take to strangers." Nick flirted unabashedly.

"Right." Jaz cooled that shit fast, and he chuckled as he escorted her to the door. "Well, Mr. Santucci—"

"Nick." A smile split his handsome face.

"I'll draw up some plans for your approval and get back to you."

"Any ideas off the top of your head?"

"Well, you have only a few options so as not to destroy the integrity of the existing house. A simple plan would be to add your study to the other side of the fireplace, open it up so both rooms could enjoy it and extend your terrace. Another option would be to place the study right next to the living room, but you'd give up some of your light and compromise the glass catwalk."

"Tell me the one you like," he said.

"A silo addition. A semicircular attachment built onto your kitchen, giving you the office, a den/guest room, and a laundry room."

"I like that. I'm interested in seeing what you come up with." Nick paused, asking with a glint in his eye, "Will you be working on this project until completion or just until Kyle comes back?"

"Completion."

"Good, so you'll be in touch?"

"Yes. I'll call you for an appointment."

"No need. I'm always here or on the beach, just Beau and me."

Sure, a handsome stud like you couldn't pick up a loaf of bread at the corner store without causing a riot, and you expect me to believe that "boy and his dog" are here all alone. Yeah, right, Jaz thought.

"You know Kyle pulled some long hours," he said as he guided her down to the front door. "Night and day." He opened it and leaned against it with a boyish, devilish grin. "I don't want to cause any problems between you and Mr. Chandler."

Obviously fishing to see if she was really married or if the rings were a protective ruse, she replied, "You can't." Jaz watched a pleased smile stretch into a wide grin. "He's MIA in Vietnam."

Nick's face dropped. "Oh, I'm sorry."

"So am I. If you don't mind, I'll walk around the house before I leave."

"Fine," he said, still stunned when Jaz stuck out her hand for a professional shake.

"Thank you, Mr. Santucci."

"Yeah, sure, Mrs. Chandler. Thank you."

"Bye, Beau." Jaz removed her shoes and walked in the warm sand, passing underneath the house by his all-black Porsche, reminiscent of TC's beloved car.

As she viewed the house from the ocean side she thought of Qwayz, not knowing whether she had said what she did out of habit or necessity. The wind whipped her hair and the hem of her dress as she surveyed the impressive beach house. Perhaps she should give the Great White Bwana more credit... it was magnificent. With her back to the beautiful fuchsia sunset, she saw neither it nor the man of the house with the aquamarine eyes, the brown hair, and the cleft chin who looked down upon her.

~*~

"Hello, Zeke, welcome back," Jaz sang brightly as she entered the elevator.

"Sounds like someone had a good weekend," the old man inquired as he handed her the daily pink rose.

"I missed these... and you. How are you feelin'?"

"Fair to middlin'." He sighed, cranking up the controls.

Jaz spoke to everyone as she went to her office and her secretary followed. "Addie, tell me what you know about Nick Santucci."

"Oh, he called you today. Haven't you read any of his books? He's a bestselling author who writes novels about love and romance, with strong women and lots of sex. Three have been made into movies: *Distant Rhapsody* was the best. Fine for a white boy. But I don't have to tell you that, you lucky dog."

Jaz spread out the designs for the Santucci addition on her drafting table. She had worked on them Sunday, thinking about him in the process, and wondering what he did for a living. At lunch, she sauntered into the bookstore to buy *To Catch the Wind*. As she stood in line to pay for the item, she tried not to look at his picture on the back cover, his eyes penetrating. She told herself this purchase was research, merely to get an understanding of her client.

Jaz swung by the Vanderpools to check the progress on their lap pool, in-house gym and sauna before going on to Santucci's beach house.

"Right on time." He opened the door as wide as his smile and Jaz sashayed up the steps in the multi-colored Chinese quilted jacket that Claire Vanderpool had drooled over. "How was your Thanksgiving?" he asked casually as Jaz spread out the blueprints on the dining room table for his inspection.

"Fine. Quiet," she answered abruptly. He didn't need to know that Mel and Hud flew up for the big dinner at their folks. Or, that she spent the weekend reading *To Catch the Wind* and was both surprised and moved to tears by his sensitivity. "How about yours?" She tried hard not to notice how his sweater hung over his body.

"Quiet. Just me, Beau, and Tom turkey. I talked to the family on the East Coast, though."

They pored over the plans and he asked questions about structure and integrity before deciding on the silo.

"I'll be in touch," Jaz said when they finished, and she turned to go out the door.

"Mrs. Chandler?"

"Yes?" Jaz looked directly into his eyes, fighting the urge to look away, as if the intensity of his gaze hurt hers. "Do you ever wear your hair down?" Their eyes held each other's for an awkward moment.

"Sometimes. Good night, Mr. Santucci."

"Nick." He corrected her with a smile.

Jaz undid the buttons to her Chinese jacket as she opened up the sunroof and the engine of her Jag. Suddenly she was hot. Though it had been months since Solomon Noble, Jaz had been successful in replacing sex with Amber, family, friends and work. Her life so full and exhausting, she hadn't the time or disposition to think about it and rarely did until she saw a couple so in love that they didn't see her. How wonderful, she'd think with a bit of envy and then dismiss it. Prior to Solomon Noble, Jaz hadn't wanted sex, didn't know where to find it, and couldn't get it if she did. Clearly a nonpriority... until Noble. She'd put it to rest squarely behind her again and then Whammo! One day you open a door and there it is: Sex in a five foot ten, healthy, living, breathing, gorgeous package reminding you of what you're missing. Nick Santucci's mere presence pushed past her veneer of cool, and labyrinth of career and personal obligations blaring "I'm next." Just by being, he dared her to deny her animal urges, desires and taking that heart break.

"Well, Nick," she chuckled into the assaulting warm air, "we'll have to give you extra time and get this project over ASAP. That's my only salvation."

~*~

"I don't believe I left them in my desk drawer," Jaz lamented as AJ turned the corner in front of CE and stopped.

"I do. You spend your life there," AJ teased.

"Can I go, too?" Amber piped up from the back seat, her Shirley Temple curls already unraveling.

"No, I'll be right back," Jaz said, opening the passenger side door.

"You'd better go with her," AJ agreed, to the little girl's glee. "Or, she'll start working and forget all about us."

"Wait, I'm going, too." Amber lit from the car and grabbed Jaz's hand as they walked to the elevator.

Their collective heels tapped on the marble flooring. The pretty brown women, dressed in red velvet...Jaz's off the shoulder with a sweetheart neckline and Amber's adorned with a bib of cream French lace and matching tights.

"Hello, Zeke." Jaz climbed aboard the elevator. "You still here?"

"Ooow!" Amber shrieked-screamed.

"Amber, what's the matter?" Jaz ran out to get the petrified little girl.

"It's a monster!" she cried in terror, cowering in the folds of Jaz's soft red gown. "He'll eat me!"

"Amber." Jaz chided both amazed and embarrassed. "This is Zeke. He's my friend and a very nice man." She coaxed her into the small chamber.

"He's going to kill us!"

"Amber!"

"That's a mighty pretty name," Zeke commented, closing the door.

"She's not acting very pretty. I'm sorry, Zeke."

"Aw, guess I'm kinda scary to children. You all are mighty pretty, dressed up and all." He spoke facing the closed doors.

"Yes, we're going to see The Nutcracker at the Opera House." Jaz wiped Amber's face, as the little girl whimpered and stood on the bench, clinging to Jaz. "I left the tickets in my desk drawer."

Amber wouldn't let go of Jaz's hand, but she snuck peeks at the man's back as they descended to the ground floor. Once Zeke opened the door, Amber bolted straight into the arms of AJ a few feet away.

"AJ, there is a monster in that elevator!" She pointed as he walked toward her, and Jaz fanned him back.

"I'm really sorry, Zeke," Jaz apologized, knowing it must have hurt him despite his brave front.

"Have a nice time at the ballet, Miss Jaz," he said, but when she turned to join the pair, he wiped a single tear from his one eye.

Amber forgot all about "the monster in the elevator" as the music, costumes, and dancing of the troupe captured her attention. Jaz couldn't stop feeling sorry for the lonely old operator. By intermission, however, even Jaz had pushed Zeke into the back of her mind.

"Aunt Jaz." Amber pulled on her gown, interrupting her adult conversation. "I saw him! Prince Charming. He was right over there." Amber pointed. "He said we looked really pretty, like princesses, and he was glad my daddy was back," she giggled. "He thinks AJ is my daddy." Amber loved when adults were wrong.

"What? What's this?" AJ asked.

"It's Amber's Prince Charming," Jaz said and acknowledged the flashing lights by taking Amber's hand. "She's Tracy's child. I'll explain later."

"I'm her father?" AJ was confused and amused.

At the ballet's end, Prince Charming, on the arm of his anchorwoman princess, watched the reunited family leave. He had seen Amber away from her mother on the ferry and asked about her father, and the little girl had stated that they "were waiting for him to come back." What a nice Christmas gift, a family reunited for the holidays. As he watched the lucky man escort his two ladies outside to the waiting Jaguar, both happiness and envy claimed his smile.

"Take care of them, my brother," he advised sotto voce.

"What?" the anchorwoman princess inquired.

Chapter 10

"Jaz, are you coming to Kyle's later?" Addie breezed in from the office Christmas party.

"No." Jaz looked up. "I've got to finish this and I'm outta here. Besides, I wasn't invited."

"No invite required. He has an open house once a year when he's here, and he does all the cooking. We thought we'd miss it this year with him traveling so much, but he's here and we'll all be there."

"That's nice." Jaz wasn't even listening.

"Everybody loved your bread pudding," Addie added.

Jaz paused, biting the eraser of the pencil and remembering Qwayz and that bread pudding. "My mother-in-law's recipe. My husband loved—"

"And thanks for my belt, it is 'bad.' Well, Merry Christmas. Don't work too late."

"Bye, Addie." Jaz chuckled, realizing her secretary had a Yuletide buzz.

Finishing the final review and approval on the Santucci addition, she felt a presence darken the doorway, but the liniment smell caused her to look up. "Hi, Zeke. C'mon in." Jaz put down her pencil.

"You wanted to see me, Miss Jaz?" He shuffled in, negotiating the threshold with care. "I've never been in here before." He talked to pass the time it took for him to reach her desk.

"Lemme turn on the overhead light."

"I'd rather you not," he said quietly.

"All right."

"Lotta little doodads." He eyed her picture frames, music box, rock, and desk clock, breathing heavily and catching his breath.

"Want to sit down?" He shook his head no.

"Might . . . never . . . get . . . up," he managed with some difficulty.

Jaz never realized how overexerted he got with the simplest of tasks. "Merry Christmas, Zeke." She presented him with a large box and cleared a space on the desk, since he couldn't hold it with both hands.

"Oh, Miss Jaz, that bread pudding was gift enough. Everybody liked it, even the young folks."

Zeke began scratching at the box, not denting the foil paper, so Jaz opened it for him, pulling a raincoat from the tissue paper.

"Oh my, isn't that nice."

"It's got a lining for those cool days." She had noticed he didn't have one.

He held on to a nearby chair for support. "I don't have a thing for you, Miss Jaz."

"Oh, Zeke, I don't give to get. 'Sides, you give to me every day, not just the rose but your optimistic spirit."

"Aw, thank you, Miss Jaz."·

For him, even talking seemed labor intensive, but he wanted to, so Jaz let him tell her of his plans to call his family in St. Louis. Of friends, he had in his apartment building who were also alone. Jaz shared her plans before he said he was returning to the party, but she suspected he was so exhausted he'd just go home.

Jaz made her Yuletide circuit in L.A., eating and visiting from home to home, often with Amber in tow. She could be found at one of three places: Tracy's and Scoey's, Denny's and Lloyd's, or Mel's and Lee Harker's. She returned to San Francisco in time for her parents' New Year's Eve bash, and then, with eagerness, back to work. Seeing everyone moving on, married with children and happy lives...especially Denny, spurned a melancholia in her she couldn't shake despite her best efforts. Another year without Qwayz.

~*~

Jaz gathered her files together on the Vanderpool and Santucci additions, placing them in her briefcase.

"Fixin' to leave?" Addie swung in, fluttering her hand about like a bad impersonation of the Ink Spots.

"Yeah, I'm going out for the final inspection of the Vanderpool and Santucci additions if the engineers followed my instructions."

"Why would you want that to end?" Addie held her hand out. "Your father wants to see you first."

"Okay."

"Jaz!" Addie scolded, and stuck the third finger of her left hand right under Jaz's nose.

"Addie, you and Bob?"

"Yes! I want a May wedding. Everybody gets hitched in June."

"Congratulations! You two have renewed my faith in true love." They hugged, and Jaz left a giggling Addie for her father's office.

"Hey, Dad." She stuck her face in, and he invited in the rest.

"Well, how about a late Christmas and Happy New Year gift? Your very own project from the ground up."

"No lie? It's not a bowling alley or a waste refuse plant, is it?"

"No. It's luxury homes on prime real estate. We think you're ready. Of course, Kyle will continue to oversee your projects."

"I'm sure he's real good at 'overseeing.'"

"What is it with you and him? He's really a very nice—"

"Spare me. Gimme the lowdown...the location and preliminary surveys."

"I knew you'd ask." He handed her the waiting portfolio.

"Hot damn, near the bridge? I'm going out for the final walk-throughs on the Vanderpool and Santucci projects, but I'm checking this out on my way. You won't be sorry."

An excited Jaz pulled up to the land in question and noted the project's terrain, roughly hewn from mountains overlooking the bay with Sausalito in the distance, a prime location. Jaz envisioned houses spilling down the cliffs Amalfi-coast style, but knowing the California codes would never permit such a design and people wouldn't buy them in this earthquake-prone area, she regrouped. Every home would be situated to take advantage of the spectacular views of the bay, and she would incorporate as many European features as feasible and cost effective. The Cliffs, she'd call it. Glancing at her watch, she jetted to the Vanderpools', where the gym, sauna and the lap pool passed inspection.

196

Jaz then led the way for the final walk-through at the Santucci addition, where Nick had already moved into his office.

"How do you like it?" Jaz asked.

"I love it, can't you tell? Like it was always here." He smiled. "Kyle couldn't have done better." He crossed his hands over his chest in a stance he'd come to own.

"Well, Nick Santucci, it's been a pleasure." She extended her hand for a final shake.

"Hey, we gotta celebrate. Isn't this your first project? What do I gotta do, build onto my house to get to see you again? C'mon, we can celebrate up the road. A little place only us locals know about."

"Can I go like this?" Jaz asked of her jeans.

"Required dress, ponytail and all. Hold on a sec." He went to let Beau in and get his wallet and keys.

"My dad would love this car," Jaz said, thinking again of TC but deciding not to mention him as they sped down the highway.

"It's a 1954 three fifty-six Speedster in premium shape. Your dad into classic cars?"

"Is water wet? He has my grandfather's Doozy and a—"

"A Duesenberg? He's a serious collector." They turned off the road and went a mile or so to Pancho's Hideaway.

"Little Italian place I like," he said as he opened the door for her and took her arm, escorting her as if she were dripping in diamonds and furs.

Jaz and Nick exchanged family histories over chicken cacciatore and fettuccine Alfredo. They talked about their works-in-progress. His *Shadow in the Sky* and her The Cliffs project until they closed the restaurant and drove back to his house.

"I really enjoyed myself." Jaz stood with her car door open between them. He was leaning dangerously close. She warded off the urge to taste his lips.

"I'm glad," he answered simply. The tension of desire radiated between them.

"Well, bye," Jaz said weakly, not wanting to go, but afraid to stay.

"Wait!" he almost shouted, like a little boy with a line in the Christmas pageant. "Forgive me. I'm sorry, but I just can't let you leave like this." Jaz stood only inches away; she could feel his breath on her skin as he spoke. "I know you'll think me terrible, self-centered, and I'm not really, but I'd like to kiss you if I may. I've wanted to since the day I first saw you. I know about your husband and I'm truly sorry, I really am," he added quickly, his eyes unable to look directly into hers until now. "But if you leave tonight I'll never see you again, no matter how many additions I put on this house. I'll call, and you won't call back. It's now or never. And I want it to be now. I couldn't take never."

Surprised by his openness, his lack of game playing, Jaz likened him to the character he created in *To Catch the Wind*.

"Don't think I'm a sleaze. If your husband comes back, I'm outta the picture in a flash. I respect and accept that even if—"

Fortified with Chianti and desire, Jaz directed, "Shut up and kiss me."

Nick grabbed her hand and pulled her into the house. Once the door closed, Nick took her in his arms and brushed his lips gently across hers, as if savoring the taste of a fine vintage before devouring the red liquid. His hands caressed her back and she sank into him, feeling the urgency of his maleness, even though his lips spelled patience. The faint smell of the garlic and wine they'd just consumed mingled with a hint of cologne from

198

earlier that day. His taste was urbane: sweet and salt, tinged with a thin film of sweat that their body heat produced. He suckled her lips first gently, then more deliberately, and his hands, now beneath her blouse, blazed pure heat upon her naked back. Her eyes opened at the rhythm established by the kissing and caught glimpses of his dark hair, curling in the torrid intensity of the moment, his fabulous eyes hooded by long lashes. The sound of the distant ocean gave way to throaty moans, his or hers—soon she didn't care. Swept up in the tide of passion, she'd seen him towering over her, removing his shirt, baring his muscled chest. Her hands ran up his moist flesh as she encircled his neck, pulling him down upon her. Sure, she'd be taken on the steps, but was surprised when he swept her up to the landing under the circle window and the sky-lit cathedral ceiling. As if his reserve gave out and he could resist no longer, he entered her deeply, fluidly, insatiably as her pulsating orifice accepted him willingly, continually, hungrily, with such fierceness she shocked herself.

They lay in their exhausted nakedness, the moon peeking in on the contours of two exquisitely satisfied bodies. Nick carried her the few feet more into the living room, where they stretched out in front of an unlit fireplace, covered by a throw he retrieved from the couch.

"I guess you could tell this wasn't planned," he said, offering that same infectious smile.

"I would have worn better underwear," Jaz quipped, trying to sound worldly.

"Where is it?" He smiled, looking about.

"We left it on the steps." In their mutual awkwardness they began to chuckle. "I'm relatively new at this," Jaz admitted, thinking about how he was only the third man in nearly thirty years of life she'd ever slept with besides Qwayz.

"We'll get better with time." He brushed her nose with his, and she thought him the most handsome of men.

"I gotta go." Jaz panicked and tried to raise herself against him.

"Oh, I was just going to offer you some wine...something to eat."

"I think we've covered that." She reared up on her elbows in time to catch Nick blush momentarily. She wanted to go. She wanted to stay and maybe do it once more, enough to last her awhile, or in case she'd never have him again. She wondered how many women he'd had in his life. Surely, more than three. She still didn't know where the condom came from...he was not only worldly but out of her league.

"Do you really want to go?" He rubbed her arm gently and felt himself rise against her thigh. "Maybe we could make it up the stairs to the bedroom this time." He smiled, his hand crossing her shoulder blade and inching down to her erect nipples.

They made it to the bed this time, barely, and afterwards fell into a deep sleep. Jaz awoke at the first hint of distant light. She lay in the crevice of his arm. The beginnings of a shadow played about his sensuous lips and Romanesque jaw-line. He was almost too gorgeous to be real. Without removing her gaze from him, she tried to untangle his legs from hers. In the process, his eyes flew open.

"Good morning! Gosh, you're an early riser." He reached for his dead arm and shook life back into it.

"I gotta go." This time Jaz rose, gathering the sheet about her like a robe, and descended the stairs to her clothes.

"Hey, what about breakfast?" Nick wrapped himself in the spread, not fully understanding this false modesty.

"I'm sorry. I thought I could, but I can't." She jumped into her panties and jeans, pulled on her blouse, and moved toward the front door, opened it and out she went.

Heading toward Paradise Rock as if it were her one salvation, Jaz recognized that in affairs of the heart she was still lost without Qwayz. Not that this or any other liaison could approximate what she'd had with her husband, but she was unnerved by it. The fantasy of Prince Omar. The dalliance with Solomon Noble, but Nick was reality, here in California, close to her loved ones, her job, her parents and more importantly, his style of loving approximated that of her one true love. It scared her. But unlike the sordid farce with the prince, she could lend the unattached Nick her body, never getting in so deep she couldn't pull out at a moment's notice; that'd be her protection. The stage was set, and Nick understood, so what's the harm? Was she seriously considering doing this again?

"Damn!" she shouted, hitting the steering wheel. If Qwayz had been here, there wouldn't have been a Prince Omar, Solomon Noble or a Nick Santucci—she would never have needed them.

She cut the engine and closed her eyes, absorbing the sounds and rhythms of her surroundings—the crash of the sea below, the feel of the wind caressing her face and the smell of the salty air. She purged herself of all thoughts because when she entered Paradise Rock, she entered alone, with no thoughts other than those of her beloved husband. For in Paradise Rock, Qwayz reigned supreme. This was his house, and she respected him and it.

As if cleansing herself of impure thoughts and deeds, Jaz cut off the alarm, slid back the door and stepped into the cathedral ceilings of natural light and presence.

"Qwayz, I'm home!"

"I hate it when she goes to that damn beach house," Hep said, redoing his tie "It's a goddamn mausoleum to a dead man." He finally turned to let his wife work her magic.

"It's a place for her to relax and get away," Lorette said. "It's a place for her to remember."

"It's not natural. She should have been over this years ago." He yanked his jacket from the stationary valet. "Then she drags that music box and rock with her everywhere. Puts them out on her desk every Monday morning. It's been nearly ten years—the girl's almost thirty. AJ's marrying Avia, for chrissakes. Jaz ought to get on with her life."

"Maybe this is her life, Hep, and we have to accept it. She's happy—"

"She is not happy."

"You're not happy that she's missing this dinner meeting. She gives you twelve-hour days in the office; she doesn't owe you her weekends, too."

"Is it wrong to want what we have for our daughters?"

"No. But Jaz had it with Qwayz. I wouldn't want the impossible task of finding your replacement."

"You couldn't!" Hep boomed, and Lorette smiled.

~*~

"Hi, how are you?" Jaz could hear Nick smile.

"Hey! I was just thinking about you." He'd thought of nothing else for the past five days. "I was going to call and invite you to Beau's birthday party." He'd picked up the phone a thousand times but decided that this relationship had to be her call or not at all. "Made a big pot of marinara, even got a cake."

"Sounds good." She fanned Addie in. "What time?"

"Seven-ish."

202

"Can I bring anything?" Jaz watched Addie's approving smile. "Great! See you then." She hung up. "Wipe that grin off your face."

"I don't know who, where, or when, but I'm happy for you." Addie set the papers on the desk.

"Nothing from Kyle yet?" Jaz riffled through the papers, looking for his approval of her specs on The Cliffs. He tap-danced on her last good nerve. She'd assembled her team: Marc and Derek as collaborating architects, Dory for landscaping, Tre' for finance, all stood ready to proceed.

"He hasn't returned my call? No overseas communique? Damn! He's holding up production."

"Nothing yet."

Jaz waited until afternoon and still no return call or word from the Great Bwana. Her guys had inquired about the final approval, and Addie had asked if Jaz wanted her to wait around after five.

"No, you and your fiancé have a wedding to finish planning."

"About that," Addie began. "I was wondering if you'd do a big favor for me. In lieu of a gift, even." Jaz looked evenly at her assistant. "Bring Zeke for me," Addie asked and read her reluctance. "I want him there and you are the only one I would dare ask besides Kyle, but he'll still be in Hong Kong. It'll be our last goodbye, since I'll be leaving for our honeymoon and then we'll be in Atlanta for good."

"Don't remind me." Jaz stroked the bridge of her nose, thinking of the headache it would be to replace her and break in a new secretary.

"One of those days, huh?"

"One of those months." Jaz picked through the papers on her desk.

"Well, will you be Zeke's date, so to speak?"

203

"Yeah, yeah."

"If you have to leave early with him or something, I'll understand."

"Great."

"I wouldn't go in there if I were you," Addie warned Marc on her way out.

"Hey, boss, wanna go boogie at the disco tonight?" He did a twisty movement.

"Have a nice weekend, Marc." Jaz waved him off playfully. She recalled how hard her team had worked, giving up a Saturday afternoon for The Cliffs when Jaz enticed them with a home cooked lunch and a celebratory dinner at Giuseppe's. The session produced the flawless plans on which Kyle now sat in Hong Kong. Jaz snatched up the phone.

"Kyle Jagger of Culhane Enterprises please." Jaz sounded as official as possible.

"Sorree," the heavily accented woman apologized. "'He in meeting now, no disturb."

"I'm calling for his boss, Hepburn Culhane." Her information and tone caused the secretary to think better of Mr. Jagger's instructions.

"Hold on, please."

Jaz wasn't lying. Hep too wanted to get on with building the luxury homes.

"Yeah, boss?" A male voice spoke after two expensive minutes.

"This is Jasmine Chandler and we're waiting for the final approval and specs on The Cliffs." There was a long pause. "Hello?"

"Mrs. Chandler," he began tightly in a lethally low tone. "The information you request is on its way. I can neither do anything to expedite that process nor communicate the changes to you

204

over the phone. Therefore, you will have to exercise some professional patience." There was a brief pause before he continued, "Never, I repeat, never call me out of a conference again." The slam of the phone caused Jaz to jump; the sound of the dial tone infuriated her.

"Bastard!" She retaliated in kind. "Arrogant, shriveled-up old honky."

Across the ocean, as Kyle walked back to the meeting, he had thoughts of his own on the boss's spoiled daughter. While he personified grace under pressure and maintained the outer presence of cool, calm, and control, underneath he seethed at her audacity. She'd irked him to distraction with her demands, as if expert work could be rushed. She was a young, pampered, indulged brat whose father probably bought her the degrees here and abroad. He admired and respected Hep's business acumen and vision, but the man had a blind spot when it came to his daughters, both of them—the star and this one, for whom he'd actually saved an office for three years until she was ready to go to work.

He'd heard she was drop-dead gorgeous, and knowing her type, was sure to be on to something else soon when architecture bored her. She was special to her daddy, but was nothing to him . . . except a nuisance. If he never met the woman, it would be too soon.

"Now, gentlemen." Kyle reentered the conference room, unbuttoning his jacket. "Where were we?" An easy smile claimed his face as he spoke to his Hong Kong investors.

~*~

"How was Miss Checole's wedding to that handsome son of a gun?" Zeke asked Jaz as she returned from the weekend festivities.

"It was dazzling," Jaz said. She'd stood in as Avia's "family" as well as AJ's aunt. "I feel a certain amount of responsibility for that one. Hope St. Theresa's has a christening soon."

"Not too soon," Zeke said, his chuckle leading to a phlegmy cough.

"You okay?" Jaz asked once he caught his breath.

"Fine, Miss Jaz. Have a nice day." Zeke closed the elevator doors between them, and Jaz proceeded to her office.

As Jaz entered through her door, Addie danced in and closed the door. "Here ya go!" Addie slapped the overseas mailer from Kyle on Jaz's desk.

"It's about time."

She opened the package, thinking of the compromises she'd made to Kyle's queries: adding the skylight in the master bedroom for more natural light and making the industrial kitchen appliances optional instead of standard. She'd bumped heads with him and won over the adjoining European courtyards; the tri-level master bedroom, fireplace, and picture window, the first-floor atrium, and the number of houses to be constructed.

"Yes!" she yelled when she saw in his chicken scratch, "*Okay. Good job. May buy one myself. KJ,*" noted before her overseas call.

"So was I, but rather than have you as a neighbor . . . hey, it's yours."

She hoisted the markups on the board. It was pure genius. A big outer courtyard with flowerbeds and trees secured by wrought-iron gates and three huge configurations, each with two detached houses sharing an open marble vestibule with fountain. There were six houses per outer courtyard construction, and Jaz had put four, making it a twenty-four-house project. And it was ready to go!

"To The Cliffs!" Nick toasted at Pancho's Hideaway.

"And *Shadow in the Sky*!" Jaz countered, and their glasses clinked in unison. "We done Little Italy and Watts proud."

For dessert, they'd devoured each other at his place. "Yeah, we're pretty damn lucky," Nick said, groaning and stretching in satisfaction.

"Shower?" Jaz asked, kissing him on the nose and climbing off him.

"Let's just lie and bask for a while." He caught her and rolled her onto her back. "Maybe the good-time fairy will call again."

"Somehow fairy and Santucci just don't belong in the same sentence. Besides, I have a wedding to go to."

Jaz sprang for the shower and he listened to the water begin to flow. Their time together went too fast for Nick. They'd settled into a comfortable existence even though he never had enough time with Jaz. He understood her reluctance with going public, but he grew tired of getting reports on, not invitations to, important events in her life. The anniversary party for Denny and Lloyd, Brittany's and Bethany's birthday party, the AIA banquet, her sister Mel's and Lee Harker's engagement soiree. He knew he'd never win over the protective AJ, but he could melt Amber's little heart. So Nick showed her the way; gave her a key to his house when he had never even seen hers, had her speak to his mother in New York when he was never included in dinners with her parents; the couple had dined with his sister when she visited California. He had told Jaz how he felt about her, but she either minimized or ignored it. No reciprocity. Patience. Slowly she would have to come around.

"Mama wants me to bring you out for Christmas," he said when she returned, dressed in an exquisite peach suit. "You look great. Comin' back after the wedding?"

"Probably not. I've got that business brunch on Sunday, and work to make up 'cause I'm here today. You understand." She kissed him goodbye. "I'll call."

"What about Christmas at Mama's?" He yelled after her.

"Sure! Bye." Jaz walked out to the car and started it up. Christmas, dag, she thought. Anything can happen between now and then.

Jaz sat beside Zeke in the church and teared up as Addie, having spoken her vows and heading back up the aisle, stopped with her new husband at Zeke and touched his hand. At the reception, while Jaz worried about the stares Zeke would get, she found that the acorn doesn't fall far from the tree. Addie's family filed by Zeke as if he were the guest of honor, and it warmed Jaz's heart. She recalled picking him up earlier. Entering his stark, brightly lit, squeaky-clean one-room efficiency, with no rugs so the wheelchair and oxygen tank could move freely. The radiators puffed steam into the stale, hot room, and mixed with the hospital smell of antiseptics, rubbing alcohol, and unguents; the smells making Jaz just as nauseous and light-headed as riding in the elevator. As he strapped on his leg behind a curtain, she studied the clean kitchenette, with its one plate, one fork, one spoon, and cup neatly draining near the sink next to a long row of pill bottles. An expensive component set with a remote seemed out of character; perhaps a gift from his daughter and family in St. Louis, or even her father, known for his generosity to people he liked.

When the wedding reception was over, it seemed a shame to return Zeke to that mean little room, so he popped a few more pills and consented to take a ride with her to her beach house. He wasn't much company, as he slept on the way. She tipped from the car to the house so as not to disturb him, retrieved her papers and looked up, surprised to see him standing there. "Not much to it," he'd said.

"My husband and I loved it here," Jaz answered and looked around with a hopeful smile. "We found it when we were in college and came her every chance we got. Our sanctuary." Jaz watched the setting sun dance on the floor-to-ceiling split rock fireplace of the sunken living. "One day we came and they'd built this house on it. Qwayz was so mad." Jaz stopped. "I bought it as a surprise for him when he came home. He never knew it. But his spirt is here. I never feel more connected to him than here. Where he has never been."

An exhausted Zeke leaned against the wall and let her ramble.

"You're the first man to visit here…"

"Zat right?" he managed.

"God, I loved that man."

"I'm sure the feeling was mutual."

Jaz eyed Zeke almost forgetting she was not alone. "Let me get you home. It's been a long day."

As Jaz locked up, Zeke shuffled to the passenger's side. Jaz opened his door, positioned his prosthetic leg inside, and as she strapped him into his seatbelt, he asked quietly, "You think we can stop by the drugstore on the way back?"

"Sure," Jaz said cheerily as she slid behind the wheel and started the car. "Thanks for listening to me. I rarely get the chance to talk about him out loud." Zeke was asleep before they reached the end of the driveway. She went in and got the few items he wanted and when she returned she shooed teen boys away from the car. "You ought to be ashamed of yourself. He is a veteran who fought so you all could be free. He's the reason you're not speaking German now."

A furious Jaz entered her car and Zeke was calm like he was with Amber.

"Hoodlums."

"You get used to it."

Jaz helped him to his apartment, and he tolerated her as she stood between his rest and sleep. "See you Monday morning," he dismissed. "And thank you."

Jaz returned to her apartment, eyed Qwayz's red baseball cap, and stroked his bomber jacket hanging on the hall tree. She showered, braided her hair, climbed into bed, and touched Qwayz's face on the Malibu picture by the lamp before cutting it off. A shaft of light escaped the shutters and shone on their images: he in his peach Banlon, holding Jaz in front of him. Their smiles as big as the heavens above and the bright future that lay before them. Although physically exhausted, Jaz's mind was full of thoughts of him; the wedding ceremony of Addie and Bob and their new beginnings only emphasized Jaz's lack thereof. Loneliness surrounded her like a cloying embrace…but not enough for her to settle for life with a man she did not truly love; deep down to her toes love. Qwayz-love. Intellectually, she knew she'd never find that again. She had to let it go. She had backed herself into a corner and had to stop dating unacceptable men. Men she wouldn't consider marrying; after all, she was pushing up on thirty, she was too old for that. Yet, she wasn't desperate enough to have a man for having a man's sake. She'd had brief conversations with Denny and recently Aunt Selena about how they'd moved on. None of it resonated with Jaz. So she'd continue to live her life full of friends, family and her career and maybe, when she wasn't looking, her Prince Charming would come along; she longed to love somebody and have him love her back. Being Auntie Jaz was not a bad existence; she'd already had the best that this life had to offer,

210

and his name was Quinton Regis Chandler IV. Jaz balled up a pillow that held his faint scent and fell asleep.

~*~

During her waking hours, Jaz could be found at an onsite trailer at The Cliffs where the project progressed with such ease it was scary. She chastised herself for resenting the break when she flew to L.A. for fittings for the matron-of-honor dress she was wearing in Mel's wedding to Lee Harker, the only black executive at NBC, and the executive producer of her show. Using the company jet enabled Jaz to slip in and out of L.A. undetected by Amber, but Nick was becoming more of an unwanted distraction.

After a satisfying love making session, Jaz just wanted sleep.

"You know Mama loves you," he declared.

"That's nice," Jaz had snuggled beneath him.

"Listening to you two speak fluent Italian with one another is priceless."

"Umm-hmm." Good gravy he was chatty tonight, she thought.

"I could write a book about the way you make me feel." He held her. "She asked me why I was dragging my feet. I told her I was way ahead of her." He reached into the drawer by his nightstand. "You know they call you *unicorno nero magico*. And I totally agree." He kissed her shoulder.

"See. That—" She sat up and faced him.

"It's a compliment, magical black unicorn? How can that be offensive?"

"I'm not magical or a unicorn. Millions of black people have the same achievements and accomplishments. Even better. Still millions more could do the same thing if they were given the opportunity. So folks like me are not unusual. Or magical. I worked hard for where I am and so did they. You can't dismiss that and think—"

"Jaz. Jaz," he soothed, brushing his lips against her bare skin.

Jaz paused, breathed deeply and then heard the squeak of a box opening.

"Will you marry me? Take my name and become Jasmine Santucci?"

Jaz looked into the aura of a gigantic sparking solitaire diamond perched on black velvet surrounded by Tiffany blue; it soaked up the moonlight and shoved it back.

Jaz froze.

"You must know how crazy I am about you. Once the family agreed. It was a cinch."

Speechless, Jaz just stared from him to that ring, so big it looked fake.

She turned toward him and treaded lightly. Nick had been good *for* and *to* her. "I care for you. I even love you in my own way, but I am not *in* love with you. Not the way you deserve someone to be."

It was Nick's turn to return the stare. He'd never heard a woman declare she did not love him. It'd always been the opposite. Most of his life he'd spent running from women.

"Nick," she tempered her stance realizing it had been a mistake to visit him today when she was so dog-tired. "If I ever consider marriage again... it's going to be someone like me. Who shares the same past and heritage—"

"You're a bigot."

Jaz chuckled wryly. "Why is it that when an Italian, Jew, or Vanderpool wants to marry their own kind, they're applauded? For upholding tradition. Let a black person show a little racial pride—"

"It's 1976. Why can't two people of different races fall in love, and marry?"

"Many do, but not me. I have a wonderful responsibility to the ancestors before me, and my children to come."

"Our children will be a blend of two magnificent races."

"No. My children will be black. Thoroughbreds. No cultural treason here."

Nick was eerily quiet.

"Listen, I want a man like my daddy, my granddaddy, my brother. Of all the things you can give me, Nick, you can't give me that." Suddenly, it felt strangely hypocritical to be in bed with him, literally and figuratively. She got up and stood by the dresser. Like with Prince Omar, she'd thought they were on the same page. How can she be this bad at picking men? "So this is as good as it gets, and as far as it goes for us. Besides you knew the deal when we started. I have a husband—"

"Here we go with the sainted-husband routine," Nick wailed out of hurt and rejection. "You pull his memory out, dust it off and tote it around for your convenience. You know he's not coming back, Jaz. He's not MIA...he's dead." He saw her face and heard the irrevocable rip of their relationship.

"You bastard." Jaz cut him with her eyes, pulled out her suitcase, and filled it with her belongings.

"Jaz." He was immediately, irreversibly, irretrievably sorry as he watched her pack her things to take a permanent trip out of his life. He wondered how a simple marriage proposal had turned into the end of a spectacular love affair. He watched her walk down two flights of steps and get into her car. He cursed himself and laughed wryly as "Hey Girl" play softly on the radio. It played out like a scene from one of his novels, only this was too real. Bad fiction. He had ruined his own life. "How am

213

I supposed to exist without you? Bye. Bye. Baby. Don't go away…" the crooner lamented.

Chapter 11

L ast Christmas and the first of the year were dominated by previous events: Zack's untimely death, Mel's wedding, The Cliffs, Nick, Amber, the twins, but Jaz relished spending more time with family. But summers in Colt, Texas had always been exceptional, and she looked forward to its spiritual reaffirmation and rejuvenation. She drove towards her family's homestead, and at first sight of Cherokee Ranch, the crest where Papa Colt first brought his bride Keely, Jaz relaxed. She paused only feet from where her father walked from World War II back home. She supposed everyone who'd been here had that first reaction to the sight of Cherokee. She'd missed being here. There was something soothing about being in a place of your ancestral home where, though you may change, everything remains the same. Remains welcoming, and brims with unconditional love and support. Grandma Keely, Aunt Star, Aunt O and, since Zack's passing, Aunt Selena. Jaz'd had many long distance conversations that began with, "How do you get over this, Jazzy? Does the pain of losing the love of your life ever end?" All the times her aunt had been there for her, Jaz felt woefully inadequate. Jaz was the wrong person to ask about getting over your one true love. She never mastered how not to think about Qwayz.

Jaz cut the engine, opened the door and then the gate, approaching the porch. "Aunt Jaz!" Hud barreled out as he ran and jumped into her arms.

"Oh, boy! You're getting too big for this." She kissed his forehead. "You're gonna break my back." She ruffled his hair and he blushed a smile. "How you doing?"

"Fine," he answered too quickly.

"Really?" She knew his mother's recent marriage and blossoming pregnancy had to be difficult for the almost eleven year old. "We'll talk later. Just you and me."

"OK." He spotted the Jaguar. "I love your new car. So cool!"

"Hey, Dad." Jaz walked up the steps to the porch where he stood, looking like the cat that swallowed the canary. "So I'm here. What's the big deal about all of us being here *now* especially?"

Like an ersatz receiving line, her father stood next to Grandma Keely, Aunt Selena, Aunt Star, Keely J and Aunt O.

Jaz's heart caught. For one crazy, golden moment she expected Qwayz to join them on the porch… Papa Colt's porch, where he'd first declared his love for her when she was fifteen…maybe with a broken or missing leg, but she couldn't stop her heart from triple beating. Qwayz'd do something classically poetic like this. "What is it?"

"Hey, Hud?" A little boy about Hud's age pushed open the screen door. "You coming or not?"

Jaz looked at him. Familiar eyes stared back at her. "Oh, my goodness," Jaz muttered.

"Cully," Hep's booming voice introduced. "This is your Aunt Jaz. Your father's sister."

216

"Pleased to meet you," he said politely.

Tears sprang to Jaz's eyes. It wasn't Qwayz—it was TC. "Hello, Cully," she managed as wetness cascaded down her cheeks. "My, you are the spitting-image of your daddy."

"That's what everybody says."

"C'mon," Hud beckoned to his cousin.

"See you later," Cully said and fell in behind Hud.

"How? When? What dad? His mother is LeLani isn't it?"

"Yep."

"Is she here?"

"Not this year. She came the first time. But this year she let him come by himself. Once I convinced her I meant neither of them harm and I wasn't trying to steal him away from her."

After supplying hello kisses for the ladies, Jaz watched her grandmother and aunts file back into the house to finish dinner. "During Qwayz's R&R in Hawaii I ran into LeLani and saw him as a boy but wasn't sure. Qwayz and I had other things on our minds." Practicing to conceive a child of their own, Jaz thought. "We didn't pursue it while there. Qwayz didn't see him up close like I did. It was one of the things we were going to do when Qwayz came home. How?"

"I got wind of the possibility. Went to LeLani's father's funeral in Watts, but she didn't bring him. So I pursued it and here we are."

"I bet it was nowhere near that simple."

"Some things are just worth it, Punkin. Some things take time."

Jaz's eyes asked for more, so Hep sat on the porch swing and continued, "A lot of visits back and forth. Reassurances. Restraining orders. And finally, a Hawaiian maternal grandmother as an ally. Made all the difference." His foot put the swing in motion. "Offered LeLani a house anywhere in L.A.

217

she wanted. To get her a job at any bank or financial institution she wanted; she was quite clear she did not want to work for CE." He chuckled. "Who doesn't want better for their children? Access to better schools. More activities. Hawaii is nice, but paradise isn't suited for constant wear."

"Was she ever going to tell TC?"

"She says she intended to, but the first time she came back to the states, she found out he'd gone to Vietnam. She thought she'd tell him when he returned." But he never did, hung unsaid, between father and daughter. "Says she didn't mean to get pregnant, but when she did, she decided to keep the child. But couldn't stay and watch TC fall in love with another woman… so she left."

"Yeah. That's rough." Jaz thought of Beverly Nash.

He and Jaz watched the boys' horses kick up dust as they rode in the prairie across the wide open spaces. Just like him and Range. Like TC and Qwayz and now Hud and Cully. "History repeating," Hep said quietly. "Only this time, they're really related. I hope they become close. Hope their bond is never broken, hope no white man's war separates them. I'm hoping for a better outcome."

Jaz joined her father on the swing. "Wouldn't TC be crazy about that boy? A son." She rested her head on his shoulder. "You can really keep a secret."

"You have no idea." He kissed the top of Jaz's head.

"Now you and Qwayz can pursue something else when he comes back," Hep offered quietly. Always supporting his daughter's notion that his return was eminent.

Falling from her father's lips, it sounded idiotic. "He's not coming back, Dad," she whispered sotto voce. "If he could, he would have been here by now."

Hep looked down at his daughter, wanting to applaud her forward movement but not trusting himself to comment on it. Had his prayers finally been answered? He patted her hand in response.

"He was the Christmas surprise that no one found out because of Zack's passing."

"Everybody knew but me?"

"Well, it evolved organically. Cully met Hud, which meant Mel and LeLani. Then grandma Keely and Star. Selena when they visited here the first time."

"That's a yes, Dad."

"No one wanted to tell you and have to answer a million and one questions. Besides, you are the eyewitness type. You need proof."

"Like my Daddy. Show me. Well, it is clear as can be."

"That's the scientist in you. Tracy, Denny or Scoey didn't know."

"Unfunny, Dad. Look at him ride. That's more than a couple of Colt, Texas visits. Where'd he learn to sit a horse like that?" Jaz asked of Cully's ability.

"Rides horses in Hawaii and can surf with the best of them...swimming hole doesn't have waves...but he can stroke."

Jaz fought hard not to marvel and stare at this pint-sized version of her big brother. "I can't believe you kept this from me, Dad."

"You had other fish to fry," he teased.

"So how's it been? He and Hud? LeLani?"

"After the initial glitches and mistrusting, it smoothed out considerably. I've slowly introduced him to his father and his father's world. Always making him question instead of inundating him with TC. Zion Blassingame and Jaxson Henderson came to visit him in San Francisco, saying they wanted to 'see him.' Then I arranged for a heritage tour of sorts when Roosevelt's Chandler-Culhane Music Program honored the scholarship recipients."

Hep smiled remembering. Once the boy and LeLani moved to L.A., Hep'd taken his grandson on short excursions. Fishing first from a pier, then on a small boat before he sprang his yacht on him. At Culley's request, they went to a baseball came. Brutal for Hep but his grandson enjoyed it. After the third ride, Cully adjusted to private plane rides up and down the coast. He'd not only taken Cully to the award program but to Champion Studios, where it all jelled for the young boy. Z and Jax, to whom TC had rightfully bequeathed his beloved creation, squired him around the studio his father had built. The pair had kept Champion Studio viable and innovative, so it remained one of the top five studios in the nation. As the youngster walked the halls, you could see Cully's intelligent eyes absorbing everything around him including his upstairs apartment with the round bed. Z and Jax had assembled video of his father in action... conducting recording sessions, playing all the instruments, directing vocals, writing music, leading orchestras, and playing basketball with Qwayz on the small outdoor court. Luckily, TC taped everything; he and Zack did that for posterity. Neither could have known how prophetic this gesture would be. LeLani appeared in many of the films which made Cully smile. Had he ever seen his mother "in love" before? The way she looked at TC... and he her at times, priceless. In Studio 3, Blassingame asked Cully if he'd like to try the piano or guitar. Cully said, "Sure." The boy, born and bred in Hawaii who'd never taken a music lesson or held an instrument besides triangles, sat at the piano and fiddled with the keys before plucking out the scale. All went back to doing what they did and then...He picked out a tune. "Beauty Black." The next go around, he improved upon it. But the next time…his playing mesmerized them all. At the end of the piece…Hep, Z and Cully were all in tears. "I don't know what happened," Cully said quietly. "Your father was here? That was your father's first piece he wrote for Aunt Selena." Hep shared reverently. "TC was here…with you. With us…"

"So can he play?" Jaz asked, bringing her father back to the present.

"For someone who just started? He's got talent."

"Not like TC."

"No one is like TC."

"True. Are the cousins getting along? I know Hud."

"He seems to be dealing with him fine.. We're going to have them transferred to the same school. So time will tell."

"You mean you're having Cully attend Melbourne Prep Academy. Hope you asked Hud first."

"Yeah. We did. He hunched his shoulders."

"They seem to be bonding. They both have daddy-issues. One absent altogether and one living but abandoned his son."

"Different sides of the same coin. Hud knows his father but doesn't think much of him."

"Which was Big Hud's doing. Cully never knew his father at all and now discovers him but can't see or touch or feel him."

That's where you're wrong, Punkin. He figures when he gets older, he'll go by CT. For Culhane Troop."

"The reverse of TC? Mature."

"Like his daddy before him."

"Must be in the DNA."

Grandma Keely called for dinner. "C'mon, Punkin."

"I am just floored."

"Hasn't taken your appetite?"

"Well, no."

Chapter 12

The rest of the year sped by, catching Jaz in a whirlwind of activity. Mostly trips to L.A. for Mel's tapings for her hit show, attending Denny's surprise birthday party for her husband, Lloyd, and trips to see Amber. In San Francisco, the completed The Cliffs was fully occupied, and Hep promised her a multimillion-dollar project in New Orleans; he and Kyle thought her ready. Jaz helped Avia adjust to becoming an interpreter and executive assistant at Culhane Enterprises, San Francisco as AJ completed his third year of med school in June. Life chugged along.

The American Institute of Architects awards banquet was extra-special this year. Not because of the absence of Kyle for yet another year. Not because the handsome "Doc AJ," as Amber called him, escorted her. Not because she wore the brand-new Russian lynx that she had treated herself to, but because Jasmine Bianca Culhane Chandler received the Trailblazing Design Award for The Cliffs. A proud and ecstatic Hep had to be quieted so Jaz could make her acceptance speech.

When Jaz went home, she placed the award on her mantel beside TC's Grammy and underneath Papa Colt's pearl-handled guns and Stetson hat. Finally, something she'd achieved and could display. Her professional career progressed at warp speed, even if romantically she remained stalled in 1968.

The presenter's words about the "innovative, groundbreaking design" still rang in her ears. Maybe Kyle should have flown in from Japan just to see her get her due. She'd bought a house in The Cliffs, since Kyle had not. It'd be fun decorating and having a larger place in which to entertain. Amber, Hud and hopefully CT would relish having their own rooms when they visited, and the one hundred fifty-thousand-dollar appreciation of the property since sales began, just a bonus.

Jaz dropped the car key in the palm of the smiling valet as she sashayed into the elegant lobby of The Fairmount Hotel. Her luck had run out. Her father had arranged a lunch meeting for her and the Great Bwana since they were to "share" the New Orleans project. She perched on the corner of the sofa, impeccably dressed and feeling like a natural-born child about to meet an adopted, "preferred" one. Glancing out the window she observed a small crowd admiring a fancy car the same color as that Bugatti Royale Amber's Prince Charming drove. Jaz hadn't seen Amber's prince since the opera. No sooner did the thought enter Jaz's mind than she spotted him gliding past the doorman. Reflex propelled her to the lobby door, where she coyly dropped a glove which was retrieved by a man as the prince was stopped by a hotel attendant.

"Thanks," Jaz snapped, jerking her glove from the clutches of the man. I was never any good at this game-playing crap, Jaz sighed. How to approach a man 101 had eluded her.

"Hello." Jaz jumped at the greeting. "Didn't mean to startle you." A slow, easy grin spread across the prince's face. "But I thought it was you."

"Hello." Jaz couldn't suppress her grin, noticing for the first time, deep dimples framing his smile.

"How's Amber?"

"Fine."

"Tell her hello. So are you here for lunch?"

"Yes, business meeting actually. And you?"

"Same. We must be a couple of workaholics to be here on a Saturday afternoon."

"What business are you in?" They asked each other simultaneously and laughed, just as Hep approached, his booming voice preceding his body.

"I love punctuality in my people." Hep came between them, then called to a man coming in, "Charlie Barnes!" and went off to greet an old friend, leaving the gap-mouthed couple there.

"Wait. You're Kyle Jagger?"

"You're Jaz Chandler?"

"But I thought you were an old white man!"

"What?" Kyle joined her in laughter as Hep returned.

"Ready?" Hep walked between them again, ushering them toward the elevator. "I knew Charlie Barnes at Fisk, haven't seen him in years."

Entering the elevator, Hep went on about Charlie Barnes, as Jaz and Kyle became absorbed in thoughts about each other. Seeing him now explained his house in Africa, his office motif, his voice not matching that of an old codger, as well as why the female student interns always wanted Mr. Jagger and why the secretaries were both protective and enamored of him.

Kyle stood on the other side of Hep, racking his brain for the details Hep had given about his two daughters. Topaz eyes was Hep's daughter and Amber's mother. She wasn't the one who just got married, that was the star or was it? Topaz had a wedding ring, she was married to Amber's father. Someone had a husband who died in Vietnam, was that Hud or Amber's father? No, they never had children.

The three discussed the plans for the New Orleans project, the conversion of the old railway station into a pricey luxury hotel and mezzanine shops. As Hep reviewed the project, he noticed the preoccupation between the two.

"Is there something going on here?" he asked abruptly, like a teacher accosting two mischievous pupils.

"No, Daddy."

"It's just so ironic that we've seen each other around all this time and never—"

"Well, of course you've seen each other around. You've worked together for almost two years."

"This is our first meeting," Kyle said, simply.

"I've never seen him in the office before, Dad. Only around San Francisco."

"But your offices are right next to each other. The Cliffs—"

"All memo and specs sent from the Orient. And a very nasty phone call."

"Believe me, I didn't know," Kyle apologized with a smile. "May I drop you somewhere?" Kyle asked Jaz while Hep paid the bill.

"No, I have my car."

"An aquamarine Jag."

"Right. How do you know that?"

"Ahh, didn't your father tell you I was the best?"

"Best male."

"So I guess we'll be seeing more of each other."

"'Spec so. Enjoy the rest of your weekend."

Later that day, Jaz surprised her parents by accepting their dinner invitation on Sunday.

"It was great, Millie," Jaz said as she removed the dishes. "I thought Kyle might be here today." She tried to sound casual.

"Kyle doesn't hang out with us old folks any more than you do. On a day like today you'll find him on his boat," Hep said. "Did you know that they didn't know each other before yesterday?"

"Yes, dear, you told me," Lorette drawled.

"I guess I had him traveling more than I realized."

"Told you so. Kyle is a sweetie." Lorette sipped her coffee.

"Why did I think Kyle was an old white man who managed your assets before you went to Italy?"

"You're on your own with that one," Hep dodged.

"You know who she means, Hep?" Lorette said, "Tippy . . . Kylerton. He ran things while we were in Italy. He is old and white, and retired when we came back."

"Oh no. I met Kyle Jagger at an antique car show in Scottsdale, Arizona. Then I saw him in Cannes, lured him away from a New York firm with big bucks and complete autonomy. Comes from a good family with solid values, morals, and pride. Jeremiah Jagger, a Texan, moved his family to Chicago in the 1900s and started The Negro Voice, which became The Negro Gazette in the twenties. His son, Buck, Kyle's father, parlayed it into the highly successful, nationally distributed Chicago Journal, the only black-owned paper of its status in the United States."

"His mother, Dallas, is the most genuine woman. You'd never suspect she grew up filthy rich," Lorette said.

"Her daddy was a Texas wildcatter who struck it rich before the federal regulations," said Hep.

"And they have the nicest children—"

"Six of them, two boys and four girls," Hep interrupted again. Jaz's head volleyed back and forth between the two old married people who slipped in and out of each other's conversations.

226

"You know them?" Jaz asked.

"Sure, they have a big Texas barbecue every summer at their Winnetka estate outside Chicago."

"All their children are as accomplished as mine," Lorette beamed.

"A great big old house with its own lake where all the kids grew up. Full of pictures, trophies, and awards . . . real homey and strong."

"Sounds like a house I know in Colt, Texas." Jaz smiled. "The kind Grandma Keely created."

"The woman sets the tone of a home. Remember that," Hep instructed.

"Sounds like a Hep-saying to me," Jaz told her mother, and they giggled, just as Akira came in and sat by Jaz's feet.

"Oh, Lawd, am I old enough to create 'sayings' like Papa Colt?" Hep joined in the fun.

Over the next several weeks, staff began noticing the path worn between the offices of Kyle and Jaz. They worked long hours on the New Orleans project, often lunching in, hunched over a drafting table. Hep had been right. Kyle was brilliant, innovative, and knowledgeable about everything from budget considerations to stresses of materials. Despite his proven genius, he was always open to Marc's and Derek's suggestions, accepting the plausible ones, discarding the others after he explained why.

Only Zeke was treated to the after-work conversation, and the nosy, disfigured man strained his one "good" ear to hear the end-of-the-week invites.

"Do you like boating?" Kyle would ask Jaz on a Friday.

"Not especially. Have a good weekend!" Jaz would pop off toward the parking lot.

"Hang in there, Kyle," Zeke said.

"I dunno, man. I ask the lady if she wants to go out for a drink. She doesn't drink. Dinner? She's not hungry. I don't think she's interested in a personal relationship. We get along great in the office, but once I suggest something after five, Boom . . . the shield." Kyle caught himself wondering why he was telling the elevator man.

"She's scared."

"Scared? She doesn't strike me as a lady who's scared of a thing."

"Take it from me. I hear it all in here. You'd be surprised. You gotta slow-walk her. It's that first husband, he still got a hold on her, but she ain't dealing with nobody. Wait till you get her to New Orleans. Nice and easy does it. Have a good weekend," Zeke dismissed him.

"Yeah." Kyle looked at the sad old man. "You too."

The following Friday as they finished up, Kyle mentioned having a brainstorming session aboard his boat. Intentionally, waiting until the last minute so Jaz couldn't make up an excuse; he thought he would make it more comfortable by having her guys out with them, while easing Jaz out of the office setting.

"Sorry, Mel's coming up for the weekend." Her eyes locked with his as she went off to answer her telephone.

He didn't pull rank.

The relationship jelled into a wonderful working one Monday through Friday, but when the sun went down, her defenses went up. Nice and easy does it, Kyle kept singing the jazzy song suggested by Zeke. It hadn't taken Kyle Rawlings Jagger long to decide that Jasmine Bianca Culhane Chandler was the woman for him. He hadn't been so sure about any female since his last year at Princeton. Every time he saw Jaz, his heart went aflutter: a whiff of her perfume as they worked, the way her hair curled around her neck in coppery swirls, the

228

turn of her head when she asked a question, those glasses perched on her nose or worn across her head like a headband. He saw in her qualities that were missing in his other female contenders. Jaz enjoyed her job, but she didn't have the blind ambition of Beverly Nash, for instance. Bev and women like her had something to prove; wanted to "be" somebody. Jaz just was. She possessed a confident sense of being and self. Jaz wanted more than "a career at the top" at the end of her days and had interests beyond working, which he'd seen with her care for Amber and Hud. Being raised not to judge a person's choices unless he knew the options from which they had to choose; he didn't begrudge Bev Nash's passion. He just wanted more in a partner.

Kyle decided that Jaz was the prize of his life, the reason he hadn't married yet. He'd worked through all the others just to get to Jaz. He decided not only to ride the course out, but to manipulate it. To have her think it was her idea to fall for him. It wasn't going to be easy, but nothing worth having ever was. He visualized them as a couple; the image he wanted and would get. Kyle Rawlings Jagger always got what he went after.

~*~

The cousins found themselves in Colt, Texas for a holiday again. Now, thanks to their grandfather, Cully'd joined Hud at the same private school though they didn't live in close proximity. Initially, Hud was happy to have a "brother" especially after he learned the birth of a sister was eminent. The first visit to Colt, Texas, Hud liked the idea of having a long-lost cousin and being the one to squire Cully around to meet all of Hud's old friends. He'd been coming to Colt, Texas since he was small. This guy, brand new. Still Hud understood. Or so he thought. Back then, they both lived in LA, different

229

neighborhoods and schools and no shared activities. It required too much coordination between the "star" Mel and LeLani, the working mother.

At the end of that initial first week of the very first visit, Cully had gotten used to the pitiful-bunch of Colt, Texas adults with their leaky eyes and sad smiles. Colt, Texas was not Hawaii. But Cully visited his father's grave, heard stories about him and his exploits, had seen his pictures, the organ he played in Mt. Moriah, and the swimming hole was no comparison with the surf of the Pacific Ocean, but he continued to ride his horses which he loved almost as much as flying in the plane to get here. After the second week, the adults began to perk up and he really liked his Great-Grandma Keely, the mercurial Aunt Star was a little rough, and hard to figure out but seemed to have a gooey center. Grandma Lorette and Grandpa Hep seemed cool. The third week his mother returned to Hawaii alone as Cully began to like the family and friends he made in Colt, Texas. Neither having siblings, by then, Cully and Hud opted to share Grandpa Hep's and Henley's room and became fast friends.

The second visit at Cherokee Ranch, Hud began to take issue with everyone who liked the newest Culhane but the novelty for Hud was wearing off. He wanted things back to when he was the exotic import for the summer or holidays. Cully tried to introduce the Colt boys to surfing as he rode well, a skill he brought from Hawaii. Hud heard Cully offer to help around the house and listened to his old friends responding to this new cousin in a way Hud did not appreciate. Finally, he asked his grandfather Hep, "When is he going back to Hawaii? "

The question took Hep by surprise.

"He's here all the time. Wherever I go. There he is."

"Well, he visits to be with you and us."

"I see him all the time, now. Here and at home. A guy needs a break."

"You sound like an old man," Hep teased.

"You like him better than me, G'Pa?" he asked Hep.

"Of course not. I love you both." Hep rubbed Hud's head roughly as he always had. "You are both my grandsons." Hep beamed at the mere thought. "You have a lot in common and some things are different. You know your Dad. He didn't know his. Both of you are being raised by wonderful mothers. But you are both Culhane men-in-the-making and I expect you two to look out for one another. Now and always. You can teach him a few things and maybe learn some things from him."

"He's from Hawaii. He ought to go back there."

Hep lovingly put his arm around his grandson, "You've had us for a long time. Since before you were born. Cully is new. We're just trying to make him feel comfortable and loved...the way you have always felt and been. We hope these vacations will happen for you both. "

"Every summer? All summer?" Hud repeated.

Seeing his Aunt Jaz respond the way she did to the new interloper brought all of Hud's old feelings back. Instead of just him and Aunt Jaz, Cully always went along. The three of them practically inseparable.

With apparently no help from the adults, Hud grew consumed with how Cully had taken over his family, his friends, his place and fixated on how he could get rid of him. Hud didn't want to share them. They were his. Had always been. He didn't want Cully to die, just go away.

About 2 a.m., Hud snuck down the steps, stole to the corral, unhitched the gate and slipped back up the steps to bed.

That morning, Star's loud cussing, rampant chaos and the pounding sounds of horses' hooves awakened the quiet household. Having already run through the bunk house, she roused every available rider to help round up the fleeing equines. "The horses got out! Will take the better part of this day and probably the next to round them up." Hep tried to calm her, but she was unapologetic. "Who secured the corral gate last night?" Her eyes volleyed accusingly between the two cousins.

"I did," Cully spoke up.

"No, you didn't," Star spat.

"But I did."

"You sassin' me, boy?"

"No, ma'am."

"Maybe you thought you did, or you did a piss-poor job." Star bucked.

"Now, Star…" Hep began.

"Saddle up. We got horses to catch. A full day's work, maybe two. Shit. If they eat the green hay and bloat they can't work, and we'll lose a whole week. These little bastards let this happen," she fumed, pulling on her gloves as she left the house.

"But I did," Cully pled to Hep.

"We all make mistakes, son," Hep began while Hud watched.

The entire day was spent capturing runaway horses. Out all day, they managed to choke down dinner while preparing for more of the same the next day. Hud sought his G'Pa Hep on the porch swing and asked, "So I guess you'll have to send Cully all the way back to Hawaii."

"Only if he wants to go. I hope he stays."

"But why? He left the corral gate open. That's just sloppy."

"You never made a mistake, Hud? Remember when you let the water run and it flooded the floor in your apartment and the one below? Your mom was none too happy with you."

"Yeah, but that's different."

"Do tell?"

Hud squirmed and Hep knew. "You know there'll be a lot of times we make mistakes. There are really no mistakes. Only lessons from which to learn. So as not to repeat them. There'll be times when we fail... but failure is all part of life. That's how the universe lets you know you're on the wrong path. So you readjust and try again. But lying? Whew. That's about the worst thing you can do. Lie, cheat or steal."

Hud fiddled with his fingers without looking at his grandfather.

"You're not going to get everything you want in this life. That's just the way this life works. But you decide what you want from it and go after it with all your might. But that green-eyed monster can really steer you wrong."

"A green monster?" Hud looked up at his grandfather.

"Jealousy. Makes you do stupid things. You've heard Grandma Keely say, 'What God has for you...He has for you?'"

"Yeah."

"Nobody else. So there is no need to envy anybody anything. You just be the best Hud you can be. No one can do you, any better. You be you and don't worry about other folk unless they do you harm."

They sat in silence for a few minutes while Hep let him soak up his words.

"I'm going to turn in now," Hud announced and stood.

"OK," Hep said. "Can I get a hug?"

Hud leaned in and Hep embraced him. "I love you. Don't ever forget that. I may not like your behavior or your choices ... but never question whether I love you. Continue to make me proud."

After a fitful night's sleep, Hud sought out Aunt Star early the next morning while she swallowed a cup of coffee, and choked back a biscuit and bacon before mounting up again.

"Cully did latch the gate. I unhooked it," he confessed. Star had been warned by her brother that Hud had done something.

"Humm. Was that right?"

"No, ma'am."

"Why'd you do that?" Star asked and Hud hunched in answer. "You plan on doing something like that again?"

No'mam."

"What did you learn from that little episode?"

"That it was a bad thing to do and inconvenienced a lot of people."

"What about the horses."

"It could hurt them too."

"Cost the ranch a lot of time and money. Did you get what you wanted for doing it?"

"No ma'am."

"That was a colossal waste, wasn't it?"

"Yessum."

"God don't like ugly, Hud. Don't let it happen again." She pulled on her gloves. "Mount up."

"Are you going to tell my mother? Can I still come here for the summers?"

"You learned that what you did compromised the operation of this ranch? Your ranch? Your future?"

"Yes."

"You're a Culhane in the making… don't mess it up again."

"No, ma'am."

"You got one more apology to make. To your cousin. You lied on him. That's a cowardly thing to do."

Hud found Cully in the barn and confessed. Cully jumped from his horse and started to punch out his cousin, asking instead, "But why? What did I ever do to you?'

234

"I guess I was jealous because everyone liked you better than me. I wanted you gone so I'd get all the attention again. You know, be top dog again."

"My dad's name was 'TC' which stood for Top Cat. All I know of him is what they tell me and visiting his grave up there. You have a dad. I think you never have to worry about me outdoing you in anything. You already won. You have more people in your life pulling for you. Always will."

"You and your dad have a special bond. I'd rather my dad be dead and gone, than be here and ignore me."

"Don't say that. At least you have a chance of seeing your dad and talking to him."

"He abandoned me years ago. Now he's married and has another family. Another son. You'll never know what it's like to wait for your father to come and pick you up and he never shows." Hud fought back tears. "Or miss your birthday…'cause you don't matter."

"I know what it's like not to have a father at all. To wonder who he was. The sound of his voice. . If you would have gotten along or not. It's a crapshoot for us all. But we can't make it bad for us. You and me. Like G'pa Hep says, we are Culhane men in the making. We have to stick together and be like him. I think he's a good person for us to be like."

"I guess." Hud wiped his nose on his sleeve.

"You guess? He's alive and cares about us. We don't have nobody else."

"I know," Hud relented. "I'm sorry, Cully. Friends?" Hud stuck out his hand.

"Cousins," Cully clarified. "I decided something else."

"What?"

"I'm changing my name to CT. For Culhane Troop. For me and for my dad…TC."

"That's good. I'm already named for my dad. Maybe I'll change it to 'Not-a-asshole.'"

The cousins laughed.

"Let's go, CT."

Hep sank against the doorjamb. Admiring how the two young boys resolved the situation themselves. Maybe this was the beginning of a great union. Maybe not. Hud had a mean streak like his daddy. But Hep felt the spirit of another Culhane... his daddy, Papa Colt. Hep would do all he could to maintain and foster an alliance between them. The sons of a musical genius and a Broadway actor. Even if this relationship were not in the stars, Hep prayed that both of his grandsons would find their own way.

~*~

"What's a bastard?" It'd taken till the next visit before Hud asked his aunt Star.

"Where'd you hear that word?" Star snapped, immediately pissed that anyone used such a disparaging remark on her nephews. She'd whip whomever herself. Having gone through this with her beloved daughter, Keely J when she was small, she wouldn't tolerate such a word now.

"From you."

"Me?" She challenged, eyeing them both.

"You called me and CT 'bastards when the horses got out."

Star pinched the bridge between her eyes. "Well, that was wrong of me. I was upset and I should not have said that. I apologize."

Hud and CT's eyes grew saucer-wide. Never had they heard their Aunt Star take such a conciliatory stance...and apologize. She gathered them both by the scruff of their necks then began to rub them in turn. She stooped to where they were, noticing how much they had grown since their last visit. "You know I

236

love you…both. Like you're my own. Well, hell you are. Oh, sorry. I love you like sons I don't have and sometimes, I may be a little harsh. But you two are Culhanes. And I'm proud of the young men you're growing up to be." Neither could contain their smiles. "Besides, you are *my* little bastards…and I love you." She grabbed them in a hug of three. "Don't let nobody call you out your name. But me." She winked. "That'll be our little secret. Our little joke."

"She never did explain what "bastard" meant," Hud said.

"I guess we ought to look it up," CT suggested.

"I don't much care. I'll take the love," Hud concluded.

Chapter 13

When Kyle combined an on-site inspection review with a Rawlings family reunion down in New Orleans, Jaz scheduled a session with her team at her apartment in San Francisco.

"Well, if we augment this here..." Jaz drew a line on one side as Marc held the blueprint in place. The doorbell rang. Jaz jumped up from the floor, her ponytail swinging in the breeze. "Ahh!" she gasped, seeing Kyle leaning against the woodwork, wearing a short tan leather jacket, a pair of brown slacks with a matching shirt, and his patented smile. "You've canceled your trip?"

"No, the wonderful world of private jetting gets you where you want to go and back in hours. Hope you don't mind." He knew she did.

"Not at all." She opened the door wide and saw the Bugatti parked below. "First time I've seen it without a crowd. What is it again?"

"Bugatti Royale," he said, hanging his jacket on the hall tree next to Qwayz's, not noticing Jaz's horrified expression. "Gentlemen, help has arrived." He slapped his hands eagerly, but Jaz's eyes remained riveted to his jacket hanging next to Qwayz's. She removed it and put it in the closet with the others.

238

She returned to the floor with Marc and the specs. Toward the end, Dory led Kyle through the buffet while Jaz accepted over-the-shoulder compliments. "Dessert time!" Jaz jumped up once the last pencil mark was accurate.

"Reward time!" Derek said, slapping five with Marc.

"That's quite a machine you've got there," Kyle said as Jaz allowed the espresso to flow from its brass recesses.

"Thanks." Jaz tried to ignore the fact that he was there. She hoped to conjure up the camaraderie here that they enjoyed in the office, but it wouldn't translate. Everyone had spread out to enjoy the delectable homemade sweets, and when Jaz didn't see Kyle, she relaxed. Good, he's gone, she thought. Then he emerged from her bedroom, and it rattled her to the core. Get a grip, girlie. He only used the bathroom, she thought.

The younger guys were leaving to go to the Sly and Family Stone concert, and Jaz teased them for not asking her.

"You said you'd never go with us to a concert again," Marc reminded her.

"Except for Earth, Wind & Fire," Derek added.

"You got it. Well, I hope they show," Jaz said. ·

"It's their hometown, they'd better show;" said Marc.

"Good luck. Have fun, guys." Jaz waved them off, returning to face Kyle and Dory. "Well, you two got big plans?" she said brightly.

"May I have another cup of coffee?" Kyle asked, relaxed, crossing his legs. "Do you have any cardamom?"

"Cardamom . . . the spice?"

"Yeah. I picked up the taste for it in Kuwait."

"Make that two, Jaz," Dory said.

"Two cardamom-laced coffees coming up."

"How's your coffee plantation in Kenya doing?" Jaz could hear Dory ask Kyle.

Why not go visit it right now? Jaz thought.

The three chitchatted until Kyle offered to help Jaz clean up, which she declined. He asked if she had any plans this evening. As he could have predicted, she begged off, being tired.

"Maybe some other time." Kyle smiled, reaching for his missing jacket.

"Enjoy your reunion tomorrow." Jaz whipped the jacket out of the closet. "Bye."

"You all right?" Dory asked as Kyle jogged down the steps, aware of the unnerving effect Kyle had on her.

"Sure. Thanks. See you Monday, my friend."

Armed with all the recent information on the New Orleans project, Kyle scheduled a meeting at his house the next weekend, and Jaz could not refuse. She and Dory came together. Dory proved to be a wonderful ally, noting how "the Chief" disturbed her but never said anything about it directly.

Parking in the visitors' lot for Secret Harbor guests, the two traversed a footbridge over a meandering canal full of quacking ducks.

"This is quaint," Jaz said of the section of town she hadn't known existed.

"Built in the twenties by a millionaire who fell in love with Venice, Italy," Dory said as they approached the foliage-hidden homes. "There're only about fifteen houses along here . . . all different."

"I know Kyle doesn't park that Bugatti out there."

"Oh no, he has a two-car garage next to his house, one for it and one for his Ferrari."

"A Ferrari? Figures." As Jaz followed Dory up the winding, flagstone steps, she noticed that the homes were situated on a peninsula, with the canal on one side and the San Francisco Bay on the other.

240

"There's an access road back there for homeowners complete with a guard and gate," Dory told her. "All the residents have boat garages in the bay for their yachts."

Jaz followed the unique walkway past explosions of colorful flowers to a richly-hewn door with a Tiffany inset of colorful, beveled glass. Dory turned the ornate knob, and once inside, she was dwarfed by the cavernous A-frame structure with exposed beams and a mammoth stone fireplace stretching from the floor to the ceiling. Arranged around it were leather sofas, chairs, and smooth slabs of wood nailed together as a table. The floors, with a rug under the conversation area only, buffed to slipperiness. Opposite the fireplace, a twenty-foot African print hung on the wall from the rafters, stopped by another conversation area filled with more leather chairs and divided by a long table, currently laden with all sorts of goodies.

Dory found Kyle in the kitchen and Jaz could see Kyle's sleeves rolled up to the elbow. She walked toward the African print and looked out a set of double French doors that led to a spacious wooden-floored terrace with built-in stone seats. On the other side of the French doors, near the fireplace wall, a built-in étagère housed an elaborate component system and record collection.

"Jazz," she scoffed as she read the titles. "Figures." She read the selections in the Wurlitzer jukebox as well. The doorbell rang and she went to answer the door.

"Hi, Jaz." Kyle's greeting stopped her. "Would you get that for me?" he asked, as easy and unhurried as you please.

"Sure."

The rest of the crew was familiar with their environs, and Jaz watched Derek open cabinets she'd overlooked that hid the bar. "I aspire to be just like Kyle Jagger when I grow up. To live in a million-dollar, one-bedroom lodge with two cars, one boat, and security to keep all you triflin' Negroes out," he said.

As Kyle ushered Marc out of his kitchen, Jaz sauntered through the first set of French doors into Kyle's office—a long, organized space with a desk, matching cabinets, his awards, and a drafting table. Traipsing through the second set of French doors brought her to the terrace, where she couldn't see the bay for the trees, but she could hear the lapping waves and smell the wet saltiness.

Despite its uncomfortable beginning for Jaz, the day proved to be productive and relaxing.

"Jaz, you wanna help me clean up a bit?" Kyle asked casually.

"No, I don't. You asked me just because I'm the only woman here, you chauvinist pig," she kidded him. The guys loved it. "I'm the guest, you're the host."

"Coming here once you're a guest. Next time you're not," Kyle quipped as he brought out the coffee.

"Might I have a little cardamom with that?" she asked as Kyle and Dory laughed.

"Must be an over-thirty joke," Tre' said with a raised eyebrow.

"Watch it. I'm not there yet. Can't speak for these two fossils," Jaz said.

"Since this is your first visit here, you're entitled to the fifty-cent tour." Kyle extended his hand to Jaz, who grew immediately unnerved. "It's not as comfy as yours, but my life hasn't been as full," Kyle said and Jaz stepped into a large comfortable professionally functional kitchen. An eight-burner stove, a double farmhouse sink, two ovens, two dishwashers, stood next to the door leading outside to the deck; a pantry as big as her bedroom, and next to it, a closet full of all sorts of kitchen equipment neatly shelved and ready for use.

"You like to cook?"

"And eat." He smiled, guiding her back into the hallway past the powder room toward his bedroom.

Jaz stepped into the large room with a huge fireplace, and two rocks on its mantel caught her interest.

"Amber?" she asked, picking up the rough rock.

"In its natural ore state," Kyle informed her as she picked up the deep gold transparent rock. "Topaz." He decided not to tell Jaz that Topaz was the pet name he'd given her when he'd seen her about town, before he knew who she was.

"Nice view." Jaz was stopped by the sight of the bay, with boats bobbing in the distance beyond the terrace.

"Would you like to go out and sit?"

"No, the tour."

"Sure. Closets on either side, bathroom through there." He pointed and Jaz tried not to look at the exquisite, four-poster antique Chinese bed.

"Make-out city!" Marc walked in and looked around.

"When you get to be my age, you'll find that quality far exceeds quantity." He spoke directly to Jaz.

"Then I hope I never reach your age, man," Marc joked as they returned to the living room.

"What can we do to entice you to take the Golden Lady out for a quick spin in the bay?" Tre' asked.

"All right, lemme get my jacket and keys."

"Well, I'm off," Jaz announced.

"No ride on the bay?" Kyle's smile slid from his face.

"Not this time, I'm going to L.A. I'll be back in the office by Tuesday."

"You'll be missed." Kyle's easy smile returned.

"I can see why you haven't lost any weight," Jaz teased her friend as she sliced a hunk of cheesecake.

"That is so cold." Denny twirled the knife playfully. "Lloyd likes it."

"That's who counts, girl." As if on cue, Denny's husband, Lloyd, walked in carrying a tired Little Lloyd. "Hey, cutie." Jaz jumped up to hold him, but he shrugged away.

"What's the matter, Champ?" his father asked him. "I'm going to put him to bed, and I'll be right behind him." He kissed his wife, then Jaz. "See you next time, Jaz." Father and son disappeared.

"You done good, Denny. Give him a daughter."

"Not in this life, I'm too old. So what's on your wee little mind?"

"In L.A. Just stopped by to see my old ace boon coon."

"Mm-hmm. Just spit it out, girl. I've known you 'long time.'"

"Okay. There's this guy—"

"Really?"

"It's not what you think, so don't get happy," Jaz warned. "He bothers me."

"What do you mean, 'bothers' you?"

"I mean he gets under my skin." She stabbed the cheesecake with the fork. "He works at CE, my father's right-hand man, and we have to work closely together. We work very well together, actually, he's brilliant and we relate to most things. We have lunch in, usually in my office. We've been out on a couple of dinner meetings with clients. I drove and he drove."

"So what's the problem?"

"He won't stay put." Jaz looked at her friend. "Our relationship is a working one, and he keeps trying to move it to another level. He asks me out for dinner or a concert or a movie or to go out on his boat—"

"So did you put this offensive slime-ball in his place?" Denny asked with a laugh, knowing Jaz wouldn't have any problem telling him where to get off if she so desired.

"He's very nice, gentlemanly. Amber calls him her Prince Charming."

"Amber?"

"We used to see him around Frisco before I knew who he was, and Amber called him her Prince Charming."

"Outta the mouths of babes. So what is it, Jaz?"

"I feel out of control, like I can't keep him where I want him."

"He doesn't sound like a man who lets anyone put limits on him."

"When he came to the session at my house, he put his jacket on the hall tree right next to Qwayz's. I was appalled. And he used my personal bathroom when the powder room was occupied. In there with my toothbrush, soap and my tampons! He was in my bedroom with my private things, commenting on my antiques and—"

"Well, Lloyd, Scoey and AJ use that bathroom all the time."

"Not the same thing," Jaz snapped.

"Do other team members use your 'personal' bath?"

"Yes, but I know them."

And they're no threat, Denny thought, and asked, "Is this guy married?"

"No, no time, with all the traveling he does." Jaz walked to the window.

"So what's wrong, Jaz?"

"Intellectually, I know Qwayz is not coming back to me. The only way he could is if he'd been a POW with years of torture, but emotionally, I haven't let go. I don't think I ever can or will. But if I did, Kyle would be the type I'd think about dating."

And there it was. After all these years, Jaz was letting go. Denny's eyes brimmed with tears of joy she wouldn't let fall. After all these years, Jasmine Bianca Culhane Chandler was moving on, accepting instead of denying, and it warmed her heart. This Kyle guy might not be the one, but he was a start, a rung on the ladder to ultimate happiness, and Denny welcomed him.

"He's not Qwayz," Jaz spoke of the first man who threatened his memory. "Not even close. He eats blood-red meat, can't carry a tune in a bucket, drinks scotch on the rocks, makes his own beer and loves buttermilk, boating, skiing, and jazz."

"Can he dance?" Denny got up to freshen their coffee.

"I dunno. I guess he can waltz."

"Jaz, I was just kidding."

"And he plays tennis," Jaz scoffed.

"Oh the horror!" Denny said sarcastically. "Lloyd plays tennis. He'll have another partner."

"I won't be out of control again."

"You think you were out of control with Qwayz?"

"I think we were both out of control." She smiled.

"You were both young and in love. It was allowed."

"Qwayz was my spirit in the dark. All I wanted was to love and be loved by him, but life beat us up like two doves in a hurricane. I could never be in love like that again. Never."

"You know why? 'Cause you'll never be sixteen or twenty-one again."

"I always had his hand to hold," Jaz whispered, wistfully. "No matter what. Loving Qwayz was transformative. I don't know who, where or what I'd be if it weren't for him loving me so deeply, so completely. I've never felt that way about a man

246

before or since him. Doubt that I ever will again. It's one thing to love and be loved, but to be *understood* is… profound. That man knew me."

Jaz thought of the three men she'd had in her life and what they taught her. From Prince Omar, Jaz learned no matter the stature of a man, if he tells you he and his wife have an understanding …check with the wife for verification first. From Solomon Noble, no matter how tempted, and despite all the positive vibes and connection, don't make him your priority if you are just his backup. Sometimes love is not enough. From Nick Santucci, your pride versus his sensitivity does not equal capitulation. And from Kyle? What would be the lesson? That you can love again.

"I tell you, Denny, the idea of reservations for two scares the shit outta me. I'm not ready for a friendship with a future."

"Take it slow. This will be your first since Qwayz." Again, Jaz thought of Prince Omar, Solomon Noble and Nick, but she had felt in control of those situations. "Go out with Kyle. He might be lame, doofus, or gay. Then you went through all this for nothing." Denny hunched her friend. "It's almost the eighties, you can sleep with men and still be a good girl."

"How do you move on?"

"When you're tired of being abjectly alone and a man walks into your life and you know that you cannot consider your future without him? That's the litmus test."

"Well, I am nowhere near that," Jaz dismissed, swiping another finger-full of cheesecake. "What I wouldn't give to watch Qwayz walk into a room again. He owned that Qwayz athletic swagger-sway." Jaz smiled remembering. "I'll never forget your brother, Denny. Never stop loving him."

"No one's asking you to, sweetie."

Chapter 14

"**M**an, you know this is not my thing." Kyle took his chair under the thatched cabana out of the sun. "If I'm in the sun, I want to be on my boat."

"Bitch, bitch," his cousin and best friend Cass answered, catching sight of a scantily clad beige beauty. "Look, cuz, it's more than your environs. You don't want to be in beautiful St. Jermaine because your mind is elsewhere. Rap to me, brother. Lawd have mercy!" He fanned himself as two plum-hewed natives sashayed by.

"Grow up, Cass."

"And be a stick in the mud like you? No, thanks. I'm young and single and ready to mingle."

"Two out of three ain't bad." Kyle sipped his tropical drink.

"Okay, man, who is she? This babe that's got your nose? I don't remember you being this bad off since Marisa Margeaux at Tulane."

"Ancient history."

"You know she's divorced, no children."

"How nice."

"Who is this lady of yours, man?" Cass watched the familiar smile glide across his cousin's features.

"Let's say, I think you'd approve."

"You in love or what?"

"Yes, I am." He smiled wide enough to wet both ears, and continued, "She turned around and my world spun before I had any idea of who she was. I thought she was a single mother shopping at the Farmer's Market. She makes the whole word sparkle, man. The sun waits for her to get up."

"Aw, man, I'm happy for you." Cass slapped him five, pivoting off to pour a toast of Chivas Regal. "Here's to you and her, man."

"Thanks." The gold liquid slid down his throat easy as you please.

"So when can I meet her?"

"Gotta bide my time. I'm the one with a love jones. I gotta convince her before I speak her name, especially to you."

"Aw, man, I'm the one from New Orleans who should believe in jinxes, haints, voodoo, and shit."

"You'll be the first to find out if it works out."

"And I'll be the first to find out if it doesn't." They chuckled. "You did the right thing, man, waiting till the right one," Cass said, reflecting on his own two failed marriages and two children. The cousins talked until the sun went down and came up again. "Timing is everything, man. Raina and I were too young to get married."

"You're a good daddy, Cass."

"Yeah, meant to be a father but not a husband."

"I think your lifestyle might have something to do with finding a good woman."

"Man, I can't give up my night spots in Houston. Gold mines."

"All depends on what you want, man. I know what I want, and I'm gonna get it. The whole shebang."

"I wish you luck, my brother."

~*~

The CE team's arrival in New Orleans garnered the kind of fanfare usually reserved for Mardi Gras, but that was months off, and the party people wanted an excuse now. The conversion and restoration of the old railway station into a luxury waterfront hotel and shops in the French Quarter had been the commerce and tourism department's coup, and hiring the prestigious Culhane Enterprises reason enough for celebration. The Harbor View ribbon cutting ceremony in the afternoon and gala banquet the same night had been sold out for months, as were all the promotional weekend activities.

The Culhane entourage flew in for the festivities, occupying the three-bedroom suite at the small, elegant Chalfonte, where Kyle joined them. Hep and Lorette's room immediately to the left of the entrance, Jaz's a few steps into the living room on the right, and Kyle's past the fireplace and conversation area in the far left corner.

The mayor of New Orleans, the major financier, Mr. Ribauld, and the Culhanes were the most photographed folks at the afternoon groundbreaking ceremony. Hep and Kyle stood side by side like a pair of black Adonises, looking cool in the sweltering New Orleans heat while Lorette, refined elegance in a coral Yves Saint Laurent suit, and Jaz in an impeccable Gianni alabaster linen suit with embroidered lapels, rounded out the pictures. The crowd cheered as Hep pitched the first shovel of dirt, and again when Lorette cut the red ribbon releasing thousands of colorful balloons into the steamy blue sky.

Having gotten wind of Lorette's heritage, the tabloids almost ignored The Harbor View project as the headlines read: "Return of the Native Daughter." Lorette had graciously accepted the request to be the guest of honor at a luncheon hosted by the Creole Daughters of Fine Lineage.

"Jaz, the invitation includes you," Lorette said.

"Kyle offered to show me around," Jaz countered.

"Sure did," he agreed, trying to hide his surprise.

"Just don't be late for the banquet tonight," Lorette threw over her shoulder as she went to her room to change. "We'll meet here at six."

"I owe you one, Jagger." Jaz stepped out of her heels. "Not since D.C. have I felt hot like this."

"New Orleans hot. I suggest you wear shorts," he said, backing into his room.

"Listen, I was only kidding. I thought I'd just stay in here and cool out until—"

"Uh-uh. You're not making a liar out of me. Get dressed and wear comfortable shoes." He wasn't about to pass up private time with his newest project, slow-walking Jaz Chandler. "That's quite a hat." He joned on her wide straw bowler as they climbed into the air-conditioned cab. With relish, Kyle escorted Jaz around the hallowed halls of Tulane University, his old alma mater and stomping grounds.

"Then you went to Princeton. Impressive for a black guy in the sixties."

"Ain't no thang."

Jaz chuckled at his slang. Despite the Ivy League grooming, Kyle knew who and what he was, where he'd come from and where he was going. She was impressed.

"You know, I'm at a disadvantage." She took off her hat and fanned herself. "You're used to this heat."

"No one gets used to New Orleans hot, you just learn to respect it." They walked by the small shops, hotels, and restaurants of the French Quarter. "This is why Harbor View is going to be so successful. We need a large, first-class luxury hotel. We'll have time to check out all of these," he mused as they passed the quiet jazz clubs, which would be jumping later tonight.

"You know my Aunt Selena started down here at The Onyx, after a short stint at Chez Amour. That's where she met Zack."

"It's a romantic city." Kyle smiled as they crossed over to look at an overgrown, abandoned house.

"Just like in *A Streetcar Named Desire*." Jaz pulled some of the vines off the gate, making space enough to peer inside.

"Suppose the owners just wanted to keep nosy voyeurs out?" Kyle teased.

"No one's lived here for eons. I bet it was something in its day."

They both marveled at the classic French motif. The two-story building with louvered doors on the second floor that opened onto the terraced galleries. Downstairs the French doors stood sentry, just beyond a magnificent stone courtyard complete with fountain, statues, and the remnants of a once manicured garden.

"The people who must have visited this place in the 1800s." Kyle didn't remove his eyes from the structure.

"You think it's that old?"

"Easily. It would make a fine small hotel or restaurant. Look at these gold Js on the gate. That alone cost a fortune in those days. J for Jagger."

"Negro, please. Javier is more likely," Jaz quipped. "Javier. I wonder if this could be my mother's people?"

"Were they rich?"

"Filthy. But my grandfather J's folks cut him off when he married a brown-skinned woman from Tennessee."

"Sounds 'bout right."

"Imagine stumbling over your roots like that?"

"That's the way we have to do it most times. Right now we gotta head back. It's showtime."

Jaz and Kyle returned before Lorette, and Hep was busy on the phone, so Jaz went in to bathe and dress. When she emerged hours later, their restful living room had been converted into a hospitality suite.

As the guests began filing out for the big bash, Jaz fell back. "C'mon, Punkin." Hep stopped to hurry her up.

"Aren't you waiting for Kyle?"

"He's not here, he went on with his aunt, uncle, and cousins."

If Jaz felt self-conscious accompanying her parents to the gala, she felt even more so when all the attention focused upon her. She remained aloof, distantly friendly, shimmering in a halter-topped, chocolate-brown gown that dipped low to the small of her back as the split rose up, treating spectators to an occasional glimpse of a shapely bronze leg.

"Holy moley." Cass slapped Kyle on the arm. "Lookit there. She is one F-I-N-E fox!" Before Cass could finish his comment, Kyle had strutted to her side, much to his cousin's amazement. "Well, excuse the hell outta me!"

"You look like a million bucks," Kyle said, escorting Jaz to her seat.

"I know," she said without looking at him, though she heard him chuckle.

"Won't you save me a dance, Mrs. Chandler?" Kyle inclined his head as he slid the chair up under her perfect derrière.

"I can't make any promises." She tossed her wild coppery mane, which, by design, fell right back over her eye.

The evening progressed nicely, with Kyle paying the right amount of discreet attention to Jaz. When the dancing commenced, Jaz danced first with the mayor and an assortment of his staffers until her father rescued her before Kyle cut in.

"What took you so long, Jagger?"

"I thought I'd give everyone their chance up front, because I don't plan to give you up without a fight." He twirled her around on the dance floor, and Jaz made a mental note to tell Denny that the brother could dance.

"You kids coming back to the hotel now?" Hep asked.

"I thought we'd go on down and catch a few sets. Why don't you two come?" Kyle asked.

"Ah, no," Lorette nixed it.

"The boss has spoken." Hep followed his wife into the sleek black limo.

"You know you have superb bone structure." Kyle fell back as his eyes followed Jaz's bare back down to her waist and back up.

"And you have exquisite taste." She glided ahead of him.

The next morning, when Jaz emerged from her room clad in shorts and a NOLA T shirt, no makeup, her hair combed to one side in a lopsided ponytail, Kyle bellowed, "Oh, Cinderella! What happened?" He was dapper even in casual clothes.

"The ball is over." Jaz reached for juice.

"This is the real Jaz," Hep said. "Not pleasant until noon. In fact, she doesn't usually rise until then. What's the occasion?"

"Gladys Ann is here for a medical conference. I'm meeting her for lunch before she catches a plane back to D.C."

"So you'll be back by, say, three?" Kyle asked. Jaz looked at him as if he were daft and he continued, "I have a surprise for you and your mom. Hep, you're welcome, too. I managed to get keys to the old Javier mansion."

254

"Sorry, but I meet Ribauld at two-thirty." Hep chowed down on a piece of French toast. "Followed by a dinner meeting at seven."

Later that afternoon, Jaz and Lorette followed Kyle as he used a key to open the wrought-iron gates of the mansion. A total surprise to Lorette, it took longer for the significance of the house to register. When it did, her hand flew to her mouth and she approached the inner courtyard, mustering old memories of being here in her father's house years ago when she was just a small child. She looked up at the open galleries, at the faded elegance, perhaps hearing sounds and seeing sights that Kyle and Jaz were not privy to. Remembering her grandmother, the Grand Dame Gabrielle Giselle, talk so despairingly of her father and mother. For his marrying an obviously colored woman of African descent and having many children, accepting only one, Lorette, with the French name and pleasant demeanor. For many years hence, Lorette thought the woman, who wanted her granddaughter to move and live with her in New Orleans, was not only foolish but white. Turned out, she was neither.

As they were leaving the mansion, Lorette thanked Kyle again for bringing her face-to-face with part of her past. "Got rid of some bigoted old ghosts," she told Jaz, looping her hand through Jaz's arm.

The next day, Jaz stood perplexed by the bellmen who loaded her parents' luggage and left hers. Hep explained that he thought she knew she would be staying in New Orleans for the duration of the project.

"That's what it means to have a Culhane contract. Kyle, you didn't tell her?"

"Hey, Hep, I don't make that kind of money."

"But, Dad, I have a few things on my agenda and I'm not prepared for this wardrobe-wise. I still have to go home and pack for—"

"Is it all right if she comes back tomorrow, Kyle?"

"What the hell are you asking him for?"

"It's his baby, Jaz. He's the boss."

"Sure, tomorrow will be fine." Kyle grinned knowingly.

"You already closed up your houses and your Jag is in my garage. You can buy clothes and clear your calendar from here," Hep logically concluded.

"Since you put it that way," Jaz said tightly.

Later, once her parents departed and she remained ensconced, bag and baggage, with Kyle here in New Orleans, she realized the implications of this project. It had been fun and games, flirter and flirtee, but never had she focused on the fact that it would be the two of them alone in a suite for months. Scoey's words came back to haunt her, "Your mouth, Squirt. Always writing checks your body can't cash."

The law of propinquity reigned in full effect as the talented architectural duo spent mornings, noons, and nights in each other's company. Kyle and Jaz accepted but essentially bypassed the offices offered by the mayor, working mostly from the on-site trailer and their three-bedroom suite. They preferred to work hard all day, dine at one of the local cafes in the evening, walk the meal off, and catch a little jazz before heading back to the hotel. It was over those cozy dinners that self-revelations unfolded. Jaz listened as Kyle told the story of his grandparents and parents, of his Tulane college days, Princeton, and the trials and victories of his career in New York before he was lured away by Hep Culhane.

Over the next few weeks, Jaz shared her Watts upbringing, all her friends, Roosevelt High, Berkeley, Paris, Italy, and back again. She spoke easily of Qwayz without realizing it. Kyle, the first male in whom she'd confided, who didn't know her history with her husband, attentively listened. It felt good to sing Qwayz's praises to someone new, like keeping him alive and passing him on.

"Do you think he's coming back?" Kyle asked after one such conversation.

"Yes, I do." It was the first time she'd lied to Kyle, and intentionally lied about Qwayz. She thought the inner turmoil was all over, but the lump of untruth stuck in her throat and she couldn't swallow. Kyle touched her hand reassuringly and suggested they get some air. He didn't press her for conversation as they strolled back to the hotel.

Once they returned to the suite, Kyle asked, "Can I get you anything before I turn in?"

"No thanks."

"Goodnight, then." He went into his room and left Jaz standing by her door like a date without a goodnight kiss. Once inside her room, she realized why she felt so badly. She'd used Qwayz's memory to keep Kyle at a distance, neither of which she wanted to do.

During their subsequent dinners, Kyle enjoyed hearing about Jaz's studies in Italy, while the descriptions of his retreat in Kenya, his coffee plantation and its operation intrigued Jaz. As they sipped cappuccino at the Black Dove, Kyle spoke of the investments Hep had roped him into: an Australian vineyard that they sold for a Hawaiian coffee plantation, and an olive and avocado oil operation in Napa Valley. Kyle had maintained his vanilla and clove farms in Madagascar, oil in Nigeria, cocoa on the Ivory Coast, and ginger in Australia, all lucrative on their own. Jaz mentioned her real estate holdings.

"Lemme guess. The San Francisco apartment you live in, The Cliffs, and the beach house."

Jaz, startled by his referral to Paradise Rock, added, "And those my brother left me."

"I suppose you'll meet my brother sooner or later. I'll be forever grateful to him for going into business with my father at the paper, allowing me to become an architect."

"When did you know that's what you wanted to do?"

"When my grandpa gave me Lincoln logs and an erector set one Christmas, that was all she wrote. I still made excellent grades in English, more for my dad's benefit. Couldn't have the son of the only successful, nationally distributed black daily paper getting Cs. My father worked so hard, he was seldom home before we went to bed and was always gone when we got up in the morning." He twirled the swizzle stick around the ice. "Then when I was about eight, my folks gave up three upstairs bedrooms to create the Great Room, which would double as a den for the family and an office for my dad, so he could always see us when he worked at home. Funny, it takes being a grown man to understand why my father missed all the scout meetings, track meets, and basketball games. Not because he wanted to. Anyway, I followed that work crew around forever, and knew I wanted to build and create spaces for work and leisure."

"You any good at B-ball?"

"One of the best." The easy smile stole across his face.

They walked past small brick houses toward their home away from home.

"You grow up in a big house, Jagger?"

"No. At least it didn't seem big to me at the time. You think that everyone grows up the way you do, regardless. I suppose it would be considered large by some. All of us had our own rooms with adjoining baths, but my mom made it feel cozy.

We're all close." He smiled at her as they reached the suite door. He wasn't used to talking about his growing up... people weren't interested in that. He was constantly dealing with tomorrow.

Over the next month, Jaz watched Kyle's close friends rotate in and out of the suite. His crazy cousin, Cass, and Stovall and his "boys" from college, who, with Kyle, had constituted the "wild bunch" when they partied at Dillard and Xavier, showing out in their crimson and cream. Kyle had met Jaz's aunts and cousins, as well as Sloane and Gladys Ann when they came through for their sorority's Boule.

As the pair drove to his aunt's and uncle's Saturday night house party for Cass's birthday, Jaz felt a little trepidation, which diffused quickly once she was greeted by the family. Kyle set her back by introducing her as "his colleague on the Harbor View project." "Friend" would have described their relationship nicely, but "colleague" suggested she didn't have anything to do, so he brought her along. Jaz didn't relish the "pity" reference but the decadently sinful food, good and fattening, and the room full of old anecdotes, lots of laughter, and music took over, totally relaxing her, until the news of Marisa Margeaux's return demanded an announced quiet. "...Supposed to stop by tonight."

"Who is Marisa?" Jaz asked Genna, Cass's equally crazy sister.

"She and Kyle were an item back when he was at Tulane and she at Dillard. Against her wishes, Kyle took the scholarship to Princeton, and Miss Lady, invited to come along, decided not to, so she stayed back here." Genna spooned more of the luscious reddish-brown gumbo into the serving kettle that Jaz held. "So while he's up there studying, she up and marries a doctor and moves to—guess where?"

"New Jersey?"

"Bingo, girl, Montclair. Kyle pays her no mind, graduates, works in New York, then on to California. Closed chapter. These romantic voodoo who-doo fools should let sleeping dogs lie. My cousin is not interested in and is far too good for her. Ass-backwards, Marisa decides letting Kyle go was her big mistake. Look again, he was the one who did the letting go and the leavin'. The sorry heffa. Now I suppose she thinks her divorced butt is just gonna stroll in and capture his heart again." She replaced the lid. "Nothin' you have to worry about."

"Me?"

"You. My money's on you." Genna winked and carried the steaming delicacy to the waiting guests.

Marisa Margeaux never showed. Jaz didn't ask about her. She wasn't even curious…so she told herself.

Chapter 15

"Hello!" Jaz ran into the suite to catch the telephone. "Hey, Amber." Jaz perched herself on the back of the sofa; Kyle removed his jacket and disappeared into his room. "Of course I'll be there for your dance recital. Wouldn't miss it for the world."

"Is Prince Charming coming?" she asked.

"I don't think so, Amber, and his name is not Prince Charming."

"Is she talking about me?" Kyle asked, reentering the living room.

"Is he there?" Amber asked.

"Yes." Jaz gave Kyle the phone and walked to the bar for bottled water.

"She says she'll see us next Thursday night," Kyle informed as he hung up.

"You're going?"

"Why not? I was invited by the Sun and Rainbow herself." He watched Jaz go into her act. He'd become used to it, whenever he mentioned their being together somewhere outside the New Orleans city limits. "Told her we'd be in early, about four, and maybe we could take her for ice cream—"

"She has parents, you know," Jaz snapped. "I won't be ready to catch the plane that early. I speak at St. Gabriel's of the Sacred Heart Girls School that morning."

"Okay." He came up close to her in a stance she'd never seen him take before. "Tell you what, Jaz. I'll take one plane and you can take another, even though we're going to the same place. I'll take one cab and you take another. Maybe we can trade our seats, so we can sit on opposite sides of the auditorium." He cut his eyes, turned away from her and disappeared into his room, where he remained the night.

The following day Kyle's cordial but curt attitude wasn't much improved. At the end of the workday, Jaz returned to the suite alone, since Kyle had told her to "go on," he'd be busy on the site for a while. So she ordered up room service and settled in to watch *South Pacific* on the smaller set in her room.

Later, Jaz heard Kyle come in and go directly to his room. Shortly thereafter, when the telephone rang, Jaz decided to let Kyle answer it. But he didn't, so she went out into the living room to find his door closed. She picked up. "Hello."

"Kyle Jagger, please," the female voice requested.

"May I ask who's calling?"

"Marisa."

"Hold on." Who does she think she is, Cher? Jaz knocked on the door, then rang up his bathroom extension. "I'm sorry, Marisa, he's not available. Is there a message?"

"Just tell him I called. My number is—" Jaz smiled like a Cheshire cat as she took the number, which meant he didn't already have it.

"All right, I'll see that he gets it." Jaz hung up and taped the message on his door.

262

She'd fallen asleep after the movie, and when she got up to turn the television off, she noticed the telephone light was lit. Opening her door a crack, she checked Kyle's door. The message was gone, and now Jaz was pissed.

The next morning Kyle's attitude was much improved, but by then Tracy had called reporting that Amber and half of Ms. Terrell's dance class had chicken pox, so the show was off.

"Well, how lucky for you," Kyle remarked.

"I'm going up to see her if you can spare me for a couple of days."

"No sweat. Tell her there'll be other Suns and Rainbows." He smiled, and Jaz seethed beneath her facade.

Aunt Jaz flew in to soothe Amber as much as possible, then, with both Bethany and Brittany, sought less baby and more adult conversation, visited Denny, ready to discuss her feelings about Kyle.

"Well now, as the Dragons used to say, 'not gonna give him any grass and gonna tell him where to graze'?" Denny said, and Jaz laughed. "Lemme get this straight, for the record. He hasn't, that is, has *not* made any advances toward you?" Jaz shook her head. "Not a rub of the arm. A kiss on the cheek, a hand slipped around the waist?"

"Nope."

"Well, congratulations, you've gotten just what you wanted from him. A nice working, platonic relationship. That is what you wanted?" Denny's dark ebony eyes pierced Jaz's.

"I'm not sure," Jaz said slowly.

"Well, if you don't know what you want, then how can you go about getting it? It's obvious that if you want the relationship to change, you're gonna have to be the one to make the first move. He's not going to do anything to mess it up. The ball is in your court."

"Enter player number two, Marisa, an old college sweetheart."

"Oooh, the plot thickens. Anything you have to worry about?"

"Probably screwing their brains out in all three bedrooms as we speak."

"First, you have to decide if you want this guy, and then go for it. If it's not too late." Denny watched the panic in Jaz's face. "Well, you said there was this old gal come back."

"I just dunno." Jaz stood and began pacing. "I don't want him right now, maybe later."

"So you're going to be another Marisa? Years later realize that you missed the boat and try to come back to the pier, only to find the ship has sailed."

"I'll decide soon. We're going to the AIA next week. He asked. Let me rephrase that. What he said was 'since we've both got to attend, we might as well go together.'"

"He said it that way because of your ornery attitude." Denny wanted her friend to pursue this man so badly. "The man's no fool."

"Well, if he hasn't announced his engagement when I get back, I'll consider this thing more seriously." The idea of his being engaged to someone else struck her as weird. She didn't see him with anyone else, yet she didn't see herself with him.

"While you're at it," Denny teased., "perhaps tennis lessons are in order."

~*~

Cass and Jaz came into the Chalfonte suite laughing as Kyle rose from the drafting table.

"What have you two been up to?" he asked of his cousin and his colleague.

264

"Jaz is teaching me what classy women want in their men," Cass said, placing some of Jaz's purchases on the sofa.

"Can't teach an old dog new tricks," Kyle said, and Cass barked on cue.

"Dory will be down tomorrow," Kyle told Jaz as she went into her bedroom.

"I like her," Cass said to his cousin quietly. "She's good peeps."

"What you doin' with my woman, huh?" They started sparring like they were kids.

"Okay, boys," Jaz reentered like a scolding mother. "Are we gonna eat?"

"We just ate. Jeez, I'd hate to be the man who feeds you," Cass quipped.

"I feed myself. In fact, I'll feed you both. My treat. Let's move out," Jaz said.

Kyle had tried backing off, distancing himself from her, but when he did that, Cass was flying in routinely to fill the void. He was glad she got along with his friends and their wives, even his cousin Genna, who didn't take a liking to anybody, all of which made his parents curious about Hep and Lorette Culhane's daughter. Kyle reassured them that they were just friends. He wanted their relationship made or broken just between the two of them, not the in- or the out-laws. Knowing what a private person he was, everyone respected his wishes and kept their hopes to themselves, not so much regarding Jaz but anyone. His mother decreed to his father, that "it was time for the boy to settle down and make a family."

Kyle and Jaz flew to San Francisco for the AIA banquet. CE had four tables and received eight of the twenty-six awards; Kyle's Seattle restoration project being the most notable. They danced, went past the Culhanes for the after party celebration, danced and ate some more, before Kyle saw her home.

"I had a really good time. It's good to be back where I can breathe easy." Jaz fished for her house keys.

"New Orleans is not that bad," Kyle defended his second home.

"You wanna come in?" was out before she realized it, an invitation made of wine and good feelings.

"I'd better not." He wanted to, longed for the day when they could go in together, slip off their clothes together, slip underneath the covers together, and stay there until death do them part. "We've got to get back to the real world tomorrow."

"It's really going well."

"We should be finished by January or February, if the weather doesn't hold us up."

"Then we'll be back here for good." Jaz hoped her disappointment didn't register on her face.

"Hey, let's not get maudlin, we got a few more months in Nawlins. See you tomorrow. Need a ride to the plane?" Wanting to kiss her, he backed away.

"Yep. Bye." She wanted to kiss him, just on the cheek like she did AJ, she told herself before admitting, Naw, as they used to say back-in-the-day, I want to bust some slobs.

She watched him drive off and closed her door. Turning to the hall tree, she looked at her fedora hat and buckskin jacket, stroking Qwayz's brown leather bomber and his red baseball cap out of habit.

"You'd like him, Qwayz. You two coulda been friends," she said aloud, leaving her shoes where she'd stepped from them. We did make a striking couple, she thought undressing, washing her face, brushing her teeth, and falling into bed. She reached for the picture of Qwayz and her, kissed him, and decided to let the

266

music box put her to sleep before remembering it was on her desk at CE along with her Hawaiian rock. She sighed and rolled onto her side in the darkness. The phone jangled in the quiet.

"Hello!" She hoped it was Kyle.

"Are you alone? Is he there with you?" Denny whispered into the phone.

"I am all by myself. Thanks for pointing that out."

"Good, gimme the details."

The line was busy, so Kyle returned the phone to its receiver. He'd gotten used to telling Jaz goodnight, but he'd see her in a few hours anyway. He shed the thick, plush-piled paisley robe Jaz had given him as a birthday gift and got into bed wondering who she was talking to this time of morning.

~*~

Back in New Orleans at the Chalfonte suite, Kyle spoke into the telephone. "I'll ask her, Mom." Kyle invited Jaz to Winnetka for Thanksgiving, but he knew better.

"Thank your mother, but I have plans," was her reply.

"You know Moms. No matter how old you are—"

"I got one too."

"I think that's really a nice idea, you all going back to the Evelyn, Tennessee homestead for the holiday."

"I haven't been there since I was a kid. We always went to Colt, Texas, 'cause it was closer and there was more to do... I'm still dropping by to see Hud and CT." She ordered her papers and continued, "Then my maternal grandparents, Javier, died, and my aunt and her husband took over the place. I've only seen my Aunt Coke and Vashti to remember. I can't wait to see my other aunts again, to meet all my cousins." She settled down on the couch to watch an old movie. "In a way, we have you to thank for it. Getting us into that old Javier place started Lorette thinking about lost time. The reunion was her idea."

267

"I couldn't figure out her reaction at the time," Kyle said.

"Well, I'm still naming my daughter after the bigoted old bat, Lorette's grandmere."

"A known racist. Why?"

"I fell in love with the name before I knew anything about the woman. 'A rose by any other name.'"

"Which is?"

"Gabrielle Giselle," Jaz said, and Kyle repeated it.

"It's lyrical. Does your husband have anything to say about this?"

"If I have one, he can name the boy, which will probably be a junior. You guys have no imagination."

Kyle left Jaz watching *Back Street*, mentally retaliating that he had more imagination than she thought. Gabrielle Giselle Jagger sounded almost as good as Mrs. Jasmine Jagger.

As wonderful as the separate Thanksgivings were, the two couldn't wait to get back to the suite at the Chalfonte, with their respective reports on their families. They eagerly fell into their former routines, relishing their time together. Kyle invited Jaz to accompany him and Cass skiing.

"I hate cold weather. Genna and I may go to the Caribbean."

"What? Oh no," he'd answered before realizing.

"It's no different than you and Cass going skiing," she said, surprisingly pleased by his reaction. She and Genna had discussed no such thing.

"We're only going to Gstaad, and may I add that you wear a lotta clothes when you ski."

"Which come off when you dine at the lodge."

"There won't be bikinis."

"How do you know what I wear?"

"I can imagine." He smiled. Then the suite door flew open, with Marc and Derek lugging their own bags.

"Oops, did we interrupt something?"

"No!" Jaz and Kyle answered in unison.

"This place is like Grand Central," Kyle said.

"Too cheap to tip a bellman?" Jaz teased from her desk.

"Speaking of cheap," Kyle began, "only you two are to come up here to this suite. No girls, women, or members of the opposite sex."

"He covered all the bases, didn't he?" Marc asked Derek. "Where to?"

"Straight down the hall," Kyle said.

"Oh, wow! Get a load of this crib!" Derek said loudly.

The following day he greeted Jaz. "For you," Kyle said, handing Jaz a wrapped gift. "Happy birthday."

"Why, thank you." She opened it. "You're early."

"That didn't stop you from opening it." He had thought about replacing the gold star she wore, but learned it was a gift from her husband, which she never removed.

"Earth, Wind & Fire tickets! You do listen. Thank you!" She cheek-kissed and hugged him. "In San Francisco?"

"No problem, you can fly up to catch the concert, then come back."

"Oh no sir, Buster." She leaned over his back to say, "You gave them to me, you take me. Besides, you need the cultural exposure."

"I was afraid of that." He looked at her with a grin.

~*~

They flew up and entered the stadium. Jaz sang along with the group. Kyle awed by the prim, proper professional sophisticate partying hardy with the concert audience. "Ah! I had the best time!" she enthused, skipping with excitement to the car, holding his hand as she would have AJ's or Scoey's. "It was the perfect gift. Have you changed your mind about their talents?"

"I must say I was pleasantly surprised. I like that song about 'needing a woman like the air you breathe,' and the other one, 'making love till you're satisfied.'"

"'Lover's Holiday' and 'I Need You,'" Jaz identified. "You would. Stick with me, Jagger, there's hope for you yet." She stood with the car door between them. "Really. Thank you," she said, their eyes feeding from one another's. At that very moment, if she could spirit them into bed by magic, she would have.

Still wound up, Kyle listened as she spoke of Qwayz and TC's group. "Earth, Wind & Fire remind me of Raw Cilk's instrumental roots...innovative, relevant, and ahead of their time. I'm hungry. You hungry?"

"Hungry?" Kyle said with a chuckle.

"We have time to eat, don't we?"

"Just so we're back in time for our A.M., meeting with Ribauld."

"You're joking, aren't you?" The idea of your place or mine evaporated with the moon. "A Saturday morning meeting? In Nawlins? Surely, you jest."

"Couldn't be helped." He snapped his fingers. "That reminds me. I gotta go past Hep's to pick up something." He U-turned in the middle of the block.

"At this time of night?" She checked her watch. "Good luck, Lorette's been in bed... for hours, and so have Tennyson and Millie. Dad might be working in his downstairs office, but he won't hear the bell."

"I better call." He found a pay phone, used it, and returned. "He says to use your key; he'll put it by the door."

270

They pulled into the circular driveway and Jaz opened the door, feeling around for the light switch. "Surprise!" The lights came on as folks shouted, and in reaction, Jaz slammed the door shut.

"Good reflexes for a thirty-year-old," Kyle teased from behind.

"C'mon, Punkin." Hep reopened the door. "We've seen you now." He pulled his daughter into the house as the group sang "Happy Birthday."

"See, I can keep a secret." Aunt Selena was the first to catch her in a hug.

"I just talked to you!"

"Happy birthday, Jazzy."

Jaz filled with an indescribable sense of joy swelling her heart as all of her friends from various stages of her life gathered to help celebrate this milestone. They mingled in comfortable groups, holding mini-reunions. At one point she looked around and thought, Qwayz would have loved this.

As usual, Selena fiddled on the ivories, and a group of music lovers gathered around her to sing old songs. But when Hep cut up the volume on the oldies tape, the dancing antics started. They formed Madison and stroll lines, and started dancing the pony, hitchhike, monkey, cool jerk, Philly dog, and boogaloo. When Junior Walker's "Road Runner" came on, Jaz and Gladys Ann cut loose like they were teens outside Champion's Studio 3 again.

Jaz, Gladys Ann, Mel, and Selena blew guests away with four-part harmony on a few a cappella songs before Jaz said to her aunt, "C'mon, let's do 'Dr. Feelgood.'"

"You sure?" Selena hedged.

Finishing that song signified the end of the singing. No one could top the aunt/niece rendition of that bluesy, funky finale. Jaz saw Zeke way off in the distance, and she went over to him.

"You're leavin'?"

"Yes, Addie and I are going to lunch tomorrow, so I gotta rest up," Zeke said in his scratchy voice.

"Did you get enough to eat?"

"Aplenty, although there wasn't no bread puddin'," he joked.

"Well, my mother planned this one." Jaz winked. "Wait." She went and cut the first piece of cake for him.

"Oh, Miss Jaz, you didn't have to do that," he said, so touched a tear threatened to fall from his one good eye.

"I never do what I don't want to, Zeke. Your cab is here. Take care," Jaz said as Mel pulled her away.

"She's a fine woman." AJ sidled up to Kyle as they both watched the birthday girl mingle.

"Yes, she is."

"She's very special to all of us," AJ continued as Jaz convulsed with laughter. "We'd hate to see anything or anybody hurt her." AJ's cold stare penetrated Kyle's casual gaze.

"I can understand that, doc." He knew this little punk wasn't threatening him. "I don't think anyone would intentionally hurt her."

"Haven't I seen you someplace before?" AJ couldn't remember where, but thought it had something to do with sports. Basketball maybe.

"Anything's possible," Kyle said, and left to join Jaz.

"Kyle, this is Denny," Jaz introduced him, eager to see what she thought of him.

"Hello, Kyle," Denny said, sticking out her hand for a shake.

"Dr. Denise Winslow."

"Don't believe a word Jaz says about me."

"It's all been good, 'a brilliant psychologist married to a handsome psychiatrist who have one cute little big-head boy.'" They shared a laugh and Jaz relaxed.

The party broke up around four, with the last of the revelers bidding adieu as the sun peeked over the garden wall.

"He really is a Prince Charming," Denny whispered to her friend. "You didn't tell me he was fine, with those cute dimples. From the mouth of babes." As Kyle turned toward her, Denny said, "It was so nice to have met you, Kyle. I hope to see you again soon." She purposely didn't look at Jaz's scolding eyes.

"That was great. Thanks, Dad, Mom." Jaz hugged her parents.

"We had co-conspirators; Kyle was one of them."

"I suppose there's no meeting with Ribauld this morning?" Jaz asked Kyle.

"Would I do that to you on your thirtieth birthday?"

"You know, if you never mention my exact age to me ever again in life, I wouldn't mind."

"Thirty? That was an excellent year, wasn't it, Hep?"

"Too long gone for me to remember," Hep passed.

"How many birthdays since for you, Jagger?"

"A few."

"Oooh! You are old. Here." Jaz handed him an Earth, Wind & Fire tape. "A little positive reinforcement for your ride home… and thanks again."

"My pleasure." A smile split his face. "See ya, Hep."

~*~

"What's this?" Kyle entered the New Orleans suite to find Jaz decorating a small table-top tree.

"Now that my birthday is over, it is officially Christmas. Ta-dah." She turned on the lights.

273

"Nice touch." He placed his briefcase by the drafting table. "The food's all arranged. We better get dressed."

Moments later, Jaz emerged dressed for the Christmas party they were hosting together as Kyle adjusted the music on the stereo. The ebony pair had been on the party circuit as a couple; one was seldom invited without the other, but their friends were never part of that inner circle, so they decided to throw this one for them.

They met in the middle of the room. Kyle bowed and held out his hands for a slow dance to Babyface asking, "Where Will You Go?" and Jaz fit comfortably in his arms. At the song's end, she looked up at him. He brushed a tendril from her face and their lips drew closer.

The door chimed.

"Saved by the bell," Jaz taunted as Kyle went to let in their first guest.

With excesses of food, drink, music and merriment, the party reigned as one of the best. Cass passed out and slept on the couch. In the morning, when Jaz and Kyle each appeared from their separate rooms, Cass sat up puzzled.

"You guys are unreal. Live together and don't ... aren't—"

"Can I drop you somewhere?" Jaz asked, picking up her purse.

"On his head," Kyle suggested.

"Oh, no, please, I've been through enough." Cass massaged his hangover-temples and followed Jaz from the room.

After a grueling day, Jaz relaxed in her comfy sweats, preparing to watch *Pocketful of Miracles* with Chinese take-out, when Kyle bounded in. With a quick "Hey," he disappeared into his bedroom. There were only a couple more social obligations; one was the Grand Ball, then the CE couple was off duty until Mardi Gras time, and perhaps they'd be gone by then. Jaz considered taking the St. Gabriel's church project gratis, since she liked the all-girl parochial school. "Oh God, what did I forget?" Jaz questioned as Kyle emerged from his room tuxed down.

"Relax. It's just me." He inserted a cuff link as the phone rang.

"Your limo is downstairs." Jaz hung up the phone. "Where to?"

"Just a soiree Courtney wanted me to escort her to. I envy you." He almost started to kiss her goodbye, but headed for the door. "Enjoy!"

She threw her moo shu pork across the room as Glenn Ford bought an apple from Bette Davis in front of the swank hotel. She thought of hurling the pancakes and plum sauce, too, but tossed the chopsticks she'd formerly reserved for Kyle instead. So Courtney, the mayor's assistant, asked him to escort her to a soiree! Jaz thought. "So you say thanks, but no thanks. You don't go... you *man*, you!"

Jaz recalled a brief conversation with the woman when she'd asked if Jaz and Kyle were dating. "We're just colleagues," Jaz had answered brusquely, a la Kyle.

"So he's a free agent? Great. 'Cause there are so few good black men around here, you wouldn't believe it," Courtney'd said, and Jaz hadn't thought any more about it until now. I can't win for losing, Jaz thought.

Jaz heard Kyle return to the dark suite at about two. He came to her door and left. The next morning he was up and eating breakfast as usual, sitting next to the Christmas tree.

"Mornin'." He folded the paper and laid it down.

"How was the party?" Jaz poured juice and slathered apricot marmalade onto a waiting croissant.

"Great, it was at the governor's mansion. Made a few new contacts. Everybody asked about you," he offered with that infectious smile.

"You tell them I was partyin' with Bette Davis?"

"Not exactly. Listen, since you won't go to Gstaad with Cass and me and won't invite me to the Caribbean, why don't you consider coming to Kenya when we have a longer break? You'd love it, Jaz. It's as wild, untamed, earthy and natural as you."

"Won't your staff get me mixed up with all your other Afro-American women guests?"

"No." He stood and placed his napkin beside his plate. "You'd be the first." His sincere ebony eyes caused her topaz pools to look away. She didn't mean to always antagonize and push him away, but she always did.

Despite the season, New Orleans still served up hot and humid like a seafood etouffee.

"You ready?" Kyle asked, returning from his room and putting on his suit jacket.

"Yep." Jaz stood, gathering her attaché.

"We're ready for Ribauld in every sense of the word. Madame," he said, holding the door for her. She looked so fresh and professional in her chocolate wrap dress accented by the ecru lapels and matching French cuffs. "We're still on for the Grand Masquerade Ball, aren't we?"

"Yeah. But I'll be coming in from L.A.," she told him, as they waited for the elevator.

"L.A.?"

"Yeah, Amber and I are doing our traditional *Nutcracker* in San Fran. Then I have to take her home."

"That's right. Just don't let all of this running around tire you out," he teased.

276

"Me tired? I'm a nighthawk." Jaz winced as the strong New Orleans sun assaulted her eyes. "It's the mornings I have problems with." Donning her shades, she nodded a greeting to the chauffeur.

"Lemme know if you want tickets to the Dance Theatre of Harlem. My sister dances with them."

"What? Avia and I saw them at the Festival of Two Worlds in Rome in '71, then in Milan in '72. Yes, I want tickets whenever they're within a two-state radius. What else don't I know about you?"

"Plenty." That easy smile spread across his handsome face like a wet spot on a thirsty paper towel.

With Amber safely at home, Jaz found herself in front of Ma Vy's house. The front door wide open with the screen locked, as usual. She could see Qwayz's mom taking down clothes from the line in the back yard. Jaz purposely dropped Amber off, a smart move or the nosy girl would have asked a thousand questions by now. Instead, Jaz savored the quiet and leisure of remembering, alone. She hadn't seen Ma Vy since Denny's wedding when she'd avoided her.

"Jaz?" The woman came to the door where Jaz waited, almost unaware that she had walked up the path and rung the bell. "Jaz," Ma Vy soothed at the sight of her daughter- in-law.

"Hello, Ma Vy. Merry Christmas."

"Come in, child."

Jaz hesitated in the doorway, knowing that to step back into that living room was to step back in time. Seeing the staircase up to the second floor she recalled how Qwayz used to jump the last four steps, to the chagrin of his mother. Jaz imagined his room upstairs, just as he'd left it on his way to Stanford. Full of basketballs, athletic trophies and academic certificates on the wall, next to a blown-up picture of Jaz and Reds, his new car. A

277

cherished varsity jacket of three years, and the All-American one he gave up to wear the brown bomber jacket, which now hung on her hall tree next to his red baseball cap.

"Come, please," Ma Vy repeated with a smile. Jaz sighed loudly.

The place hadn't changed at all: the same furniture, the same impeccable cleanliness and order. Jaz looked at the mantel, seeing again the pictures of all three Chandler children at various stages of development with snaggle-teeth and braids. Jaz looked away, but her gaze was drawn back. Qwayz's trophies from swimming, track, football, and basketball...so many they spilled off the high perch onto the floor around the fireplace. Then there were medals from Vietnam, a replicated dog tag with his name engraved on cheap metal, and a heavy bronze urn. Jaz held on to the mantel for support and cried, as she should have years ago.

"He never did like the idea of being put into the ground." Ma Vy had taken the silent journey with her.

"This is all that's left of him?" Jaz sobbed, and Ma Vy held her. "How can that be? We were so happy. So in love."

"I know, child."

"I still miss him." And her body shook as she wept.

Hours later, Jaz's face, swollen with puffiness from tears, her eyes red, but finally seeing. "I still talk to him, Ma Vy."

"Me too. I talk to father and son—they are together."

They fell into comfortable silence.

"He is never coming back to me; and I'm so tired of being alone and lonely. I want to be somebody's somebody again. But I can't move on."

"You must."

"I just can't."

278

"Who is holding you back? Certainly not Qwayz. If he were here, just for a split second, what would he tell you? Not to keep on as you have, Jaz. He loved you and he would want you happy, not sad."

"But you didn't, Ma Vy."

"And now I am alone." She stroked the girl's brow. "I had children, which was my gift, and now I have a grandson. And Hanie is now pregnant even though still living with her husband in London." Ma Vy shrugged her shoulders. "But there is still time for you, Jasmine, and for the children you have to bear. No one can say you didn't grieve for my son. It's been ten years. It's time, just like I told Denny when it was time. Profit from my mistakes. He was my only son, who is gone now, but you are here."

During the return flight to New Orleans, Jaz recognized that it may have been ten years since Qwayz's death, but it had only been months since she'd finally accepted it. Ma Vy was right. As the plane banked and landed, Jaz thought, but the realization was a far cry from the action.

~*~

The Governor's Grand Ball evoked all the high drama and theatrics of a Hollywood premiere. An ebony couple stood in the center of the action: a handsome man in exquisite tails and a dashing red tie, cummerbund, and boutonniere. The woman, a symphony in a dripping-gold ball gown, plucked from an Italian opera.

"You better give that dress back to Deborah Kerr in *The King and I*," Cass joned.

"Don't tease her, she feels like Scarlett O'Hara as it is," Kyle warned him.

"Well, it is the south," Cass conceded, winking at Jaz. "But you outdo them all. Belle of the Ball."

"Who let you in here?" Kyle joked.

"I just told them I was a friend of Jaz's. In like Flynn." He snapped his fingers. "Shall we dance?" He crooked his arm, Jaz took it, and they waltzed on the huge dance floor, ignoring the swooshing of hooped gowns fighting for territory.

"You know my cousin's in love," Cass tested her, during a turn.

"Is that right?" Jaz didn't want to know "who with," in case it wasn't her, and she didn't want it to be her...not yet. She wasn't ready for him. She wanted to try her shaky freedom out on a couple of guys first, and then come back and marry Kyle, after all her excess baggage had been launched overboard. He deserved that.

"Aren't you curious?" Cass pressed.

"Nope."

"Speak of the devil." Cass allowed Kyle to cut in.

"What's he jawjackin' about?"

"Nothing special. You know Cass."

"He really likes you."

"Am I breathing?" Jaz said, insinuating Cass's only requisite for females.

"He's not that bad. Just a little scared."

Aren't we all, Jaz wanted to say, but asked instead, "Of another failed marriage? It takes two to tango."

"He's still in love with Raina, his first wife." Kyle double-spun her. "Some people don't know what they have until it's gone."

The Ball ended followed by powdered beignets from Café Dumont and piping hot coffee. Night-folks lingered until the bitter end until finally at four, the guests dispersed.

"That was a wonderful Grand Ball!" Jaz whirled around the suite, kicking off her gold-sequined shoes. "I could have danced all night." She flipped on the stereo, switching the dial from his jazz to her soul station.

"You did." Kyle removed his tails, loosened his tie, stoked the fire the hotel built on winter weekends, and plopped on the sofa to watch Jaz sway to the mellow sounds.

He loved her in those slinky, knock-out gowns that invited attention but denied access. The ones with high slits and backless halters, spun from fine fabrics. But in this Cinderella extravaganza, she looked magical. The gigantic puffed sleeves decorated with gold braid that resembled beveled glass. The same braid bordered the plunging sweetheart neckline, challenging the right side of propriety. She was gorgeous.

"C'mon, Jagger." Jaz pulled him up from the couch. "You're not that old. Let's see if you've perfected the D.C. bop yet. I love this tempo. You know I was quite a party animal in my day." He whirled her around. "Very good."

"You're a good teacher." He held her close, his hands on her back, before releasing her for another volley of fancy footwork. Then they were groin-close again.

Jaz held her breath at the nearness of him, her champagne buzz evaporating as his hand ever-so- gently caressed her bare skin. This wasn't the governor's ball. This was one-on-one in a top floor hotel suite, dancing in a fire's glow. He spun her twice in a row and her head reeled and though it was a mid-tempo song, Jaz felt swept away as they touched cheek to cheek, heartbeat to heartbeat, the intermittent rustle of her gown masking her breathlessness. Kyle's dip coincided with the final note of the song and the last bobby pins fell from her French roll. As he pulled Jaz back up to him, her hair fell wildly about her shoulders.

Jaz wanted to say something flippant and witty, but the words stuck in her throat, and her eyes couldn't bear to pull away from his. She melted into Kyle's body as his arms encircled her even tighter, his lips brushed the side of her cheek, and the DJ from heaven spun right into the next slow jam.

Jaz just knew she'd stopped breathing and only the sight of Kyle sustained her in this world. The warm, sweet wind from his parted lips landed on her own, but she turned hers in upon themselves like a child resisting spoonfuls of cod liver oil. Then Earth, Wind & Fire sang "I Need You" from the concert, and Jaz's lips sprang loose like the tight blossoms of some deprived plant responding to the sun: opening and ready to accept the rain. And finally, Kyle Jagger and Jasmine Chandler kissed.

Still locked in an embrace, Jaz attempted to unfasten the zipper of her ball gown, but Kyle stopped her, his eyes questioning her readiness. She reassured him with a kiss, and began unbuttoning his tux shirt while he unzipped and peeled the gold fabric from her body.

Her fairytale ball gown collapsed to the middle of the floor and Jaz's breasts bloomed in their freedom then grew taut with desire. Kyle rolled her hot pink panties over her flat abdomen down to her feet, and scooped her up in his arms to lie her on the sofa, as the their bodies basked in the glow of the fireplace. Jaz fingered his chest, her eyes exploring the wonders of his lean body and his projectile just within her reach. He leaned over her, kissing, prolonging the delicious inevitability of events.

Jaz awakened in Kyle's bed, not knowing when they'd moved from the couch, but remembering every spectacular movement. She felt energized and alive again… all silly and giddy.

"Good morning." His stretch included her in an embrace.

"Morning." She smile-smirked as she watched his nature rise with its own greeting.

"What's say we freshen up and I meet you back here in ten minutes?"

282

"Sounds like heaven to me."

They did, making love more deliberately but just as satisfyingly. "Ah, Topaz, you are—"

"Topaz!" Jaz shot up and was out of bed with a robe like a bullet. "Who the hell is Topaz?"

"Oh, Jaz, lemme explain—"

"There's nothing to explain." She gathered her earrings. "You're a free agent, neither of us are kids. You have your—"

"Jaz." He surprised her by grabbing her wrists.

"Let go of me!" She jerked away.

"*You* are Topaz."

"Nice try, but I'm from Watts. You can't pull that BS on me."

"Jaz, you are Topaz. That's what I called you when I thought you were Amber's mother. Get it? Amber, Topaz… your eyes. I had to call you something. You kept creeping into my dreams." He watched her eyes zero in on him as if she could tell if he was lying just by looking at him. "Remember the two mineral chunks on my bedroom mantel? You and Amber." Confident he'd calmed her down, he climbed back into bed. "You'll never guess who I thought your husband was."

"Who?" She wanted to believe him, had to believe him because if she didn't, she would have been totally wrong about him. She would have to concede that everything she previously thought she knew of him was completely incorrect. Then where would they be? Where would she be?

"AJ. I see this pretty little girl with a woman she tells me is her mom. Then I ask her about her father, and she says you two are 'waiting for him to come back.' Then I see you three at the ballet and in the park flying kites, and I figure, Dad's back." Jaz, giggling down deep in her stomach, began climbing toward him from the foot of the bed like a cat on all fours. He tackled her and playfully pinned her down. "We're gonna have to talk to that girl about her imagination." He kissed her.

"Oh, I dunno." She kissed him back. "She was right about you, Prince Charming."

"Ah, Topi—my variation on Topaz," he explained hastily, and they made love all over again. Prince Charming and Topi.

Chapter 16

The couple enjoyed two more uninterrupted days of glorious lovemaking in the third-floor suite before they went their separate ways. Despite Kyle's plea that Jaz join him for his mother's famous meatball chili with dumplings, a Jagger Christmas and skiing in Gstaad, she stuck to her usual California plans.

"You have your obligations and I have mine," Jaz said.

"You don't want to go public with this just yet?"

Jaz remained amazed and relieved by his refreshing directness and continuous honesty.

"Yeah, it's been a while for me, and well, I haven't even gotten used to it."

"I have, but I respect what you're going through."

Jaz pirouetted through her usual Christmas visits and rituals in San Francisco, Colt, Texas and L.A. These festivities, formerly so satisfying, were now lacking. They were Kyle-less, though the smell, sight, and sound of him accompanied her everywhere. Although he called her from the Jagger estate and Gstaad, it wasn't the same as seeing him daily, sharing events at day's end, or lounging lazily in bed in fluffy robes with the paper and a breakfast tray on a Sunday morning.

Kyle had snuck up on her, whisking her away to a new horizon. Only in retrospect and away from him, had Jaz convinced herself she was in complete control of the situation. But her inner voice laughed and told her she was kidding herself; she was already in too deep to pull out.

In L.A., Denny noticed Jaz's preoccupation, and in San Francisco at her parents' annual New Year's Eve party, Selena, while tickling the ivories as the guests sang, caught a glimpse of her thoughtful niece. Denny and Selena both inquired regarding Jaz's pensive mood. Jaz feigned innocence and thought, just one more stop, back down to see Hud, Mel and Lee Harker's new baby girl and CT who was staying there, before she could get back to New Orleans and Kyle. She could hardly wait.

"Hello, handsome." Jaz entered the Chalfonte suite and hurried to him.

"Hello, Auntie Jaz." Kyle put down his papers in time to accept her embrace. "Why didn't you call and lemme know you were coming? I'd have sent a car. I missed you."

"Me too." She returned the kiss before he swirled her around.

"How are mother, baby, daddy and Hud?"

"All are fine. They loved your flowers, but the diaper service was really a big hit with Mel. How'd you get so smart?"

"I have sisters, remember?"

"Ah yes." She bent her head way back so he could kiss her neck. "Keep going," she moaned.

Their relationship flourished. Kyle brought music back into her dreary life. After Qwayz, Jaz had shunned listening to the radio; new songs of longing made her feel empty, old songs made her cry. With Kyle, she danced and sang again. Now she could listen to old Raw Cilk songs without turning the station. She could remember the day and what they did before and after recording, and smile. Kyle was almost everything Qwayz wasn't. Obvious differences in personality and demeanor, musical ability and taste, and packaging, yet there were similarities; both possessing an understated confidence and a coolness, an intelligence, pride, and honesty. True, she didn't know how Qwayz would have been at thirty-something or how Kyle was at twenty, but Kyle's slow, deliberate speech was as much of a turn-on as his full, parenthetical smile. She never compared Kyle to Qwayz the way she had Prince Omar, Solomon Noble and Nick. As she snuggled beneath their chins and slowly looked up into their eyes, she'd always hoped one day, if only for a moment, hazel eyes would penetrate her honey. Just once again. But Kyle stood on his own. She didn't know why, but she didn't feel as if she were cheating on Qwayz with Kyle.

Finally, The Grand Opening of Harbor View was an affaire finis and celebrated in magnificent style.

"That went well," Jaz said, reentering the suite and dropping her purse on the table as Kyle stole a kiss. "Kyle!" Jaz reprimanded him, eyeing the door waiting for her parents to return from the festivities.

"We're not teenagers. Meet me in my room after they go to bed."

"No way."

"Okay. The Rousseau served us well the last time they were here."

The small, boutique Rousseau Hotel served them well again, until Hep and Lorette left, freeing them to roam the Chalfonte suite anew.

"It feels strange making love in the bed my parents did," Jaz mused as Kyle went for clean champagne flutes.

"You so sure they did?" Kyle jumped back in.

"I know my daddy." She licked her lips at the sight of chocolate-covered strawberries.

"Think we'll be like that?" Kyle held a succulent red ball above her mouth before he let her devour it, then licked the chocolate from her lips.

"Humm, just as good as the berry," Jaz moaned. "I bet the maid service thinks we're demented, hopping from bed to bed."

"They're paid well. Besides, we'll be gone in a couple of weeks." Kyle settled back on the mountains of pillows as Jaz joined him. "I was thinking, why don't we do something super special for Valentine's Day? We can go to someplace close. Acapulco or the Caribbean. Your choice."

Jaz soberly sat up in bed. "No, I have something else to do."

"What?" Kyle sat up with her. He knew her schedule as well as she knew his.

"I can't do anything on the fourteenth," she said, climbing out of bed.

"Jaz?" Kyle grabbed her arm. "What is it?" He walked her around to his side of the bed. "Ah! Your anniversary, no problem, we can do it later. It's OK."

"Okay." She resumed lying on his chest, overwhelmed by his understanding and not having to explain.

"We're still on for Mardi Gras, right?"

"Right." She accepted his kiss on her forehead. As she drifted off to sleep, she thought it appropriate that the decadent carnival observance would mark the end of their New Orleans closeness. She missed him already.

~*~

Kyle turned to his panoramic view of San Francisco, trying to find the answer to Jaz's abrupt change of temperament in its skyline. They'd returned from New Orleans three weeks ago, and she offered him only vagueness, indifference, and preoccupation. They hadn't dined together for lunch or dinner, and hadn't made love. His mind, body, and soul ached for the nearness of her, but he was left famished.

On one weekend, she was off to AJ and Avia's, the next, flying down in Hep's sleek new Harker 800 to see Amber in a recital. He wondered what she'd let come between them this weekend. She informed him of her activities as if he was her secretary, not the man who'd become her lover. He swiveled around with a sigh just as Maxine came into the office with finished contracts.

"Thanks, Maxi." He hoped everything between them would be straightened out next week, when they were flying to Hawaii for the botanical garden project. It was the reason he'd been so patient.

"Hep wants to see you," Maxine said.

"Thanks." Kyle used the private passage linking the two offices. "Yeah, Hep."

"Ready for Hawaii, my tireless wonder?" Hep asked, slapping him on the back. "New Orleans was a charm."

"That it was." Kyle's grin spread for different reasons. "But I'm looking forward to this smaller project." In a romantic setting with Jaz and the islands all to ourselves went unsaid. "I think Jaz is too."

"Jaz isn't going. She's taking a hospital project in San Diego. She wants to work solo," Hep said as Kyle disappeared.

The words "Jaz isn't going" rang in his ears as Kyle strode down the hall and into her office.

He barged in on her team's meeting. "Jaz, we have to talk." He leaned directly over her, as everyone looked up, surprised at the usually super-cool Kyle.

"I'm in the middle of a meeting," Jaz stated the obvious.

"You'll excuse us, won't you, gentlemen?" Kyle's knuckles never left the mahogany of her desk as he turned his steely cold ebony eyes upon each of them. "Close the door behind you, Marc, thanks," he directed, and they filed out without comment. As soon as the door closed, Kyle whirled back to Jaz, who sprang into action.

"I don't appreciate your coming in here, disrupting my meeting and dismissing my team—"

"Best defense is an offense," Kyle said. "I don't appreciate the runaround and cold shoulder you've given me since we got back from New Orleans." He continued in that killer low voice she had to strain to hear. "I don't appreciate spending my days and nights alone when I'm used to having you with me. I don't appreciate an empty bed." Jaz jumped up from her desk and turned toward her view of the city, folding her arms across her chest. "Jaz," he said, softly, moving his body, between her and the view. "I know we had something special all those months in New Orleans. We come back here and I'm cut off at the knees. I miss the you I knew there. I want to know why it went away, and I want it back."

Jaz couldn't get herself to speak, so she just shook her head, only fueling Kyle's press.

"I know for some insane reason you think this is for the best, but it isn't. Only the lucky ones find what we have… again. We can't throw it away because we came back to a place and people who knew you as a married woman. They'll get used to the idea; you did."

290

"No!" Her feelings found voice. "I thought about it and I decided."

"'I?' Excuse me, but there are two of us in this relationship, which means some discussion—"

"No. It's over. It was great while it lasted—"

"Hold up. You've been looking at too many old movies. This was not something to occupy my time while I was in New Orleans. I could've had that with Marisa, Courtney, or any number of women." He held her by the shoulders to get her to listen. "This was something deeper, stronger, and far more lasting then just a roll in the hay."

"I'm sorry." She broke away. "But that's all it was for me, okay?"

"You're a liar."

"You men. Just can't believe a girl can have a purely physical relationship with a guy."

"Oh, I can believe it, but not of you. Casual sex? Naw. No way." He stalked her move for move. "I know you're anxious, scared of commitment—"

"Ah! Dr. Jagger!" Jaz threw up her hands. "I've heard the 'you're scared' routine before."

"You're scared that I'm gonna do the same thing Qwayz did."

Her head jerked at yet another man daring to speak his name.

"You're afraid that you'll love me, and I'll abandon you like he did."

"Now wait just a damn minute!"

"You're afraid that somewhere down the line I'll leave you for some noble cause."

"You are way out of line!" Jaz shrieked against his calm, slamming things into her attaché case. "You have no right to discuss him and me."

"I have every right. I'm here and I'm staying. I'm in love with you. I want to marry you, and I'm tired of seeing your life wasted on a ghost."

"Damn you to hell! Let go of me."

"He's dead, Jaz, and he's not coming back. Let go of him. Let go." He spoke in soothing mantra-like tones. "He chose his relationship with your brother over you.

But he wouldn't want—"

"Don't even pretend to know him or what he would want." She grew as eerily calm as he. "You shouldn't be allowed to speak his name."

"I promise I won't leave you, Jaz."

"Yeah, well, so did he." Jaz ran tearfully down the hall, pressing the elevator button a zillion times before Zeke opened the door. "Close it!" she ordered, just as Kyle reached the shaft. "Down!" Jaz spat when she realized that Zeke had closed the doors, but hadn't put the elevator into motion.

"Is that a commentary on your life?"

"Mind your own damn business!" She collapsed onto the bench, fishing for her sunglasses, car keys, and a tissue.

"Yes, Miss Jaz."

"Don't call me Miss Jaz."

"I don't think you should drive, Miss—" Zeke caught himself, but not her before she was through the garage doors and in her Jag burning rubber out of the lot.

Jaz yanked a tissue from its box, the tears flying as fast as the car was going, her hair trailing in the wind. Inside, she wailed aloud like a wounded animal, talking to herself, wavering between trying to calm herself down and inciting herself up. For the first time she admitted that she was mad at Qwayz for making a decision to leave her, and then for not coming back; a promise broken.

292

"Damn you, Qwayz, for leaving me!" she screamed within the confines of the car. Mad at a dead man and scared to try again…to open herself up for hurt again. To love and be loved copiously and be left again.

Then her anger turned on the man who brought it to the forefront, who had the guts and caring enough to risk it all to heal her. To force her to come to grips with the total reality of the situation. Qwayz chose his relationship with TC over her…to avenge his buddy's death, and in so doing, caused his own. Stupid. Stupid man. She choked on her own tears.

"Kyle." She banged on the steering wheel. "Arrogant SOB. Let go. Let go. I let *you* go." She turned up the volume of the radio and laughed at the irony of vintage Jackie Ross taunting her with "Selfish One."

"Qwayz, Qwayz," she said dreamily. "If only you had come back to me or hadn't gone at all, I wouldn't be in this fix now." She almost missed the turn to Ruidoso Canyon Road. She slammed on the brakes and turned the wheel, and the car skidded out, clinging to the side of the cliff before cutting itself off. Jaz banged her head on the padded steering wheel.

"Aw, damn!" Jaz looked at the blood trickling from her forehead, and sighed. "C'mon, do what you always do," she instructed herself after eliciting only a mocking whine from her car. "Call on your ancestors from the past who know you can handle this and anything else life has to dish out." She rested her head on the backrest and became mesmerized by the ocean. The image of calm and infinity.

She fell asleep until a Ruidoso Canyon cop found her and escorted her to Paradise Rock, where she made Formosa oolong tea, lit a roaring fire, and went to bed.

After a restless night, the brightness of the rising sun and the flickering red light of her answering service woke her. Deleting

Kyle's messages, she called her parents to assure them that she was fine, that she didn't want company, and she'd return to work in a couple of days. Her father didn't mention Kyle, which meant he hadn't said anything to her father.

There at Paradise Rock, Jaz sorted out her emotions. That Qwayz was as irrevocably in love and flawed as she, and his decision forever affected her...them. The dreams they had and future they planned were all lost. Gone forever as was Qwayz. During the course of the next few days of solitude, Jaz forgave him for going and not coming back, and herself for harboring such feelings for so long. She reconciled herself with Qwayz in his absence, and finally Jaz accepted his death on all levels; there was nothing else she could do.

She didn't return any of Kyle's phone calls before he left for Hawaii. Walking the beach of Paradise Rock, she admitted to herself, if to no one else, that she did love Kyle Rawlins Jagger. Denny had been right. When you cannot conceive a life, a future without him in it...you know. Jaz couldn't fathom existing alone. She'd held her breath for a decade waiting for Qwayz, and now, letting him go...so, finally, she could breathe again. By the time she returned to work, Kyle had stopped calling her. When he called Hep, he did not inquire about her.

The following weekend, Jaz treated AJ and Avia to lunch at Gary's Seaside Restaurant in Monterey, telling them about the times she and TC had their May dates there and how she and Qwayz had frequented the popular bistro. Both AJ and Avia silently marveled at Jaz's being able to speak of Qwayz in the past tense at last. Then she led them from the restaurant down Ruidoso Canyon Road to the house perched upon the rock. Jaz watched the couple marvel at the house and the view. AJ spotted the familiar tarp-wrapped red Karmann Ghia in the carport.

294

"Is that...?" A wide smile washed over his face. "I always wondered what happened to the old girl. May I?" AJ untied and whipped off the cover. "The hours I spent in this car. I was small enough to fit back here."

"At one time," Jaz agreed, and Avia let the two venture down memory lane without explaining the details to her. "I want you to have it." Jaz dangled the keys in front of him. "If you promise to take care of her."

"Most definitely, just like I did Akira. Thanks." He hugged his Aunt Jaz. "I'll take her home and polish her." He began removing the car keys from the chain.

"Keep all the keys. This car comes with the carport and the house."

"What house? This? We can't afford this." He gathered Avia in his arms. "Not for a while yet. Maybe never."

"It's a gift. From Qwayz and me to you. I bought it as a welcome-home gift for him." They fell into silence. "This house was built and designed for lovers, and that's what you two are, even if you are married."

"Ah, man, can you believe this!" AJ swung Avia around. "Jaz, are you sure?"

"I am. Qwayz would want you to have her and this house. We called it Paradise Rock, but I'd appreciate it if you'd call it something else."

"Home," Avia said simply.

"I like that." Jaz smiled at the handsome young couple.

Over the next couple of months, Jaz quietly made the transition from Qwayz's wife to widow to single woman, doing so without outside pressure. Completing her hospital project in San Diego, she survived without Kyle's attention. She missed him, hoping that in the interim he was not engaged in another out-of-state project or another relationship. If he was, then

295

perhaps they were not meant to be, but that little reserved piece of her heart had reintegrated with the rest, making him the center of its attraction. When he got back, Jaz decided she would initiate the long-awaited discussion of feelings and future. Jaz had grown up and caught up with the tail end of the seventies, and her perspective was clear.

~*~

Although in town, Kyle didn't join the Culhanes for the Fourth of July celebration on Hep's boat in the bay. Jaz's disappointment continued when Kyle didn't come in to work for several more days during normal working hours. Jaz thought of going to his house but decided she wasn't ready for the possible rejection on his front steps or worse, have her replacement answer the door. At least at work, she could slither down the hallway, close her door, and busy herself.

"Okay, that looks good," Jaz complimented Dory on his work. "The Chancellors are gonna love it. I heard we're talking award time for the Botanical Gardens of Hawaii."

"That was a good project. You know Kyle . . . perfection personified."

Jaz didn't bite. The couple had been the talk of her team since Kyle put them out of her office months ago. "He worked us with a vengeance," Dory continued. "But it's a fantastic piece of real estate now."

"'That's good. Where's he off to next?" Jaz tried sounding nonchalant.

"Not sure. Why not ask him?" Dory smiled. "He's in his office."

"He is?" Panic hit her face as she bit her bottom lip.

"Go on. It's worth a try. All he can do is tell you to get lost."

That's exactly what I'm afraid of, Jaz thought as she smoothed her hair, straightened her hands over her suit skirt, tugged on her jacket and walked down the corridor, musing how Scoey had been right, "Your mouth. Always getting you into trouble."

Jaz knocked and opened the door with the same motion. "Hello, Kyle."

"Jaz." He acknowledged her without getting up, not trusting himself to look at her.

"How was the project?" Ah, yeah! With one glance, Jaz knew she was stone-in-love with this brother. You can play games with your mind when miles separate you, but up close and personal...seeing him... she loved this man. Tennis anyone?

"Almost complete."

"That was fast."

"I had a lot of time on my hands."

"AJ and Avia are expecting."

"That's nice. Listen, I have a lot to catch up on, so if you'll excuse me." He riffled papers, returning to them in a blink.

He didn't want to be cruel, but he wanted it known that his time chasing her was up. His father and grandfather had taught all six of them that if you want something badly, go after it with all your might; give it your best shot, and when the deed is done, good, bad or ugly, rest easy and move on. Know the difference between what can be got and what can't. Know when it's time to give up the reins and try another filly. It'd be a while before he could, but Jaz had let him know the filly wasn't going to be her.

"Fish or cut bait," Jaz whispered one of Papa Colt's sayings to herself. "Kyle Rawlings Jagger, I got some talk for you."

"Listen, Jaz, if this is the speech about how we should be friends for the sake of our professional careers. No. I don't want to do lunch or an occasional dinner meeting. I don't want to work on any joint projects—"

"What do you want?"

"I'm not up for playing games." He looked at her for the first time.

"Neither am I." Their eyes locked. "What do you want?" she repeated. "An open public relationship with a future?"

Kyle reared back in his seat but didn't utter a word. His eyes never left hers as he held an inner conversation with his wants, his needs, and the reality. He wasn't going to be jerked around, especially by someone he loved. The one who put the weak in his knees.

"With whom?"

"With me!"

He stared at her for seemingly an eternity. "Let me get this straight." He got up and rounded his desk toward her. "You are offering me an open, 'normal' exclusive adult relationship?"

"Yeah."

"Why?" A smile began to play at the corners of his luscious lips.

An immediately relieved Jaz began, "Because . . ."

"Because what, Jaz?" He moved within inches of her, looking playfully down at her, egging her on with his eyes.

"Because… " She wanted him to touch her, to hold her, to stroke her. "Because… "

"Good start. Because what?"

"Because… I love you."

"Was that so hard?" He took her in his arms.

"That was physical blackmail."

"I didn't touch you." He kissed her cheek. "I missed you, Topi. Being in a romantic place like that without you. Torture." He kissed her again. "Set a date."

"It just so happens I'm free this evening. We could eat out at The Cliffs, get baked goods from Grimaldi's."

"Cute. I'm talking wedding date."

"What?" Jaz reared back.

"You said a relationship, and I quote, 'with a future.'"

"I didn't mean now… this year."

"Hey, time is of the essence when you fall in love with an old broad like you. Tick, tick."

"That's cold-blooded."

"Why wait? We know we're compatible, we have no money problems, and now we're both in love. Oh. There is one thing we have to get straight up front." He walked her to the couch, and they sat over the lion skin. "If we are to continue to have an honest, trusting relationship, I have to say something about Qwayz."

"I can't let go of him completely."

"No one's asking you to. The love you shared will always be. There's no trading one love for another, Jaz. There will always be a special place for him that no one else can occupy. But because of your love for Qwayz, you can love again. It was never my intention to replace his memory with ours; it cannot be done. To pretend Qwayz never existed is to court misery." He lifted her chin in his hands, so their eyes met.

"I have a big heart, Jaz. Big enough for you, me, and Qwayz 's memory. As long as we can talk about him, he'll never come between us. I choose to make a place for him because I'd be no place without you." He wiped a solitary tear from her cheek. "I love you because you had the capacity to love him so deeply." He hugged her. "But there's something else, Jaz." Kyle stopped and, looking down, began playing with her fingers. "Just recently, I realized that I've met Qwayz."

"When?"

"Remember the hyped Tulane/Stanford game of '66 between Magic and Midas?" Jaz nodded.

"He hated that guy."

"Really. Did he?"

Jaz continued thoughtfully, "Actually, he admired and respected him because he didn't fall for the press's attempt to pit them against each other. 'Two black bucks fighting for the pleasure of massa basketball,'" Jaz quoted and chuckled.

"I'm Midas."

"What?"

"After the game, when Stovall and I walked toward Qwayz, I nodded at him in the lobby. Giving him his props. And saw this beautiful girl beside him. It was you. I guess in a way, I've been looking for you all my life."

"Oh, Kyle."

"Didn't seem fair that he won the game and the girl. Now, I have no more secrets, now you know that Qwayz and I have the same taste in women." He brushed his lips against hers and they kissed.

"You're some piece of work, Jagger. And I do love you."

"So what do you say, do we pick a date?" He pulled her to her feet.

"Isn't the fact that I love you enough?"

"No. I didn't get where I am today by half-steppin'." His deep-dimpled smile claimed

his face.

"What do you mean, 'we,' white man? I thought you said I could pick a date?"

"Nag, nag, nag already. You wanted to pick the date? Pick it." He encircled and hugged her in a slow dance.

"I know you'll be there."

"With bells on." As he bent to kiss her, neither heard Hep walk in, excuse himself, and walk back out.

As Hep retraced his steps back down the hall, he pondered how unusual it was for Kyle to breech his office etiquette. "Jaz is a lucky lady." He stopped abruptly in his tracks. "Jaz?" He catapulted back. "What's going on?"

"You're going to be invited to a wedding as soon as my fiancée picks a date." Kyle beamed.

"Who? Jaz?"

"Yes, Daddy; although I haven't been asked properly yet." Kyle sat her down and sank to one knee.

"Jasmine Bianca Culhane Chandler, would you do me the honor of becoming my wife to love, honor, and—"

"Uh-uh," Jaz nixed the "obey."

"Love and honor... until death us do part?"

"I do."

"I'll be damned." Hep remained flabbergasted. "When did all this happen? How did it? If I'd known, I would have promoted it." The realization began to hit him, and he slapped Kyle's back heartily. "Congratulations! I never thought of you two together. I thought of you as a son. Well, this is downright incestuous! I couldn't be happier. Lemme go call Lorette. Son of a gun."

~*~

The couple lived between his place, Secret Harbor on the Canal, and hers at The Cliffs. Kyle loved to cook and displayed his culinary prowess nightly if he arrived home first. Being exposed to different cuisines all over the world, he developed this passion as the one thing he could do while on travel acquiring, augmenting and discarding recipes as he saw fit. Despite the beauty and newness of The Cliffs, Kyle preferred his own kitchen and he loved cooking for Jaz. He could start a pot of duck and andouille sausage gumbo, leave it to simmering on the stove while they made love and it'd be ready by the time they were. He could whip up his own caramel sauce or hot

301

fudge topping to put over desserts and she couldn't believe the chocolate mousse he made from avocado and garnished with Persian mulberries. The things he could do with Brazino, coulibiac grilled salmon with mint sauce, or osso buco over asparagus risotto or porchetta, the dukkah sauce he paired with mint and poured over broccoli and charred Chinese long beans or the spicy harrisa from Morocco. His replication of piri piri chicken from South Africa, outstanding, as was the lemon curd whipped cream he spooned on a blackberry pavlova. "I am going to weigh a ton," Jaz lamented while scarfing the deliciousness down without shame.

"More of you to love," he quipped. Saturday mornings often found the couple at the local farmer's market shopping for vegetables for him to set to his artistic, edible music. "Besides the fact that there are no preservatives and we eat in season...we'll find inventive ways to work it all off."

When they invited friends to dinner the question was often, "Is Kyle cooking?" Jaz took no offense. He couldn't do bread, so she learned how to whip up and fold tasty and tender naan within minutes. When Amber visited, fresh strawberries was a given over Uncle Kyle's pound cake and homemade whipped cream, and when the boys came, Hud and CT preferred anything Uncle Kyle barbequed on the grill. While watching a movie from the couch, Kyle elevated their snacks not only limited to flavored popcorn but Sichuan chicken or squid, flash fried in a thin cornstarch batter instead of flour for lightness and crunch with an accompanying tahini sauce.

On this night, Kyle prepared a splendid meal of succulent lamb, a prelude to a torrid night of passion to exercise the calories off. Jaz stretched and lazed in bed thinking, finally, a man who lingers and lays with me. Nothing they loved more than to be tangled up with one another with no place to go or nowhere they'd rather be. While Jaz adored the love-making, the ensuing pillow talk was the cherry on top.

"Heaven can't be any better than this," Kyle said as he kissed her nose and handed her cardamom-laced coffee.

"I'm not sure I like this," Jaz stated, accepting the mug next to the tray of homemade macaroons. "Just how many other women have preceded me in this bed of hedonism?" she challenged from a kneeling position.

"No shame in my game. Admittedly, I was an equal opportunity lover in my day," Kyle teased. "Responsibly of course. Before I can be old and wise I gotta be young and crazy. Not too crazy," he added. "I was raised by Dallas Rawlings Jagger who wasn't going to let our lives get too outrageous."

"Of course." Jaz sipped and thought of how she had no intention of disclosing her past…limited as it was. She'd share with her husband on an as-needed basis. When they visited Italy's Lake Como and he wanted to visit the Villa Nubia given to a black beauty from South America by a Saudi Prince; after the affair ended, she gifted it to Como District. Jaz may tell her husband that "I am her." Or on the news, when a certain Saudi Crown Prince visited the White House she'd say, "I did him," like the guys do. Or when Nick Santucci receives another Academy Award nomination for the movie adaption of his novel, Jaz'd reveal that he proposed to her with a blinding, solitaire Tiffany diamond. Or when Solomon Noble becomes the first black president of these United States, she'd divulge, "I could have been first lady, but he messed up." Otherwise, Jaz would leave her past where it belonged. Kyle knew about the most significant love of her life. A woman must have some mystery to her marriage, she chuckled and sipped.

"All those years I searched the whole world over and the love of my life was in the office next door. Besides, it doesn't matter who was here before you. You're here now, to stay forever and ever." He gathered her to him, unfurling the sheets they'd knotted. "If you'd prefer, we could trade this bed for that gorgeous brass bed of yours…and that cappuccino machine."

"Never mind," Jaz vetoed, both slated to join the rest of her life with Qwayz in her parents' attic. "I'll wipe out every memory you ever made here with any other heifer."

"You already have. Before I even knew your name, all I had to do was look at that topaz on my mantel there, and it was you I was with." He kissed her again.

"Negro, puleeze." She resettled on his chest. "I may have been out of circulation for a while, but I'm not fresh from the farm."

"Why is it that when a guy finally finds someone he's committed to for the rest of his natural born days and finally speaks from the heart, his woman never believes him?"

"Oh, I believe you, but I don't believe this is your first time loving—"

"You are the first woman I've loved enough to propose to. I love you with everything I have. Everything I am…"

"I can never hear it enough, Jagger, don't forget that. I don't wanna spend my days remindin' you either."

"You won't have to, I guarantee it." Jaz intertwined her bronze legs with his brown ones.

She played with his long fingers, the same ones that'd just pleasured her in every way imaginable.

"You set a date yet?"

"No. I will. What is the rush?" She sat straight up, her brown nipples as piercing as her eyes.

"There's so much to clear up. Where to live? I suppose between here and The Cliffs until we decide where along the coast we want to live. Then we'll buy the land and build."

"Suppose we find one already built that we can renovate to our liking?"

"Just so it has a fireplace in the bedroom and in the bathroom."

"The bathroom?"

"Right next to the sunken tub with an ocean view. My kids will have close to what I had growing up. Not too big. First things first: When will you make me an honest man? When will you walk down the aisle with me and tell thousands of folks you love me and want me forever?" He turned her over, devouring her with kisses, which tickled her. "You could have this every morning, noon, and night."

"I already do."

"Aww, I make it too easy for you," he lamented playfully.

"I'd marry you in a second if we eloped," Jaz said after a gulp of spicy coffee. "It's so romantic, just the two of us, all alone, private, intimate, maybe a very few close friends."

"Sounds like you've had experience."

"I have, and it's highly recommended."

"Then definitely not. Not for us. I waited too long for this day. It's gonna be my first and last marriage." Jaz looked at him quizzically. "There were two things I envisioned growing up. One was becoming an architect and the other my wedding day."

"Oh Jagger, you would never have made it in Watts."

"Naw, now, you're jumping to conclusions. All men have an idea of how they want their lives to pan out. Mine included a wife and children. I guess I've been looking for you since my senior year in college. I decided that when I found you, I wanted a big wedding with all the trimmings."

"Kyle, I don't want a circus; those marriages are over before the warranties on the gifts run out. And I hate that wedding march. I'm not dressing up in all that fussy, frilly, fru-fru stuff and I won't—"

"Jaz, Jaz," he soothed, holding her close. "How about a nice garden wedding in your folks' side yard around the fountain? You can wear whatever kind or color of dress you want. All I want is to marry you."

"No press or media."

"Not a one."

"They're already having a field day since you gave me the ring. 'Money Begets Money,' 'The Merger of a Lifetime—Jagger and Culhane,' 'The Black Dynasty,' 'Heirs Extraordinaire-Publishing and Building.' It's offensive!"

"No press. Two hundred white lawn chairs arranged in rows, with flowers everywhere. A harpist."

"Harpist? I want my aunt and sister to sing."

"Great." It was the first progress he'd made with her. "One hundred ultra-close family and friends each." He extended his index and thumb at an angle and Jaz followed suit so that their joined fingers formed an open-heart. They giggled at their invention and kissed. "Deal," he concluded. "One hundred… that'll be just my family." He chuckled and then he began to sing "When We Get Married" a la the Intruders and later, Larry Graham. Jaz chimed in. Kyle got out of bed and took Jaz's hand as they sang and D.C. bopped in the nude.

Was his voice improving, Jaz thought and then said, "I don't need a dress." Jaz could barely speak through convulsive laughter. "I'll wear my birthday suit."

"We'll be the talk of the wedding circuit. An original gown!" They laughed at themselves.

"Honeymoon."

"Kyle."

"We're on a roll. Definitely Kenya, the rest of Africa and Europe."

"You've been to Europe a thousand times."

"True, but never with you. I want you to show me your Italy. So what do you say?"

"I say..." Jaz looked at him intently, "that I'm pretty damn lucky."

"I'm the man with the plan." He moved close to her, matching his body parts with hers.

"I'd say you're a man with much more than a plan." Jaz felt his nature rise, and their lovemaking began once again.

~*~

With only six weeks until their wedding day, both Jaz and Kyle tried to clear their desks and calendars to accommodate the one-month Kenyan-Italian honeymoon. Jaz made a call to Glaviano, a designer from her Tawny days, who agreed to make the wedding dress she'd designed; a tea-length peach chiffon with a bugle-beaded drop waist and sheer bodice and fitted sleeves complete with Juliet points. Jaz also commissioned an exquisite matching peach-beaded cap, which would fit snugly on her head with only an opening for her chignon in the back and a short veil over the front.

When Jaz ended her phone call to Glaviano, she grabbed the structure analysis and estimates from her desk and rode down to Finance. Tre' wasn't around, so Jaz left a note. She then pressed the executive elevator button, deciding to wait for Zeke.

"Miss Jaz?" Zeke slid open the elevator door.

"Not for long." Jaz stepped into the tiny hot chamber.

"Marryin' a good man. Couldn't do no better."

"I kinda like him, too. If I died tomorrow, I must say I've loved and been loved by two of the most exceptional black men ever to grace this earth."

"You said a mouthful, Miss Jaz." He opened the door for her.

"What will you call me after I get married?" Jaz paused over the threshold as Zeke thought.

"Mrs. Jaz," he said finally, and they enjoyed a laugh.

"You're wanted in the conference room," Lita said in passing. Jaz checked her watch and opened the door. "Surprise!" yelled Tre', Marc, Derek, Dory, and the rest of the crew.

"Guys," Jaz closed the door behind her, accepting kisses, presents, and a cake that read, "Another One Bites the Dust."

"So romantic."

Everyone lapped up expensive champagne and eats. While Jaz opened her gifts of lingerie, they made wise-cracks about her getting pregnant on the honeymoon and never coming back to work. Her guys' surprise shower had been the first of three; the other two were hosted by Denny and Tracy in L.A. and Lorette in Frisco. The former ambassador's wife, in her world, reveled in planning an "impossibly small" but elegant wedding. TC didn't have one. Mel did her own, so this was the first she'd planned for any of her children.

As Lorette's mind conjured up fantastic images of ideas she could set to money and music, Jaz addressed more realistic concerns... cleaning out her closet at the apartment. Pulling out Qwayz's Air Force trunk, Jaz opened it and the smell of Southeast Asia stung her nostrils. She paused a moment to look at the contents, which he had packed himself before taking that fateful flight; the last things he touched. Over the years, she hadn't disturbed the trunk except to move it from one house to another. She eyed the things she'd placed in there. Bypassing their love tapes and her letters, neatly secured with a red ribbon, she went straight to the Rolex box. She held the watch he never received. "Till the end of time," engraved on the back, shiny and brand new.

She patted her heart as if to quiet it, returned the watch to its box, and reached for the deed to Paradise Rock. She thought how he loved that place and how surprised he would have been when she led him to it. The documents shared an envelope with the tickets to Myrtle Beach, yellowed and unused. "Qwayz, Qwayz, Qwayz," she lamented.

Pictures of them peeked out from under his neatly placed clothes. Of her leaning against his red car when she couldn't have been more than fifteen; of both of them dressed to kill...him in jeans and Chuck Taylors, her in a mini and fringed buckskin jacket. Then with Akira. She in stirrup stretch pants and he in bell-bottoms, and, of course, his everlasting leather bomber jacket.

Jaz wiped away her tears, accepting them as fact, and went to the hall tree. She stared at his red baseball cap with the white S and jacket for a long time before she slipped them from their brass hooks. Hugging, then folding them, she returned to the trunk. She knelt, closed her eyes tightly as she unhooked the gold star her husband had placed around her neck when she was sixteen years old. She held the necklace, the bracelet of interlocking hearts, and her wedding rings in the palm of her hand, looking at them for the last time. When the sight became too painful, she balled up her fist and tears fell upon her closed fingers. She slipped them into the pocket of the leather bomber, and placed the jacket and red baseball cap in the trunk as if it were a grave accepting a long-awaited body. "Goodbye, Qwayz." She closed the lid, locked the lock, and kissed its brass edges. "Loved you then. Love you still. Always have. Always will."

She pushed the trunk as close as she could to the covered wedding portrait, Chesterfield couch, his leather Murphy chair and matching hassock on which they made young, energetic decadent love. Most of the things slated for the Culhane attic. Then she walked to the fireplace, picked up Amber, and strummed it the way he'd taught her to. There was only one place for Amber to go.

~*~

"Jasmine!" The surprised lady backed away from the door to let her in.

"Hello, Ma Vy." She kissed her on the cheek.

"I wasn't expecting to see you for another eight days."

"Then you're coming?"

"I wouldn't miss it for the world. Hanie is flying in from London. I've been waiting for this day for a long time."

"Well, good. I brought something for you." Jaz unstrapped the guitar, which hung over her back, so Ma Vy hadn't seen it until this instant. "There was no place else for it to be but here with you."

"Oh my." Ma Vy began crying. "Those men of mine sure loved this guitar."

"Yeah, they did."

"Got just the place for it." Ma Vy propped it against the fireplace near the picture of Qwayz and his dad.

"Perfect. I don't know why I didn't think of giving it to you before."

"It was where it needed to be. Now you don't need it anymore."

"I dunno 'bout that, Ma Vy."

"Just butterflies."

"I didn't have them with Qwayz."

"You had pimples with Qwayz," she chuckled. "You're braver when you're younger. You don't know no better." She patted Jaz's hand. "That Kyle, he's a good man, Jaz. I like him.

It's clear to see he's crazy about you. All we ever want is for our children to be happy. I think he can make you so."

"He brought music, humor, and happiness back into my life, Ma Vy... I gotta go." Jaz could barely speak as she turned and walked toward the door. "Next time I see you, I'll be marrying somebody else."

"Well, at least I get to go to this one," she said. "I envy you, Jasmine. To start over again. It takes courage and the love of a good man. I think you got both." She patted her cheek. "See you in eight days."

As Jaz drove back to San Francisco she thought of the important men in her life. Papa Colt, her father, her brother, even Scoey, all of whom set the bar high as to how a man was supposed to be. How she was to be treated by a man. Perfect? Not one of them but proud, respectful, honest. And Qwayz. Jaz thought, everything I am was because he loved me.

Chapter 17

Jaz sat at the vanity, staring at, but not seeing, her image in the mirror. Her wedding day had come, her make-up as perfect as her manicure and pedicure, her twisted chignon coiled at the base of her neck, not a wild, loose tendril in sight.

"I wish we had eloped," she said to her mirrored reflection as she sprang from the vanity stool in the room she used at her parents' house. "You're a wreck."

She paced, trying to calm herself.

Why are you so apprehensive? Kyle is a great man from a terrific family. You liked his parents, his brother and his brother's wife, the sisters and their spouses. What is the problem?

She peered out the window at the gathering crowd below. On the front row, an empty space for her parents, then Mel and Lee Harker sat with their daughter, who climbed from one to the other. AJ, Avia, Ma Vy, Melie, Aubrey Sr., a pregnant Hanie and her spouse of three years, the London-based actor with the Jamaican heritage who'd taken Hollywood by storm, comprised the second row.

Jaz sipped lemon water as she eyed the third row comprised of the guys from work, Gladys Ann, Sloane, and their husbands and Scoey looking lost without his wife and daughters... and his boys TC and Qwayz.

Jaz elated that Gladys Ann could come despite her heavy surgical calendar. "Hey, I missed the first one," she'd quipped to Jaz. "You weren't invited to the first one," Jaz teased, and they laughed.

"Jaz! You're not dressed yet?" Denny entered, a whirlwind of activity.

"All I need to do is put on my dress, my cap and step into my shoes."

"Well do it! Do it!" She held the dress over the bride's head. "It's gorgeous." Denny smoothed it down. "You know the trades have guesstimated the price of this Glaviano original at twenty thousand."

"I wish."

"Where's your cap? Oh, Lordy!" Denny ran from the room, returning in seconds with it. "Don't move, you'll get all sweaty!" Then disappeared again.

Jaz looked beyond the eight-foot wall that surrounded the grounds to the arriving limos. A crowd of folks in the street out front, a mixture of press and the fans of Selena and Zack, and of Mel, the Broadway and television star, pregnant again, who had recently given up her hit variety show to stay at home and raise her family. Hired security kept the onlookers at bay, but it was as festive outside the walls as it was elegant inside.

Jaz saw Lloyd, lead Little Lloyd to an aisle seat as Denny rushed in, this time with Tracy.

"You all look really nice." Jaz eyed the pale green attendants' dresses.

"Thank you." Tracy beamed.

"Will you go and get her shoes . . . please?" Denny snapped.

"Okay." Tracy sauntered off.

Sloane slid in for a hug and kiss. "I have a message for you from Solomon. He promised it would not upset you. Only make you laugh. So, he said 'Tell Reese's I hope she will be as happy as I am.'"

Jaz chuckled. "Who'd he marry?"

"I told you he relocated to Chicago and Logan followed."

"Oh right. The Pekinese." They both laughed.

"Well, she got him."

"They are perfectly matched," Jaz decreed. "That's good."

"Sloane!" Denny assaulted.

"I'm gone! See you later when you're Mrs. Jagger. Love you, girl."

"Denny, calm down. I'm the one getting married." With those words out of her mouth, panic set in on the bride. "Oh, Denny... I'm getting married?"

"Shush, shush," Denny calmed, placing the jeweled cap upon her head like a queenly crown. "Oh, Jaz, you are simply breathtaking!" A tear fell from her eye.

"Don't start, Denny, or I'll be forced to join you."

"We can't have that." She blotted her eye carefully. "I'm so happy for you. How do you feel?"

"I'm happy for me, too." They smiled. "I've had fun and good times, but not since your brother have I been lit from within with such indescribable joy. He gives me joy, Denny. Like I thought I'd never feel again."

Tracy poured into the room with Amber, a junior bridesmaid in a muted peach and green floral dress. Hud and CT tuxed out as junior groomsmen. Kyle's niece and nephew; the flower girl and ring bearer, were ushered in by Mrs. Pemberton, the wedding coordinator hired by Lorette, who fluttered about announcing "picture time," and the photographer orchestrated various poses.

"It's time! It's time!" the rotund woman sang as she escorted them to the bottom of the back stairs off the kitchen, setting the pace.

"You okay?" Denny asked before descending the steps.

"I'll be glad when it's over. Where's my father?"

"Here I am, Punkin." Hep wrapped her hand over his arm. "You okay?"

"Yes, jeez . I'm OK. I really hate all this!"

"Uh-oh, that's classic Jaz pissed off." They chuckled. "Punkin, I think you got a good deal. I think you both did."

"Well, I'll give it the old Culhane shot."

"Your grandparents would be proud."

So anxious to meet his bride, Kyle and Cass entered the floral-strewed bridal trellis well before time. Father McCaffery, who had baptized the groom, laughed at his eagerness. They watched as the procession began.

"Finally," Kyle said.

"I've never seen a man so intent to end life as we know it," Cass teased.

"You don't have a woman like Jaz."

"You got me there, brother." They watched as one of the ushers escorted Addie, her husband, and Zeke to seats in the back.

"Oh God, Daddy." Jaz shook as father and daughter stood on the back stoop waiting for their musical cue.

"It's all right, Punkin, I'm here," he said, and stroked her hand. The harpist began her solo.

Jaz stepped onto the ivory carpet that led to the trellis and saw Kyle. Her eyes fastened to her future husband and her lips smiled when she recognized the stringed rendition of "When We Get Married," recalling how they'd danced nude to it and decided to use it instead of that clichéd wedding march.

"I dunno, man," Cass said. "Mixed marriage may not work."

"Wha?" Kyle asked without removing his gaze from the vision of his bride.

"You're jazz and she's strictly rock and roll."

"If that's all we have to deal with, we'll be just fine." Kyle could see that beneath her veil, Jaz was wearing the diamond earrings he'd given her. A mutual compromise when she balked at the nine-carat diamond engagement ring, calling it gaudy and pretentious. So they'd decided on a five-carat, rare pink Australian diamond ring if she'd let him put five on her ears, "two and a half on each precious lobe."

"You'll spoil me."

"That's the plan."

Jaz joined Kyle beneath the perfumed arch, laden with imported Casablanca orchids. The magical trickling from the Italian fountain interrupted by the light laughter of the guests when Jaz anxiously took his hand before being directed to do so. He squeezed and held it firmly, and wrapped in the hush of their moment, they barely took their eyes from one another during the ceremony.

Forced to look at the priest when vows were exchanged, Jaz caught a glimpse of another wedding party behind the clergyman and the trellis, beside the ivory baby grand where Selena sat, and beyond the imported fountain. Wavery, filmy images of her ancestors, on whose shoulders she stood. She couldn't make out the ones in the back, but was sure the dark-purple-blue-black woman was Great-Grandma Saida, who stood next to her son Papa Colt. There were her grandparents Javier, with a tribe of folks of many hues behind them, and TC—all her friends and relatives from the world beyond ventured back to bear witness and show their approval of this happy union.

316

"TC," Jaz whispered as he tipped his porkpie hat, winked and smiled.

"Jaz?" Kyle said gently. She looked at him, not realizing it was time to repeat her vows. She did, and returned her gaze for ancestral approval, but only sunlight shone where they'd been, and a lone, milky…ghostly outline of Qwayz.

"I now pronounce you man and wife. What God has joined together, let no man put asunder. You may kiss the bride."

Kyle slowly lifted the gossamer tulle from Jaz's face, allowing it to fall over her chignon. Taking her chin in his hand, he raised her lips toward him and kissed her tenderly. The guests shrieked.

"I give you Mr. and Mrs. Kyle Rawlings Jagger," the priest said, as doves fluttered amid helium-filled balloons exploding into the heavens and the kids ran around with sparklers.

"This is where our happy ending begins, Jaz," Kyle vowed as if they were the only two people in the universe.

The next few hours, a cacophony of best wishes, congratulations, picture posing, hugs and kisses, champagne toasts, and dancing, with music provided by Aunt Selena's jazz combo. A happy, gracious yet ravenous Jaz held court sneaking sushi or a lobster salad boat or a beggar's pouch filled with succulent pork from any traveling waiter. The Jaggers held on to one another tightly seeing only each other as the Temptations crooned "Night and Day," their last song before being directed to more picture posing.

Finally, the cake was cut, the bouquet thrown, and the bride and groom had transformed from wedding attire into traveling suits. The newlyweds ran full gallop down the circular staircase across the Harlequin tile to the waiting ivory antique car. The license read: TOPI.

"Your first gift from me as Mrs. Kyle Jagger." Kyle kissed Jaz as he opened the door to her ecru Excalibur amid the rice-throwing.

"We decorated the car, Aunt Jaz." Hud Jr. and CT ran up to kiss her goodbye.

"My boys. You did a wonderful job. Thank you."

"Be happy, Jasmine!" Ma Vy elbowed her way to Jaz for an embrace and final kiss.

"Thank you, Ma Vy."

The Jaggers pulled away from jubilant family and close friends into their future.

"Oh, Kyle, it's over." She nestled right up to him.

"Happy?" His dimpled smile was never wider.

"Indescribably. And famished beyond words."

"First stop, a full meal."

"Bless you." She kissed him. "Oh, I have to stop by the office."

"What?"

"C'mon. I have to get something. It's my first marital request."

He pulled onto the plaza as Jaz jumped out and grabbed the first available elevator and zoomed to the thirty-fifth floor. Jaz ran around to her office and seized the music box and the rock, juggling with them before realizing she hadn't brought her purse, so she left the music box and palmed the rock.

"I'll get you later. Goodbye, office! At least for a while!"

When she returned, Zeke awaited her in the executive elevator.

"Sure was some wedding," Zeke said, closing the elevator.

"It was rather nice." Jaz didn't remember his being there. "Why did you leave so early?"

"Ah, I'm not much for crowds. A lot of those children didn't know me."

"Well, I'm glad you came." It was suffocating in the tiny little cubicle, made worse by her lack of eating, the wine bubbling in her head, and the excitement.

"What's that you got in your hand?"

"It's a lucky rock from Hawaii. Good-luck charm... part of my dowry." She chuckled.

"You know, Mrs. Jaz, you and Kyle are special people. He's a good man, didn't just tolerate me, but actually cared about me. One of the few genuine men I've had the pleasure to meet in my long life. You? Well, you take some getting used to." He chuckled and coughed. "I think you two deserve a shot. Got a real good chance of making it."

"Why, thank you, Zeke. I agree."

"So is that rock a wedding gift to your husband?"

"No, not exactly, but I carry it with me all the time."

"Didn't you tell me it was from your first husband?" He slowed up the elevator a bit.

"Did I? It's the last thing he gave to me on a runway in Hawaii." Jaz's breathe grew shallow. "Jeez, it's hot in here."

"Why take it on your honeymoon?"

"Why not?"

"Because you're starting out a new life and there should be nothing between you and Mr. Kyle." He slowed the elevator down even more so it drifted from floor to floor. "If you're not going to tell him about the rock, you shouldn't take it. You startin' off on the wrong foot, with a rock between you that can grow into a mountain."

"Zeke," Jaz began. Weariness, nerves, and a lack of sleep had caught up with the bride, and she felt a weird weightlessness.

Her head began spinning in the heat of the dark chamber, and the smell of liniment only added to her dizziness.

"You can have no hope for the future, if your past keeps crossing it. One foot in yesterday and one in tomorrow is only a half-assed commitment." Jaz had never heard the old man curse before and she looked at him as he went on. "You love that man downstairs waitin' on you, don't you? And it's easy to see how he feels about you. You're starting a new life. Don't carry old baggage."

She felt faint but said, "I don't need a sermon—"

"Listen to me, girl…" The old man had turned toward her, grabbing her about the shoulders. "You're gonna have to let Qwayz go. All of him. He's not coming back, and you can't hold on to him any longer." Jaz stared at Zeke's one good eye, which changed from black to brown to hazel and back to black again.

"He's dead. Bury him and the love you had for him… now. Jaz, let go. Let him go. Let me go, please. You gave me paradise here on earth, but you're making my life in heaven… hell. Qwayz and Jaz? It's over. We are no longer the couple everyone wished they were."

Jaz eyed the old man, upon whose melted face a superimposed chalky, ghostly vision of Qwayz reappeared.

"Qwayz?" Jaz rocked and swayed. She thought she heard the lilt of his voice, his familiar cadence, or was it a carryover of Ma Vy's, Melie's and Hanie's she'd heard only moments before?

"Qwayz is gone forever, Jas-of-mine. Let me go, Jaz, so you can live again, so my heart can rejoice in your happiness and my tired soul can rest in peace. I loved you more than life itself, but we are not together and won't be for all eternity. Go. Be happy. You have my blessing."

Jaz stared at the image on the contorted face. Had Qwayz used Zeke for his blessing and the sign she sought all along? As the elevator reached the ground floor, the vision of him disappeared.

"Goodbye, Qwayz."

Zeke opened the elevator door and a shaft of sunlight lit the eerie chamber. Jaz eyed the grotesque man, not sure of what, if anything, had just occurred.

"Zeke, would you take care of this for me?" She handed him the rock.

"Sure, Mrs. Jaz." He tipped his hat and smiled on the side of his face that could.

"Jaz?" Kyle met her halfway in the open foyer, and they walked off together into the ray of light. Zeke watched them pull away in the new automobile.

"Did you get what you wanted?" Kyle asked, negotiating traffic.

"I decided I didn't need it. I've got everything I'll ever need right here." And she lifted her lips to his as from the radio, Jeffrey Osborne told them they were going all the way.

Chapter 18

As planned, the newlyweds' first stop, Cherokee Ranch to visit Grandma Keely and Aunt Star who couldn't travel to San Francisco. They stayed a couple of days before jetting on to Kenya. Keely'd shared that she hadn't left this ranch since attending the World's Fair with her husband. "Everything I ever needed or wanted was here." Kyle admitted how much he liked Grandma Keely and wished he'd met Papa Colt. "You remind me of him in some ways," Jaz confessed. "I hope you two will be as happy as we were," Grandma Keely blessed them upon their leaving.

"That is quite a ranch," Kyle stated, and Jaz shared her Papa Colt's vision and how Star sustained it through her foresight and innovations, making it the formidable operation it is today. How Star was already on the lookout for Cherokee's successor about twenty years from now. "Someone who shares the same passion and love for the land and its inhabitants."

Two months later, Keely Ross Culhane passed. Star went into the room to wake her mother one morning and she had a contented smile on her face, but no breath in her cold body. "Daddy came and took Ma last night," is how she broke the news to Hep and Selena. With her children and grands doing so well Papa Colt, tired of waiting on her, called her home.

Everyone envisioned him coming back, taking her hand and their walking into the light...together again. She was 101. After the funeral service and all had vacated Colt, Texas, Star and Selena sat on the porch in a pair of wicker rockers and witnessed the setting of the sun. Selena'd sold Chateau Jazz but kept her spacious Paris flat and her club SELENA'S where four times a year she returned to an SRO crowd. As they both sipped spiked tea from mason jars like their daddy had, Star told Selena, "Thomas Wolfe was wrong. You can go home again."

"Amen," Selena toasted.

Time both collapsed and exploded. Over the ensuing years all those who touched and were touched by Cherokee Ranch in Colt, Texas flourished. Probably from the nurturing time spent in this magically mystical spot on the horizon of America. What they learned and experienced here, the love and resilience, followed them wherever they went.

Although Lee Harker proved to be an excellent surrogate father for Hud and uncle to CT, he and Mel went on to have three more children while she made special guest appearances on occasion, including a six month appearance in a Broadway show and one film. She decided to let Lee Harker be he breadwinner and relished the role of "housewife." Be careful what you ask for.

Keely's Soul Food restaurant in Paris continued to thrive as a welcome alternative to all the fancy French cuisine with their butter sauces, and a beacon to homesick travelers. She did not pretend that her fare was any healthier. She met, and later married, the farmer who resided outside of Paris and provided most of the organic vegetables for Paris restaurants when she requested that he grow more collard greens for her establishment.

AJ and Avia, remained blissfully happy. The doctor and his accomplished wife had three children, lived in town near the hospital but to get away from time to time frequented their beach home... renamed Oasis, that jutted out into the Pacific Ocean on a tongue of granite. Hanie's handsome husband with his British accent had become the heart-throb of Hollywood.

Even though told not to, Dr. Ulery Menair disobeyed and called Jaz, telling her that her old friend was having a mastectomy. Jaz flew to Gladys Ann's side, arriving while she was in recovery and staying with her for the first few rounds of chemo. The pair ate popsicles while reminiscing about old times from eight years old to the present. Once Jaz returned home, they replaced their bi-weekly letter-writing with weekly telephone conversations. A year later, Jaz and Kyle flew to D.C. to attend the christening of Michael, the little boy they adopted. A lucky family, indeed.

Scoey and Tracy finally added a boy to their three girls. Ellis Carlton Scofield III decided not to honor a father who had walked out on his mother and him when he was 11 and chose to honor men of stature and grace and named their son Tavio Quinton Ellis, after his two best buddies who died in Vietnam. Tav Ellis would play football and follow his father into law, Scofield and Son.

Kyle and Jaz Jagger found a 1927 Tudor home built by an old film studio head, and restored it to their liking, adding tennis courts, and adding a pool house casita complete with two bedrooms, a Jack and Jill bath and small kitchen, which they used as a guest house. Their substantial five bedroom home eventually filled with their children. In 1982, while accompanying Kyle on a trip to D.C. to testify on The Hill as an expert witness regarding California Building Codes, Jaz, pregnant with their second child, stood in front of the polished black granite Vietnam Memorial. While three year old Gabrielle Giselle, whose father called her "GG Jagger," napped with grandma Dallas at the hotel suite, Jaz and Hud watched CT trace his father's name, Tavio Culhane, on a piece of white paper. Her fourteen-year-old nephews had never been to the Nation's Capital and Aunt Jaz thought it time; after all, she was 14 when she attended the March on Washington and first visited the capital of the free world. TC's name was etched into the black granite as was Sinclair Cosgrove, an old high school classmate, but not Qwayz. Jaz hid her outrage from her nephews and her husband, but called her father irate that the name Quinton Regis Chandler IV was omitted. Hep said he'd look into it.

In a few years the Culhane cousins, Hud and CT, whose bond began and was seared at Colt, Texas, frayed during their late teen years and they found themselves in different places. Offered a part in a play in New York City and despite his mother Mel wanting him to complete high school, Hud took the role and left for NYC mimicking the acclaim of his mother and surpassing that of his father. For about five years, like his father before him, Hud fell into the hype of being a young star, garnering a Tony award for the part he played, which led to film roles and the high life. Realizing that his major reason for succeeding was to show his father up, which he did, he burned out, spun out of control and crashed. Harkening back to when and where he was truly happy, he found himself and decided to return to the welcoming refuge of Colt, Texas and a young lady he left behind.

CT's teen years proved far less mercurial and more staid. He completed high school and accepted admission to a veterinary college in St. Kitts where he pursued and attained his degree; he remained on the island a few years with a young lady he thought would be his wife, but it didn't work out. He loved the piano but steered closer to guitar which soothed him in difficult times, but he never reached nor tried to the heights of his father's popularity and acclaim. Preferring the company and care of animals to people, he eventually settled in Colt, Texas and in his late twenties married Evangeline "Vangi" Criqui, the two of them occupying a second floor bedroom at Cherokee Ranch when Hud came to visit.

"Well, what do you think, cuz?" Hud posed.

"About Aunt Star's proposition? She seems to think we are the heirs apparent to this Culhane dynasty," CT asked and smiled. "The yen and yang of it."

"Nobody can run this ranch like us. I been out there and it ain't all it's cracked up to be."

"The hot head and the cool breeze?" CT looked out over the prairie recalling his first visit. "We'd balance each other out."

"The bastards of Cherokee Ranch," Hud teased. They laughed at Aunt Star's redemptive sobriquet for them.

"Once she leaves, there'll be no one left that loves this land like we do."

"True that."

Hud settled down and married Juanita Redbird whose uncle had broken aunt Jaz's heart when she was 14. Juanita, the only woman who could both fascinate and tame her wild husband.

Like so many other black folks in America, the Culhanes not only survived but prevailed.

Not ready to give up the reins yet, Star continued to groom the legacy. "My bastards of Cherokee. Don't matter what they call you... it's what you answer to," she told them. "You got legacy and land; they got nothing. You'll make them take notice by 'being who you are,' like, your great-great grandma Saida said. . Force them to deal with you equally or not at all. 'Cause

326

you two are living the epitome of what your great-grandfather, Colt Culhane, always claimed… the best in the west."

"To the Pride of Cherokee," they all toasted.

MYRTLE BEACH, SOUTH CAROLINA

1985

Far from the beaten path in a small cottage on its own private inlet, the flickering of a projector shot light into the darkness of the house and its surroundings. From the back pier through the kitchen, voices from long ago cut through the heat and the smell of medicines and human decay. In a comer of the overheated house, an artificial leg was propped against an antique hall tree with brass hooks. There was a wheelchair by the table that held an imported music box, which played Nat King Cole's "Too Young," and next to it was a rock from a Hawaiian runway. Dozens of photographs of the young lovers littered the room. Old European magazines with Tawny gracing their covers and some more recent ones with articles on Culhane Enterprises, rare pictures of Kyle and Jaz. Jackie Wilson, Johnny Mathis, and Nat King Cole albums scattered about the floor. Words from "Everlastin' Love" pumped life, hope, and romance into the otherwise dreary dankness.

The film showed Qwayz and Jaz singing one of his songs, then leaving the control booth into the congratulatory arms of Selena, Zack, Hep, TC, and Gladys Ann. As the old man rewound that segment, he started the VHS tape that showed Jaz and Qwayz frolicking on the beach that Malibu summer. From there, the old man rewound and replayed the young lovers again.

Zeke sat alone, watching the images of two very young, very in love people singing to each other as if there was no one else in the world. It was the usual way he spent his time—fishing or watching every inch of film he could get on these young lovers. When the film ran out, he had a series of photos made into slides, and for hours he'd press that single button that would project their larger-than-life images up on the giant screen.

"It's four in the morning." His gnarled hand reached over to cut off the projector, plummeting the room into pitch darkness except for a lone, naked bulb in the kitchen.

This was the dog's cue that his day was beginning. The old man seldom slept. These days he couldn't lie flat and had to sit in his overstuffed Murphy chair with its hassock, surrounded by bottles of pills and liquid medicines he couldn't take without choking.

"Time for some fresh air." He maneuvered his stiff leg onto the floor and shifted his weight to scoot to the front of the seat. He sighed heavily and the dog relaxed, knowing it would be some time before the man mobilized himself.

"Better take these pills before that witch-nurse badgers me to death today." He struggled to pour lukewarm water from a carafe into a glass. "Is Hep supposed to come today, or is it my IV day?" he asked his canine companion. "He'll bitch at me, too." He screwed the pills into the side of his mouth and choked on the first swig of water, coughing convulsively, causing him to collapse back into the chair. Exhausted.

"Whew!" He sighed, rewinding the VHS as the dog resumed a sleeping position. "Hep thinks this is unhealthy. What else I got to do?" he asked the dog and began coughing again. "Won't be the first time we disagreed, won't be the last." His breathing remained difficult and labored. "Not the first time we haven't seen eye to eye. Get it? Eye." He pointed to his one good one, then the one gone bad. "To eye."

Hep had nixed his request of a picture of Jaz pregnant or with one of her babies or with her "sharp new" haircut. The old man hadn't confessed that he'd called her a couple of times. He got her number from the address book Hep left during one of his monthly visits. Every time he called, the housekeeper answered. What did Hep think he was going to do anyway? He would never hurt Jaz or destroy what she had.

He couldn't complain about Hepburn Culhane. Over the years he'd been mighty generous: the job, setting him up in this house with everything he could possibly ask for and some things he didn't. He thought of the seven phones in this tiny little place, so when Hep called daily to check up on him, the old man wouldn't be taxed. And the nurses who came daily from ten to ten. Hep had provided him with several live-ins over the years, but he'd chase them off until they had finally compromised on a twelve-hour shift about ten years ago. Neither he nor Hep thought he'd live this long.

After all these years, hard as he tried; he still couldn't remember the actual explosion. Whether they had drawn enemy fire or if it was engine malfunction. He just remembered waking up in a pool of his own blood in the midst of the most excruciating pain his taut athletic body had ever experienced. Surrounded by an eerie quiet only a jungle forest can produce, one in which a thousand pairs of eyes watch your every move. It was still and dim, the sun blotted out by the dense foliage. He called out, but only a monkey's high cackle answered. He didn't know how many hours he'd been there before the pain awoke him. A merciful pain caused him to shut down and black out again. Sometimes when he woke it was pitch-black, as if his eyes were still closed. The acrid smell of burned flesh undeniable.

He finally decided to move at least out from his own liquid, and in determining his direction, he noticed he could see through only one eye. Struggling to move, he noticed his blood-soaked clothing had become encrusted with tiny bugs feeding on his plasma. One arm was burned beyond repair, and a leg held on by a thread of flesh. It was himself he smelled. The sight and realization of his condition, coupled with the pain, caused him to black out once again.

The next few hours and days a blur. An unending series of him hurling what was left of his charred, shattered body down the hillside. He crawled through thick vegetation, through buffalo dung, over rocks and ridges. In and out of various stages of consciousness, of sleeping and waking and talking to himself.

He prayed that Jaz wouldn't mind his missing a limb or eye. That their love was strong enough to endure the physical infirmities. He also prayed that he was rolling toward a road and not a river. He didn't have the strength or limbs to negotiate the water.

The hot dusty roadway accepted the lump of humanity, baking him unmercifully in its heat. Qwayz could roll no farther on the flat surface, so he lay there sizzling in the sun's rays until he could feel the vibrations of an approaching platoon.

"Make 'em mine, Lord, not VC. If they're mine, I go home to Jaz. If they're Charlie, I'm gonna die. It's your call, Lord."

The scuff of marching feet shuffled around the pile of rags in the roadway. Qwayz hadn't strength to raise his arm or the voice to cry out as his own men passed him by.

"Hendrick!" A commanding officer barked after identifying the uniform as theirs: "Get this carcass in a body bag!" He marched on.

"Whew!" Hendrick fanned off the stink. "Wonder how long this has been lyin' here."

"Why bother?" The other soldier bent beside him, arranging a body bag.

"I guess the folks back home will be glad to get anything," Hendrick said, looking for dog tags but finding none.

"Could be a gook for all we know," the other soldier surmised. "Got no face, just a little beady eye."

"Looks like he was cooked pretty bad," Hendrick said as they placed the torso with a dangling leg into the plastic.

"Hendrick, look . . . is that eye moving?"

"Can't be." Hendrick began zipping up the heavy black plastic.

"It blinked!"

"Impossible, lemme see." Hendrick spit out his toothpick and straddled the body, blocking out the sun, so he could see the eye himself.

Qwayz tried with every fiber of his mangled body to blink the eye over which he no longer had control. He knew that if they zipped him up in that plastic bag, he'd suffocate. He moved his fingers, but they weren't looking. And suddenly his hand grabbed the ankle of the soldier.

"Shit!" The soldier jumped, scared.

"I'll be damned!" Hendrick bent to one knee and listened for a heartbeat. Feeling for the familiar pounding, he saw the mush of lips moving. He held his nose and inclined his ear to the lips of the man.

"What's he saying? Kill me? It's the humane thing to do, man. Shit."

"Naw... he said jazz." Hendrick stood. "I guess he wants us to know he's a brother. No sweat, blood, me and Anderson will take real good care of you, soul brother," Hendrick pledged as Qwayz passed out.

Qwayz was told he went from a MASH unit to a sea hospital on to Japan, where he awakened from a coma six months later. He'd undergone several extensive operations, was bandaged from head to toe and on life sustaining equipment when he came out of his deep sleep. He'd become the challenge and pet project of Dr. Maeda Yamamoto, who was hoping the GI would remember who he was, since there was no ID and his fingerprints had been burned off. According to all practical indications this soldier should have been dead, but he had an insatiable will to live against all odds and Dr. Yamamoto felt it his mission to help him. This story astounded the medical community as much as Qwayz's awakening.

The trauma from all the operations, sedations and the painkillers, caused Qwayz to suffer from a medically induced amnesia. It took another six months before he finally realized who he was... and he cried. Not tears of joy but tears of despair.

He had once been a robust, talented basketball player, a musician with a future as a brilliant lawyer and had an adoring family, and the most beautiful, devoted wife in the world, now reduced to a grotesque piece of flesh, with one eye, one arm, and one leg and paralyzed on one side. He'd been burned over most of his body, and the little skin left had been harvested and scarred from grafting. His handsome face, now a melted contortion of pinkish flesh with a Cyclops eye, a collapsed nose, sealed lips, and no hair. Hooked on morphine and wanting to die, he tried suicide several times. Dr. Yamamoto believed Qwayz knew who he was, but when asked, he'd simply answer, "Frankenstein."

In February 1972, Qwayz began the long road to rehabilitation. With severely atrophied muscles, he began

333

slowly with bed exercises before learning to walk with an artificial leg. He labored to maneuver his arm, care for himself, and feed himself; quite a task for the superb athlete who had broken records, packed sports arenas, and graced the covers of notable sports magazines. The only way he could reconcile himself was to believe *that* Qwayz had died in Vietnam. This was the Qwayz of today. This was who he had to deal with, live with, and be. His only inspiration was Jaz and his family. He didn't want to contact anyone until he was ready. He hoped Jaz wouldn't remarry, she just couldn't take another man so soon, not if what they had was real, and he knew it was.

Almost a year later, he finally contacted Ambassador Culhane in Italy. It took several attempts.

"Yes? Ambassador Culhane here." Hep had taken the phone from his secretary. He listened in horror as a cracked old voice claimed to be his son-in-law. "This is some kind of sick, demented joke. Do not call here again!" he boomed, and hung up. But the calls kept coming on his private line, which only his family was privy to. For that reason he couldn't tell Antonella not to put the man through.

"I'm afraid you leave me no choice but to contact Jaz directly," Qwayz threatened, not really knowing where Jaz was, knowing Hep's number only because of their scheduled trip to Italy in 1965.

"That would not be advisable!" Hep thundered, closing the door to the sight of his precious daughter and Antonella conversing in his outer office. "Just so happens that I will be in Tokyo next week," he lied. "Perhaps I'll stop by then."

Qwayz's memorial had been over long ago, the calls had begun two months ago, and with their persistence, Hep hadn't slept much in the past few weeks. Perhaps the art of denial was an inherited trait; Jaz denying Qwayz's death, and him denying his existence. Hep thought of calling in an investigator, but he didn't want anyone else to know about this man. Hep hadn't confided in anyone, not even his wife, which worried him as much as the use of his private line. If those calls were really nothing, as he pretended, he would have told Lorette.

The voice sounded old and weary, not one of a man in his early twenties, but it had a familiar cadence and rhythm, a familiar unusual choice of words. If it were Qwayz, in what kind of shape would he be? But of course it couldn't be him. What could this man want from him... money? On what basis could he make such a claim? Blackmail? Was Qwayz living in Vietnam with another family? No way! Was he a prisoner of war, and this guy the link to getting him out? There were no dog tags, as with TC. No body, not even part of one, just the Air Force's word that Quinton Regis Chandler IV had been Killed In Action.

Upon his arrival, Hep walked the long antiseptic hallway of the hospital with its medicinal smell and an occasional unbearable vision of the remains of a man lumped in a wheelchair. It was all too painful. "Here we are, sir," the nurse said. "Sorry to stare, but Jazzman hasn't had any visitors."

"Jazzman?"

"Used to call himself Frankenstein, but now he's the Jazzman. We're fellow music lovers." She didn't go into the private room. "I'll get his doctor."

Hep didn't want to be alone, but the nurse disappeared. He approached the back of the shrunken man, immediately convinced that it couldn't be Qwayz. He was about to leave before the doctor came, but the shriveled hand of the old man fanned Hep closer.

"I am Ambassador Culhane," Hep boomed in his usual vocally intimidating ploy, but the old man didn't respond with the characteristic jerk.

"Don't be so relieved, Mr. C," the man turned slowly, facing him, his voice coming from a hole in his neck. "It's me. And you're still doing that thing with your voice, huh?"

Hep almost collapsed at the sheer sight of this monstrous mush of a face. Ribbons of pink scar tissue about his face and neck covered one eye completely and left only a pinhole of a pupil in the other. Hep fought the fact that this could be his son-in-law, but in some deep recess of consciousness... he knew. For the first time, he was glad that TC had died and had not come back... not like this.

Hep fired questions about Ma Vy, Denny, and Hanie, about Qwayz's sports records, his singing and affiliation with Champion Studios and Raw Cilk. Qwayz answered them all without hesitation.

"For all I know, you could have been in a prison camp with Qwayz. That would certainly give you time enough to study up on him."

"I know you wish, Mr. C. You have no idea how many times I've tried to kill myself, but I'm still here." He lay back on the pillows. "You've asked about everyone who's dear to me but the two I loved best, TC and Jaz."

Hep began to pace nervously. Trying to deny that this man was his Qwayz, the pride of Watts. The prize sought by nine colleges and six Ivy League universities. The most superb athlete of the sixties. Magic Chandler of Stanford. Scholarship to law school. The love of his daughter's life.

Outside the hospital room, Dr. Yamamoto allowed Hep to read the medical chart which revealed that this man's only word on the dusty road in Vietnam had been his daughter's name. He reviewed what this young man had endured over the past few years—the operations, addiction, rehabilitation—only proved that one man could survive a tremendous agony for the love of one woman.

In the hallway, Hep openly wept for Qwayz, for TC, and for Jaz.

The doctor shared that there were a few more procedures necessary before Jazzman could be released. Hep returned to the room and after several hours of telling Qwayz all he knew about Jaz, he quietly concluded, "After your upcoming operations. I'll make arrangements to take you home."

"I figured a little house in Myrtle Beach would be nice."

"Jaz is in Italy right now. She could get here—"

"I'm not going to see Jaz. She was my reason for getting better, but I'd be a burden, pure and simple."

"No. That girl has never given up hope on you. Even when *everyone* else considered you dead, she never let anyone say differently."

"She was wrong, Mr. C. The Qwayz she knew is dead. Scattered in Laos. I ruined her life once by leaving. I won't do it again by returning."

"You can't be serious."

"But I am. I've had plenty of time to figure out all the angles. I couldn't live with her pity, her sense of duty and obligation. It would be no life for her. You remember once I told you I loved Jaz more than life itself, and I'd do anything to prove it. You told me you hoped it'd never come to that. Well, it has. The ultimate price of my love is to live out my remaining days without her and to let her get on with her life. I could be selfish and let her be my nursemaid, but I'm not that kinda guy. I guess this proves that my love for her is everlasting after all."

"But she's convinced you're alive."

"So what do we do after she gets an A on the big test and an F in the course?"

"Boy, we went around and around with that one, didn't we?" The old man's voice pierced the silence and the dog looked up. "Then Jaz came back home and went to work at CE, and I just had to see her, be around her as often as my health allowed. It was hard to ride in that Jaguar she'd wanted all her life, going to Addie's wedding with her, sitting beside her and hearing vows of love until death do us part. I lost it when we went to Paradise Rock. When she said, 'God, I loved that man.' I fell against the wall." He looked about his dismal surroundings and grunted. "She went on about how it was a surprise for me when I got back. We went to the drugstore afterwards only because I wasn't ready to leave her. But I just couldn't stay awake." He sucked air in from his oxygen tank.

"Amber really hurt me when she called me a monster on the elevator. The little girl I named. I expected as much from Scoey, but it still hurt. Then there was AJ." His voice choked. "All grown up, handsome in med school, and I wanted to say, 'I am your Uncle Qwayz.' I wanted to stand in the middle of Jaz's thirtieth birthday party and say, 'Hey! Ma, Denny, Selena, I am here!' That would have been something, huh? Then what? Everyone would cower and cry. Well." His voice broke and he thought of Jaz's wedding, when he saw both of his sisters and their spouses and his mother, who all avoided him like the plague. Denny looking at Jaz and Kyle, giving her non-verbal approval for his wife moving on. All of it hurt like the inflicted wounds never did.

"Love supreme, Akira II," he said aloud and the dog, a five year old Irish setter, rose at the sound of its name. "The supreme sacrifice… so that all the folks I care about can remember me as I was. Even though that's what I wanted, it was too painful seeing Jaz happy with someone else. I still couldn't take it. So, thanks to Hep, I finally got my house in Myrtle Beach. Ready for some fishing, girl?"

He maneuvered his stiff leg, ignoring the wheelchair, and grabbed the cane Kyle brought him from Africa. "He's a good man, a lucky man." He shuffle-scraped toward the linoleum kitchen door, quietly remembering that Hep said Jaz asked about Zeke's absence when they returned from their honeymoon. He glanced at their oil wedding portrait, which hung over the splendid brass bed, as he steadied himself; the bed that still smelled faintly of Jaz's essence. The picture she immediately knew was missing when she came back unannounced from Italy. Hep would let him visit her house about once a month, to just be in her space. Their furniture, record collection which he'd left out once. The male attendant would sit in the car while Qwayz enjoyed the environs without interruption. "We got the picture back to her and she was none the wiser." He'd told Hep about the possibility that TC had a son with LeLani. He'd dropped that dime not folks around Watts. LeLani had succeeded in keeping the parentage of her son's father private. When Jaz'd said to her father, "You can really keep a secret." And Hep answered, "You have no idea," he was speaking of the Qwayz-Zeke connection. TC has a son and is not here. I am here and have no children. Ain't that a blip?

"Ah." He made it to the doorjamb. As the screen scraped open, the dog accompanied its master for the two-minute walk down the pier, which took him fifteen. He thought of Jaz and how if he hadn't prodded Hep for information, he wouldn't know anything of her life now. Hep was stingy and made Zeke work for every morsel. But he persisted. Otherwise he wouldn't have known that Jaz took only three projects a year to keep professionally fit so that when her youngest daughter, Savannah,

339

began school, Jaz could resume her career. He wouldn't have known that Kyle came home from work nightly in time for dinner, baths and prayers with his wife and three children. That they took three vacations a year: one to their Kenyan retreat, another to their villa in St. John, and the third a trip dictated by Gabrielle, or their son, Kyle Culhane Jagger; KC he was called. Hep was most guarded in describing the Jagger home, but over the years Zeke had gleaned that it was an Italian-style villa, with Tudor accents built of limestone and split rock in the 1920s, remodeled by the Jaggers, and situated on ten prime acres of Santa Barbara coastline.

As he moved slowly down the wooden plank, Zeke recalled how Hep'd told him when Jaz took the boys, Hud and CT, to Washington D.C. and they'd visited the Vietnam Memorial, they found TC's name, but Quinton Chandler was missing. How an enraged Jaz had called him complaining at the omission of Qwayz's name and Hep said he'd look into it.

Zeke sighed and plopped on the custom bench Hep had had built for him by the water. It housed duplicates of his oxygen tank, medicine, spring water, cups, dog food, and his fishing gear. He looked to the mouth of his inlet, where the ocean and wider horizon met. "Looks like it's gonna be a good day. Huh, girlie?" He patted his dog clumsily. "Ah, death is a slow process." He kissed this Irish setter. "Jaz wouldn't like that. Does she have a dog? Oh yeah, two Airedales named Osiris and Isis after those black Egyptian gods. That's Kyle's doing, I bet. Those kids know their roots. Our kids would have known theirs, too." He patted the dog once more before dropping his line in the water.

"Yep, yep, yep, another beautiful Myrtle Beach morning will be breaking soon." He resituated himself on the bench and began coughing convulsively, hacking and sucking up the thin oxygen.

"Whew!" He wiped his brow, wanting a sip of water, but dared not drink. The man and his dog sat in silence for a while and he finally murmured. "The stars are in their heavens and all's right with the world." Tired and spent, he closed his eyes and his rod fell into the water.

~*~

Jubal Rudd Criqui dropped dead at 91. Late for a Criqui man. When the gravedigger was commissioned to dig a grave, Hep paid him to dig two. Paid him well to do the deed and to keep it secret. One in the Criqui section of Mt. Moriah Gethsemane Baptist Church cemetery and the other in the Culhane family plot.

On a starless night after the Criqui funeral, Hep arranged to bring a coffin escorted by two unknown men who deposited the gleaming bronze casket into the ground and buried it. He paid these men well before they drove the hearse back to the private plane which awaited them in an open field five miles outside of town. Hep looked at the graves side by side. One was years old with a marker that read: Tavio Culhane. The other, a freshly turned grave.

"Brothers," Hep whispered and then saluted. "Together again."

The next morning, Star asked her brother of the suspicious nocturnal doings. "Who's up there?"

Hep held her gaze and finally said, "You don't want to know."

Star smiled cryptically and answered, "Probably not."

About a year later, after the ground settled and no one noticed the latest entry into the Culhane plot, a granite tombstone found its place at the head of the grave.

It read simply: Unknown Soldier.

~*~

In the end whose love was everlastin'?

Discussion Questions

1. Characterize and contrast your two favorite female characters. Your two favorite male characters and why?
2. What scenes/scenarios resonated most with you and why?
3. Given the adage, "careful how you treat people," all people, regardless of their presentation, should be treated with respect and compassion. How is this applicable to Qwayz/Zeke?
4. Some secrets are best kept. Agree or disagree? For example, Hep kept his secret regarding Qwayz from Jaz and his mother and sisters.
5. What kind of life would they have lived if...
   a) TC had never gone to Vietnam?
   b) Qwayz had returned to Jaz?
   c) Hep had told Jaz about Qwayz?
6. Family dynamics remain an important theme in this author's novels. Characterize the interactions between the women of the Culhane family -- Keely and her daughters, Orelia, Star, and Selena.
   a) Between siblings Mel and Jaz and their mother, Lorette

b) Friends -- Gladys Ann, Denny, Tracy and Sloane -- and how they helped Jaz deal with the love and loss of Qwayz.

7. Explore the relationships of the men:
   a) Fathers and sons -- Papa Colt and Hep, Hep and TC
   b) Friends -- TC, Scoey and Qwayz
   c) Cousins -- Hud and CT

8. Discuss Jaz and her three lovers: Prince Omar, Solomon Noble and Nick Santucci

9. Describe and compare Jaz's relationships with the loves of her life: Qwayz and Kyle Jagger.

10. Years ago the working title of this book was *This Father's Daughter*, centering on the relationship between Jaz and Hep. It has evolved into her relationships with her brother, TC, her lovers and the loves of her life: Qwayz and Kyle. Based on your own experience and Jaz's, do women always date a certain type of man?

344